PENGUIN  CLASSICS

THE HARBOR

ERNEST POOLE was born in 1880 in Chicago, where he grew up in a politically progressive middle-class family. After graduating from Princeton in 1902 he set out to be become a writer, working initially as a muckraking journalist in New York City. In 1905 he traveled to Russia for *Outlook* magazine to report on the aftermath of a failed anticzarist uprising and investigate European socialism firsthand. Over the next decade he wrote numerous short stories, an undistinguished first novel, and a dozen plays, three of which were produced. Poole's greatest success came in 1915 with the publication of *The Harbor*, a bestselling and controversial socialist novel that described the political conversion of a middle-class young man to active sympathy with the labor movement during a violent waterfront strike. After *The Harbor* made him famous, Poole's literary reputation reached its peak when his next novel, *His Family*, won the first-ever Pulitzer Prize for fiction in 1918, an award that some saw as belated recognition for *The Harbor*. Poole published several moderately successful novels in the 1920s, but his work gradually fell out of favor with critics. During the Depression he largely gave up fiction to write class-conscious journalism about economic conditions in the United States and Europe. His autobiography, *The Bridge*, appeared in 1940. He died in 1950 having published twenty-four books, including fiction, history, and reform-oriented journalism.

PATRICK CHURA is associate professor of English at the University of Akron, where he teaches courses in American literature. He is the author of two books—*Vital Contact* in 2005 and *Thoreau the Land Surveyor* in 2010—and has published articles on a variety of literary-historical topics. He is a former Peace Corps volunteer and Fulbright lecturer in the Republic of Lithuania, and has received research grants from the European Union, the Fulbright Foundation, and the University of Akron.

ERNEST POOLE

The Harbor

Introduction and Notes by
PATRICK CHURA

PENGUIN BOOKS

PENGUIN BOOKS
Published by the Penguin Group
Penguin Group (USA) Inc., 375 Hudson Street,
New York, New York 10014, U.S.A.
Penguin Group (Canada), 90 Eglinton Avenue East, Suite 700, Toronto,
Ontario, Canada M4P 2Y3 (a division of Pearson Penguin Canada Inc.)
Penguin Books Ltd, 80 Strand, London WC2R 0RL, England
Penguin Ireland, 25 St Stephen's Green, Dublin 2,
Ireland (a division of Penguin Books Ltd)
Penguin Group (Australia), 250 Camberwell Road,
Camberwell, Victoria 3124, Australia
(a division of Pearson Australia Group Pty Ltd)
Penguin Books India Pvt Ltd, 11 Community Centre,
Panchsheel Park, New Delhi - 110 017, India
Penguin Group (NZ), 67 Apollo Drive, Rosedale, Auckland 0632,
New Zealand (a division of Pearson New Zealand Ltd)
Penguin Books (South Africa) (Pty) Ltd, 24 Sturdee Avenue,
Rosebank, Johannesburg 2196, South Africa

Penguin Books Ltd, Registered Offices:
80 Strand, London WC2R 0RL, England

First published in the United States of America by The Macmillan Company 1915
This edition with an introduction by Patrick Chura published in Penguin Books 2011

3 5 7 9 10 8 6 4 2

Introduction copyright © Patrick Chura, 2011
All rights reserved

LIBRARY OF CONGRESS CATALOGING IN PUBLICATION DATA
Poole, Ernest, 1880–1950.
The harbor / Ernest Poole ; introduction and notes by Patrick Chura.
p. cm.
Includes bibliographical references.
ISBN 978-0-14-310644-9
1. Labor unions—Fiction. 2. Brooklyn (New York, N.Y.)—Fiction. I. Chura, Patrick, 1964– II. Title.
PS3531.O53H37 2011
813'.52—dc23   2011033847

Printed in the United States of America

To M.A.

Contents

Introduction

Critics from several eras have described *The Harbor* as "the best Socialist novel of all," the "best radical novel written in the 1910s," and "the best fictional account of the Paterson strike by a participant."[1] Like a number of muckraking classics, the book both recorded history and made history. It was the highly controversial eighth bestseller of 1915, going through seventy-eight thousand copies and twenty-two printings in a matter of months. The *New York Times* reviewer called it "the best American novel that has appeared in many a long day" and added, "It is difficult to give more than the faintest hint of the scope and power of this very unusual book within the limits of a review. Here in this vision of the harbor is focused much of our modern world."[2] After *The Harbor* made him famous, Ernest Poole's career reached its zenith when his next novel, *His Family*, won the first-ever Pulitzer Prize for fiction in 1918, an award that some saw as belated recognition for Poole's more celebrated earlier book.[3] *The Harbor* had a strong influence on the generation of radicals and progressives that came of age during World War I, and its significance was not lost on major writers with leftist leanings, including John Dos Passos, Upton Sinclair, and Eugene O'Neill.

For the class-conscious writer of the early 1910s, evidence was all around the United States that the labor-capital conflict was reaching a critical stage. In 1912, Socialist candidate Eugene V. Debs won over nine hundred thousand votes for president, and a successful textile workers' strike in Lawrence, Massachusetts, brought "Big Bill" Haywood and his labor organization, the Industrial Workers of the World (IWW), to their peak of influence and power. Dues-paying membership in the Socialist Party reached an all-time high of 120,000. Nationwide, at least 435 socialists held public office, including 21 state legislators and the mayor of Milwaukee.[4] Beginning in 1913, a long, ugly coal strike in the Trinidad-Ludlow area of southern Colorado drew public attention to appalling conditions in the western mines. Headlines in the national press described increasingly violent attempts of industrial "combinations" to break strikes and destroy unions—along with the increasing political effectiveness of the labor movement itself. What newspaper editors referred to with interest and trepidation as "The Rising Tide of Socialism" was a real phenomenon. At no previous time in U.S. history did a turn toward a collectivist economic future seem quite so possible.

The year 1913 is often cited as a watershed in both labor history and art history, a moment in which the contradictions of capitalism determined multiple aesthetic forms and filtered into popular culture. In February, the epoch-making New York Armory Show ushered in modernism in the visual and plastic arts, and in June, a silk workers' strike in Paterson, New Jersey, brought Greenwich Village intellectuals and the working class together to create the spectacular Paterson Strike Pageant, an unprecedented example of revolutionary élan that is now understood as a turning point in the evolution of public art and radical self-consciousness.[5] "Looking back on it now," wrote the millionaire labor sympathizer Mabel Dodge Luhan, "it seems as though everywhere, in that year of 1913, barriers went down and people reached each other who had never been in touch before; there were all sorts of new ways to communicate, as well as new communications."[6]

Among the most admired and evocative new communications in this period was Poole's *The Harbor*, a culturally revealing, politically embedded novel that Poole began writing in 1912, completed in 1914, and published in the spring of 1915 to instant acclaim. The making of *The Harbor* was directly influenced by concurrent events, some of which are now forgotten. Poole's initial impulse for a story about the rise of labor came from the Lawrence strike. The fierce political tensions he described were the product of his contact with Bill Haywood and IWW organizers. The author gained further impetus, along with fresh insights about the class system, from his direct participation in the Paterson strike and Paterson pageant. The Colorado coal strikes added material that heightened the violence and shock value of the book's main labor action.

Finally, in a direct convergence of literature and world events, the novel's conclusion was shaped by the outbreak of World War I. When *The Harbor* was accepted by the Macmillan Company in early 1914, Poole believed the book finished, but after European hostilities broke out in July of that year, he asked the publisher to return the manuscript and then spent a month rewriting the final chapters. As he explained in his autobiography, *The Bridge*, the new ending incorporated the onset of the Great War by "showing the whole world in chaos."[7]

Though Poole's success came suddenly, it had a long foreground in the study of serious social issues. Born in 1880 into a securely middle-class Chicago family, he probably imbibed his interest in reform movements from his mother, Mary Howe Poole, who taught tolerance and generosity toward the underprivileged as an extension of her Christian ethics. In *The Bridge*, the author recalled childhood friendships with indigent boys who played in the city dumps, experiences he would recycle as part of his main character's background in *The Harbor*. Poole's reformist sympathies were further inspired in his teenage years by reading Jacob Riis's *How the Other Half Lives*. From 1898 to 1902 he attended Princeton, where he was a mediocre student during his first two years. By the time he graduated he was ranked in the top quarter of his class and had earned As from Woodrow Wilson in history and political science.

Influenced by his study of Tolstoy, Turgenev, Balzac, and Kipling, Poole set out to become a fiction writer after graduation. Like many well-educated children of middle-class political progressives at the turn of the century, he chose a settlement house in the slums as a setting for his research into the lives of the poor. As he explained in *The Bridge*, "Tenement life appealed to me as a tremendous new field, scarcely touched by American writers as yet."[8] In September 1902 Poole took up residence at the University Settlement house on New York's Lower East Side. His arrival coincided with the rise of social exposé literature—what was later known as muckraking journalism for its focus on urban squalor and the victims of poverty. His first writing project was a report on child labor that appeared in the April 1903 *McClure's* under the title "Waifs of the Street."

While living in University Settlement off and on from 1902 to early 1905, Poole wrote dozens of articles and pamphlets about slum perils ranging from rampant tuberculosis to venereal disease. In 1904 he returned to Chicago for six weeks to research a packinghouse strike. He lived in a tenement near the stockyards and produced articles that Upton Sinclair later drew from in writing *The Jungle*. Poole's memoir describes meeting Sinclair while *The Jungle* was in progress and giving his fellow muckraker "the inside dope on conditions in the Yards," along with "some tips on where to get more." On the same trip, Poole visited Jane Addams at Hull House and enlisted her aid in raising money for starving strikers.[9]

A year later Poole traveled to Russia, Georgia, and Ukraine for *Outlook* magazine to investigate the aftermath of the failed socialist uprising of January 1905, making him one of the earliest American writers to study European socialism firsthand. He interviewed party leaders in St. Petersburg and Moscow before venturing into the rural villages, where he lived with peasant families and recorded their stories of recent czarist atrocities. The vivid and perceptive local descriptions Poole produced on this assignment are often considered his best journalism. During a stopover in London on the way home, the young author traded political insights and discussed socialist theory with George Bernard Shaw.

In the years between his Russian trip and the writing of *The Harbor* Poole pursued a literary career in New York, selling an occasional work of fiction to *The Saturday Evening Post* and publishing more articles on slum conditions that won the praise of Theodore Roosevelt. Friends and influences in this phase of apprenticeship included liberal journalist Lincoln Steffens, immigrant newspaper editor Abraham Cahan, and writer-activist Mary Heaton Vorse. Before he turned thirty Poole had written a somewhat amateurish first novel, sold a handful of stories, and written perhaps a dozen full-length plays, three of which had been produced. In October 1908, impressed by the political success of moderate socialist leader and state congressional candidate Morris Hillquit, Poole joined the Socialist Party and began contributing regular articles to New York's socialist organ, the *Call*.

When Big Bill Haywood's aggressive labor organization, the

Industrial Workers of the World, came east from Colorado in 1912 to take the lead in a major strike in the textile mills of Lowell and Lawrence, Poole naturally became involved. He organized a well-attended mass meeting in New York's Carnegie Hall to raise funds for the jailed Italian strike leaders Joseph Ettor and Arturo Giovannitti. Poole not only followed the strike closely, in the process learning valuable political lessons; he played a tangential role in the IWW's greatest victory, an event then widely viewed as the first battle in the coming class war. The Lawrence strike opened up the eastern states to agitation through the preaching and practice of the controversial IWW doctrine of "direct action." By all accounts it was this strike that prompted Poole to begin the novel he had been contemplating for years—a work that would transmit to a wide audience the dynamic of a radical labor conflict and offer a vision of a world run by workers.

But *The Harbor* could not have taken final shape without the stimulus of the silk workers' strike in Paterson, New Jersey, that began in February 1913. During this strike, Ernest Poole came to Paterson more than any other prominent Socialist and took more away with him. He often accompanied Bill Haywood and feminist labor leader Elizabeth Gurley Flynn to Turn Hall in New York, where strike rallies were held, and gave speeches to the workers at the weekly Sunday striker gatherings at the New Jersey town of Haledon. Poole was also deeply involved in the Paterson Strike Pageant, a moving reenactment of the events of the strike before an audience of twenty thousand in Madison Square Garden. This groundbreaking performance used several hundred real strikers as actors portraying themselves in dramatized scenes from the Paterson conflict, including the initial walkout, picket lines at the mills, mass meetings and speeches by Haywood, police violence, the funeral of a murdered striker, and the singing of the *Internationale* as a finale. Working with future Communist revolutionary John Reed and set designer Robert Edmond Jones, Poole drew on his stage experience to help plan the logistics of the production. In newspaper accounts on the morning after the pageant, he was named as one of the "bright lights who worked up the show" and one of the four writers of the pageant script.[10]

Over the years, pageant witnesses, participants, and historians have outdone themselves in their attempts to adequately extol the emotive power of the event. Flynn called the pageant "the most beautiful and realistic example of art that has been put on stage in the last half century." Upton Sinclair, who advertised his latest novel in the event program, was moved to tears by the show, which he avowed "would never pass from [his] memory." Theater scholars now generally agree that the pageant sparked the development of American drama, preparing the way for the labor plays of the Provincetown Players.[11] A number of the founding members of the players—including George Cram Cook, Susan Glaspell, and John Reed—were involved in or present at the pageant. Cook referred to it as "the first labor play" and praised the "feeling of oneness" with the strikers that Poole and the other pageant organizers had conveyed.[12]

Ultimately, perhaps, nothing better expresses the event's power than an artifact that actually predated it—Robert Edmond Jones's compelling publicity illustration, which doubled as the cover of the pageant program and now serves as the cover of this book. In Jones's sketch, an intent, confident young worker emerges from the factory, surging upward under a boldly emblazoned "I.W.W." as if in answer to the organization's call to action. This image—championing anticapitalist revolution and forcefully asserting the rising might of the working class—has become the strike's chief symbol and an icon of labor history.

While Jones and the Provincetowners expressed their feeling of "oneness" with workers through visual art and drama, Poole found a way to put this sentiment into fiction. One evening during the Paterson strike, while Haywood was having dinner at Poole's home in New York, the Wobbly leader mentioned that he planned "to strike New York Harbor and shut it up tight" the following spring. When Poole replied that he knew of this plan and had learned of it from a young IWW organizer he'd been interviewing on the waterfront, the surprised Haywood asked the purpose of his research. "I'm writing a book called The Harbor," Poole replied.[13]

The book Poole alluded to, a largely forgotten landmark in American literary history, offers a detailed treatment of economic and social conditions in New York from the 1880s to the outbreak of the Great War. While Poole's novel spans decades, one of its chief merits is that it preserves in literary form a brilliant but short-lived episode in the history of the radical labor movement. In book III of The Harbor, when a militant organizer leads the middle-class main character into the hold of an ocean liner to view the working conditions of stevedores and stokers and declares, "[T]hey're waking up fast—all over the world," he is putting on display the kind of energy captured visually by Jones and harnessed in the Lawrence and Paterson strikes. This energy, glimpsed by Poole at Paterson, is reconstituted in the closing chapters of his novel when the "great spirit of the crowd" is born in a violent dockworkers' action.

Fittingly, the basic tension in Poole's representation of the prewar national mood involves the question of political conversion to socialism. The novel's protagonist, Billy (he is not given a surname), is an aspiring writer who struggles to reconcile his sympathy for oppressed workers with his middle-class loyalties and basic faith in capitalist progress. The other central characters in the novel—Dillon and Joe Kramer—are aligned on opposite sides of the class war, with Billy in a complicated position between them. Dillon, an acclaimed engineer, city planner, and "priest of big business," urges Billy to use his literary talents to write politically conservative "glory stories," thinly disguised paeans to the "great men" at the top of the industrial system. Kramer, a radical activist whose character is based on the organizer Poole met at Paterson, renounces his ties to the respectable classes to go among slum dwellers and stokers, preach syndicalism, and lead strikes. He introduces Billy to working-class misery, warns him against the brutality of business interests, and insists that Billy use his literary talents to further the international labor movement.

While the socialist "conversion novel"—exemplified in works by Sinclair, Jack London, Isaac Friedman, Arthur Bullard, and others—had already become a known genre by 1915, Poole's work depicts the process with distinctive intensity. At a moment when labor activism and the Industrial Workers of the World were, as Poole claimed, "spreading with amazing speed all over the land," the author quotes and paraphrases from actual IWW speeches, giving voice to the proponents of industrial sabotage and anticapitalist violence in an unusually direct way.[14] Before Poole, perhaps only Friedman's *By Bread Alone*, a much lesser novel, had taken the conflict of the middle-class sympathizer to the level of civil war in which neutrality was impossible and the necessity to "decide which side you're on" was mandated by both conscience and historical circumstance.[15] And in *The Harbor* the pull toward the left is felt not only by the protagonist but by a credible group of secondary characters who also afford legitimacy to radicalism and are also from the middle class. The root conflicts they embody go deeper than politics, involving ties of blood and marriage. Billy's family, for example, is split down the middle, a condition that forces the main character to weigh loyalties to his leisure-class wife, his labor-leader sister, his businessman father, and the anarchist who may become his brother-in-law. Within this network of relations all choices carry tragic potential, and yet a choice must be made; as the book's ending suggests, 1914 is "no year for compromise."

What follows from this material is a realistic consideration of questions that self-conscious liberals, then and now, cannot avoid: Is calculated violence against corporations justified by the calculated violence they do every day to people and to the planet? What actually can and should be done about poverty by members of the middle class? How practical is the idea of political union between destitute workers and sympathetic bourgeois intellectuals? Can a middle-class writer truly understand workers' hardships or interpret their lives without condescension and in ways that aid them in the class struggle? What are the real and intended effects—for both socially aware writers and their working-class subjects—of politically engaged literature? Viable questions today, as they were for the educated men and women who were famously active for reform causes during the novel's historical present.

In *The Harbor*, Poole follows the progress of an autobiographical main character from a genteel childhood to the advent of his career as a serious novelist. By tracing the struggles of the artist toward maturity, the author works in the fixed and familiar vein of the Künstlerroman. The book's twist on this traditional genre is that in Billy's case political growth is the single factor that precedes and enables artistic growth. For twenty-first-century readers, however, Billy's development as an artist will probably be overshadowed by the book's inspired setting: the vast harbor itself, which Poole calls "the world's first port." New York Harbor, in all of its magnificence and ugliness, gives Poole a comprehensive metaphor for the implacable creative-destructive forces behind what we now think of as the American century. Teeming with men and machines, raw industry and abundant consumer goods, the place is a magnet for Billy's imagination and a catalyst to his development. From the opening pages, when the seven-year-old boy attends a sermon by the great preacher Henry Ward Beecher and hears Beecher refer lyrically to "the harbor of life" as a place of safety and rest, Billy is fixated on the waterfront as a source of vital knowledge. His direct experience on the docks, where he befriends gang toughs, "micks," and ragged street urchins, tells him that Beecher is wrong about the harbor—it is not a refuge from the world's cares. As he already senses, it is a place "close to the deep rough tides of life," where immigrants, stokers, deckhands, and prostitutes struggle for survival. Later in the novel Billy comes to a more complex appreciation of the harbor as "a symbol of the changing world that I had seen with my changing eyes."[16]

Understanding the harbor this way—as a measure of both inner psychological and outward material change—actually works generally, offering a means of gauging the sympathies of each major character. Billy's mother, his first influence, tries to keep her son away from the sordid life on the docks. She fails, but she gives Billy the desire to be a writer along with a value system—a broad-minded Christian ethos resembling that of the nineteenth-century social gospelers—that ultimately draws him toward the labor movement. Billy's father, the owner of a waterfront warehouse, is subjected to wrenching economic transformations. Unprepared for the era of big companies and Standard Oil, he watches his harbor become "clouded in the smoke and soot of an age of steam and iron" and longs nostalgically for the bygone age of towering sails and Yankee clippers. He fails to understand or adapt to the crude industrial forces that have destroyed the old harbor and "crushed the life out of" his commercial hopes and stable worldview.

Poole's younger characters are less static—they change with the harbor, sometimes painfully, and reflect fascinating stages in the evolution of American class and gender attitudes. Raised in an atmosphere of progressive optimism, Billy initially yearns to escape the waterfront and avoid his father's business by writing novels. Since Art is Billy's first godlike principle, his youthful religion is style, technique, and form. The problem, however, is that Billy has nothing to say, no idea of what view of reality his writing should espouse or what social meaning, if any, his novels should have. The notion that it is enough to simply create beauty, an idea derived from his elite education, buoys his fantasy that a sojourn in Paris after college graduation will make him a genuine writer, free of all loyalties except to his romanticized aesthetic ideal. But when Billy returns to the harbor following the death of his mother, his politically indeterminate creativity is exposed as naive when measured against the more dynamic lives of Dillon and Kramer.

Dillon, who helps build global capitalism while promising to "cure" its endemic side effects—massive human suffering and environmental destruction—exemplifies "the real strength of Wall Street." He embodies what Poole calls the "new god . . . of Efficiency," and his great dream in the novel is to organize the harbor according to the theory of scientific management. This principle is described in terms reminiscent of Taylorism: "[A]rmed with Science, its feet stood firm on mechanical laws and in its head were all the brains of all the strong men at the top." Dillon's efficiency becomes a second godlike principle to Billy, who gives up his attempts at abstruse fiction to follow the urban engineer's political lead and write articles in praise of corporate power. As Billy acknowledges, "The first social vision of my life I had through Dillon's field glass."

While this is happening, however, Kramer relentlessly assails Billy's conservatism, reminding him of the "millions of people . . . getting a raw deal and getting mad about it" and warning against the hypocrisy of the "damned respectable upper class." Kramer's impassioned pleas for economic reforms derive directly from the IWW lexicon and carry significant weight in the novel. His declarations of an imminent "age of force"—in which violent exploits by "prodigious masses of men" will tear down the institutional order through "direct action"—challenge the belief models of Poole's main character and struck a powerful chord with Poole's 1915 readership. As Billy's social awareness develops he comes variously under the sway of two formidable personalities at ideological war with each other, with Dillon initially more credible and compelling.

Eleanore Dillon, a childhood playmate of Billy's and the daughter of the great industrial engineer, enters the novel as an urbane moderate and vicarious participant in her father's work of remaking New York's maritime infrastructure. An adherent to her father's views, she explores the harbor in her personal motorboat, sometimes with Billy aboard, running business errands and occasionally putting her own engineering knowledge to use in geographic studies that further exploitation of the waterfront. After marrying Billy, however, her sensibilities broaden, less from Billy's urging than from her conversations with Kramer, who forces her to think about class war. She also bonds with Billy's sister, Sue, a nascent feminist who introduces her to the women's movement. Under these two influences, Eleanore evolves politically from suffrage marcher to settlement worker to intrepid relief worker in the novel's great harbor strike. Like the well-dressed Chicago settlement worker that Upton Sinclair had briefly sketched in *The Jungle*, Eleanore is not above using her influence with corporate bosses to help relieve misery in the slums created by those same corporate bosses. At the novel's end her visits to the poorest dockside tenements with a female strike leader tip the balance, pulling her away from conventional identification with the leisure class and toward a life lived in closer contact with poverty. "I've changed," she announces, "I saw the worst of it, things so wrong in the tenements that big reforms are needed."

By pursuing deep involvements in social causes, Billy's younger sister, Sue, takes advantage of one of the few career options available to unmarried middle-class women in the early twentieth century. Like the altruistic Gertie Ferish in Edith Wharton's 1905 novel *The House of Mirth*, Sue volunteers at the working girls' clubs that were active in New York around the turn of the century. She does not merely march in suffrage parades but helps organize them. She hosts radical gatherings and makes speeches at both women's meetings and workers' rallies. Finally, Sue falls in love with the revolutionary Joe Kramer and becomes what he calls "a regular organizer." Sue is the real revolutionary in Billy's family, a woman who does not shy away even from the idea of direct industrial sabotage. She, as much as any of the book's core personalities, inhabits and expresses what Poole calls "this glorious age of deep radical changes going on." As her relationship with Kramer develops, the question becomes whether it is actually possible for her to sunder all class ties to accept a bitter, hand-to-mouth existence as the wife of an outlaw labor agitator. Perhaps more seriously than Billy, she contemplates the permanent sacrifice of bourgeois privilege.

In creating the character of Billy's sister, Poole did not need a specific historical model; rather, Sue is a much advanced composite of the independent-minded New Woman who was already making waves on the American social scene. Poole's fictional strike heroine Nora Ganey, however, seems an interesting composite of two historical figures. She resembles both Elizabeth Gurley Flynn—the fearless IWW Rebel Girl who was often called the Joan of Arc of the labor movement—and seventeen-year-old millworker Hannah Silverman, the "Paterson firebrand" whom Flynn came to admire as one of the leading figures of the strike. Through their courage and effectiveness as speakers and protesters, these women defied gender stereotypes and showed what female activists could do during strikes if given the chance. Flynn agitated for both the IWW and an early but potent form of feminism. She built confidence among the women strikers and broke down the resistance of male strikers toward female leadership. Silverman was repeatedly arrested at Paterson but always quickly rejoined picket lines to lift morale. She was given the honor of leading the parade of workers to Madison Square Garden on the day of the Paterson Pageant. In Poole's novel, Nora Ganey speaks to an audience of twenty thousand at the Garden, an event that Billy calls "the one great miracle of the strike." Ganey, Sue, and to some extent Eleanore Dillon reflect the emergence of the female labor leader, a phenomenon that was one of the most exciting developments at Paterson and Lawrence.

Considering Poole's evident responsiveness to current social history in *The Harbor*, it would have been surprising if he hadn't reserved a prominent role for the arch-revolutionist and prime force of American syndicalism, Bill Haywood. In labor leader Jim Marsh, Poole paints an accurate portrait of Haywood, one that captures the man's magnetism at the height of his power. When Billy meets Marsh, described as "the great mob agitator and notorious leader of strikes," he feels an "electric shock" with effects less physical than ideological. While still a skeptic of radical change, Billy gets a quick education from Marsh, who shares appalling statistics about workplace conditions, worker death rates, and other indices of lower-class misery. Billy had been introduced to Marsh for the purpose of "writing up" the labor leader in a large circulation journal, something he had already done for Marsh's businessmen enemies. Approaching Marsh with conventionally shaped ideas, Billy is promptly overwhelmed by the other side of the story: "I could feel him taking my harbor to pieces, transforming each piece into something grim and so building a harbor of his own."

Aside from the Paterson-inspired presentation of Billy's involvements, many of the structural details of *The Harbor* have direct analogues in the 1913 silk workers' strike. The Farm in Poole's novel, an outdoor site near the harbor where strikers meet for rallies, is a version of Haledon, where the Paterson silk workers held peaceful Sunday afternoon mass gatherings, listened to talks by Poole, Haywood, Flynn, and Carlo Tresca, and sang football songs led by former Harvard cheerleader John Reed. Described in Poole's novel as the open shore space in front of a dock, the Farm is where thirty thousand "intensely alive" workers gather and where Ganey, Marsh, and Kramer use rousing speeches to unify the ethnically diverse strikers.

At one particularly stirring meeting the trio of agitators takes turns exhorting the crowd. Ganey mourns the thousands of deaths caused by big companies, urging the workers to "strike and strike and strike again—till you make these tenements own the ships—and a life won't be thrown away for a dollar." Marsh makes his class-based point by alluding to press accounts of the wealthy women who had recently died in the sinking of the *Titanic*. "We heard a lot about their screams," Marsh recalls, but the "millions more" killed in "mines and mills and stinking slums" have yet to be heard. Kramer, whose health has been ruined by two years spent shoveling coal in a ship's engine room, speaks directly to the "men who work in the stokeholes naked" and asks for a moment of silence as "a tribute to all the dead stokers." The chapter closes with prophecies from Marsh that could well have been uttered by Haywood and repeated as Wobbly policy: "Until we get our share, this labor war will have no end! . . . You will rise—and the world will be free."

In the next chapter, a version of the Paterson Pageant takes place; even the process by which the pageant was reportedly initiated by Haywood is re-created: "Marsh proposed a parade, and the Farm took it up with prompt acclaim." The entire polyglot "strike family" marches down Fifth Avenue, causing the shutting down of the retail stores and displacing the well-dressed shoppers, suggesting the antagonism between the labor movement and middle-class consumerism. The event actually resembles a pageant much more than a parade, with dirgelike funeral music and banners announcing OUR WOUNDED and OUR DEAD, followed by a procession of coffins that recasts the most moving scene of the Paterson Pageant: the funeral of striker Modestino Valentino. Mirroring the basic dynamic of the original pageant, this mass action prompts Billy, who is marching with the workers, to recognize the dissonance of his own loyalties. Though he is deeply moved by a spontaneous expression of joy among the strikers, he reflects, "You can't join in a laugh like that—you're no real member of this crowd—their world is not where you belong."

As Billy considers this class-based limitation, the theme of *The Harbor* becomes his own relationship—and the relationship of his writing—to the labor struggle. For a time after he fell in love with Eleanore Dillon, he had submitted wholly to the worldview of capitalist efficiency and written in praise of its power. But a key stage in the reversal of his worldview comes when Kramer leads Billy into the stokehole of an ocean liner for a shocking glimpse of bestial half-naked workers shoveling coal into the ship's furnace. Poole's rendering of the hellish scene—where there is "no day and no night, only steel walls and electric light"—recalls the working conditions described in several of Eugene O'Neill's early sea plays, most notably *The Hairy Ape*. As in O'Neill's play, which was almost certainly thematically influenced by *The Harbor*, a visit to the stokehole by the slumming adventurer has profound psychological effects: Billy is traumatized by his intrusion into workers' lives. Noticing his distress, Kramer remarks, "That look at a stokehole got hold of you hard." Billy's insistent questions about industrial conditions at his next meeting with Dillon signal a change in attitude—his faith in efficiency has weakened. Essentially, Billy realizes that his picture of the class struggle had been woefully incomplete. He now decides to forgo the glory stories, write what he sees and feels during his excursions into the labor movement, and present his perceptions to the public with all the realism he can marshal.

When Billy becomes personally involved in a massive strike of stokers and longshoremen, his conversion to socialism accelerates. While attending a worker rally, he is overwhelmed by police, beaten to unconsciousness, and taken to prison with the strikers. Poole describes the various nationalities of the imprisoned workers, their spirited singing, and Billy's newfound solidarity with the poor: "At last with a deep warm certainty I felt myself where I belonged." In his prison cell Poole's alter ego poses the profound questions that are on trial for the rest of the novel and are still on trial for anyone concerned with social justice: "What has all this to do with me? What is it going to mean in my life?"

The paradigm for muckraking novels takes for granted the subject's eventual adoption of a revolutionary stance, and for most of *The Harbor* this seems to be exactly where Billy is headed. The actual outcome of his struggle, however, is not a conversion to political certainty but to a state of inquiry, posing a series of unresolved questions about class relationships. Even when the strike is crushed and the voice of the workers ceases, Billy wonders, "Would that crowd spirit rise again? Could it be that the time was near?" Whatever conversion these thoughts imply remains incomplete because Billy's judgment is intruded upon by a new factor. Before his leftism can fully crystallize, the "first low grumble of war" is heard, and the cause of labor is superseded by what may only be called a more immediate historical concern: the "crashing down" of civilization itself.

Poole's novel closes with an analysis of the incipient war—one of the first in an American novel and one of the most prescient. Months before trench warfare and machine-driven death were generally known horrors, Billy describes efficient, modernized slaughter.

> I thought of the long lines of fire at dawn spurting from the mouths of guns . . . from trenches in fast blackening fields—and of men in endless multitudes pitching on their faces as the fire mowed them down.

And five years before F. Scott Fitzgerald's first hero, Amory Blaine, would famously describe the spiritual effects of the war's end in *This Side of Paradise*—"all Gods dead, all wars fought, all faiths in man shaken"—Poole offers a valedictory to the "gods of civilization and peace" that were shattered in the war's beginning. While Billy remains hopeful but uncertain that the class struggle can be won, he does know that on the battlefields of Europe the god of his mother's church, the god of corporate efficiency, and the god of the working masses were being plunged into a "furnace of war" from which each would emerge in radically altered form.

Largely because Poole's rise as a writer was so closely tied to the shifting fortunes of history and politics, the national celebrity that he achieved with *The Harbor* did not last. With American entry into the European conflict in 1917, the desire for patriotic unity gave license to the severe curtailment of civil liberties and touched off strong antileft persecutions. Strikes and labor actions of the type depicted by Poole in *The Harbor* were not only no longer front-page news; they soon became illegal under the Sedition Act of 1918. Though Poole initially supported American war aims, after the November 1918 Armistice he was severely disillusioned by reactionary trends in the United States. Events of 1919—the first Red scare, the lynching of Wobblies, the sentencing of socialists to long prison terms—made it clear that his brand of liberalism was out of step with postwar "normalcy." Though he continued to produce fiction and journalism, the 1920s and 1930s saw Poole's gradual fall from prominence as a cultural figure.

When he died in 1950, Poole's *New York Times* obituary stated correctly that he had won the first Pulitzer Prize for fiction ever awarded, and that he was best known for his acclaimed novel of 1915. But the *Times* did scant justice to Poole's most influential book, blandly misdescribing *The Harbor* only as an "intimate picture of this city." Someone must have realized that the novel's importance had been slighted, for the *Times* immediately prepared an addendum. Published two days later, "The Days of Ernest Poole" better served the historical record by relating the real subject matter of *The Harbor* and placing it in distinguished literary company. The book, it was now acknowledged, stood up to comparisons with Upton Sinclair's *The Jungle*, Frank Norris's *The Octopus*, and the novels of the great naturalist Theodore Dreiser. It was a work that helped define the muckraking era, a "golden age" of American fiction in which powerful "cries of indignation" from American writers registered stark economic injustice and explosive political tensions.[17]

Even this assessment, however, fails to account for all aspects of the novel's contemporary significance. Reading *The Harbor* today, we recognize among its many modern attributes an early warning about the destruction of an ecosystem by corporate greed and consumerism. Almost a century before the Gulf of Mexico oil spill of 2010, Poole's central character wonders whether he should be impressed by the "hundreds of millions of dollars that are being spent on engineering to make the harbor like it should be"—or appalled by the "loathsome blotches and streaks of oil" in the East River, the "foul, sluggish columns of smoke on the Jersey shore," and the hideous miles of acrid-smelling black water poisoned by Standard Oil. Dillon the engineer, one of the earliest depictions in our literature of a corporate talking head, claims despite appalling evidence to the contrary that CEOs know best. His assurances that the pollution problem is being "worked on" call to mind the early twenty-first-century assurances from oil industry executives about the safety of deep-water drilling in environmentally sensitive areas.

In his autobiography, Poole found it interesting that three hundred copies of *The Harbor*, bound for British readers in Liverpool, went down with the RMS *Lusitania* on May 7, 1915. Compared to the nearly twelve hundred lives lost in the sinking of the British liner by a German U-boat, the copies of Poole's book mean nothing materially. But they do make a good symbol, a reminder of the political conditions that often decide the fate of artistic efforts. And the fact that a chain of events beginning with the sinking of the *Lusitania* ended with U.S. entry into a war that throttled socialism at home and ultimately marginalized Ernest Poole as a writer is telling. While the war explains the short-lived viability of American radicalism, making it easy for historians to minimize its importance, it also explains why *The Harbor* was forgotten for much of the twentieth century, and why a new edition of the novel is so necessary. Reissuing this book doesn't change history, but it repairs a loss to our literary history by ensuring that the quintessential story of prewar radicalism did not, in the end, go down with the *Lusitania*.

PATRICK CHURA

Notes

1. Rideout, 56; Keefer, 54; Golin, 235.
2. "Current Fiction." *New York Times*, February 7, 1915.
3. Keefer considers it possible that the Pulitzer Poole received for *His Family* just after the success of *The Harbor* was "in part recognition of the importance of its predecessor" (55). In *The Pulitzer Prizes* (New York: Columbia University Press, 1974), John Hohenberg analyzed the prize committee's deliberations and noted that *His Family* "had not made anything like the impression of Poole's earlier and more successful work, *The Harbor*" (57).
4. Rideout, 48. For a synopsis of Socialist political gains in the period, see Rideout, 47–48.
5. For detailed accounts of the Paterson Pageant, see Anne Huber Tripp, Steve Golin, and Linda Nochlin.
6. Mabel Dodge Luhan, *Intimate Memories*, v. 3, *Movers and Shakers* (New York: Harcourt, Brace and Company, 1936), 39.
7. *The Bridge*, 216.
8. Ibid., 66.
9. Ibid., 95, 97.
10. Reed, Mabel Dodge Luhan, and Thompson Buchanan were the other three (New York *Tribune*, June 8, 1913).
11. Leona Rust Egan, *Provincetown as a Stage* (Orleans, MA: Parnassus, 1994), 106.
12. Susan Glaspell, *The Road to the Temple* (New York: Stokes, 1941), 250.
13. *The Bridge*, 199.
14. Ibid., 199.
15. In Friedman's novel, the central character is wounded attempting to stop fighting between Pinkertons and strikers. The protagonist's love interest is the wealthy daughter of a steel mill owner.
16. *The Bridge*, 200.
17. "Ernest Poole, 69, Novelist, Is Dead." *New York Times*, January 11, 1950; "The Days of Ernest Poole." *New York Times*, January 13, 1950.

Suggestions for Further Reading

Boylan, James. *The Rise of Ernest Poole: The Making of a Social Muckraker*. Kansas City, MO: Association for Education in Journalism and Mass Communication, 1993.

Chura, Patrick. *Vital Contact: Downclassing Journeys in American Literature from Herman Melville to Richard Wright*. New York and London: Routledge, 2005.

Cuff, Robert. "Ernest Poole: Novelist as Propagandist, 1917–1918: A Note." *Canadian Review of American Studies*. 19, 2 (1995): 183–94.

Dowling, Robert. *Slumming in New York: From the Waterfront to Mythic Harlem*. Urbana: University of Illinois Press, 2007.

Dubofsky, Melvin. *We Shall Be All*. Chicago: Quadrangle Books, 1969.

Flynn, Elizabeth G. "The Truth About the Paterson Pageant," in *I Speak My Peace*. New York: Masses and Mainstream, 1955.

Freeman, Joseph. *An American Testament, a Narrative of Rebels and Romantics*. New York: Farrar & Rinehart, 1936.

Golin, Steve. *The Fragile Bridge: Paterson Silk Strike, 1913*. Philadelphia: Temple University Press, 1988.

Hapgood, Hutchins. *A Victorian in the Modern World*. New York: Harcourt Brace, 1939.

Hapke, Laura. *Labor's Text: The Worker in American Fiction*. New Brunswick, NJ: Rutgers University Press, 2001.

Hart, John E. "Heroism Through Social Awareness: Ernest Poole's *The Harbor*." *Critique: Studies in Contemporary Fiction*. 9, 3 (1967): 84–94.

Keefer, Truman Frederick. *Ernest Poole*. New York: Twayne, 1966.

Kornbluh, Joyce. *Rebel Voices: An I.W.W. Anthology*. Ann Arbor: University of Michigan Press, 1964.

Nochlin, Linda. "The Paterson Strike Pageant of 1913." *Art in America* 62 (May 1974): 64–68.

Poole, Ernest. *The Bridge: My Own Story*. New York: The Macmillan Company, 1940.

_____. *His Family*. New York: The Macmillan Company, 1917.

Rideout, Walter Bates. *The Radical Novel in the United States, 1900–1954: Some Interrelations of Literature and Society*. Cambridge, MA: Harvard University Press, 1956.

Sinclair, Upton, *American Outpost*. Port Washington, NY: Kennikat Press, 1932.

Tripp, Anne Huber. *The IWW and the Paterson Silk Strike of 1913*. Urbana: University of Illinois Press, 1987.

The Harbor

BOOK I

CHAPTER I

"You chump," I thought contemptuously. I was seven years old at the time, and the gentleman to whom I referred was Henry Ward Beecher. What it was that aroused my contempt for the man will be more fully understood if I tell first of the grudge that I bore him.

I was sitting in my mother's pew in the old church in Brooklyn. I was altogether too small for the pew, it was much too wide for the bend at my knees; and my legs which were very short and fat, stuck straight out before me. I was not allowed to move, I was most uncomfortable, and for this Sabbath torture I laid all the blame on the preacher. For my mother had once told me that I was brought to church so small in order that when I grew up I could say I had heard the great man preach before he died. Hence the deep grudge that I bore him. Sitting here this morning, it seemed to me for hours and hours, I had been meditating upon my hard lot. From time to time, as was my habit when thinking or feeling deeply, one hand would unconsciously go to my head and slowly stroke my bang. My hair was short and had no curls, its only glory was this bang, which was deliciously soft to my hand and shone like a mirror from much reflective stroking. Presently my mother would notice and with a smile she would put down my hand, but a few moments later up it would come and would continue its stroking. For I felt both abused and puzzled. What was there in the talk of the large white-haired old man in the pulpit to make my mother's eyes so queer, to make her sit so stiff and still? What good would it do me when I grew up to say that I had heard him?

"I don't believe I will ever say it," I reasoned doggedly to myself. "And even if I do, I don't believe any other man will care

whether I say it to him or not." I felt sure my father wouldn't. He
never even came to church.

At the thought of my strange silent father, my mind leaped to
his warehouse, his dock, the ships and the harbor. Like him, they
were all so strange. And my hands grew a little cold and moist as
I thought of the terribly risky thing I had planned to do all by
myself that very afternoon. I thought about it for a long time
with my eyes tight shut. Then the voice of the minister brought
me back, I found myself sitting here in church and went on with
this less shivery thinking.

"I wouldn't care myself," I decided. "If I were a man and another
man met me on the street and said, 'Look here. When I was a boy
I heard Henry Ward Beecher before he died,' I guess I would just
say to him, 'You mind your business and I'll mind mine.'" This
phrase I had heard from the corner grocer, and I liked the sound of
it. I repeated it now with an added zest.

Again I opened my eyes and again I found myself here in
church. Still here. I heaved a weary sigh.

"If you were dead already," I thought as I looked up at the
preacher, "my mother wouldn't bring me here." I found this an
exceedingly cheering thought. I had once overheard our cook
Anny describe how her old father had dropped dead. I eyed the
old minister hopefully.

But what was this he was saying? Something about "the harbor of life." The harbor! In an instant I was listening hard, for
this was something I knew about.

"Safe into the harbor," I heard him say. "Home to the harbor
at last to rest." And then, while he passed on to something else,
something I *didn't* know about, I settled disgustedly back in the
pew.

"You chump," I thought contemptuously. To hear him talk you
would have thought the harbor was a place to feel quite safe in, a
place to snuggle down in, a nice little place to come home to at
night. "I guess he has never seen it much," I snorted.

For I had. From our narrow brownstone house on the Heights,
ever since I could remember (and let me tell you that seems a long
time when you are seven years old), I had looked down from our
back windows upon a harbor that to me was strange and terrible.

I was glad that our house was up so high. Its front was on a sedate old street, and within it everything felt safe. My mother was here, and Sue, my little sister, and old Belle, our nurse, our nursery, my games, my animals, my fairy books, the small red table where I ate my supper, and the warm fur rug by my bed, where I knelt for "Now I lay me."

But from the porch at the back of our house you went three steps down to a long narrow garden—at least the garden seemed long to me—and if you walked to the end of the garden and peered through the ivy-covered bars of the fence, as I had done when I was so little that I could barely walk alone, you had the first mighty thrill of your life. For you found that through a hole in the ivy you could see a shivery distance straight down through the air to a street below. You found that the two iron posts, one at either end of the fence, were warm when you touched them, had holes in the top, had smoke coming out—were chimneys! And slowly it dawned upon your mind that this garden of yours was nothing at all but the roof of a gray old building—which your nurse told you vaguely had been a "warehouse" long ago when the waters of the harbor had come 'way in to the street below. The old "wharves" had been down there, she said. What was a "wharf"? It was a "dock," she told me. And she said that a family of "dockers" lived in the building under our garden. They were all that was left in it now but "old junk." Who was Old Junk, a man or a woman? And what in the world were Dockers?

Pursuing my adventurous ways, I found at one place in the garden, hidden by flowers near a side wall, a large heavy lid which was painted brown and felt like tin. But how much heavier than tin. Tug as I might, I could not budge it. Then I found it had an iron hook and was hooked down tight to the garden. Yes, it was true, our whole garden was a roof! I put my ear down to the lid and listened scowling, both eyes shut. I heard nothing then, but I came back and tried it many times, until once I jumped up and ran like mad. For faintly from somewhere deep down under the flower beds I had heard a baby crying! What was this baby, a Junk or a Docker? And who were these people who lived under flowers? To me they sounded suspiciously like the goblins in my goblin book. Once when I was sick in bed, Sue came shrieking into the house and said that a giant had heaved up that great lid from below. Up had come his shaggy head, his dirty face, his rolling eyes, and he had laughed and laughed at the flowers. He was a drunken man, our old nurse Belle had told her, but Sue was sure he was a giant.

"You are wrong," I said with dignity. "He is either a Junk or a Docker."

The lid was spiked down after that, and our visitor never appeared again. But I saw him vividly in my mind's eye—his shaggy wild head rising up among our flowers. Vaguely I felt that he came from the harbor.

As the exciting weeks of my life went on I discovered three good holes in that ivy-covered fence of ours. These all became my secret holes, and through them I watched the street below, a bleak bare chasm of a street which when the trucks came by echoed till it thundered. Across the street rose the high gray front of my father's warehouse. It was part of a solid line of similar gray brick buildings, and it was like my father, it was grim and silent, you could not see inside. Over its five tiers of windows black iron shutters were fastened tight. From time to time a pair of these shutters would fly open, disclosing a dark cave behind, out of which men brought barrels and crates and let them down by ropes into the trucks on the street below. How they spun round and round as they came! But most of the trucks drove rumbling into a tunnel which led through the warehouse out to my father's dock, out to the ships and the harbor. And from that mysterious region long lines of men came through the tunnel at noontime, some nearly naked, some only in shirts, men with the hairiest faces. They sat on the street with their backs to the warehouse wall, eating their dinners out of pails, and from other pails they took long drinks of a curious stuff all white on top. Some of them were always crossing the street and disappearing from my view into a little store directly underneath me. Belle spoke of this store as a "vile saloon" and of these men as "dockers." So I knew what Dockers were at last! In place of the one who lived under our garden and had burst up among the flowers, I saw now that there were hundreds and thousands of men like him down there on the docks. And all belonged to the harbor.

Their work I learned was to load the ships whose masts and spars peeped up at me over the warehouse roofs. From my nursery window above I could see them better. Sometimes they had large white sails and then they moved off somewhere. I could see them go, these tall ships, with their sails making low, mysterious sounds, flappings, spankings and deep boomings. The men on them sang the weirdest songs as they pulled all together at the ropes. Some of these songs brought a lump in your throat. Where were they going? "To heathen lands," Belle told me. What did she mean? I was just going to ask her. But then I stopped—I did not dare! From up the river, under the sweeping arch of that Great Bridge which seemed high as the clouds, came more tall ships, and low "steamers" belching smoke and "tugs" and "barges" and "ferry boats." The names of all these I learned from Belle and Anny the cook and my mother. And all were going "to heathen lands." What in the world did Belle mean by that?

Once I thought I had it. I saw that some of these smaller boats were just going across the river and stopping at the land over there, a land so crowded with buildings you could barely see into it at all. "Is that a heathen land?" I asked her. "Yes!" said Belle. And she laughed. She was Scotch and very religious. But later I heard her call it "New York" and say she was going there herself to buy herself some corsets. And so I was even more puzzled than ever. For some deep instinct told me you could buy no corsets in "heathen lands"—least of all Belle's corsets.

She often spoke of "the ocean," too, another place where the tall ships went. But what was the ocean? "It's like a lake, but mightier," Belle had said. But what was a lake? It was all so vague and confusing. Always it came back to this, that I had no more seen the "ocean" than I had seen a "heathen land," and so I did not know them.

But I knew the harbor by day and by night, on bright sunny days and in fogs and rains, in storms of wind, in whirling snow, and under the restful stars at night that twinkled down from so far above, while the shadowy region below twinkled back with stars of its own, restless, many-colored stars, yellow, green and red and blue, moving, dancing, flaring, dying. And all these stars had voices, too. By night in my bed I could hear them—hoots and shrieks from ferries and tugs, hoarse coughs from engines along the docks, the whine of wheels, the clang of bells, deep blasts and bellows from steamers. And closer still, from that "vile saloon" directly under the garden, I could hear wild shouts and songs and roars of laughter that came, I learned, not only from dockers, but from "stokers" and "drunken sailors," men who lived right inside the ships and would soon be starting for heathen lands!

"I wonder how I'd feel," I would think, "if I were out in the garden now—out in the dark all by myself—right above that vile saloon!"

This would always scare me so that I would bury my head in the covers and shake. But I often did this, for I liked to be scared. It was a game I had all by myself with the harbor.

And yet this old man in the pulpit called it a place where you went to rest!

Twenty-five years have gone since then, and all that I can remember now of anything Henry Ward Beecher said was this— that once, just once, I heard him speak of something that I knew about, and that when he did he was wrong.

And though all the years since then have been for me one long story of a harbor, restless, heaving, changing, always changing— it has never changed for me in this—it has never seemed a haven where ships come to dock, but always a place from which ships start out—into the storms and the fogs of the seas, over the "ocean" to "heathen lands." For so I saw it when I was a child, the threshold of adventures.

CHAPTER II

As I walked home from church with my mother that day the streets seemed as quiet and safe as her eyes. How suddenly tempting it seemed to me, this quiet and this safety, compared to the place where I was going. For I had decided to run away from my home and my mother that afternoon, down to the harbor to see the world. What would become of me 'way down there? What would she do if I never came back? A lump rose in my throat at the thought of her tears. It was terrible.

"All the same I am going to do it," I kept thinking doggedly. And yet suddenly, as we reached our front steps, how near I came to telling her. But no, she would only spoil it all. She wanted me always up in the garden, she wanted me never to have any thrills.

My mother knew me so well. She had seen that when she read stories of fairies, witches and goblins out of my books to Sue and me, while Sue, though two years younger, would sit there like a little dark imp, her black eyes snapping over the fights, I would creep softly out of the room, ashamed and shaken, and would wait in the hall outside till the happy ending was in plain view. So my mother had gradually toned down all the fights and the killings, the witches and the monsters, and much to my disappointment had wholly shut out the gory pirates who were for me the most frightfully fascinating of all. Sometimes I felt vaguely that for this she had her own reason, too—that my mother hated everything that had to do with the ocean, especially my father's dock that made him so gloomy and silent. But of this I could never be quite sure. I would often watch her intently, with a sudden sharp anxiety, for I loved my mother with all my soul and I could not bear to see her unhappy.

"Never on any account," I heard her say to Belle, "are the children to go down the street toward the docks."

"Yes, ma'am," said Belle. "I'll see to it."

At once I wanted to go there. The street in front of our house sloped abruptly down at the next corner two blocks through poorer and smaller houses to a cobblestone space below, over which trucks clattered, plainly on their way to the docks. So I could go down and around by that way. How tempting it all looked down there. Above the roofs of the houses, the elevated railroad made a sharp bend on its way to the Bridge, trains roared by, high over all the Great Bridge swept across the sky. And below all this and more thrilling than all, I caught glimpses of strange, ragged boys. "Micks," Belle sometimes called them, and sometimes, "Finian Mickies." Up here I had no playmates.

From now on, our garden lost its charms. Up the narrow courtway which ran along the side of the house I would slip stealthily to the front gate and often get a good look down the street before Belle sharply called me back. The longest looks, I found, were always on Sunday afternoons, when Belle would sit back there in the garden, close to the bed of red tulips which encircled a small fountain made of two white angels. Belle, who was bony, tall and grim, would sit by the little angels reading her shabby Bible. Her face was wrinkled and almost brown, her eyes now kind, now gloomy. She had a song she would sing now and then. "For beneath the Union Jack we will drive the Finians back"—is all I can remember. She told me of witches in the Scotch hills. At her touch horrible monsters rose in the most surprising places. In the bathtub, for example, when I stayed in the bath too long she would jerk out the stopper, and as from the hole there came a loud gurgle—"It's the Were-shark," Belle would mutter. And I would leap out trembling.

This old "Were-shark" had his home in the very middle of the ocean. In one gulp he could swallow a boy of my size, and this he did three times each day. The boys were brought to him by the "Condor," a perfectly hideous bird as large as a cow and as fierce as a tiger. If ever I dared go down that street and disobey my mother, the Condor would "swoop" down over the roofs, snatch me up in his long yellow beak with the blood of the last boy on it, and with thunder and lightning would carry me off far over the clouds and drop me into the Were-shark's mouth.

Then Belle would sit down to her Bible.

Sunday after Sunday passed, and still in fascinated dread I would steal quietly out to the gate and watch this street forbidden. Pointing to it one day, Belle had declared in awful tones, "Broad is the way that leadeth to destruction." But it was not broad. In that at least she was all wrong. It was in fact so narrow that a Condor as big as a cow might easily bump himself when he "swooped." Besides, there were good strong lamp-posts where a little boy could cling and scream, and almost always somewhere in sight was a policeman so fat and heavy that even two Condors could hardly lift him from the ground. This policeman would come running. My mother had said I must never be scared by policemen, because they were really good kind men. In fact, she said, it was foolish to be scared by anything ever. She never knew of Belle's methods with me.

So at last I had decided to risk it, and now the fearful day had come. I could barely eat my dinner. My courage was fast ebbing away. In the dining-room the sunlight was for a time wiped out by clouds, and I grew suddenly happy. It might rain and then I could not go. But it did not rain nor did anything I hoped for happen to prevent my plan. Belle sat down by the angels and was soon so deep in her Bible that it was plain I could easily slip up the path. Sue never looked up from her sand-pile to say, "Stop Billy! He's running away from home!" With a gulp I passed my mother's window. She did not happen to look out. Now I had reached the very gate. "I can't go! I can't open the gate!" But the old gate opened with one push. "I can't go! There is no policeman!" But yes, there he was on my side of the street slowly walking toward me. My heart thumped, I could hardly breathe. In a moment with a frantic rush I had reached the nearest lamp-post and was clinging breathless. I could not scream, I shut my eyes in sickening fear and waited for the rushing of enormous wings.

But there came no Condor swooping.

Another rush—another post—another and another!

"What's the matter with you, little feller?"

I looked up at the big safe policeman and laughed.

"I'm playing a game," I almost shouted, and ran without touching another post two blocks to the cobblestone space below. I ran blindly around it several times, I bumped into a man who said, "Heigh there! Look out!" After that I strutted proudly, then turned and ran back with all my might up the street, and into our house and up to my room. And there on my bed to my great surprise I found myself sobbing and sobbing. It was a long time before I could stop. I had had my first adventure.

I made many Sunday trips after that, and on no one of them was I caught. For delighted and proud at what I had done I kept asking Belle to talk of the Condor, gloomily she piled on the terrors, and seeing the awed look in my eyes (awe at my own courage in defying such a bird), she felt so sure of my safety that often she would barely look up from her Bible the whole afternoon. Even on workdays over her sewing she would forget. And so I went "to destruction."

At first I stayed but a little while and never left the cobblestone space, only peering up into the steep little streets that led to the fearsome homes of the "Micks." But then I made the acquaintance of Sam. It happened through a small toy boat which I had taken down there with the purpose of starting it off for "heathen lands." As I headed across the railroad tracks that led to the docks, suddenly Sam and his gang appeared from around a freight car. I stood stock-still. They were certainly "Micks"— ragged and dirty, with holes in their shoes and soot on their faces. Sam was smoking a cigarette.

"Heigh, fellers," he said, "look at Willy's boat."

I clutched my boat tighter and turned to run. But the next moment Sam had me by the arm.

"Look here, young feller," he growled. "You've got the wrong man to do business with this time."

"I don't want to do any business," I gasped.

"Smash him, Sam—smash in his nut for him," piped the smallest Micky cheerfully. And this Sam promptly proceeded to do. It was a wild and painful time. But though Sam was two years older, he was barely any larger than I, and when he and his gang had gone off with my boat, as I stood there breathing hard, I was filled with a grim satisfaction. For once when he tried to wrench the boat from me I had hit him with it right on the face, and I had had a glimpse of a thick red mark across his cheek. I tasted something new in my mouth and spit it out. It was blood. I did this several times, slowly and impressively, till it made a good big spot on the railroad tie at my feet. Then I walked with dignity back across the tracks and up "the way of destruction" home. I walked slowly, planning as I went. At the gate I climbed up on it and swung. Then with a sudden loud cry I fell off and ran back into the garden crying, "I fell off the gate! I fell on my face!" So my cut and swollen lip was explained, and my trips were not discovered.

I felt myself growing older fast. For I knew that I could both fight and tell lies, besides defying the Condor.

In the next years, for weeks at a time my life was centered on Sam and his gang. How we became friends, how often we met, by just what means I evaded my nurse, all these details are vague to me now. I am not even sure I was never caught. But it seems to me that I was not. For as I grew to be eight years old, Belle turned her attention more and more to that impish little sister of mine who was always up to some mischief or other. There was the corner grocer, too, with whom I pretended to be staunch friends. "I'm going to see the grocer," I would say, when I heard Sam's cautious whistle in front of the house—and so presently I would join the gang. I followed Sam with a doglike devotion, giving up my weekly twenty-five cents instead of saving it for Christmas, and in return receiving from him all the world-old wisdom stored in that bullet-shaped head of his which sat so tight on his round little shoulders.

And though I did not realize it then, in my tense crowded childhood, through Sam and his companions I learned something else that was to stand me in good stead years later on. I learned how to make friends with "the slums." I discovered that by making friends with "Micks" and "Dockers" and the like, you find they are no fearful goblins, giants bursting savagely up among the flowers of your life, but people as human as yourself, or rather, much more human, because they live so close to the harbor, close to the deep rough tides of life.

Into these tides I was now drawn down—and it did me some

good and a great deal of harm. For I was too little those days for the harbor.

Sam had the most wonderful life in the world. He could go wherever he liked and at any hour day or night. Once, he said, when a "feller" was drowned, he had stayed out on the docks all night. His mother always let him alone. An enormous woman with heavy eyes, I was in awe of her from the first. The place that she kept with Sam's father was called "The Sailor's Harbor." It stood on a corner down by the docks, a long, low wooden building painted white, with twelve tight-shuttered, mysterious windows along the second story, and below them a "Ladies' Entrance." In front was a small blackboard with words in white which Sam could read. "Ten Cent Dinners" stood at the top. Below came, "Coffee and rolls." Next, "Ham and eggs." Then "Bacon and eggs." And then, "To-day"—with a space underneath where Sam's fat father wrote down every morning still more delicious eatables. You got whiffs of these things and they made your mouth water, they made your stomach fairly turn against your nursery supper.

But most of our time we spent on the docks. All were roofed, and exploring the long dock sheds and climbing down into the dark holds of the square-rigged ships called "clippers," we found logs of curious mottled wood, huge baskets of sugar, odorous spices, indigo, camphor, tea, coffee, jute and endless other things. Sam knew their names and the names of the wonder-places they came from—Manila, Calcutta, Bombay, Ceylon. He knew besides such words as "hawser," "bulkhead" and "ebb-tide." And Sam knew how to swear. He swore with a fascinating ease such words as made me shiver and stare. And then he would look at me and chuckle.

"You think I'll go to hell for this, don't you," he asked me once. And my face grew hot with embarrassment, for I thought that he assuredly would.

I asked him what were heathen lands, and he said they were countries where heathen lived. And what were heathen? Cannibals. And what were they?

"Fellers that eat fellers," he said.

"Alive?" I inquired. He turned to the gang:

"Listen to the kid! He wants to know if they eat 'em alive!" Sam spat disgustedly. "Naw," he said. "First they roast 'em like any meat. They roast 'em," he added reflectively, "until their skin gets brown and bubbles out and busts."

One afternoon a carriage brought three travelers for one of the ships, a man, his wife and a little girl with shining yellow pigtails. "To be et," Sam whispered as we stood close beside them. And then, pointing to some of the half-naked brown men that made the crew of the ship near by—"cannibals," he muttered. For a long time I stared at these eaters, especially at their lean brown stomachs.

"We're safe enough," Sam told me. "They ain't allowed to come ashore." I found this very comforting.

But what a frightful fate lay in store for the little girl with pigtails. As I watched her I felt worse and worse. Why couldn't somebody warn her in time? At last I decided to do it myself. Procuring a scrap of paper I retired behind a pile of crates and wrote in my large, clumsy hand, "You look out—you are going to be et." Watching my chance, I slipped this into her satchel and hoped that she would read it soon. Then I promptly forgot all about her and ran off into a warehouse where the gang had gone to slide.

These warehouses had cavernous rooms, so dark you could not see to the ends, and there from between the wooden columns the things from the ships loomed out of the dark like so many ghosts. There were strange sweet smells. And from a hole in the ceiling there was a twisting chute of steel down which you could slide with terrific speed. We used to slide by the hour.

Outside were freight cars in long lines, some motionless, some suddenly lurching forward or back, with a grinding and screeching of wheels and a puffing and coughing from engines ahead. Sam taught me how to climb on the cars and how to swing off while they were going. He had learned from watching the brakemen that dangerous backward left-hand swing that lands you stock-still in your tracks. It is a splendid feeling. Only once Sam's left hand caught, I heard a low cry, and after I jumped I found him standing there with a white face. His left hand hung straight down from the wrist and blood was dripping from it.

"Shut up, you damn fool!" he said fiercely.

"I wasn't saying nothing," I gasped.

"Yes, you was—you was startin' to cry! Holy Christ!" He sat down suddenly, then rolled over and lay still. Some one ran for his mother, and after a time he was carried away. I did not see him again for some weeks.

We did things that were bad for a boy of my size, and I saw things that I shouldn't have seen—a docker crushed upon one of the docks and brought out on a stretcher dead, a stoker as drunk as though he were dead being wheeled on a wheelbarrow to a ship by the man called a "crimp," who sold this drunken body for an advance on its future pay. Sam told me in detail of these things. There came a strike, and once in the darkness of a cold November twilight I saw some dockers rush on a "scab," I heard the dull sickening thumps as they beat him.

And one day Sam took me to the door of his father's saloon and pointed out a man in there who had an admiring circle around him.

"He's going to jump from the Bridge on a bet," Sam whispered. I saw the man go. For what seemed to me hours I watched the Great Bridge up there in the sky, with its crawling processions of trolleys and wagons, its whole moving armies of little black men. Suddenly one of these tiny specks shot out and down, I saw it fall below the roofs, I felt Sam's hand like ice in mine. And this was not good for a boy of ten.

But the sight that ended it all for me was not a man, but a woman. It happened one chilly March afternoon when I fell from a dock into water covered with grease and foam, came up spluttering and terrified, was quickly hauled to the dock by a man and then hustled by Sam and the gang to his home, to have my clothes dried and so not get caught by my mother. Scolded by Sam's mother and given something fiery hot to drink, stripped naked and wrapped in an old flannel night-gown and told to sit by the stove in the kitchen—I was then left alone with Sam. And then Sam with a curious light in his eyes took me to a door which he opened just a crack. Through the crack he showed me a small back room full of round iron tables. And at one of these a man, stoker or sailor I don't know which, his face flushed red under dirt and hair, held in his lap a big fat girl half dressed, giggling and queer, quite drunk. And then while Sam whispered on and on about the shuttered rooms upstairs, I felt a rush of such sickening fear and loathing that I wanted to scream—but I turned too faint.

I remember awakening on the floor, Sam's mother furiously slapping Sam, then dressing me quickly, gripping me tight by both my arms and saying,

"You tell a word of this to your pa and we'll come up and kill you!"

That night at home I did not sleep. I lay in my bed and shivered and burned. My first long exciting adventure was over. Ended were all the thrills, the wild fun. It was a spree I had had with the harbor, from the time I was seven until I was ten. It had taken me at seven, a plump sturdy little boy, and at ten it had left me wiry, thin, with quick, nervous movements and often dark shadows under my eyes. And it left a deep scar on my early life. For over all the adventures and over my whole childhood loomed this last thing I had seen, hideous, disgusting. For years after that, when I saw or even thought of the harbor, I felt the taste of foul, greasy water in my mouth and in my soul.

So ended the first lesson.

CHAPTER III

The next morning as I started for school, suddenly in the hallway I thought of what my mother had told me—always when I was frightened to shut my eyes and speak to Jesus and he would be sure to make everything right. I had not spoken to Jesus of late except to say "Holy Christ!" like Sam. But now, so sickened by Sam and his docks, my head throbbing from the sleepless night, on the impulse I kneeled quickly with my face on a chair right there in the hall. But I found I was too ashamed to begin.

"If he would only ask me," I thought. Why didn't he ask me, "What's the matter, little son?" or say, "Now, you must tell me and then you'll feel better"—as my mother always did. But Jesus did not help me out. I could not even feel him near me. "I will never tell anyone," I thought. And I felt myself horribly alone.

Help came from a quite different source.

"There he is! Look!"

I heard Sue's eager whisper. Jumping quickly to my feet, I saw in the library doorway Sue's dark little figure and her mocking, dancing eyes as she pointed me out to our father, her chum, whose face wore a smile of amusement. In a moment I had rushed out of doors and was running angrily to school, furious at myself for praying, furious at Sue for spying and at my father for that smile. My terror was forgotten. No more telling Jesus things! I retreated deep inside of myself and worked out of my troubles as best I could.

From that day the harbor became for me a big grim place to be let alone—like my father. A place immeasurably stronger than I—like my father—and like him harsh and indifferent, not caring whether when I fell into it I was pulled up to safety or drawn far down into grease and slime. It made no difference. I was nothing to it one way or the other. And I was nothing to my father.

Of course this was by no means true. As I look back now I know that often he must have tried to be kind, that in the jar and worry of his own absorbing troubled life he must have often turned to me and tried to make himself my friend. But children pass hard judgments. And if my father was friendly at times it did no good. For he was a man—big and strong—and I was a small boy craving his love.

Why couldn't he really love me? Why couldn't he ask me how I felt or pull my ear and say "Hello, Puss?" He was always saying these things to Sue, and caring about her very hard and trying to understand her, although she was nothing but a girl, two years younger and smaller than I and far less interesting. And yet with her he was kind and tender, curious and smiling, he watched her with wholly different eyes. My father was a short, powerful man, and though he was nearly fifty years old his hair was black and thick and coarse. At night he would rub his unshaven cheek on Sue's small cheek and tickle her. She would chuckle and wriggle as though it were fun. I used to watch this hungrily, and once I awkwardly drew close and offered my cheek to be tickled. My father at once grew as awkward as I, and he gave me a rub so rough it stung. And this wasn't fair—I had hoped for a cuddle. Besides, he was always praising Sue when I knew she didn't deserve it. He called her brave. Once when he took us duck shooting together a squall came up and he rowed hard, and Sue sat with her eyes on his, smiling and quite unafraid. At home that night I heard him tell my mother how wonderfully brave she had been, and of how I, on the other hand, had gripped the boat and turned white with fear, while little Sue just sat and smiled.

"We'll see how brave she is," I thought, and the next day I hit her in Sam's best style, fairly "knocked her nut off," in fact, with one quick blow. "There," I said to myself while she screamed. "I guess that shows how brave you are. I didn't scream when Sam hit me."

He said she was quicker than I at her lessons. And this rankled the deeper because it was true. But I would never admit it.

"Of course she's quick, when he's always helping her. Why

doesn't he ever come and help me?" I would burst into tears of vexation. My father was unfair!

More than that, it was he and his dock and his warehouse, in the years that followed my thrills with Sam, that stripped all these thrills away. A great ship with her spreading, booming white sails might move up the river from heathen lands as wonderful and strange as you please. But the moment she reached my father's dock she became a dirty, spotted thing, just a common everyday part of his business.

He himself was nothing but business. His business was with ships and the sea, and yet he had never once in his life taken a long sea voyage. "Why doesn't he? Why does he like only tiresome things?" I argued secretly to myself. "Why does he always come ashore?" He always did. In my memories of ships sailing I see him always there on deck talking to the captain, scowling, wrinkling his eyes over the smoke of his cigar, but always coming down the gang-plank at the end, unconcernedly turning his back on all the excitement and going back to his warehouse.

He could get excited about ships, but only in the queerest way that had something to do with his business. Late one night from my bed I heard his voice downstairs, cutting and snarling through other voices. I got out of bed and stole downstairs and along the half-lit hall to the library door, and there from behind the curtain I watched what was going on inside. The library was full of men, grave, courteous-looking gentlemen, some of them angry, some merely amused. My father was leaning over his table talking of ships, of mysterious things that he said must be done with battleships and tariffs.

"And mark me, gentlemen," he cried. "If we don't do these things in time American sails will be swept from the seas!"

Listening, I got a picture of an immense broom reaching out of the clouds and sweeping American ships off the ocean. But I could make nothing of this at the time. I only watched his face and eyes and his fist that came down with a crash on the table. And I was afraid of my father.

When ships lay at his dock the captains often came up to dinner. But even these marvelous creatures lost in my father's presence all that Sam had given them in my eyes. They did not like my mother, they ate in uneasy silence, or spoke gruffly of their dull affairs. Once or twice I heard talk of mutinies, of sailors shot down or put in irons, but all in a matter-of-fact sort of way. Mere grunts came from my father. Steadily drearier grew the ocean, flatter all the heathen lands.

One stout, red-faced captain, jovial even in spite of my mother, would annoy me frightfully by joking about my going to sea. He was always asking me when I meant to run away and be "a bloody pirate." He took it for granted I liked the sea, was thrilled by the sea, when the truth of it was that I hated the sea! It was business now, only business!

My father's warehouse, too, lost its mystery as I grew older. For exploring into its darkness I found that of course it did have walls like any common building. The things in it, too, lost their wonder. It was as though my father had packed all the rich and romantic Far East into common barrels and crates and then nailed down the covers. And he himself became for me as common as his warehouse. For in his case, too, I could see the walls.

"I know you now," I thought to myself. He could sit through supper night after night and not utter a word in his gloom. But the mystery in him was gone. Business, nothing but business. A man and a place to be let alone.

But it was my mother more than anyone else who drew me away from the harbor. All through those early years she was the one who never changed, the strong sure friend I could always come back to. My mother was as safe as our house.

She was a small, slender woman grown bodily stronger year by year by the sheer force of her spirit. I remember her smoothly parted hair, brown but showing gray at forty, the strong, lined face and the kindly eyes which I saw so often lighted by that loving smile of hers for me. If my father didn't care for me, I was always sure she did. I could feel her always watching, trying to understand what I was thinking and feeling. As when I was very small she toned down the stories she read, so she did in everything else for me, even in her religion. Though she was a strong church woman, I heard little from her of the terrors of hell. But I heard much of heaven and more still of a heaven on earth. "Thy will be done on earth as it is in heaven." I can never forget how she spoke those words as I knelt and repeated them after

her—not so much in the tone of a prayer to a higher being as in
one of quiet resolve to herself. To do her share, through church
and hospital and charity work and the bringing up of her children, her share in the establishment of a heaven upon the earth,
this was her religion.

And this heaven on earth of my mother's was made up of all
that was "fine" in humanity past and present. "Fine, fine!" she
would say of some kind deed, of some new plan for bettering life,
or of some book she was reading, some music she had heard, or
of a photograph of some great painting over in Europe. All her
life she had wanted to go abroad.

My mother was one of those first American women who went
to college, and one of that army sent out from college as school
teachers all over the land. She had taught school in frontier hamlets far out West, homesick she had looked back on the old college town in New England, and those ten years of her life out
West had been bare and hard, an exile. At last she had secured a
position in an expensive girls' school in New York, and from
there a few years later she had married my father. I think they
had been happy at first, I think that his work with the ships had
seemed to her a gateway leading out to Europe, to all the very
"finest" things. But later, as he set his whole mind upon his warehouse worries, upon his fight for Yankee ships, a navy, subsidies,
tariffs, and shut out all thought of travel, culture, friends, all but
the bare, ugly business of life—my mother had rebelled against
this, had come to hate his harbor, and had determinedly set herself to help me get what she had missed.

I don't mean that she babied me. She was too good a teacher
for that. I mean she steered me through hard work away from
what she saw in the harbor up toward what she felt was fine. She
began when I was very little giving me daily lessons at home in
the brief time she had to spare from her house and charity work.
She made me study and she studied me. My mother, sooner or
later, seemed to find out all I did or felt.

Often I would hold stubbornly back. While I was going with
Sam to the docks I never once gave her a hint of my rovings. It
was not until two years after that drunken woman disaster that I
suddenly told my mother about it. I remember then she did not
chide. Instead she caught the chance to draw out of me all I had

learned from the harbor. I talked to her long that night, but she said little in reply. I can vividly remember, though, how she came to me a few days later and placed a "book for young men" in my hands.

"You are only twelve," she said. "It's a pity. But after what you have seen, my son, it is better that you know."

She did this twenty years ago. It was far in advance of what most parents did then or are doing even now for their children. And it threw a flood of light into the darkest place in my mind, swept away endless forebodings, secret broodings over what until then had seemed to me the ugliest, the dirtiest, the most frightening thing I had found in life.

"When you meet anything ugly or bad," she told me, "I don't want you to turn away at once, I want you to face it and see what it is. Understand it and then leave it, and then it won't follow you in the dark."

"Keep clean," she said. And understanding me as she did, I think she added to herself, "And I must keep you quiet." She once told me she hoped that when I grew up I might become a professor in one of those college towns she loved, where I might work all my life in peace.

Although she never said anything to me against the harbor, I knew that my mother put all the ugliest things in life down there. And the things that were fine were all up here.

"I always like the front door of a house," she used to say, "to be wide and low with only a step or two leading up. I like it to look hospitable, as though always waiting for friends to come in."

Our front door was like that, and the neighborhood it waited for was one of the quietest, the cleanest and the finest, according to her view, of any in the country. The narrow little street had wide, leisurely sidewalks and old-fashioned houses on either side, a few of red brick, but more of brown stone with spotless white-sashed windows which were tall and narrow and rounded at the top. There were no trees, but there were many smooth, orderly vines. Almost all the houses had wide, inviting doorways like ours, but the people they invited in were only those who lived quietly here, shutting out New York and all the toots and rumblings of the ships and warehouses and docks below, of which they themselves were the owners.

These people in their leisurely way talked of literature and music, of sculpture and painting and travel abroad, as their fathers and even grandfathers had done—in times when the rest of the country, like one colossal harbor, changing, heaving, seething, had had time for only the crudest things, for railroads, mining camps, belching mills, vast herds of cattle and droves of sheep, for the frontier towns my mother had loathed, for a Civil War, for a Tweed Ring, for the Knights of Labor, a Haymarket riot, for the astounding growth of cities, slums, corporations and trusts, in this deep turbulent onward rush, this peopling of a continent.

And because my father, crude and self-made and come out of the West, was of this present country, he was an intruder politely avoided by these people of the past. The men would come sometimes at night, but they came only on business. They went straight through to the library, whence I could hear my father's voice, loud, impatient, angry, talking of what must be done soon, or Germany and England would drive the American flag from the ocean and make us beggars on the seas, humbly asking the ships of our rivals to give us a share in the trade of the world. To such disturbing meetings these grave and courteous gentlemen came less and less as the years went by.

And so that hospitable front door of ours waited long for neighbors.

CHAPTER IV

But if my father was an intruder, a disturber of the peace of these contented gentlemen, my mother was more and more liked by their wives. As time wore on they came to our house in the afternoons, upon hospital and church affairs. And first in the church and then in a private school near by I grew to be friends with their children.

Across the street from us at the corner there stood a huge, square brownstone house with a garden and a wide yard around it. Two boys and a little girl lived here, and about them our small circle centered. Here we played hockey in winter, part of the yard being flooded for our use; and in Spring and Autumn, ball, tag, I spy, prisoner's base and other games. They were all well enough as far as they went, but all were so very young and tame compared to my former adventures with Sam. Adventures, that was the difference. These were only games.

I felt poor beside these boys, in this ample yard by their grandfather's house. I often saw his great carriage roll out of the stable behind the yard. "Coach," they called it. It had rich silver trimmings and a red thing called a "crest," and a footman and coachman in top boots. Inside the house was a butler who was still more imposing, and a lofty room with spacious windows called the picture gallery. But by far the most awesome of all was the white-headed grandfather of these boys, who had been to Europe twenty-eight times and could read and speak "every language on earth," as I was told in whispers while we peeped in through his library door. There he sat with all his books, a man so rich he never even went to his office, a man who had owned not only warehouses but hundreds of ships and had sent them to every land in the world! While, as for me, my grandfather was not even alive. I felt poor and small, and I did not like it.

Besides, these unadventurous boys all put me down as "a queer kid." I was middling good at most of their games and would get sudden spurts when I would become almost a leader. But at other times, often right in the middle of a game, I would suddenly forget where I was and would think of Sam, of the cannibals that I had seen, of the man who had jumped from the Great Bridge, or of that drunken woman. They would catch me at it and call me queer. And I would grow hot and feel ashamed.

On the other hand, poor and queer as I felt at times, at others I would swell with my wisdom and importance. For what did they know, these respectable boys, about the docks and the gangs of "Micks" deep down there below us all as we played about in our nice little gardens. When they called me queer, sometimes I would retort with dark hints, all games would stop, they would gather close, and then I would tell these intense eager boys the things I had learned from the harbor. And I had the more pleasure in the telling from the feeling of relief that now I was safe away from it all.

"That's the real thing, that is," I would declare impressively. But how good it felt to me to be free of such reality.

At such times we made "the Chips" stay over on their side of the yard. "The Chips" were three small admiring girls. One was my young sister Sue, who was then about nine years old, long-legged, skinny and quick as a flash, her black hair always flying. The second, a plump freckled girl, was the younger sister of the boys who lived here. And the third was a quiet little thing who lived around the corner. We called them "Chips" to annoy them. We got the term from the stout coachman in the barn who used it with a fine sweeping contempt that included all his lady friends. We ourselves had the most profound contempt for these girls who kept poking into our games. At times we would stop everything and take the utmost pains to explain to them that they were nothing whatever but girls. And this would make Sue furious. She would screw up her snapping black eyes and viciously stick out her tongue and stamp her foot and say "darn!" to show she could swear like a regular kid. And still they hung around us.

But as time wore on we grew more indulgent, we included them more and more. And this was largely due to me. For I took a vague curious interest in the one who lived around the corner.

Her name was Eleanore Dillon and her age was eight, and she had attractions that slowly grew. To begin with, as I became gradually aware, she was much the prettiest of the three. She had light curly hair tied up in red ribbons, always *fresh* red ribbons. Everything about her was always fresh and clean. She had the most serious blue eyes, which at times would grow intent on what a tall chap of twelve like myself condescended to tell her, and at other times wondrously confiding.

Eleanore first attracted me by making me a hero. It was a warm May afternoon and she was sitting on the grass with her doll and her two companions. Sue had stolen some matches and was using them as Jackstraws. Suddenly I heard a scream, then I saw Sue racing like mad toward the garden hose, and I saw that the white skirt of Eleanore's dress had caught fire. As yet there was only a little flame. She was sitting still motionless on the grass, hugging her doll, with scared round eyes. I got to her first and with my cap I beat out the flame. I was suddenly panting, my hands were cold. But a few moments later, when Sue and two of the boys came tugging the hose, it as suddenly flashed upon me that I had done a heroic thing.

"Get out!" I shouted scornfully, as they started to play the hose on her. "Can't you see the whole fire is out?"

And then while the plump freckled girl came screeching out of the kitchen with half the servants behind her, and presently these servants all called me "a little heero"—the one whom I had rescued looked up at me very gratefully and said,

"Thank you, Boy, for not letting them squirt water on my dolly's clean dress."

"Aw, what do I care for a doll?" I retorted ungraciously.

But I liked her from that day. She was not at all like Sue. She was quiet and knew her place. She knew that she was only a girl, how thoroughly well she knew it. And yet, although so feminine, so deliberate and sedate, she had "a pile of ginger" deep down inside of her. In our games, whenever allowed to play, with a dogged resolution she would come pegging along in the rear, she was a sticker, she never gave up. In winter when they flooded the yard she was the poorest skater of all, but patiently plodding along on the ice, each time she fell down she would pick herself up with such determination that at last with a jerk at her arm I said,

"Here, Chip, come on and I'll teach you."

She came on. I can still feel her soft determined clutch on my elbow. When I said, "That's enough," she said, "Thank you, Boy," and went quietly on alone.

After that I taught her many times. One afternoon when there was a thaw, I said,

"Gee, but this ice is rotten." And then Eleanore asked me placidly,

"Do you like my pretty new shoes?"

"What's that got to do with it?" I demanded indignantly.

"Nothing, I guess," she said meekly.

This girl was full of mysteries. One great point in her favor was that she had a mother "at death's door." This appealed to me tremendously. It was so unusual.

"How's your mother?" I would ask her often, just for the pleasure of hearing her answer softly,

"She's at death's door, thank you."

She soon learned to skate much better, and I remember quite vividly still the January afternoon when as the darkness deepened a silvery moon appeared overhead. I had not skated with her for a week, but now we'd been skating for nearly an hour. One by one the others went home, and the plump girl turned at the kitchen door to call back to Eleanore tauntingly,

"You'll catch it, going home so late!"

"Never mind," said a gentle voice at my side, and round and round we skated. The moon grew steadily brighter. Still that soft steady clutch on my arm.

"Now you'd better go home," I said gruffly at last.

"What time is it?" she asked me. I looked at my watch.

"Gee! It's nearly seven o'clock!"

"What a pretty watch that is," she said in a pleased, quiet voice, but I was not to be diverted.

"Go on home, I tell you. Sit down and I'll take off your skates." She sighed regretfully but obeyed.

"What'll they do to you?" I asked her when we stopped in front of her house.

"They'll try to punish me," she answered. I looked down at her anxiously.

"Hard?" I inquired. She smiled at me.

"What time is it now?" she asked.

"Ten minutes after seven."

"Then they won't punish me," she said. "My father always comes home at seven." And she went placidly into the house.

"A mighty smart Chip," I said to myself.

I had told her a little about the docks, and one day she asked me to take her there. I promptly refused, but patiently from time to time she repeated her request. She wanted me to take her "just for a little walk" down there, or she would run if I preferred. She wanted to come out after supper into her garden, which was only the third from ours, and then she would sing and I would whistle. Then I would come around by the street and she would meet me at her front gate. I don't know how she ever persuaded me, but she did, and the plan worked splendidly. At the gate without a word I took her hand and ran down the street. Soon we were flying. Down to the open space we came, and around across the railroad tracks. In and out among grimy freight cars we sped. I would not stop.

"Christ!" I thought in terror. "Suppose Sam and the gang come around this way!" I had not seen them now for years. What might not they do to her?

But she made me stop by my father's dock. She was gasping and her face was red, but with her hand like a little vise on mine she stood there staring at the ship.

"Where are the heathen?" she asked at last, in a queer choking voice.

"There." I pointed to a small brown man with a white skull-cap on his head. "There's one. See him? Now come home!"

"Wait a minute, please," she begged very softly. A moment longer she stared at him. "All right, now we'll go," she said.

When I got her safe inside my gate I was in a cold sweat. This adventure, to my surprise, had been one of the most thrilling of all. And who'd have thought *her* an adventurer?

Her mother died that summer while we were up in the mountains, and when we came back we found the house empty. Her father had taken her out West.

I remember being distinctly relieved when I heard that she had gone away. For now there was something uncanny about her. It was one thing to have a mother "at death's door." That had been quite exciting. But to have one dead! There was something too awful about it. I would not have known what to say to the girl. And, besides, the thought suddenly entered my mind—suppose my own mother were to die!

We had been splendid chums, my mother and I, that long delightful summer up in the White Mountains. The mountains, we had decided together, were our favorite place to live in. "I will lift up mine eyes unto the hills," was the part of the Bible which she liked best. She loved these hills for their quiet, I loved them for the exciting adventures I had with Sue and "Stouty," the son of the farmer with whom we stayed. But these adventures were of a kind that my mother warmly approved of for me. They were not like those on the harbor.

An adventure to climb with Stouty and Sue up through the resinous branches of an enormous pine on the mountainside to the hawk's nest in the bare top branches, snatch the eggs and smash them, while Stouty with a big thick stick would beat off the mother hawk. An adventure to clamber half the day up a bouldery path through firs and birches, looking into black caves, peeping over steep cliffs, and at last reaching the wind-swept summit to look off through miles of emptiness. An adventure, coming home from a picnic as evening was falling, to sit snug in that creaking capacious wagon which belonged to Stouty's father, and to watch the lights and shadows that darted in and out of the pines as the lantern swung beneath our wheels.

But even up here in the mountains the harbor reached with its cold embrace. For at night it was an adventure hurriedly to undress and bury myself in the covers in time to hear the first low rumble of "the night freight" that went by some five miles distant. It made me think of the trains on the docks, whose voices I had heard at night, and of the things I had done with Sam. I would hear the mountain engine come panting impatiently up the grade. As it reached the top I would rise from my bed and soar off into space, in one swift rushing flight through the darkness I would be there in the nick of time, I would swing on to a freight car in the way Sam had shown me, climb to the top and crouching there I would watch the dark roadway open ahead through the silent forest. Lower would sink the voice of the engine until it became a faint confused mutter. And the rest was dreamland.

This was one of those secret games I never told my mother about—until, to my own surprise, in one of those long talks at night when she seemed drawing me to her right out through my eyes, I blurted this out. My mother wanted to know all about it. Did my hands get cold? Yes, colder and colder, as listening here in bed I heard the first muttering of the train and knew that in a few moments more I would take that five-mile flight, right through the window and over the trees to the distant track, to be there just ahead of the on-puffing engine. My voice quivered excitedly as I spoke.

"I see—I see," she said soothingly. "And when you are riding on top of a car—aren't you ever frightened?"

"No—because all the time I know that I am back there at home in my bed. I can see myself back there behind me."

"Do you fall asleep in bed—or are you still on the top of the car the last thing you can remember?"

"Most always on the top of the car."

"And when you sleep—do you always dream?"

"Yes—that's the finest part of it."

"Do you ever dream of Sam?"

"Yes."

"And all those things you did on the harbor?"

"Yes—all."

For some moments she sat by my bedside quietly stroking one of my hands.

"Billy."

"Yes, mother." I was growing impatient, I wished she would go, for now it was nearly time for the train.

"Have you ever played other games like that? I mean where you leave yourself and look back—and see your own body behind you."

"Yes—in bed in Brooklyn when I was quite little."

"Where did you go from your bed?"

"I went to the end of the garden. I heard drunken sailors and dockers shouting in that vile saloon below." This was not true.

What I had really done was to lie in bed and whisper, "*Suppose* I were out there"—which is very different. I was too young then to have learned the real trick. But now I was so proud of it that I honestly thought I had always known how. "It was a game I had with the harbor," I said.

"With the harbor." I felt her hand slowly tighten on mine. Then all at once as we heard the first low grumble of the freight train coming, my mother's hold grew tighter and tighter. "Open your eyes." I opened them quickly, for her voice was sharp and stern. She held me until the sound was gone.

"Do you hear it any longer?" she asked quietly at last.

"No," I whispered. My breath still came fast.

"Neither do I." There was another silence. "Let's go and sit by the window," she said.

And there she talked to me of the stars. How great they were and how very quiet. She said that the greatest men in the world were almost always quiet like that. They never let their hands get cold.

Often after that in the evenings just before I went to bed we had these talks about the stars. And not only in the mountains. On sparkling frosty winter nights we watched them over the harbor. And the things she said about them were so utterly absorbing that I would never think to look down, would barely hear the toots and the puffings and grinding of wheels from that infernal region below. For always when she spoke of the stars my mother spoke of great men too, the men who had done the "finest" things—a few in the clash and jar of life like Washington and Lincoln, but most of them more quietly, by preaching, writing, painting, composing, sermons, books, pictures and music so "fine" that all the best people on earth had known about them and loved them.

As I grew older she read to me more and more about these men. And sometimes I would feel deeply content as though I had found what I wanted. But more often I would feel myself swell up big inside of me, restless, worrying, groping for something. I didn't know what I wanted then, but I do know now as I look back, and I think there are thousands of children like me, the kind who are called "queer kids" by their playmates, who are all groping for much the same thing.

"Where is the Golden Age to-day?" they are asking. "We hear of all this from our mothers. We hear of brave knights and warriors, of God and Christ as they walked around on earth like regular people, of saints and preachers, writers and painters. But where are the great men living now? Not in our house nor on our street, nor in school nor in our church on the corner. There is nothing there that thrills us. Why isn't there? What is the matter? We are no longer babies, we are becoming big boys and girls. What will we do when we are grown up? Has everything fine already been done? Is there no chance for us to be great and to do them?"

It was to questionings like these that my mother had led me up from the harbor.

CHAPTER V

And to such questionings I believe that for many children of my kind there is often some familiar place—a schoolroom or a commonplace street, or a dreary farm in winter, a grimy row of factories or the ugly mouth of a mine—that mutely answers,

"No. There are no more great men for you, nor any fine things left to be done. There is nothing else left in the world but me. And you'd better stop trying to find it."

In my case this message came from the harbor, that one part of the modern world which looked up at me steadily day after day. Vaguely struggle as I would to build up fine things in the present from all that my mother brought out of the past, the harbor would not let me. For what I clothed it soon stripped naked, what I built it soon tore down.

"When you were little," it seemed to say, "for you I was filled with thrilling idols—cannibals and condors, Sam, strange wonder-ships and sailors adventuring to heathen lands. But then I dragged these idols down and made you see me as I am. And as I showed myself to you, so I'll show up all other wonderful places or men that your mother would have you believe in."

It did this, as I remember it, in the easiest most trivial ways, like some huge beast that flicks off a fly and then lumbers unconcernedly on.

My mother by years of patient work had built up my religion, filling it with the grand figures of God and Christ and his followers down to the present time, ending with Henry Ward Beecher. When this man died I felt awe at her silent grief. All at once the idea popped into my head that I too might become a great preacher. And still greater, I soon learned, I might become a preacher who went far off to heathen lands, braving cannibals and death and giving to thousands of heathen eternal happiness and life. Our church was sending out such a man. I heard him described as a hero of God, and I thought of pictures I had seen of saints and martyrs with soft haloes around their heads.

But this hero of God came down to the harbor. He was to sail for China from my father's dock. He wore, I remember, a brown derby hat and a little top coat. He was thin, with stooping shoulders, he was flustered in the excitement of leaving, nervously laughing as he shook hands with admiring women and talking fast in his high jerky voice. Two big dockers trundled his trunks. I saw them grin at the little man and spit tobacco juice his way. My father came by, shot one contemptuous glance, and then went on board to his business. I looked back at the hero. Off fell the halo from his head.

"No," I said gloomily to myself, "I never want to be like you." And drearily I looked around. What heaps and heaps of business here. What an immense gray harbor. I found no more thrills in church after that.

And as with religion, so with love. In reading of men of the Golden Age I came upon stories of high romance that made me strangely happy. But I saw no love of this kind in our house. I saw my mother and father living sharply separate lives, and I saw few kisses between them. I saw my father absorbed in his business, with little time for my mother. And I blamed this on the harbor. Long ago the same grim place had taught me something else about this many-sided passion between men and women, and one day it rose suddenly up in my mind:

I must have been about fifteen when my little friend Eleanore Dillon came back. Soon she and Sue were intimate chums, they went to school together. My mother invited her up to the mountains, and there I was with her a good deal. She was now nearly twelve years old, and the life in the West with her father had left her sturdy as you please. And yet somehow she still seemed to me the same feminine little creature, and as she told me stories of the life out West, where her father, who was an engineer, had built bridges, planned out harbors and new cities, I would wonder vaguely about her. What a fresh, clean little person to be talking of such places.

She was talking to me in this way one drowsy August afternoon.

We had been fishing down on the river, and now on our way home up the long hot slope of the meadow we had stopped to cool ourselves in the shadow of a haystack. It was fragrant there. Presently, from the top of the stack close over our heads, a bird poured forth a ravishing song. And Eleanore with a deep "Oh-h" of delight threw both her hands behind her head, sank back in the hay and lay there close beside me. Her eyes were shut and she was smiling to herself. Then as the song of the bird bubbled on, I felt suddenly a little shock, a new disturbing feeling. Breathlessly I watched her face. The song stopped and Eleanore opened her eyes, met mine, and closed them quickly. I saw a slight tightening of her features. I grew anxious at once and awkward. I wanted to get away.

But as I made a first uneasy movement, a bit of bright color caught my eye. It was one of her red garters which had slipped down from beneath her skirt. And all at once out of my memory rose a picture of years ago, a picture from the harbor, of that fat drunken girl I had seen. She too had worn red garters—in fact, little else! With disgusting vividness up she came! And I jumped trembling to my feet.

"I'm going home," I said roughly, and left my small companion.

I kept away from her after that. And even the following winter, when she came over often to our house to spend the night with Sue, I did my best to avoid her. I avoided all Sue's friends. I did not keep girls quite out of my thoughts, I had spells now and then when I would read about them in novels, papers and magazines, anything I could lay hands on. I would read hungrily, at times almost wistfully. But all the stories that I read, however romantic, could never quite overbalance for me that giggling woman I had seen.

"This is what love can be these days, foul as two pigs in a sty," said the harbor.

The same thing happened again with war and the great idea of giving one's life for one's country.

By countless eager questionings I had forced my mother to include among our heroes men like Napoleon, Nelson and Grant, and after I gave up hopes of the church these men for a time became greatest of all. You needed no mother to help you here. It was the easiest thing in the world to picture yourself leading charges or standing high up on a hill like Grant, quietly smoking a black cigar and sending your orderlies on the mad gallop out to

all corners of the field. My hill grew very real to me. It had three
wind-swept trees on top and I stood just in front of them.

When the war with Spain broke out I was still in my 'teens,
still rather thin and by no means tall, but I made up my mind to
try to enlist. Even now I can shut my eyes and see again that long
night on the docks when I watched two regiments embark on
ships which were to sail at dawn. With the uniforms, the crash of
bands, the flags, the cheers, the women laughing and crying, the
harbor seemed all on my side that night.

"This is certainly what I want!" I thought.

But my father forbade my going. He was not only stern, he was
savage. For once he came out of himself and talked. And his talk
was not only against this war but against all wars. The Civil War
was the worst of all. This was the more a surprise to me because
I knew that he himself had been with the Boys of Sixty One, I
had often boasted about it. But now I learned he had not fought
at all, he had been a mere commissary clerk moving rations and
blankets on freight trains!

"The business side of war," he said. "And when you've seen
that side of it you know how rotten a big war is! Men in the
North made millions by sending such rotten meat to the front
that we had to live on the people down South, we had to go into
their farms and plantations and plunder defenseless women and
children of all they had to eat! That's war! And war is filthy stinking camps where men die of fever and scurvy like flies—and war
is field hospitals so rotten in their management that you see the
wounded in long lines—packed together like bloody sardines—
bleeding to death for the lack of care! When they're dead you dig
big trenches and you pile 'em in like dogs! In time of war remember peace—and then you'll be ashamed you're there!"

For a moment I was struck dumb with surprise. What was this
strange fire deep down within my father's soul that could give out
such a flash? Confusedly I wondered. A sudden idea crossed my
mind.

"But if that's how you feel," I retorted, "why are you always
talking about the battleships we need? You want a big navy——"

"Yes," he snapped, "to keep this country *out* of war! If you live
long enough you'll see what I mean—remember then what I'm
telling you! This country needs a navy so big she can trade

wherever she likes and make other nations leave her alone! But she doesn't want war! Sixty One was enough! Some day when you get a man's eyes in your head you'll see what that did to this harbor!"

I had it now, the cause of all his curious wrath! War had hurt his harbor! How or why I did not care. Could this harbor of his stand nothing heroic? Patriotism, religion, love—must they all be shoved aside to make way for his dull business?

About a year later I was torn for months between two careers. Should I become a great musician or a famous writer? The idea of writing came to me first, I got it from "Pendennis," and for a time it took hold so hard I thought I was nicely settled for life. But then my mother read aloud "The Lives of Great Musicians," and within a few weeks the piano lessons which for years I had thought so dull became an absorbing passion. My mother bought me a photograph of one of the Beethoven portraits, and around it over my desk I tacked up pictures of famous pianists that I cut from magazines. I went to concerts in New York. Better still, my teacher secured me admittance to some orchestra rehearsals, where like a real professional, all mere amateurs shut out, I could sit in the dark and listen, and shut my eyes and hold my head between my hands. I was composing! After a month or two of this feverish life I remember the pride with which I wrote "Opus 38" over my last composition. My rapidity was astounding!

But one day my teacher, a kind tactful German, told me that Beethoven, when he was composing, had not always shut himself up in a room and scowled with both hands to his head, as in the portrait of him I had, but had rather gone out into the world.

"The Master found his music," he said, "by listening to the life close around him."

"He did?" I became uneasy at once, for again I felt myself being pushed toward that eternal harbor.

"If I were you," my relentless monitor went on, "and desired to become in music the great voice of my country"—I looked at him quickly but saw no smile—"I should watch the great ships down there below, I should listen to them with an artist's ears. They are here from all over the world, these ships, they are manned by men of all nations. I should listen to the songs of these men.

I have heard," he added reflectively, "that some of their songs are centuries old. Beethoven gathered only the folk songs of his country. But you in your city of all nations might gather the folk songs of all the seas."

I turned quickly. I had been walking the room.

"I have heard the sailors sing," I said, "ever since I was a little kid out there in the garden." I scowled in the effort to search my soul, my artist's soul. "Yes," I added triumphantly, "and sometimes it brought a lump in my throat!"

"Ah! Now you are a musician!"

"I will see what I can do," I said.

So again I tackled the harbor. By day it was quite impossible, all toots and blares, the most frightful discords—but at night its vulgar loudness was toned down sufficiently so that a fellow with artist's ears could really stand listening to its life, especially if I did not go too close but listened from my window. Here with uglier sounds subdued I could catch low voices, snatches of song and now and then a chorus. "The folk songs of the Seven Seas!" How that phrase took hold of me!

I went for information to an old dock watchman who had been a sailor.

"Songs? Why sure!" he answered. "It must be the chanties ye mean."

"Chanties?"

"That's it. I've been told the word's French."

"Oh! Chanter!"

"No—chanty. An' the man that sings the verses, he's called the chantyman. He sings while the crew heaves on the ropes an' they all come in on the chorus. If he's a real good chantyman he makes up new verses every time, a kind of a yarn he spins while he sings."

Soon after this, toward the end of a warm, windy April night, I awoke and heard them singing. I jumped up and went to my window. From the dock next to my father's, over the line of warehouse roofs, I could see the immense white sails already slowly rising into the starlit night. Quickly I threw on some clothes and hurried down to the docks. The waterfront was empty, swept clean of all that I disliked. Only overhead a few billowy clouds, the soft rush of the wind, a slight flush in the east, it was almost dawn. Here and there gleamed a light, red, green or yellow, with a phantom tug or barge around it, moving over the black of the water. Not silence but something richer was here—the confused mysterious murmuring, the creaking and the breathing of the sleeping port. And out of this those voices singing.

I drew nearer slowly. Hungrily I tried to take in the details of color and sound. And I felt suddenly such a deep delight as I had never dreamed of. To look around and listen and gather it into me and remember. This was great, no doubt about it—it fitted into all that was fine!

"This is really what I want to do—I'd like to learn to do it well—I'd like to do it all my life!"

Slower, more fearfully, I drew near. Would anything happen to spoil it all? There she lay, the long white ship, laden deep, settled low in the water. I could see the lines of little dark men heaving together at the ropes. Each time they hove they sang the refrain, which, no doubt, was centuries old, a song of the winds, the big bullies of the ocean, calling to each other as in some wild storm at sea they buffeted the tiny men who clung to the masts and spars of ships:

> "Blow the man down, bullies,
>   Blow him right down!
>   Hey! Hey! Blow the man down!
>   Give us the time to blow the man down!"

But what were the verses? I could hear the plaintive tenor voice of the chantyman who sang them—now low and almost mournful, now passionate, thrilling up into the night, as though yearning for all that was hid in the heavens. Could a man like that feel things like that? But what were the words he was singing, this yarn he was spinning in his song?

I came around by the foot of the slip and walked rapidly up the dockshed toward one of its wide hatchways. The singing had stopped, but as I drew close a rough voice broke the silence:

"Sing it again, Paddy!"

I looked out. Close by on the deck, in the hard blue glare of an arc-light, were some twenty men, dirty, greasy, ragged, sweating, all gripping the ropes and waiting for Paddy, who rolled his quid in his mouth, spat twice, and then began:

"As I went awalking down Paradise Street
A pretty young maiden I chanced for to meet."

A heave on the ropes and a deafening roar:

"Blow the man down, bullies,
Blow him right down!
Hey! Hey! Blow the man down!"

Again the solo voice, plaintiff and tender:

"By her build I took her for Dutch.
She was square in the stuns'l and bluff in the bow."

The rest was a detailed account of the night spent with the maiden. Roar on roar rose the boisterous chorus: "Blow the man down, bullies, blow him right down!" The big patched, dirty sails went jerking and flapping up toward the stars, which from here were so faint they could barely be seen. And the ship moved out on the harbor.

"There go the folk songs of the seas," I thought disgustedly, looking out on the water now showing itself grease-mottled in the first raw light of day.

I tried other songs with my artist's ears and found them all much like the first, the music like the very stars, the words like the grease and scum on the water. I was about giving up my search when I met my old friend, the watchman.

"Well, did ye find the chanties?" he asked.

"Yes," I said. "They can't be printed." His old eyes twinkled merrily:

"Of course they can't. An' *most* songs an' stories can't. But I'll give ye a nice little song ye can print. It's the oldest chanty of 'em all. I'll try to remember an' write it down."

Here is the song he gave me:

ROLLING HOME

To Australia's fair-haired maidens
We will bid our last good-bye.

We are going home to England,
We may never more see you.
Rolling home, rolling home,
Rolling home across the sea,
Rolling home to merry England,
Rolling home dear land to thee.
We will leave you our best wishes
As we leave your rocky shores,
We are going home to England,
We may never see you more.
Rolling home . . . . .
Up aloft amidst her rigging
Spreading out her snow white sails,
Like a bird with outstretched pinions,
On we speed before the gale.
Rolling home . . . . .
And the wild waves, as we leave them,
Seem to murmur as they roll;
There are hands and hearts to greet thee
In that land to which you go.
Rolling home . . . . .
Cheer up, Jack, fond hearts await thee,
And kind welcomes everywhere;
There are hands and hearts to greet thee,
Kind caresses from the fair.
Rolling home, rolling home,
Rolling home across the sea,
Rolling home to merry England,
Rolling home dear land to thee.

"Do they ever sing those words?" I asked suspiciously. The old Irishman looked steadily back.

"Sure they sing 'em—sometimes," he said. "It's the same thing as them other songs—only nicer put. Put to be printed," he added.

He found me others "put to be printed." Soon I had quite a collection. And with the help of my German teacher I wrote down the music.

"There are not enough for a book," he said. "Why don't you

write an article, tell where you found them, put them in, and send it to a paper? So you can give them to the world."

This I at once set out to do. In the writing I found again that deep delight I had had on the dock, just far enough off to miss the dirt, the sweat and the words of the song. I showed the article to my mother, and she was surprised and delighted. Working together, in less than a week we had polished it off. I heard her read it aloud to my father, I watched his face, and I saw the grim smile that came over it as he asked me,

"Are those the words you heard them sing?"

"Not all of them are," I answered. And suddenly, somehow or other, I felt guilty, as though I had done something wrong. But angrily I shook it off. Why should I always give in to his harbor? This that I had written was fine! This was Art! At last in spite of him and his docks I had found something great that I could do!

When the article was taken by a Sunday paper in New York and a check for eight dollars was sent me with a brief but flattering letter, my pride and hopes rose high. The eight dollars I spent on a pin for my mother, as "Pendennis" or some other boy genius had done. When the article appeared in the paper my mother bought fifty copies and gave them out to our neighbors. There was nothing to shock such neighbors here, and they praised me highly for what they called my "real descriptive power."

"That boy will go far," I heard one cultured old gentleman say. And I lost no time in starting out. No musical career for me, down came Beethoven from my wall, for I was now a writer. And not of mere articles, either. Inside of six months I had written a dozen short stories, and when each of these in turn was rejected I began to plan out a five-act play. But here my mother stopped me.

"You're trying to go too fast," she said. "Think of it, you are barely nineteen. You must give up everything else just now and spend all your time getting ready for college. For if you are going to be a strong writer, as I hope, you need to learn so many things first. And you will find them all in college—as I did once when I was young," she added a little wistfully.

CHAPTER VI

The first thing I needed in college was a good thorough dressing down. And this I got without any delay. In the first few weeks my artist's ears and eyes and soul were hazed to a frazzle. From "that boy who will go far" I became "you damn young freshman." I was told to make love to a horse's hind leg, I was made to perch on a gatepost and read the tenderest passages of "Romeo and Juliet," replacing Romeo's name by my own, and Juliet's by that of stout Mrs. Doogan, who scrubbed floors in a dormitory close by. Refusals only made matters painful. Besides, I was told by a freshman friend that I'd better fit in or I'd "queer" myself.

This dread of "queering" myself at first did me a world of good. Dumped in this community of over a thousand callow youths, three hundred in my class alone and each one absorbed in getting acquainted, fitting in, making friends and a place for himself, I was soon struggling for a foothold as hard as the rest. Within a month the thing I wanted above all else was to shed my genius and become "a good mixer" in the crowd.

This drew me at first from books to athletics. Though still slight of build I was wiry, high-strung and quick of movement. I had a snub nose and sandy hair, and I was tough, with a hard-set jaw. And I now went into the football world with a passion and a patience that landed me at the end of the season—one of the substitute quarterbacks on the freshman team. I did not get into a single game, I was only used on the "scrub" in our practice. This made for a wholesome humility and a real love of my college.

The football season over, I tried for the daily paper. One of the freshman candidates for the editorial Spring elections, I became a daily reporter slave. Here at first I drew on my "queer" past, turning all my "descriptive powers" to use. But a fat senior editor called "Pop" inquired one day with a sneer, "For God's sake, Freshman, why these flowers?" And the flowers forthwith dropped out of my style. At all hours, day and night, to the almost entire neglect of studies, I went about college digging up news—not the trivial news of the faculty's dull, puny plans for the development of our minds, but the real vital news of our college life, news of the things we were here for, the things by which a man got on, news of all the athletic teams, of the glee, mandolin and banjo clubs, of "proms," of class and fraternity elections, mass meetings and parades. Ferreting my way into all nooks and crannies of college life, ears keen for hints and rumors, alert to "scoop" my eighteen reporter rivals—the more I learned the better I loved. And when in the Spring I was one of the five freshman editors chosen, the conquest was complete. No more artist's soul for me. I was part and parcel of college life.

Together with my companions I assumed a genial tolerance toward all those poor dry devils known to us as "profs." I remember the weary sighs of our old college president as he monotoned through his lectures on ethics to the tune of the cracking of peanuts, which an old darky sold to us at the entrance to the hall. It was a case of live and let live. He let us eat and we let him talk. With the physics prof, who was known as "Madge the Scientist," our indulgence went still further. We took no disturbing peanuts there and we let him drone his hour away without an interruption, except perhaps an occasional snore. We were so good to him, I think, because of his sense of humor. He used to stop talking now and then and with a quizzical hopeless smile he would look about the hall. And we would all smile broadly back, enjoying to the full with him the droll farce of our presence there. "Go to it, Madge," someone would murmur. And the work of revealing the wonders of this material universe would limp quietly along. In examinations Madge gave no marks, at least not to the mass of us. If he had, over half of us would have been dropped, so he "flunked" the worst twenty and let the rest through.

The faculty, as a whole, appeared to me no less fatigued. Most of them lectured as though getting tired, the others as though tired out. There were a few lonely exceptions but they had to fight against heavy odds.

The hottest fighter of all against this classic torpor was a tall, joyous Frenchman who gestured not only with his hands but with his eloquent knees as well. His subject was French literature, but from this at a moment's notice he would dart off into every phase of French life. There was nothing in life, according to him, that was not a part of literature. In college he was considered quite mad.

I met him not long ago in New York. We were both hanging to straps in the subway and we had but a moment before he got off.

"I have read you," he said, "in the magazines. And from what you write I think you can tell me. What was the trouble with me at college?" I looked into his black twinkling eyes.

"Great Scott!" I said suddenly. "You were alive!"

"Merci! Au revoir, monsieur!"

What a desert of knowledge it was back there. Our placid tolerance of the profs included the books they gave us. The history prof gave us ten books of collateral reading. Each book, if we could pledge our honor as gentlemen that we had read it, counted us five in examination. On the night before the examination I happened to enter the room of one of our football giants, and found him surrounded by five freshmen, all of whom were reading aloud. One was reading a book on Russia, another the life of Frederick the Great, a third was patiently droning forth Napoleon's war on Europe, while over on the window-seat the other two were racing through volumes one and two of Carlyle's French Revolution. The room was a perfect babel of sound. But the big man sat and smoked his pipe, his honor safe and the morrow secure. In later years, whatever might happen across the sea would find this fellow fully prepared, a wise, intelligent judge of the world, with a college education.

"This reminds me," he said, "of last summer—when I did Europe in three weeks with Dad."

The main idea in all courses was to do what you had to but no more. One day an English prof called upon me to define the difference between a novel and a book of science.

"About the same difference," I replied, "as between an artist's painting and a mathematical drawing."

"Bootlick, bootlick," I heard in murmurs all over the hall.

I had answered better than I had to. Hence I had licked the professor's boots. I did not offend in this way again.

But early in my sophomore year, when the novelty had worn away, I began to do some thinking. Was there nothing else here? My mother and I had had talks at home, and she had told me plainly that unless I sent home better reports I could not finish my four years' course. And after all, she wasn't a fool, there was something in that idea of hers—that here in this quiet old town, so remote from the harbor and business, a fellow ought to be getting "fine" things, things that would help him all his life.

"But look what I've got!" I told myself. "When I came here what was I? A little damn prig! And look at me now!"

"All right, look ahead. I'm toughened up, I've had some good things knocked into me and a lot of fool things knocked out of me. But that's just it. Are all the fine things fool things? Don't I still want to write? Sure I do. Well, what am I going to write about? What do I know of the big things of life? I was always hunting for what was great. I'm never hunting for it now, and unless I get something mighty quick my father will make me go into his business. What am I going to do with my life?"

At first I honestly tried to "pole," to find whether, after all, I couldn't break through the hard dry crust of books and lectures down into what I called "the real stuff." But the deeper I dug the drier it grew. Vaguely I felt that here was crust and only crust, and that for some reason or other it was meant that this should be so, because in the fresh bubbling springs and the deep blazing fires whose presence I could feel below there was something irritating to profs and disturbing to those who paid them. These profs, I thought confusedly, had about as much to do with life as had that little "hero of God" who had cut such a pitiful figure when he came close to the harbor. And more pitiful still were the "polers," the chaps who were working for high marks. They thought of marks and little else. They thrived on crust, these fellows, cramming themselves with words and rules, with facts, dates, theorems and figures, in order to become professors themselves and teach the same stuff to other "polers." There was a story of one of them who stayed in his room and crammed all through the big football game of the season, and at night when told we had won remarked blithely,

"Oh, that's splendid! I think I'll go out and have a pretzel!"

God, what a life, I thought to myself! None of that for me! And so I left the "polers."

But now in my restless groping around for realities in life that would thrill me, things that I could write about, I began trying to test things out by talking about them with my friends. What did a fellow want most in life—what to do, what to get and to be? What was there really in business beside the making of money? In medicine, law and the other professions, in art, in getting married, in this idea of God and a heaven, or in the idea I vaguely felt now filtering through the nation, that a man owed his life to his country in time of peace as in time of war. The harbor with rough heavy jolts had long ago started me thinking about questions of this kind. Now I tackled them again and tried to talk about them.

And at once I found I was "queering" myself. For these genial companions of mine had laid a most decided taboo upon all topics of this kind. They did so because to discuss them meant to openly think and feel, and to think or feel intensely, about anything but athletics and other things prescribed by the crowd, was bad form to say the least.

Bad form to talk in any such fashion of what we were going to make of our lives. Nobody cared to warm up on the subject. Many had nothing at all in sight and put off the whole idea as a bore. Others were already fixed, they had positions waiting in law and business offices, in factories, mines, mills and banks, and they took these positions as settled and sure.

"Why?" I would argue impatiently. "How do you know it's what you want most?"

"Oh, I guess it'll do as well as another."

"But damn it all, why not have a look? We can have a big look now, we've got a chance to broaden out before we jump into our little jobs—to see all the jobs and size 'em up and look at 'em as a part of the world!"

"Oh, biff." I got little or no response. The greater part of these decent likable fellows could not warm up to anything big, they simply hadn't it in them.

"Why in hell do you want me to get all hot?" drawled one fat sluggard of a friend. "I'll keep alive when the time comes." And he and his kind set the standard for all. Sometimes a chap who could warm up, who had the real stuff in him, would "loosen up" about his life on some long tramp with me alone. But back in college his lips were sealed. It was not exactly that he was ashamed, it was simply that with his college friends such talk seemed utterly out of place.

"Look out, Bill," said one affectionately. "You'll queer yourself if you keep on."

The same held true of religion. An upper classman, if he felt he had to, might safely become a leader of freshmen in the Y. M. C. A. But when one Sunday evening I disturbed a peaceful pipe-smoking crowd by wondering why it was that we were all so bored in chapel, there fell an embarrassing silence—until someone growled good-humoredly, "Don't bite off more'n you can chew." Nobody wanted to drop his religion, he simply wanted to let it alone. I remember one Sunday in chapel, in the midst of a long sermon, how our sarcastic old president woke us up with a start.

"I was asked," he said, "if we had any free thinkers here. 'No,' I replied. 'We have not yet advanced that far. For it takes half as much thinking to be a free thinker as it does to believe in God.'"

And I remember the night in our sophomore club when the news came like a thunderclap that one of our members had been killed pole-vaulting at a track meet in New York. It was our habit, in our new-found manliness, to eat with our hats on, shout and sing, and speak of our food as "tapeworm," "hemorrhage," and the like. I remember how we sat that night, silent, not a word from the crowd—one starting to eat, then seeing it wasn't the thing to do, and staring blankly like the rest. They were terrible, those stares into reality. That clutching pain of grief was real, so real it blotted everything out. Later some of us in my room began to talk in low voices of what a good fellow he had been. Then some chap from the Y. M. C. A. proposed timidly to lead us in prayer. What a glare he got from all over the room! "Damn fool," I heard someone mutter. Bad form!

Politics also were tabooed. Here again there were exceptions. A still fiery son of the South could rail about niggers, rapes and lynchings and the need for disenfranchising the blacks. It was good fun to hear him. Moreover, a fellow who was a good speaker, and needed the money, might stump the state for either political party, and his accounts were often amusing. But to sit down and talk about the trusts, graft, trade unions, strikes, or the tariff or the navy, the Philippines, "the open door," or any other of the big questions that even then, ten years ago, were beginning to shake the country, and that we would all be voting on soon? No. The little Bryan club was a joke. And one day when a socialist speaker struck town the whole college turned out in parade, waving red sweaters and firing "bombs" and roaring a wordless Marseillaise! We wanted no solemn problems here!

Finally, it was distinctly bad form to talk about sex. Not to tell "smutty stories," they were welcomed by the average crowd. But to look at it squarely, as I tried to do, and get some light upon what would be doubtless the most vital part of our future lives— this simply wasn't done. What did women mean to us, I asked. What did prostitutes mean at present? What would wives mean later on? And all this talk about mistresses and this business of free love, and easy divorces and marriage itself—what did they all amount to? Was love really what it was cracked up to be, or had the novelists handed us guff? When I came out with questions like these, the chaps called "clean" looked rather pained; the ones who weren't, distinctly bored.

For this whole intricate subject was kept in the cellars of our minds, cellars often large but dark. Because "sex" was wholly rotten. It had nothing to do, apparently, with the girls who came chaperoned to the "proms," it had to do only with certain women in a little town close by. Plenty of chaps went there at times, and now and then women from over there would come to us on the quiet at night. But one afternoon I saw a big crowd on the front campus. It grew every moment, became a mob, shoving and surging, shouting and jeering. I climbed some steps to look into the center, and saw two painted terrified girls, hysterical, sobbing, swearing and shrieking. So they were shoved, a hidden spectacle, to the station and put on the train. Nothing like that on our front campus! Nothing like "sex" in the front rooms of our minds. The crowd returned chuckling. Immoral? Hell, no. Simply bad form.

"What am I going to write about?"

"Games," said the college. "Only games. Don't go adventuring down into life."

CHAPTER VII

Then I found Joe Kramer.

He had "queered" himself at the beginning in college. I had barely known him. He belonged to no fraternity, and except on the athletic field he kept out of all our genial life. And this life of ours, for all its thoughtlessness, was so rich in genuine friendships, so filled and bubbling over with the joy of being young, that we could not understand how any decent sort of chap could deliberately keep out of it. We put Joe Kramer down as a "grouch."

But now that I too was "queering" myself, our queerness drew us together, or rather, Joe's drew mine. In the ten years that have gone since then I have never met any man who drew me harder than he did, than he is drawing me even still—and this often in spite of my efforts to shake him off, and later of his quite evident wish to be rid of me. For Joe had what is so hard to find among us comfortable mortals, a sincerity so real and deep that it absolutely ruled his life, that it kept him exploring into things, kept him adventuring always.

In long tramps over the neighboring hills, on our backs in the grass staring up at the clouds, or in winter hugging a bonfire in the shelter of a boulder, or back in college over our beer or over countless pipes in our rooms, together we adventured through books and long hungry talks down into life—and of the paths we discovered I see even now no end.

Joe was tall and lean, with heavy shoulders stooping slightly. He was sallow, he never took care of himself. He ate his meals at all hours at a small cheap restaurant, where he bought a bunch of meal tickets each week. His face was obstinate, honest, kindly, his features were as blunt as his talk. He was the first to understand what I was so vaguely looking for, and to say, "All right,

Kid, you come right along." And as he was farther along than I, he pulled me after him on the hunt after what he called "the genuine article" in this bewildering modern life.

His own life, to begin with, was a tie with this real modern world that had forced itself on me long ago through the harbor. For Joe had been "up against it" hard. Though blunt and frank about most things he talked little about himself, but I got his story bit by bit. "Graft" had come into it at the start. In a town of the Middle West his father had been a physician with a good practice, until when Joe was eleven years old a case of smallpox was discovered. Joe's father vaccinated about a score of children that week. The "dope" he used was mailed to him by a drug firm in Chicago. It was "rotten." Over half the children were desperately ill and seven of them died. Joe's father, his mother and both older sisters did duty as nurses day and night. After that they left town, moved from town to town, that story always following, and finally both parents died. Since then Joe had been a teamster, a clerk in a hardware store, a brakeman, a telegrapher, and last, the assistant editor of a paper in a small town. He had scraped and slaved and studied throughout with the idea of coming East to college. He had come at twenty-two, beating his way on freight trains. On the top of a car one night he had fallen asleep and been knocked on the head by a steel beam jutting down under a bridge. Then, after two weeks on a hospital bed, he had arrived at college.

Here he had earned a meager way by writing football and baseball news for a string of western papers. Here he had looked for an education, and here "a bunch of dead ones" had handed him "news from the graveyard" instead.

I can still see him in classroom, head cocked to one side, grimly watching the prof. And once during a Bible course lecture I heard his voice blandly ironic behind me:

"Will somebody ask Mister Charley Darwin to be so good as to step this way?"

"We've been cheated, Bill," he told me. "We've been cheated right along. Take history, for instance, the kind of stuff we were handed in school. I got onto it first when I was fourteen. It was a rainy Saturday and my mother told me to go and clean out an old closet up in the attic. Well, I found my German grandfather's diary there, written when he was in college in Leipsic, in 1848. The way those kids jumped into things! The way they got themselves mixed up in the Revolution of Forty Eight! To hear my young grandfather talk, that year was one of the biggest times in European history. Our school history gave it five pages and then druled on about courts and kings. 'I'll go to college,' I made up my mind. 'College will put me next to the truth.' So I saved my little nickels and came. But college," he added moodily, "ain't advanced as far as it was in my young grandfather's time."

"Do you know who's to blame for this stuff?" he said. "It's not the profs, I've nothing against them, all they need is to be kicked out. No, it's us, because we stand for their line of drule. If we got right up on our honkeys and howled, all of us, for a real education, we'd get it by next Saturday night. But we don't care a damn. Why don't we? Are we all of us dubs? No we're not. Go down to the football field and see. There's as much brains in figuring out those plays as there is in mathematics. Would we stand for coaches like our profs? But that's just it. It's the thing to be alive in athletics and a dub in everything else. And because it's the thing, every fellow fits in. On the whole," he added reflectively, "I think it's this 'dear old college' feeling that's to blame for it all."

"My God, Joe!" This was high treason!

"Sure it is," he retorted. "It *is* your god and the god of us all. This dear old college feeling. It's got us all stuck together so close that nobody dares to be himself and buck against its standards."

This from Joe Kramer! How often, in a football game, have I seen him on the reporter's bench, his sallow face now all a-scowl, now beaming satisfaction as he pounded his neighbor on the back.

In pursuit of "a real education" we got into the habit of spending almost every evening in the college library, where except at examination times there was nobody but a few silent "polers."

I grew to love this place. It was so huge and shadowy, with only shaded lights here and there. It had such tempting crannies. I loved its deep quiet, so pleasantly broken now and then by a step, a whisper, the sound of a book being moved from its shelf where perhaps it had stood unread for years, or occasional voices passing outside or snatches of song from the campus. And here I thought I was finding myself. That French prof had introduced me to Voltaire, Hugo, Balzac, Maupassant and others who were becoming my new idols. This was art, this was beauty and truth, this was getting at life in a way that thrilled.

But now and then looking up from my book I would see Joe prowling about the place, taking down a book, then shoving it back and scowling as he ran his eyes along whole rows of titles.

"This darned library shut its doors," he would growl to himself, "just as the real dope was coming along. But there's been such a flood of it ever since that some leaked in in spite of 'em."

Joe would search and search until he found "it" on back shelves or stuck away in corners. Angrily he would blow off the dust and then settle himself with a sigh to read. There was always something wistful to me in the way Joe opened each new book. But what a joy when he found "it"—Darwin, Nietzsche, Henry George, Walt Whitman, Zola, Samuel Butler. What a sudden sort of glee the night he discovered Bernard Shaw!

When the library closed we adjourned for beer and a smoke, and often we would argue long about what we had been reading. Joe had little use for the stuff I liked. Beauty and form were nothing to him, it was "the meat" he was after. My mother's idols he laid low.

"The first part was big," he said one night of a recent English novel. "But the last part was the kind of thing that poor old Thackeray might have done."

In an instant I was up in arms, for to my mother and me the author of "Pendennis" had been like a great lovable patron saint, a refuge from all we abhorred in the harbor. To slight him was a sacrilege. But reverence to Joe Kramer was a thing unknown. "Show me," he said, in reply to my outburst, "a single thing he ever wrote that wasn't sentimental bosh!" And we went at it hammer and tongs.

It was so in all our talks. Nothing was too sacred. Joe always insisted on "being shown."

He had a keen liking but little respect for the nation built by our fathers. From his own father's tragedy, caused by graft, his own hard struggles in the West and the Populist doctrines he had imbibed, he had come East with a deep conviction that "things in this country are one big mess with the Constitution sitting on top." And when the term "muckraker" came into use, I remember his deep satisfaction. "Now I know my name," he said.

He was equally hard on the church. How he kicked against our compulsory chapel. "Broad, isn't it, scientific," he growled, "to yank a man out of bed every morning, throw him into his seat in chapel and tell him, 'Here. This is what you believe. Be good now, take your little dose and then you can go to breakfast.'"

"I'm no atheist," he remarked. "I'm only a poor young fellah who asks, 'Say, Mister, if you *are* up there why is it that no big scientist has brains enough to see you?'"

"Look here, J. K., that isn't so!"

"Isn't it? Show me!" And we would start in. I had a deep repugnance for his whole materialistic view. But I liked the way he jarred me.

"What I want to do," he said, "is to bust every hold that any creed ever had on me. I don't mean only creeds in churches, I mean creeds in politics, business and everywhere else. I want to get 'em all out of my eyes so I can see what's really here—because I'm so sure there's an awful lot here and an awful lot more that's coming. If I make a noise like a knocker at times you don't want to put me down as any Schopenhauer fan. None of that pessimistic dope for little Joey Kramer. I never open a new book without hoping I'll find the real stuff I want, and I never open a paper without hoping that some more of it will be right here in the news of the day. Kid," he ended intensely, "you can take it from me there are going to be big doings soon in this little old world, big doings and great big ideas, as big as what caused the Civil War and a damn sight more scientific. And the thing for you and me to do is to get ourselves in some kind of shape so we can shake hands with 'em when they arrive, and say, 'Hello, fellahs, come right in. You're just what we've been waiting for.'"

When Joe gave up college at the end of the junior year, he left a small group of us behind. "The Ishmaelites," we called ourselves. For though most of us "couldn't quite go Joe," we had all "queered" ourselves in college through the influence on us he had had.

There are thousands of Joe Kramers now in colleges scattered all over the land. Each year their numbers grow, each year more deep their vague conviction that somehow they've been cheated, more harsh and insistent every year their questioning of all "news from the graveyard," whether it comes from old fogey professors or from parents or preachers, eminent lawyers or business men, great politicians or writers of books. Arrogant and sweeping, sparing nothing sacred—young. Ignorant, confused and groping, almost wistful—new. They are becoming no insignificant part in this swiftly changing national life.

Joe Kramer was one of the pioneers.

CHAPTER VIII

It was with an unpleasant shock of surprise that I found Joe liked the harbor.

When I took him home for Christmas he spent half his time down there on the docks. He explored the whole region for miles around, in a week he spoke in familiar terms of slips and bays and rivers that to me were still nothing but names. Moreover, he liked my father. And my father, opening up by degrees, showed an unmistakable relish for Joe.

They had long talks in the study at night, where I could hear them arguing about the decline of our shipping, the growth of our trusts and railroads, graft and high finance and strikes, the swift piling up of our troubles at home—and about the great chance we were losing abroad, the blind weak part we were playing in this eager ocean world where every nation that was alive was rushing in to get a place. As their voices rose loud and excited, even my young sister Sue, who was just out of high school now and doing some groping about of her own, would go into the study to listen at times. But I kept out. For already I was tired again of all these harbor problems, I wanted to get at life through Art! And I felt besides that if I entered into long talks with my father, sooner or later he would be sure to bring up the dreaded question of my going into his business. And this I was firmly resolved not to do. For my dislike of all his work, his deepening worries, his dogged absorption in his tiresome hobby of ships, was even sharper than before.

"That dad of yours," Joe told me, "is a mighty interesting old boy. He has had a big life with a big idea."

"Has he?" said I. "Then he's lost it."

"He hasn't! That's just the trouble. He thinks he's a comer

when he's a goer—he can't see his idea is out of date. It's a pity," he added sadly. "When a man can spend his days and nights hating the trusts and the railroads as he does, it's a pity he's so darned old in his views of what ought to be done about it. Your father believes that if only we'd get a strong navy and a large mercantile marine——"

"Oh, cut it, J. K.," I said pettishly. "I tell you I don't care what he believes! The next thing you'll be telling me is that I ought to take a job in his warehouse!"

"You might do worse," said Joe.

"What?" I demanded indignantly.

"That's just what I said. If you'd go on a paper and learn to write like a regular man I'd be tickled to death. But if all you want to be in life is a young Guy de Maupassant and turn out little gems for the girls, then I say you'd be a lot better off if you went into your father's warehouse and began telling Wall Street to get off the roof!"

"Thank you," I said stiffly.

From that talk Joe and I began drifting apart. I never brought him home again, I saw less of him at college. And at the end of the college year he went to New York, where he found a job on a paper.

And so all through my senior year I was left undisturbed to "queer" myself in my own sweet way, which was to slave for hours over Guy de Maupassant and other foreign authors, write stories and sketches by the score, and with two other "Ishmaelites" plan for a year's work in Paris. The French prof was delighted and spurred us on with glowing accounts of life in "the Quarter." One of us wanted to be a painter. No place for that like Paris! Another an architect—Paris! Myself a writer—Paris! For what could American writers to-day, with their sentimental little yarns covering with a laugh or a tear all the big deep facts of life, show to compare to the unflinching powerful work of the best writers over in France? In Paris they were training men to write of life as it really is! How that prof did drum it in. Better still, how he talked it up to my mother—the last time she came to college.

I soon found she was on my side. If only she could bring father around.

I still remember vividly that exciting night in June when the three of us, back there at home, sat on the terrace and fought it out. I remember the beauty of the night, I mean of the night up there in the garden under the stars, my mother's garden and her stars, and of the hideous showing put up by my father's harbor below.

Of course he opposed my going abroad. His old indifference to me had vanished, I saw he regarded me now as worth while, grown up, a business asset worth fighting for. And my father fought. He spoke abruptly, passionately of the great chance on the docks down there. I remember being surprised at his talk, at the bigness and the intensity of this hunger of his for ships. But of what he said I remembered nothing, I did not hear, for I was eyeing my mother.

I saw she was watching him pityingly. Why? What argument had she still to use? I waited in increasing suspense.

"So that's all there is to it," I heard him end. "You might as well get it right out of your head. You're not going over to Europe to fool away any more of your time. You're going to buckle down right here."

"Billy, leave us alone," said my mother.

What in the name of all the miracles did she do to him that night—my mother so frail (she had grown so of late), my father so strong? The next day she told me he had consented.

I saw little of him in the next two weeks. He left me alone with her every evening. But when I watched him he looked changed—beaten and broken, older. In spite of myself I pitied him now, and a confused uneasiness, almost remorse, came over me at the way I had opposed him. "What's come over Dad?" I wondered. Once I saw him look at my mother, and his look was frightened, crushed. What was it she had told him?

Those evenings I read "Pendennis" aloud for the third time to my mother. It had been our favorite book, and I took anxious pains to show her how I loved it still. But once chancing to look quickly up, I caught my mother watching me with a hungriness and an utter despair such as I'd never seen before. It struck me cold, I looked away—and suddenly I realized what a selfish little beast I was, beside this woman who loved me so and whom I was now leaving. My throat contracted sharply. But when I looked back the look was gone, and in its place was a quiet smile.

"Oh, my boy, you must do fine work," she said. "I want it so much more than anything else in my whole life. In my whole life," she repeated. I came over to her chair, bent over her and kissed her hard.

"I'm sorry I'm going! I'm sorry!" I whispered. "But mammy! It's only for a year!"

Why did that make her cling to me so? If only she had told me.

But what young egotists we sons are. It was only a few days later that with my two college chums, from the deck of an ocean liner, I said good-by to the harbor.

"Thank God I'm through with you at last."

CHAPTER IX

I was in Paris for two years.

In those first weeks of deep delight I called it, "The Beautiful City of Grays." For this town was certainly mellowed down. No jar of an ugly present here, no loud disturbing harbor. But on the other hand, no dullness of a fossilized past. What college had been supposed to do this city did, it took the past and made it alive, richly, thrillingly alive, and wove it in with the present. In the first Sorbonne lectures, even with my meager French, I felt this at once, I wanted to feel it. These profs were brilliant, sparkling, gay. They talked as though Rousseau and Voltaire, Hugo, Balzac and Flaubert, Maupassant and all the rest were still vital dazzling news to the world, because these men were still molding the world. And from here exploring out over the town, I was smilingly greeted everywhere by such affable gracious old places, that seemed to say:

"We've been written about for a thousand years, and now you also wish to write. How charming of you. Please sit down. Garçon, un bock."

And I sat down. Scenes from the books of my great idols rose around every corner, or if they didn't I made them rise. There was pride in the process. To go to the Place de la République, take a seat before some cheap, jolly café, squint out at the Place with an artist's eye, reconstruct the Bastille, the Great Revolution, dream back of that to Rousseau and Voltaire and the way they shook the world by their writings—and then wake up and find that I had been at it for three mortal hours! What a chap I was for dreams. I must be quite a genius. There were hours with Hugo in Notre Dame in one of its most shadowy corners; with Zola on top of a 'bus at night as it lumbered up into the Belleville slums; with Balzac in an old garden I found; with Guy de Maupassant everywhere, in the gay hum and lights of those endless cafés, from bridges at sunset over the Seine, or far up the long rich dusk of the Champs Élysées, lights twinkling out, and *his* women laughing, chattering by.

Nothing left in this rich old world but the harbor? Nothing beautiful, fine or great for an eager, hungry, happy young man? I could laugh! I knew now that the harbor had lied! For into this radiant city not only the past but the whole present of the earth appeared to me to be pouring in. Painters, sculptors, writers and builders were here from all nations, with even some Hindus and Japs thrown in, young, bringing all their dreams and ambitions, their gaiety, their vigor and zest.

"Young men are lucky. They will see great things."

Voltaire had said that about thirty years before the French Revolution. It had been true then, true ever since, it was true to-day and here—though *our* great things I felt very sure were not to come in violence—the world had gone beyond all that. No, these immense surprises that were lurking just before us, these astounding miracles that were to rise before our eyes, would come in the unfolding of the powers in men's minds, working free and ranging wide, with a deep resistless onward rush—in the stirring times of peace!

And we were not only to see great things but we were all to do them! That was the very keynote of the place. Here a fellow could certainly write if only he had it in him. Impatiently I slaved at my French. Five hours sleep was plenty.

In the small apartment we had taken just on the edge of the Luxembourg Gardens, on the nights when we were working at home, one of us at his easel, another at his drafting board, myself at my desk, we would knock off at about eleven o'clock and come down for beer and a long smoke in front of the café below. A homely little place it was, with two rows of small iron tables in front, and at one of these we would seat ourselves. Behind us in the window was a long glass tank of gold fish, into which from time to time a huge cat would reach an omnivorous paw. Often from within the café we would hear Russian folk songs played on balalaikas by a group of Russian students there. And between the songs a low hubbub rose, in French and many other tongues, for here were French and

Germans, English and Bohemians, Russians and Italians, all gathered here while they were young.

How serene the old city seemed those nights. The street outside was quiet. The motor 'bus, that pest of Paris, had not yet appeared. Only an occasional cab would come tinkling on its way. Our street was absurdly short. At one end was a gay cluster of lights from the crowded cafés of the "Boul' Mich'," at the other were the low lighted arches at the back of the Odéon, from which when the play was over fluffy feminine figures would emerge from the stage entrance; we would hear their low musical voices as they came merrily by us in cabs. Other figures would pass. Across the street before us rose the trees and the lofty iron fence of the Gardens, with a rich gloom of shrubs behind, and against this background figures in groups and alone and in couples, would come strolling by with their happiness or hurrying eagerly toward it. Or to what else were they hurrying? From what were they coming so slowly away?

These strangers in this setting thrilled me. Comedy, tragedy, character, plot—there seemed nothing in life but the writing of tales—watching, listening, dreaming, finding, then becoming deeply excited, feeling them grow inside of you, planning them out and writing them off, then working them over and over and over, little by little building them up. What a rich absorbing life for a fellow, and for me it still lay all ahead. I had used but twenty-two years of my life, there were fifty left to write in, and what couldn't you write in fifty years!

Often, sitting here at night, I would get an idea and begin to work, and I would keep on until at last the enormous old woman who kept the café—we called her "The Blessed Damozel"—would come lumbering out and good humoredly growl,

"Couches-toi donc. Une heure vient de sonner."

There came a brief interruption. Into our street's procession one evening, over its round cobble-stones on a bicycle that wearily wobbled, there came a lean dusty figure with something distinctly familiar in the stoop of the big shoulders.

"Hello, boys," said a deep gruff voice.

"J. K.!"

It was Joe Kramer arriving in Paris at midnight on a punctured tire, and cursing the cobblestone pavements over which he had hunted us out.

A hot supper, a bottle of wine, a genial beam on all three of us, and Joe told his story. After leaving college, from New York he had gone to Kansas City, and by the "livest paper" there he had been sent abroad with a bike to do a series of "Sunday specials." He had come over steerage and written an exposé of his passage. He had two weeks for Paris and then was off to Berlin and Vienna.

"I'm just breaking ground this time, boys," he said. "I want to get the hang of the countries and a start in their infernal languages."

The next day he began to break ground in our city. Early the next morning I found Joe propped up in bed scowling into *Le Matin* as he tried to butt his way through the language into the news events of the day. What I tried to tell him of the Paris I had found made no appeal whatever.

"All right, Kid," he said indulgently. "If I had a dozen lifetimes I might be a poet. But I haven't, so I'll just be a reporter."

And he and his bike plunged into the town. He found its "newspaper row" that day and a Frenchman to whom he had a letter. With this man Joe went to the Bourse and that night to the Chamber of Deputies. He got "Sunday specials" out of them both, and then went on to the Bourse de Travail. And in the few spare moments he had, Joe told us of the things he had seen. Rumors of war and high finance, trade unions, strikes and sabotage burst on my startled artist's ears. It made me think of the harbor! *This* was not my Paris!

"It is," said J. K. stoutly. "There's no place like a newspaper office to put you right next to the heart of a town."

He would not hear to our seeing him off. I remember him that last night after supper strapping his bag onto his bike and starting off down our quiet old street on his way to the station.

"To-morrow," he said, "I'll stop off in Leipsic. I want to have a look at the college that stirred my young grandfather up for life. I've got his diary with me."

Again, in spite of the gruffness, I felt that wistful quality in him. J. K. was hunting for something too.

CHAPTER X

But what a relief to see him go, to forget his loud disturbing Paris and again drink deep of mine, the city of great writers.

"I'll never really know them," I thought, "until I can not only talk but think and feel in their language."

So I drudged for hours a day in my room. I inflicted my French on my chums at meals, on defenseless drivers of 'buses who could not rise and go away, and on the Blessed Damozel, who said:

"Va donc, cherches-toi une fille. C'est la seule manière d'apprendre le Français."

I was vaguely thrilled by this idea, the more because so far in my life I had had no experience of the kind. On the streets, in cabs, and in cafés I began watching women with different eyes, more eagerly selecting eyes that picked out of the throng the one *her* of the moment so that for me she was quite alone. She was alone for a thousand reasons, different ones in every case. She was of many ages, rich and poor, now gorgeous and now simply dressed, now a ravishing creature that took your breath and again just funny and very French with a saucy way of wearing her clothes. Her fascinations were always new. I watched her twinkling earrings, her trick of using her lips when she smiled, her hands, her silk clad ankles, her swelling young bust, the small coquettish hat she wore, her shoulders, their expressive shrugs, her quick vivacious movements—and I watched her eyes. Her eyes would meet mine now and then, often with only a challenging smile but again in an intimate dazzling way that gave me a deep swift shock of delight and left me confused and excited.

"In a little while," I thought. I decided to wait till I knew more French. "She'll be strange enough, God knows," I thought half apprehensively, "even when I can talk her language." And with a feeling almost of relief I would plunge back into my work and forget her. For me she was only an incident in this teeming radiant life.

I must learn French! I strained my ears at lectures, at plays from the top gallery, I hired a tutor to hurry it on. Years later in New York I met a Russian revolutionist come to raise money for his cause. "Three weeks have I been in this country," he said in utter exasperation. "And not yet do I speak fluently the English!" That was how I felt about French. What a delight to begin to feel easy, to catch the fine shadings, the music and color of words and of phrases. How much more pliant and smooth and brilliant than English. How remote from the harbor.

I could study my models now, not only their construction but their small character touches as well. De Maupassant was still first for me. So simple and sure, with so few strokes but each stroke counting to the full, one suggestive sentence making you imagine the rest, everything else in the world shut out, your mind gripped suddenly and held, focussed on this man and this woman who a moment before had been nothing to you but were now more real than life itself. Especially this woman, what an absorbing creature he made her—and the big human ideas he injected into these petites histoires.

I wrote short stories by the score. Each one had a perfectly huge idea but each seemed worse than the one before. I took to myself the advice of Flaubert, and from a table before a café I would watch the people around me and jot down the minutest details, I filled whole pages with my strokes. But which to choose to make this person or this scene like no other in the world? There came the rub. How had De Maupassant done it? The answer came to me one night:

"Not only by watching people. He talked to 'em, lived with 'em, knew their lives!"

The very thing my music teacher had said about Beethoven. How uneasy I had been then, how absurdly young and priggish then in the gingerly way I had gone at the harbor. Thank heaven there was no harbor here. I could enter this life with a wholehearted zest.

I began with one of my roommates. He was to be an architect. A hard-working little chap, his days were filled with sharp suspense. The Beaux Arts entrance examinations were close ahead. If he did not pass, he told me, his parents in Ohio were too poor to give him another chance.

"If I have to go back to Ohio now," he said in that soft reflective voice of his, "I'll put up cowsheds—later on, barns—and maybe when I'm fifty, a moving picture theater. If I stay here and go back a Beaux Arts man, I can go to New York or Chicago and get right into the center of the big things being done."

With a wet towel bound around his head he used to sit at his work half the night. I watched the lines tighten about his thin lips and between his gray eyes, grew to know the long weariness in them over some problem, the sudden grim joy when the problem worked out. One day he came home early.

"Queer," he said simply. "I can see one side of your face, one side of your body, one leg and one arm. But the other side don't seem to be there." I looked up at him a moment.

"Let's go out for a walk," I suggested. We went for a stroll in the Gardens. And here I was surprised and just a bit ashamed to find that while I had a real sympathy for him I had just as real curiosity. For here was a living illustration of the horror of going blind. I could see his jaws set like a vise, I could hear his low voice talking steadily on as though to keep from thinking. What was he thinking? What was he feeling? We talked of the most commonplace things. But moment by moment, through his voice and his grip on my arm, those sudden waves now of sickening fear, now of keen suspense, now of angry groping around for a foothold, seemed pouring from him right into me, became part of me—while the other part of me stood off and listened.

"By God, this is life!" said one part of me. "No, it isn't; it's hell," growled the other part. "This thing has got to be settled!"

I took him to an oculist, and there I had another close view, this time of intense relief.

"Blind? Why, no, you're not going blind," said the oculist kindly. "All you need is"—I heard nothing more. I had never had any idea before of how swift and deep relief could be. On the street outside I heard it not only in his unsteady laugh but in my own as well. We celebrated long that night, and very late he took me to his favorite place down on the lower quay of the river, where with the lights and the sounds of the city far off it felt like some old dungeon. But just over our heads hung the heavy black arch of a stone bridge, and looking up through this arch as a frame we could see close above a gray, luminous mass rising and rising in great sweeping lines till it filled half the sky—silent, tremendous, Notre Dame. From down here the old edifice seemed alive. And though my friend talked little here, I felt him again coming into me. And this time it was his religion that came, his curious passion for building.

When at last we went home he could see my whole body, and I felt as though I had seen his whole soul.

Then I carefully wrote this down on paper. I put in every touch that I could remember. I rewrote it to make it big, and I made it so big I spoiled it all. I tore this up and began again. For about two weeks I wrote nothing else. But at last I tore up everything. After all, he was a friend of mine.

"But where's the harm," I argued, "so long as I always tear it up? This is real stuff. I'll get somewhere this way if I keep on."

And I did keep on. Shamelessly I wormed my way into friends by the dozen. I found it such an absorbing pursuit I could hardly wait to finish up one before I went on to another. There were such a bewildering lot of them, now that I had pried open my eyes. Would-be painters, sculptors, poets, dramatists, novelists, rich and poor, tragic ones and comic ones, with the meanest pettiest jealousies, the most bumptious self-conceits, the blindest worship of masters, the most profound humility, ambition so savage it made men inhuman. Many were starving themselves to death.

There was a little Hungarian Jew, an ardent follower of Matisse. "Technique?" he cried. "It is nothing! To grip your soul in your two hands and press it on your canvas—that is art, that is Matisse!"

He took me night after night through old buildings up in Montparnasse, immense and dismal rookeries crowded with Poles, Bohemians and God knows what other races, all feverish post-impressionists. Often we would find three together close around one candle, scowling, and squinting at their easels, gaunt, silent, eager. Matisse—Matisse!

"Most of them," said my guide, "are just mad. They cannot paint. All think they are going to do great things, but all they are going to do is to die."

It was through this little Hungarian that I made my first study of female life.

Why delay any longer? I had been in Paris over six months, and I had qualms almost of guilt at the thought of this chastity of mine. At first I said, "Art is a jealous mistress." And this did splendidly for a time. But then a stout German youth came along and laid it down as an absolute law that no writer could do a woman right until he had lived with a dozen. Hence that scented little cat with whom he had lived for the past year. She was the first of the dozen, eh? Damn the fellow, how much was there in it? De Maupassant certainly hadn't held off. In fact there were few of my idols who had. Why not be brave and take the plunge? It need not be such a terrific plunge; no doubt if I went at it right I could find a safe, easy kind of a *her*, friendly and confiding, a thoroughly good fellow with none of these wild ups and downs. The less temperament the better; she must have a good quiet head on her shoulders; no doubt we would need it. And she must not be too young. Let her have had affairs enough to know that ours was only one more and would probably be as brief as the rest— the briefer the better.

So tamely I pictured my first love. And the gay old city of Paris smiled, and in that bantering way of hers she brought to me in a café one night a perfect young tigress of a girl, a lithe, dusky beauty with smouldering eyes, and said:

"Without doubt this one is better for you. Regard what loveliness, what fire! Oh, my son, why not be brave?"

I was not brave, I barely spoke, and my friend the little Hungarian Jew who had brought her to my table was forced to do the talking. For she, too, was silent. But how different was her silence from the quiet I had pictured. Presently, however, I became a little easier, and by degrees we began to talk. She told me she was a painter. An Armenian by birth, she had run away from home at eighteen, and here for two years in Julien's she had tried to paint till she felt she'd go mad. She talked in abrupt, eager sentences, breaking off to watch people around us. How her big eyes fastened upon them. "To watch faces until you are sure—and then paint! There is nothing else in the world!" she said. And I found this reassuring.

After that I saw her many nights. And from time to time breaking that silence of hers, she became so fiercely confiding, not only about her painting, but about what she called her innermost soul, that soon I could look my De Maupassant square in the face, man to man, for I was learning a lot about women. As yet we were friends and nothing more, but I could feel both of us changing fast. "In a little while," I thought.

But alas. One night she took me up to her room and showed me her paintings. They were bad. They were fearfully bad, and my face must have shown the impression they made.

"You consider them frightful!" she exclaimed. I stoutly denied it, but things only went from bad to worse. Here was that temperament I had dreaded. Now she was clutching both my arms.

"Mon dieu! Why not say it? Why cannot you say it?"

"No," I replied. "You have done some extremely powerful work!" Anything to quiet her nerves. "Especially this one—look—over here!" And I pointed to one of her pictures.

"I will show you how I shall look at it!" she cried in a perfect frenzy of tears. She snatched up a knife that lay on her table, a very old, curved, Armenian knife, and went at the painting and slashed it to shreds, and then scattered the shreds all over the room.

And watching this little festival, I thought to myself excitedly,

"I know enough about this girl!"

My retreat was so precipitate as to appear almost a flight.

"Yes," I said to myself, outside, "De Maupassant knew women. And he went insane at forty-five."

And so my next case was a chap from Detroit, whose aim, he told me, was no less than to make himself "by the sheer force of my will a perfect, all-round, modern man."

It was over his case that I lost what was left of my sense of honor. For I not only wrote him down, I kept what I had written. "Ten years from now," I said in excuse, "I won't believe him unless he's on paper." But having kept this, I began keeping others, until my locked drawer was filled with the dreams and ambitions and even the loves of my confiding, innocent friends. At last I was a writer.

What a relief when my mother wrote that my father had consented to a second year abroad for me. In my gratitude I even grew just a trifle homesick.

"Hadn't I better come home for the summer?" I wrote her.

"No," she replied, "we cannot afford it. I want you to keep right on with your work. I feel so sure you are working hard and will do things I shall be proud of."

I was not only working, but living, feeling, listening hard, under the stimulus day and night of the tense, rich life around me. About this time I made a friend of a gaunt, bearded Russian chap, whose dream for years had been, like mine, to become a writer of fiction. His god had been Turgenief. And a year ago, leaving his home, a little town near Moscow, with forty roubles in his purse he had set out on foot with a pack on his back to tramp the long and winding road that stretched away two thousand miles to the distant city of Paris, the place where his idol had lived and studied and written for so many years. Through this young Russian pilgrim I came to know the books of some of his countrymen, and through him I caught glimpses down into the vast, mysterious soul of that people in the North.

Through other chaps I met those days, other deep, tremendous vistas opened up as backgrounds for these Paris friends of mine. Half the night, in that café endeared to so many youths of all nations under its name of "The Dirty Spoon," I heard talk about all things under the sun, talk that was a merry war of words, ideas and points of view as wide apart as that of a Jap and a German. For every land upon the earth had sent its army of ideas, and they all charged together here, and the walls of the Dirty Spoon resounded with the battle—with roars of laughter and applause. For we were of free, tolerant minds. We were gay, young dogs of war who had left our tails behind us—our tails of prejudice, distrust—and our emancipated souls had only scorn for hatreds born of race or creed. Like J. K., we had rid ourselves of all creeds past and present—but J. K. had always been free with a scowl, his feet set grimly on the ground—we here were free with a verve and a dash that took us careering up into the stars to laugh at the very heavens.

There was breadth in our very manner of speech. For here were we from all over the earth, all speaking one tongue, the language in which half the things that had moved the world had been said by men before us. And what sparkling things there were still to be said, what dazzling things we would see and do, in this prodigious onward march of the armies of peace, out of all dark ages into a glad new world for men, where our great smiling goddess of all the arts would reign supreme, where we would dream mighty visions of life and all these visions would come true.

So we saw the world those days in the radiant city on the Seine.

And meanwhile far up in the North, the Russian Czar, having started with loud ostentation the movement for a worldwide peace, was swiftly completing his preparations to strike with his armies at Japan. And the other nations of Europe, jealous and suspicious of each other's every secret plan—they, too, were making ready for what the future years might bring.

"Young men are lucky. They will see great things."

And these young men have seen great things. But they have not been lucky.

CHAPTER XI

It was about a year after this that again Joe Kramer broke in on my dreams.

He arrived early on a raw, wet morning in the following winter. His all-night ride from Cherbourg had left him disheveled, unshaven and hungry.

"Well, boys," he asked when our greetings were over, "what do you think of the news?"

"What news?"

Joe gave us a grim, fatherly smile.

"Say. Do I have to come all the way from Chicago to tell you what's happening down the street? Well, you young beauty boosters, there's a panic on the Bourse this week that's got your fair city flat on her back. And the cause of the said panic is that France is in deep on Russian bonds, which are now worth about a cent to the dollar. Because the Russian people—already dead sick of the war with Japan—have risen in a howling mob against their government. See?"

"I did hear of that," said the painter among us. "A Polish chap in the studio said something about it yesterday."

"Now, did he?" said the ironical Joe. "Just kind of murmured it, I suppose, while bending reverently over his art." He rose. "Well, boys, I'm sorry for you, but I've only got a day in this town, I'm off for Russia on the night train. Bill, I wish you'd help me here. I've got an awful lot to do and my French is still a little weak."

It was not at all weak, it was strong and loud. I can hear it still, Joe Kramer's French, and it is a fitting memory of that devastating day.

The day began so splendidly, so big with promise of great

ideas. I grew quite excited about it. Here was Joe on his way to a real revolution. Sent out by his Chicago paper, he was going to Russia to see a whole people fight to be free—a struggle prophesied long ago by Turgenief, Tolstoy and other big Russians whose work I admired. And now it was actually coming off—and Joe, the lucky devil, was going to be right on hand! From some mysterious source in New York he had secured a letter to a Russian revolutionist leader who for many years had been an exile here in Paris. Joe was anxious to see him at once.

"All right," I said eagerly. "Give me his address."

"Hold on," J. K. retorted. "It's not so easy as all that. I want to get into Russia. This man's house in Paris is watched day and night by the Russian secret police, and nobody who's seen with him has a chance of crossing the frontier. We've got to go slow."

"What'll we do?"

"I want you to steer me first to a Frenchman. He's an anarchist. Here's his address."

The anarchist was a bit disappointing. A mild little man, we found him in an attic room receiving a vigorous scolding from the huge blonde with whom he lived. But after reading Joe's letter, he, too, took on a mysterious air. He came with us in our cab, and off we went over Paris until I thought we should never end. Again and again the cab would stop and our guide would darkly disappear. But from one of these trips he returned triumphant.

"I have found his wife," he announced. "But she says she must have a look at you first." The cab rattled off, and the next stop was in front of a public library.

"Now," said our guide, "go in and sit down at a table and pretend you are reading."

We went in and did as he said. Soon a middle-aged woman in black sat down at the other side of the table. She stared at us gloomily a moment; then with a yawn she opened a book and calmly started making notes. Presently, scowling over her work, she began muttering to herself.

"You must not look up," I heard in French. "A Russian spy sits over there. You wish to see my husband. Come to-night at nine o'clock to the second floor of the Café Voltaire. He will be at the top of the stairs. Good-by." And she yawned again over her writing.

"Now, this," I thought, "is a revolution!" I thoroughly approved of this. The Café Voltaire was an excellent choice, an almost perfect mise-en-scène. It had long been one of my favorite haunts. A tall white wooden building, so toned down, so tumbled down, so heavy laden with memories of poets, dramatists, pamphleteers and fiery young orators, who had sat here and conspired and schemed and exhorted over human rights. It had well lived up to its glorious name. What great ideas had started from here! Here French history had been made!

But alas! Into this hallowed spot that night, at nine o'clock on his way to his train, came Joe in a yellow mackintosh with a brand-new suitcase in his hand—and showed me history in the making. It was made in a small, stuffy room upstairs. On the one side J. K. with a million American readers behind him, on the other this revolutionist whose name that week had been in newspapers all over the world. So far, so good. But look at him, look at this history maker. Tall, sallow and dyspeptic, a professor of economics. Romance, liberty, history, thrill? Not at all. They talked of factories, wages, strikes, of railroads, peasants' taxes, of plows and wheat and corn and hay! They got quite excited over hay.

And all this had to come through their defenseless interpreter—me. My head ached, one foot fell asleep. The Social Democratic Party, the Social Revolutionist Party, the Constitutional Democrats, in and out of my head they trooped. If this be revolution, then God save the king! Crushed to earth, as we left at last, my head still buzzing with economics, I looked dismally back on my poor café, on liberty, justice and human rights. There was something as bad as the harbor in Joe; he was always spoiling everything.

"Why don't you take Carlyle's French Revolution along?" I suggested forlornly. "You might read it on the train."

"Because, you poor kid, he's way out of date."

It took me days to get into my work.

About two months later, back he came. From one of our front windows he looked down into the old Gardens, into all the loveliness the April twilight was bringing there, and,

"Where can I get a typewriter?" he asked. "I've got such an awful lot of stuff that I want to dictate it right off the bat."

This was *literature* in the making. For hours in Joe's room that week I sat and heard him make it. In one corner lay a heap of dirty shirts and collars, in another a stack of papers and books. An English stenographer sat at the window, J. K. strode up and down and talked. It was real enough, this narrative. Facts and figures, he had them down cold, to back up with a crushing force the points he was making against the Czar. Poverty, tyranny, bloody oppression, wholesale slaughter of a people in a half-mad monarch's war—Joe pounded them in with sledgehammer blows. He not only made you sure they were true, he made you sure that these things must be stopped and that you as a decent American certainly wanted to help with your money. And as for the revolution itself, he left no doubt in your mind about that. It was there all right, Joe had seen people give up their lives, he had seen men and women clubbed and shot down, he had been so near he had seen the blood. (But he made human blood so darned commonplace, curse him!) And in Petersburg for two long nights he had gone about a city in darkness, every street light put out by the strikers, the streets filled with surging black masses of figures. Yes, Joe had certainly seen big things.

Then what was the matter with me, I thought, that all this did not thrill me? "Young men are lucky. They will see great things." All right, here was one of *my* great things, a whole nation rising to throw off its chains, to show the world that wars must cease—and to me it didn't seem great at all, it seemed only big, and there was a world of difference. Big? It was enormous, not only what Joe had seen up there, but what he was doing right here in this room. He was talking to a million people, damn him, and doubtless this was just the kind of writing that would appeal to them. Thousands of his commonplace readers would send their dollars to Russia, where dyspeptic professors of economics would use the money to hire halls, into which millions of commonplace Russians would crowd to hear about strikes, wages, taxes and hay! And then some more commonplace blood would be shed, the dyspeptic professors would be put in office—and this was a modern revolution!

Was everything modern only big? Must I always have that feeling the harbor used to give me?

"No!" I decided angrily. The fault didn't lie in me nor in

Russia, but in J. K. and the way he was writing. As I followed that blunt narrative of his journey through cities and factory towns, into deep forests, across snowy plains and through little hamlets half buried in snow and filled with the starving families of the men who had gone to the war, I tried to picture it all to myself—not as he described it, confound him, but with all the beauty which must have been there. Ye Gods of the Road, what a journey! What tremendous canvases teeming with life, such strange, dramatic significant life! What a chance for a writer!

One night on a train whose fifth-class cars, cattle cars and nothing more, were packed with wounded men from the front, out of one of those traveling hells Joe had pulled a peasant boy half drunk, and by the display of a bottle of vodka had enticed him into his own compartment in a second-class car ahead. The boy's right arm was a loathsome sight, festering from a neglected wound. Amputation was plainly a matter of days. But it was not to forget that grim event that the boy had jumped off at each little station to spend his few kopecks on vodka. No, he was stolidly getting drunk because, as he confided to Joe, at dawn he would come to his home town and there he knew he was going to tell twenty-six wives that their men had been killed. He laboriously counted them off on his fingers—each wife and each husband by their long, homely Russian names. Then he burst into half-drunken sobs and pounded the window ledge with his fist. It was the fist of his right arm, and the kid gave a queer, sharp scream of pain.

If Voltaire had been there he would have come back and described that peasant boy he'd seen in a way that would have gripped men's souls and sent a great shudder over the world at war and what it meant to mankind—while Joe was simply slapping it down like some hustling, keen reporter.

"Look here, Joe; you make me sick!" I exploded at last. "You ought to stick right here for months and work on this wonderful stuff you've got till there's nothing left you can possibly do!"

"Be an artist, eh, a poet, a great writer." He gave me one of those fatherly smiles. "I've got some things to say to *you*, Kid. I don't like the life you're leading."

"Don't you? Why don't you?" I rejoined. And so began a fight that lasted as long as he was in Paris.

Nothing that I had been doing here made any appeal whatever to Joe. I showed him my sketch of Notre Dame from under that old bridge at night.

"Yes," he said, "this is fine writing, awful fine. But it has about as much meaning to me as a woman's left ear. What's the use of sitting down under a bridge and looking up at an ancient church and trying to feel like a two-spot? For God's sake, Bill, get it out of your system, quit getting reverent over the past. You're sitting here at the feet of the Masters, fellahs who were all right in their day, but are now every one of 'em out of date. And you're so infernally busy copying their technique and style and trying to learn just how to write, that you're getting nothing to write about. Why can't you go to life for your stuff?"

"Go to life?" I said indignantly. "I've done nothing else for over a year!"

"Show me."

"Here!"

He read more of my sketches.

"But damn it, Bill, these people aren't alive. They're only a bunch of artist kids as reverent over the past as yourself, they have about as much connection with anything live and vital to-day as so many mediæval monks. You fellahs think you're free of creeds. You're the creediest kids I ever saw, your religion is style, technique and form. For God's sake lose it and use your own eyes, forget you're an artist and be a reporter, come out in the world and have a try. You'll find so much stuff you won't need any plots, you'll simply report events as they happen. And you won't have any time for technique, the next event will be tuning up before you've got to the end of the last. With a big daily paper behind him a good reporter can follow the front page around the world. Russia's on the front page now. All right, you can go to Russia. By June it may be Hindustan, or Pittsburgh, Turkey or China. Believe me, Bill, the nations of this planet are working themselves into a state where they're ready to do things you never dreamed of. I'm not talking of kings and governments, I'm talking of the people themselves, the people in such excited crowds that nobody knows who's who or what's next.

"I saw my first crowd in Petersburg the very day I got off the train. They filled a street from wall to wall and as far as you could see. They weren't saying a word or singing a song, and there wasn't even a drum to keep time. But they moved along with their wives and kids as though they'd left home, job and church, and were looking for something else so hard they didn't care for bullets. I saw 'em shot down like so many sheep. But bullets won't stop what I saw in their eyes. God knows I don't want a religion. I'm no socialist nor anarchist. But if there's one thing I want to hang on to it's my belief in the common crowd. They've had a raw deal since the world began. They can have the whole earth whenever they want it. And they're beginning to want it hard!

"Forget your own name and jump into the crowd, write and don't stop to remember you're writing! The place *you* need is the U. S. A.—and the work you need is a job on a paper!"

"Are you through?" I snapped.

"I am!"

"All right," said I. "I'm going to stay just where I am! I'm not going to be yanked by you all over the earth, to write news articles on the run! I'm going to stick in one place—right here—and take my time and learn my job. I don't want to write news, I want to write books. I'd rather write one good novel than all the headline stuff in the world. It's books that make the headlines."

"*Books?*" Joe's look was funny.

"Sure they do. Take Russia. What started this whole revolution? Books. It didn't start with your common crowds—they were all eating fried onions. It started with a few writers of novels!"

"Who left their little mahogany desks," said Joe, "got into peasant clothes and went to live with the peasants!"

"Oh no they didn't. Only a few. Turgenief didn't. Tchernichefsky didn't. Dostoiefsky——"

"Say. Are they Russians? I never heard their names up there."

I looked at J. K. thoughtfully.

"No," I said. "You wouldn't. As yet they're not quite crowdy enough. But they are Russians and their ideas made most of the first revolutionists. The whole revolution was started by books."

"It wasn't," snapped Joe. "It was taxes. Their taxes were doubled because of the war, and——"

"Oh, damn your war taxes, and damn your plows and your corn and hay! You've got a hay mind, that's the trouble with you!

You've got so you think that hay and bread and pork and beans
are all men live and die for! They don't, Mister Reporter, they die
for ideals—freedom, democracy, human rights—which are in
'em so deep that when a big writer sees 'em there and brings 'em
out and holds 'em up and says, 'Here! This is you, this is what
you want, this is what you believe in!'—your crowd says, 'Sure!
Why didn't we see it long ago?' And then they do things that go
into headlines! But to be able to write like that a man can't go
chasing all over the earth, he's got to quit sneering at art and technique, he's got to learn how to make characters real and build
plots that make readers sit up all night to see what becomes of the
people he's made! If believing that is a creed, then I'm creedy! I'm
willing to throw over everything else, but I'll hang on to this one
thing all my life—the fact that big art means working like hell!"

"Gee," said J. K. "What an artist."

These fights of ours left me weak and sore, as though I'd been
back on the terrace at home, listening to my father talk and looking at his harbor.

CHAPTER XII

When Joe left me in peace at last, just for the sake of the rest and change I turned my attention to music, or, rather, to a musical friend, a young Bohemian composer who lived wholly in a world of his own. I explored this musical world of his, by his side in dark top galleries, in the Café Rouge on concert nights, in his room at his piano. How deliciously far away from hay was this chap's feeling for Mozart. With him I could feel sure of myself, of the way I was living for my art, of what my mother way back at the start had called the "fine things" in humanity.

I remember the night we heard "Bohème" from the gallery of the Opéra Comique. I remember the talk we had late that night, and my walk by the edge of the Gardens home—and the letter and the cable that I found waiting on my desk. The letter was from my father and told me that my mother was dying. The cable told me she was dead.

I remember learning that letter by heart on that long ocean voyage home. This was no sudden illness, I learned, my mother had known of it while I was home, known that she had it and that it was fatal. That was the news she had told my father alone that night on the terrace! That was why she had been so eager to get me away to Paris; that was why she had kept me abroad!

"She did not want you to see how she looked," my father wrote. "She wanted you to remember her always as she was when you saw her last."

I remembered her now. What a young beast I had been to forget her, to drop her so utterly out of my thoughts in that selfish happy Paris life, when it was she who had sent me there, when it was she who had set me free for a time from the harbor which was now dragging me back, when it was she from the very start who had fostered this passion for "all that is fine." I remembered her now—remembered and remembered—until her dear image filled me.

My father's letter went on to tell how she had fought for her life. Three operations, all three of them failures, but still she had held bravely on in hopes of some new discovery which science might make and so bring her a cure. A thought suddenly gripped me and struck me cold. It had all depended on science, on men working calmly and coldly along in laboratories all over the world, while my mother had held to her thread of life and hoped that these laboratory gods would hurry, hurry while yet there was time! How many thousands like her every day, every hour all over the world were watching those gods with that awful suspense. For they were the only gods that were left, and a comfortless set of gods they were! They were like J. K., they had hay minds! They were businesslike, relentless, cold, they belonged to the world of the harbor! My mother's kind god was a myth and a joke, with no power here one way or the other. I *felt* that now, I had *thought* it before, only thought it, with that gay freedom of thought we had aired back there in Paris. But I knew now that deep underneath I had believed all along in this god of hers, as I had in my beautiful goddess of art and in all the things that were fine. It had taken this news from the harbor to bring him tottering, crashing down. For no god like hers would have let her die! And I felt fear now, the fear of Death, whom I'd never really noticed before and who now seemed to say to me,

"She is nothing—has gone nowhere—she is only dead!"

And fiercely in a bewildered way I rebelled against this emptiness. I rebelled against this world of hay that was so abruptly dragging me back to a sense of its almighty grip on my life. When my ship came up the Bay, the world looked harsh and gray to me, though there was a bright and sunny glare on the muddy waves of the harbor.

BOOK II

BOOK II

CHAPTER I

My mother had been buried several days before I reached home.

I found Sue waiting on the dock, and I saw with a little shock of surprise that my young sister was grown up. I had never noticed her much before. Sue and I had never got on from the start. She had been my father's chum and I had been my mother's. I had always felt her mocking smile toward me and all my solemn thoughts. And after that small catastrophe which I had had with Eleanore, I had more than ever avoided Sue and her girl friends. Then I had gone to college, and each time that I came home she had seemed to me all arms and legs, fool secrets and fool giggles—a most uninteresting kid. I remember being distinctly surprised when I brought Joe home for Christmas to find that he thought her quite a girl. But now she was all different. She had grown tall and graceful, lithe, and in her suit of mourning she looked so much older, her face thin and worn, subdued and softened by all she'd been through. For the weight of all those weary weeks had been upon her shoulders. There was something pitiful about her. I came up and kissed her awkwardly, then found myself suddenly holding her close. She clung to me and trembled a little. I found it hard to speak.

"I wish I'd been here, too," I said gruffly.

"I wish you had, Billy—it's been a long time."

All at once Sue and I had become close friends.

We had a long talk, at home that day, and she told me how our parents had drawn together in the last years, of how my poor mother had wanted my father close by her side and of how he had responded, neglecting his business and spending his last dollar on doctors, consultations and trips to sanitariums, anything to keep up her strength. He had even read "Pendennis" aloud. How changed he must have been to do that. I knew why she had wanted to hear it again. It had been our favorite book. I remembered how I had read it to her just before I went abroad, and how I had caught her watching me with that hungry despairing look in her eyes. What a young brute I had been to go! . . . For a time Sue's voice seemed far away. Then I heard her telling how over that story of a young author my mother had talked to my father of me.

"He's going to try to know you, Billy, and help you," said Sue. "He promised her that before she died. And I hope you're going to help him, too. He needs you very badly. You never understood father, you know. I don't believe you have any idea of what he has gone through in his business."

"What do you mean? Have things gone wrong?"

"I don't understand it very well. He hardly ever speaks of it. I think he'd better tell you himself."

That evening in his library, from my seat by the table, I furtively watched my father's face. He sat in a huge chair against the wall, with a smaller chair in front for his feet, his vest unbuttoned, his short heavy body settled low as he grimly kept his eyes on his book. The strong overhead light which shone on his face showed me the deeper lines, all the wrinkles, the broad loose pouch of skin on the throat, the gray color, the pain, the weakness and the age in his motionless eyes. What was going on in there? Sometimes it would seem an hour before he turned another page. All afternoon he had been at her grave.

He had given her no happy life. Was it of that he was thinking? I felt ashamed to be wondering, for he seemed so weak and old in his grief. Two years ago his hair had been gray, but he had still looked strong and hale. I could hardly feel now that he was the same man. I felt drawn to him now, I wished he would put down his book and talk and tell me everything about her.

But what an embarrassing job it is to get acquainted with one's father. When Sue had left us after dinner, there had been a few brief remarks and then this long tense silence. I, too, pretended to be reading.

"Your mother thought a lot of you, boy." He spoke at last so abruptly that I looked up at him with a start, and saw him watching me anxiously.

"Yes, sir." I looked quickly down, and our eyes did not meet again after that.

"It was her pluck that kept you in Paris—while she was dying."

I choked:

"I know."

"You don't know—not how she wanted you back—you'll never know. I wanted to write you to come home."

"I wish you had!"

"She wouldn't hear of it!"

"I see." Another silence. Why couldn't I think of something to say?

"She kept every letter you wrote her. They're up there in her bureau drawer. She was always reading 'em—over and over. She thought a lot of your writing, boy—of what you would do when—when she was dead." The last came out almost fiercely. I waited a moment, got hold of myself.

"Yes, sir," I brought out at last.

"I hope you'll make it all worth while."

"I will. I'll try. I'll do my best." I did not look up, for I could still feel his anxious eyes upon my face.

"Do you want to go back to Paris?"

"No, sir! I want to stay right here!" What was the matter with my fool voice?

"Have you got any plans for your writing here? How are you going about it to start?"

"Well, sir, to begin with—I've got some stuff I did abroad."

"Stories?"

"Not exactly——"

"Poems?" My father's look was tragic.

"No."

And I tried to explain what I had been doing. But my attempts to tell him of my work in Paris were as forced and as pathetic as his efforts to attend. More and more halting grew our talk, and it ended in a silence that seemed to have no end. Then I went to the fireplace, knocked the ashes out of my pipe, refilled it and relit it. When I returned he was reading his book, and with deep relief I took up mine. That much of it was over.

But again I found myself watching him. What was in my father's mind? Why this anxious almost humble tone? It made me wince, it made me ashamed. I sat there all evening pretending to read and feeling that he was doing the same.

"Good night, dad—I think I'll go to bed." Even this little came clumsily. I had never called him "dad" before.

"Good night, my boy. See you at breakfast."

"Yes, sir."

I glanced back as I turned down the hall and saw him staring after me.

What was it he was thinking?

CHAPTER II

"I'm closing out my business, son," he told me the next morning. Here was another sharp surprise. I did not look at him as I asked:

"Why are you doing that, sir?"

"It's a long story. Times have changed and I'm getting old."

Again I felt suddenly drawn to him. He was old and no mistake. Why had I never known him till now?

"Look here—Dad." The last word still came awkwardly. "Can't I possibly be any help down there?" He shot an anxious look at me:

"Why, yes. Glad to have you. I still have a young clerk, but I'd rather have you."

Only one clerk! What had gone wrong with his business?

But that day in his warehouse, which was empty now and silent, the mere ghost of what it had been, he seemed in no hurry to show me. On the contrary, he went back to the ledgers of his earliest years in business, on the flimsy pretext of looking up certain figures and dates. He did not need me here, the work he gave me was absurd, I was simply taking the musty books from their piles in the closet and arranging them by years on the floor. "To save time," he said. But he himself was still on that first ledger, stopping to talk, to ramble off from the pages before him. What did it mean? As the days wore on and he still delayed and at night that strange humility crept again into his eyes, with a slowly deepening suspense I came to feel that instead of saving time my father was trying to make it, to go far back into his vigorous past for strength to meet his present—because he dreaded what we would find at the end of our work on these dusty books, the last grim figure in dollars and cents that would stand there as the result of his life, as the stepping-stone for Sue's and mine. And that was why he wanted me here, this was his way of telling me the story of his business life—before I saw what lay at the end. And as in our work that story unfolded, though at times it cast its spell on me hard, revealing what a man he had been, there were other times when from somewhere deep inside of me a small selfish voice would ask:

"What is left? How much has he saved from the wreck? What is this going to mean to my life?"

In the ledgers his story was still alive. Yellow and dusty as they were, for me day by day they revivified that still odorous old warehouse until I saw it as it had been, a huge dim caravansary for the curious products of all the earth. And that trick of feeling a man, which I had learned in Paris, made me keenly sensitive now to this lonely old stranger by my side with whom I was becoming acquainted. I could feel the pull of these books upon him, pulling him out of his cramped old age back to his glad boundless youth. How suddenly spacious they became as he slowly turned the pages. Palm oil from Africa, cotton from Bombay, coffee from Arabia, pepper from Sumatra. Turn the page. Ivory from Zanzibar, salt from Cadiz and wines from Bordeaux. Turn the page. Whale oil from the Arctic, iron from the Baltic, tortoise shell from the Fiji Islands. Turn the page! India silks and rugs and shawls, indigo, spices! Turn the page!

I began to see the sails speed out along those starlit ocean roads. I began to feel the forces that had shaped my father's life. And little by little I saw in those days what not even my mother had understood, that in my father's business life there had been more than dollars, that what to us had seemed only a hobby, a dull obstinate fixed idea, had been for him a glorious vision—the white sails of American clippers dotting all the seven seas.

So they were in the late Fifties, when leaving the farm in Illinois he came at sixteen to New York and found a job as time clerk in one of the ship yards along the East River. They are all gone now, but then they were humming and teeming with work. And my young father was deeply excited. He told me of his first day here, when he stood on the deck of a ferry and watched three great clippers go out with the tide, bound for Calcutta. There were pictures of these vessels on the walls of his office, stately East Indiamen bearing such names as *Star of Empire, Daniel Webster, Ocean*

Monarch, Flying Cloud—ships known in every port of the world for their speed. He told how a British vessel, her topsails reefed in a gale of wind, would see a white tower of swelling canvas come out of the spray behind her, come booming, staggering, plunging by—a Yankee clipper under royals. Press of sail? No other nation knew what it meant! Our owners took big chances, it was no trade for nervous men!

He found a harbor that welcomed young men, where cabin boys rose to be captains, and clerks became owners of hundreds of ships. To work! To rise! To own yards like these, build ships like these and send them rushing on their courses out to all parts of the ocean world! This had been his vision, at the time when it was bright and clear. And as now he made me feel it, the crude vital force that had been in his dream poured into me deep, made me feel how shut in and one-sided had been my own vision and standards of life, gave me that profound surprise which many sons, I suppose, never have:

"My father was once young like me—wiry, straight and tough like me, and as full of dreams of the things he would do."

But then had come the Civil War. Although only nineteen when the war broke out, he was already the head clerk in his office. "But like every other young fool those days," he said, "I was caught by the noise of a brass band!" Down South as a commissary clerk he found himself a tiny pawn in that gigantic game of graft which made fat fortunes in the North and cost tens of thousands of soldiers their lives. He himself took typhoid, and when the war was over he returned to New York, weak, penniless, to find his old work gone.

"For the war," he said, "had busted American shipping sky high. Even before it began it had made the South so bitter that just for the sake of attacking the North the Solid South in congress had joined the damn fool Farmer West and attacked our mail subventions. 'No more of the nation's money,' they said, 'for ship subsidies for New York and New England!' And so all government protection of our shipping was withdrawn. And when the war ended, with forty per cent. of our ships grabbed, sunk or sold, it was ruination to build any more, for the British and German governments were pouring millions of dollars a year into the Cunard and the North German Lloyd, and we couldn't compete against them.

"Still a few of the ship yards kept on, and in one of these at last I got a job at eight dollars a week. 'The war is over,' we told ourselves, 'and the government can't stay blind forever. They'll see what they've done, and within a few months they'll go back to the old policy.' Months? I stuck to that job and waited five years—and still no news from Washington. 'My boy,' said a doddering Brooklynite, 'the nation has turned her face westward.'"

Then he left the ship yards and went into a warehouse, where the work lay mainly in handling cargoes of foreign ships. And starting life all over again he tried to make up for lost time. The first year he was a shipping clerk; the second, a bookkeeper; the third, he kept two sets of books for two different docks, one by day and the other at night. And by forty he had become a part owner in the old warehouse in which he now sat grimly reading the record of his life—of a long stubborn losing fight, for he stuck to his dream of Yankee sails.

He married my mother when he was still strong and full of hope. He must have been so much kindlier then and brighter, more human to live with. They bought that pleasant house of ours with its hospitable front door. My father's doddering Brooklynites seemed wonderful neighbors to his young wife. And so that front door waited for friends. As the years dragged on and they did not come, she blamed it all on the harbor. She saw what it was making him, jealous of every dollar and every hour spent at home. He worked all day and half the night. It took him into politics, on countless trips to Washington, and she knew he spent thousands of dollars there in ways that were by no means "fine." It made him morose and gloomy, a man of one idea, to be shunned.

And she no more saw behind all this than I did when I was a boy. For his vision was neither of pirates nor of bringing the heathen to Christ, but of imports and of exports. (He dreamed in terms of battleships and of a mercantile marine.) Each year he watched the chances grow, vast continents opening up to commerce with hints of such riches as staggered the mind. He saw the ocean world an arena into which rushed all nations but ours.

"Everyone but us," he said, "had learned the big lesson—that you can get nothing on land or sea unless you're ready to fight for it hard!"

He saw other nations get ready to fight. He watched them build huge navies and grant heavy subsidies to their fast growing merchant fleets, send vessels by thousands over the seas. He saw their shipowners draw swiftly together in great corporations. Here was an age for immense adventures in this growing trade of the world. To wait, to hold on grimly, to keep up the fight at Washington for that miracle, Protection, which would start the boom. To see the shipping yards teeming again with the building of ships by the hundreds and thousands, to see them go out again over the seas with our flag at the mast and our sailors below. To feel the new call go over the nation—"Young men, come east and west, come out! The first place on the oceans can still be yours!" This was my father's great idea.

Ship subsidies and battleships, discriminating tariffs. What a religion. But it was his. Of the miracles these things would work my father was more sure than of a god in heaven. For he had thought very little about a god, and all his life he had thought about this. For this he had spent at least half his wealth on the congressmen that he despised. Bribery? Yes. But for a religion.

"Go all around South America and to the Far East," he told me. "And you'll see the flags at sea of England, Germany, Austria, France, of Russia, Norway, Spain, Japan. But if you see the American flag you'll see it waved by a little girl from the deck of a British liner. This means that we are losing in marine freights and foreign trade billions of dollars every year. And it means more and worse than that. For it's ship building and ship sailing that take a nation's men out of their ruts, whip up their minds and imaginations, make 'em broad as the seven seas. And we've lost all that, we've thrown it away, to breed a race of farmers—of factory hands and miners and anarchists in slums. We've built a nation of high finance—and graft—and a rising angry mob. But sooner or later, boy, this country will wake up to what it has done. And with our grip on both oceans and the blood we've still got in our veins, we'll reach out and take what is ours—as soon as we're ready to fight for it hard—the mastery of the ocean world!"

For this idea he had lived his life. For this he had neglected his business, for this he had lost favor with the usurping foreign ships—until his dock and his warehouse were often idle for weeks at a time.

And the very bigness of things, the era of big companies which at forty had thrilled him by the first signs of its coming, now crushed down upon his old age. Vaguely he knew that the harbor had changed and that he was too old to change with it. An era no longer of human adventures for young men but of financial adventures for mammoth corporations, great foreign shipping companies combining in agreements with the American railroads to freeze out all the little men and take to themselves the whole port of New York. My father was one of these little men. The huge company to which he was selling owned the docks and warehouses for over two miles, and this was only a part of their holdings.

"Nothing without fighting." That had been his motto. And he had fought and he had lost. And so in this new harbor of big companies my father was now closing out. Too late for any business here, too late for life up there in his home. He had kept my mother waiting too long, he was ready at last but she was dead. Too late. He had been born too late, had dreamed his dream of sails too late, and now he was too late in dying. There was nothing left to live for. How much better for him to be dead.

CHAPTER III

I have tried to tell his story as my father felt it, at the times when it took him out of himself and made him forget himself and me. But there were other times when he remembered himself and me, and those were the times that hurt the most. For in that new humility in his eyes and in his voice I could feel him then preparing us both—me to see why it was that he could not do for me what *she* had wished; himself to hold on grimly, to find a new job for his old age, to keep from becoming a burden—on me.

At last we were coming to the end—to that last figure in dollars and cents. I caught his suspense and we talked little now. I knew the price at which he was selling, and toward that figure I watched the debts creep slowly up. I saw them creep over, and knew that we had not a dollar left to live on. And still the debts kept mounting. How small they were, these last ones, a coil of rope, two kegs of paint—the irony of it compared to the bigness of his life. Still these little figures climbed. At last he handed me his balance. He was in debt four thousand, one hundred and forty-six dollars and seventeen cents.

He had risen from his old office chair:

"Well, son, I guess that ends our work."

"Yes, sir."

He went out of the office.

I sat there dully for some time. Then I remember there came a harsh scream from a freight engine close outside. And I looked out of the window.

The harbor of big companies, uglier than I had ever seen it, no longer dotted with white sails, but clouded with the smoke and soot of an age of steam and iron, lay sprawled out there like a thing alive. Always changing, always growing, it had crushed the life out of my father and mother, and now it was ready for Sue and me.

"I've got to stay here and make money."

Good-by to the Beautiful City of Grays. A clock in an outer room struck five. In Paris it was ten o'clock, and those friends of mine from all countries were crowding into "The Dirty Spoon." I could see them sauntering one by one on that summer's night down the gay old Boulevard Saint Michel and dropping into their seats at the table in the corner.

"How am I to make money? By writing?"

I thought of De Maupassant and the rest, and the two years I had spent in trying to make vivid and real the life I had seen. In these last anxious weeks I had sent some of my Paris sketches to magazine offices in New York. They had all been returned with printed slips of rejection, except in one case where the editor wrote, "This is a good piece of writing, but the subject is too remote. Why not try something nearer home?"

"All right," I thought, "what's near me here? Let's see. There's a cloud of yellow smoke I can do, with a brand-new tug below it dragging a string of good big barges. What are they loaded with? Standard Oil. Wait till they get closer and I can even describe the smell! No," I concluded savagely. "Let's keep my writing clean out of this hole and get the money some other way!"

Then suddenly I forgot myself and thought of my stern brave old dad. What under the sun was he going to do?

That week he mortgaged our house on the Heights for five thousand dollars. With this he paid off all his debts and put the balance in the bank. Then from the big dock company he got a job in his own warehouse at a hundred dollars a month.

"Kind of 'em," he said gruffly. He was sixty-five years old. They were even kind enough to add to that a job for me. I sat at the desk next to his and I was paid ten dollars a week.

Sue let the servants go, hired one green German girl and said she knew she could run the house on a hundred and twenty dollars a month. But the August bills went over that, so we drew money out of the bank. My father had bronchitis that week. We managed to keep him in bed for three days, but then he struggled up and dressed and went back to his desk in the warehouse.

"Keep your eye on him down there," said Sue. "He's so terribly feeble."

"This can't go on," I told her.

I must make more than ten dollars a week. Again I sent out some of my sketches, again the magazines sent them back. I went to a newspaper office, but there an ironical office boy, with the aid of the city editor, made me feel that reporting was not in my line. What other work could I find to do? How much time did I have? How long was my father going to last? I watched his face and our bank account. I studied the "want ads" in the press. But the more I studied the smaller I felt, for this was one of the years of depression. "Two Hundred Thousand In New York Idle," I read in a headline. Here was literature that gripped!

"I guess I'll stay right where I am. It's safer," I thought anxiously. "Perhaps if I work hard enough they'll give me a raise at Christmas. When Dad was my age he kept two sets of books, one by day and the other at night. How can I make my evenings pay?"

I took long walks in Brooklyn and picked up night work here and there. It was monotonous clerical work, and being slow at figures I was often at it till midnight. Very late one evening, while making out bills in a hardware store, I suddenly came to a customer whose initials were J. K. It started me thinking of Joe Kramer and our last long talk—about hay.

"So this is hay," I told myself. "How long will it take me to get a hay mind, back here by this damned harbor?"

CHAPTER IV

Then Sue began to take me in hand. From the subdued and weary girl that I had found when I came home, in the last few weeks she had blossomed out. The color had come into her cheeks, a new animation into her voice, a resolute brightness into her eyes.

"This thing has got to stop, Billy," she said determinedly. "This house has been like a tomb for months, you and Dad are so gloomy and tired you're sights. He needs a change, and so do you. You're getting into a little rut and throwing away your chance to write. You need friends who are writers, you need a lot of fresh ideas to tone you up. There's plenty of money in writing. And I need a change myself. I can't stand this house any longer. After all, I've got my own life to live. I'm going to get a job before long. In the meantime I'm going to see my friends. And what's more, I'm going to have them here to the house—just as often as they'll come! Let's brighten things up a little!"

I looked at her with interest. Here was *another* sister of mine—risen out of her sorrow and eager to live, and talking of running our lives as well, of curing us both by large, firm doses of "fresh ideas," while she herself looked around for a job that would help her to "live her own life."

"Look here, Sue," I argued vaguely. "You don't want to take a job——"

"I certainly do——"

"But you can't! Dad wouldn't hear to it!"

"He'll have to—when I've found it. No poor feeble old man supporting me, thank you—quite probably no man at all—ever! But you needn't worry. I won't take any old job that comes along. And I won't bother Dad till I've found just what I really want—something I can grow in."

"That's right, take it easy," I said.

"Where have you been?" I thought as I watched her. It came over me as a distinct surprise that Sue had been in all sorts of places and had been making all sorts of friends, had been having ambitions and dreams of her own—all the time I had been having mine. Most older brothers, I suppose, at some time or another have felt this same bewilderment. "Look here, Sis," they wonder gravely, "where in thunder have you been?"

I took a keen interest in her now. In the evenings when I wasn't out working we had long talks about our lives, which to my satisfaction became almost entirely talks about *her* life, her needs, her growth. Her delight in herself, her intensity over plans for herself, her enthusiasm for all the new "movements," reforms and ideas that she had heard of God-knows-where and felt she must gather into herself to expand herself—it was wonderful! She was like that chap from Detroit, that would-be perfect all-round man. But Sue was so much less solemn about it, one minute in art and the next in social settlements, so little hampered by ever putting through what she planned.

"In short, a woman," I thought sagely.

I felt I knew a lot about women, although I had had no more intimate talks since that affair in Paris. I had felt that would last me for quite a while. But here was something perfectly safe. A sister, decent but far from dull, well stocked with all the feminine points and only too glad to be confidential. She wanted to study for the stage! Of course that was the kind of thing that Dad and I would stop darned quick. Still—I could see Sue on the stage. She was not at all like me. I was middling small, with a square jaw, snub nose and sandy hair. Sue was tall and easy moving, with an abundance of soft brown hair worn low over large and irregular features. She had fascinating eyes. She could sprawl on a rug or a sofa as lazy and indolent as you please—all but her eyes, they were always doing something or other, letting this out or keeping that back, practicing on me!

"Oh, yes, she'll marry soon enough," I thought. "This talk of a job for life is a joke."

Some nights I would listen to her for hours. It was so good to come back to life, to feel younger than my worries, to forget for a little while that stark heavy certainty that poor old Dad would soon be a burden in spite of himself, and that with a family on my hands I'd have to spend the best years of my life slaving for a little hay.

I took the same delight in her friends.

Starting with her classmates in a Brooklyn high school, most of whom were working over in New York, Sue had followed in their trail, and at settlements, in studios and in girl bachelor flats she had picked up an amazing assortment of friends. "Radicals," they called themselves. Nothing was too wild or new for these friends of Sue's to jump into—and what was more, to tie themselves to by a regular job in some queer irregular office. "Votes for Women" was just starting up, and one of this group, a stenographer in a suffragette office, had been in the first small parade. Another, a stout florid youth who wrote poems for magazines, had paraded bravely in her wake. Here were two girls who lived in a tenement, did their own cooking and pushed East Side investigations that they said would soon "shake up the town." There were several rising muckrakers, too, some of whom did free work on the side for socialist papers. There was one real socialist, a painter, who had a red membership card in his pocket to prove that he belonged to "the Party." Others were spreading music and art and dramatics through the tenements—new music, new art and new dramatics. One young husband and wife, intensely in love with one another, were working together night and day for easier divorces which would put an end to the old-fashioned home.

These people seemed to me to be laughing at a different old thing every time. But when they weren't laughing they were scowling, over some new attack upon life—and when they did that they were laughable. At least so they were to me. Not that I minded attacking things, I had done plenty of that myself in Paris. But how different we had been back there. We, too, had thrown old creeds to the winds, but with how much more finesse and art. And there had been a large remoteness about it. Each one had tossed his far-away country into the cosmopolitan pot, our talk had been on a world-wide scale. But this crude crowd, except for occasional mental flights, kept all its attention, its laughs and its jeers, its attacks and exposures centered on this one mammoth town, against which as a background they seemed the merest pigmies. Three little muckrakers loomed against Wall Street, one small, scoffing suffragette against a hundred and eighty thousand solid stolid Brooklyn wives. They had posed themselves so absurdly close to the world of things as they are.

And they were in such a rush about their work. Over there in Paris, with all our smashing of idols, we had at least held fast to our one great goddess of art, we had slaved like dogs at the hard daily labor of honestly learning our various crafts. But here they stopped for nothing at all. The magazine writers were "tearing off copy," the painters were simply "slapping it down." One of them told me he "painted the real stuff right out of life"—dashed it off with one hand, so to speak, while he shook his fist at the town with the other. Everyone wanted to see something done—and done damn quick—about this, that or the other.

My artist's eyes surveyed this group and twinkled with amused surprise. But I could sit by the hour and listen to their talk. I found it mighty refreshing, after those bills in the hardware shop, that monotonous martyr feeling of mine and those worries down by the harbor.

But I felt the harbor always there, slowly closing in on my father, who looked older day by day, slowly bringing things to a crisis. In the garden behind our house on warm September evenings when these pigmies gathered to chatter reforms, the harbor hooted at their little plans as it had hooted at my own. One evening, I remember, when the talk had waxed hot and loud in favor of labor unions and strikes, Sue left the group and with a friend strolled to the lower end of the garden. There I saw them peer over the edge and listen to the drunken stokers singing in the bar-rooms deep under all these flower beds and all this adventurous chatter of ours. I thought of the years I had spent with Sam—and Sue, too, seemed to me to be having a spree. Poor kid, what a jolt she would get some day. She called me "our dreamer imported from France." But I was far from dreaming.

Presently the harbor just opened one of its big eyes and sent up by a messenger a little grim reality.

A Russian revolutionist had appeared among us with a letter to Sue from Joe Kramer. Joe, I found to my surprise, had seen quite a little of Sue over here while I had been in Paris—and from the various ships and hotels that had been his "home" of late, he had written her now and then. Through him Sue had joined a society known as "The Friends of Russian Freedom," and Joe wrote now from Moscow urging her to "stir up the crowd and lick this fellow into shape to talk at big meetings and raise some cash. He has the real goods," Joe added. "All he needs is the English language and a few points about making it yellow. If handled right he'll be a scream."

He was handled right and he was a scream. Three months later he finished a tour that had netted over ten thousand dollars. Now to buy guns and ship them to Russia—where in the awful poverty bequeathed to them by the war with Japan, a bitter people was still fighting hard to make an end of autocracy.

"I think I can help you, Puss," said Dad.

I looked at him with interest. I knew he had been as tickled as I by these astonishing friends of hers. "Revolooters," he called them. He was a great favorite with the girls.

"I once knew a man in a business way who dealt in guns," he explained to Sue. "He shipped some to Bolivia from my dock. I'll have him up to meet your friend."

So this messenger from the harbor, a keen lean man of business, gave one hour of his time to the problem in which the Russian dreamer had been absorbed for fifteen years. And the hour made the fifteen years look decidedly dreamy.

"Guns for Russia, eh?" he said. "How'll you get 'em into your country? Where's your frontier weakest? You don't know? Then I'll tell you." And the man of business did. "Now what kind of guns do you want? You hadn't thought? Well, my friend, you want Mausers. They happen to be cheap just now in Vienna. You should have looked into that before you traipsed way over here. You can get 'em there for three twenty apiece—they dropped three cents last Tuesday."

The dreamer dreamed hard and fast for a moment.

"Then," he cried triumphantly, "wit' ten t'ousand dollars I can buy over t'ree t'ousand guns!"

The gunman's look was patient.

"Don't you want to shoot 'em off?" he inquired. "Because if you do you'll need ammunition. You ought to have a thousand rounds, which will come to a little over three times the actual cost of the guns themselves. You see when you shoot off a gun at an army you want to have plenty of cartridges or else be ready to run like hell.

"On second thought," he added, "I advise you to give up the Mausers and go in for Springfields over here—old ones—you can get 'em cheap. They're no good at over a mile, but for the first few months your fellahs will be lucky if they hit a man at a hundred yards. And there's one good point about Springfields, they make a devil of a noise—and that's all you need for a starter, noise enough to break into headlines all over the world as a 'Brave Little Rebel Army.' If you can do that, and the word goes around on the quiet that you're using American rifles—well, there's a kind of a sentiment in our trade—you'll find us all behind you. We'll even *lose* money. We're a queer bunch."

"But wait!" cried the Russian. "Dere ees a trouble! Your tr-reaty wit' Russia! Have you not a tr-reaty which makes it forbidden to sell to me guns?"

Again that look of patience:

"Yes, General, we have a tr-reaty. But we'll ship your guns as grand pianos to Naples, from there by slow boat down to Brazil and then up to the Baltic, where they'll arrive with their pedigrees lost. Our agent will be there ahead, he'll have found a customhouse man he can fix, he'll cable us where—and when those fifty pianos are landed the said official will open the box marked twenty-two. It'll take him over an hour to do it, the boards will be nailed so cussedly tight. And he'll find a real piano inside. Then he'll look at the other forty-nine crates and say, 'Oh, Hell!' in Russian. Then they'll go on to wherever you want 'em—and you'll revolute. But don't forget that what you need most is the livest press agent you can find. I've got to go now. Think it over. And if you want to do business with me come to my office to-morrow at ten."

The man of business left us. And while the dreamer talked like mad and finally decided that as Mausers were "shoot farther guns" he had better go to Vienna, I watched the twinkle in Dad's gray eyes and thought of the cool contempt in his friend's. And from being amused I became rather sore. For, after all, this little Russian cuss had risked his life for fifteen years and expected to lose it shortly. (As a matter of fact, he was stood up against a wall and shot the following April.) Why make him look so small?

Was there nothing under the heavens that this infernal harbor didn't know all about, and "do business with" so thoroughly that it could always smile?

CHAPTER V

As I drudged on down there in the warehouse, my bitterness became an obsession. I even talked about it to Sue.

"Oh, Billy, you make me tired," she said. "Here I've taken the trouble to bring to the house every magazine writer I know. And they're all ready to help you break in—but you won't write, you won't even try!"

"How do you know I haven't tried?" I retorted hotly. "But I'm working all day as it is—and four nights a week besides. And the other three nights, when I try to think of the kind of thing that I could sell to the magazines—well, I simply can't do it, that's all—it's not my way of writing!"

"Then your way is just plain morbid," she said, "and it's about time you dropped it." She seemed to get a sudden idea. "I know the person *you* ought to meet——"

"Do you? What's his name?" I inquired.

"Eleanore Dillon," she answered. I looked up at her with a start.

"Eleanore Dillon? Is she still around?"

I hadn't thought of that girl in years.

"She is—and she's just what you need," said Sue, with that know-it-all smile of hers. Her head was now cocked a bit to one side. "Your little friend of long ago," she added sympathetically. I eyed Sue for a moment. I did not care at all for her tone.

"What do I need *her* for?" I asked.

"To talk to you of the harbor, of course—that's her especial line these days."

"The harbor?" I demanded. "That girl?"

"Yes—the harbor, that girl." Sue seemed to be having quite a good time. My jaw set tight.

"What does she do down there?" I asked.

"She worships her father. Don't you remember? An engineer. He's doing a big piece of work on the harbor and Eleanore is wrapped up in his work, she's a beautiful case of how a fond parent can literally swallow up his child. There used to be nothing whatever that Eleanore Dillon wasn't going to do in life. Don't you remember, when she was small, that little determined air she had in the way she went at every game? Well, she grew even more like that. From school she went to college and worked herself to a frazzle. Then she broke down and had to drop out, and now that she's strong again she's changed. She used to go in for everything. Now she goes in for nothing at all except her father and his work. She thinks we're all a lot of young fools."

"Oh, now, Sue," I put in derisively. "You people fools? How could she?"

"You'll see," my sister sweetly replied, "for she'll probably think you're another. She detests morbid people, they're not her kind. But if she'll give you a talking to it may do you a lot of good."

She did give me a talking to and it did do me a lot of good, although when I came to think of it I found she had barely talked at all.

She wasn't the sort who liked to talk, she was just as quiet as before. When she arrived rather late one evening and Sue brought her out on the verandah into a group of those radical friends who were a committee for something or other, after the general greetings were over she settled back in a corner with the air of one who likes just to listen to people, no matter whether they're fools or not. But as I watched her I decided she did not consider these people fools. That quiet smile that came on her face showed a comfortable curiosity and now and then a gleam of amusement, but no contempt whatever. She seemed a girl so well pleased with her life that she could be pleased with the world besides and keep her eyes open for all there was in it. Although she was still rather small and still demurely feminine, with the same grave sweetness in her eyes, that same enchanting freshness about everything she wore, she struck me at once as having changed, as having grown tremendously, as having somehow filled herself deep with a quiet abundant vitality. "Where have *you* been," I wondered.

There came a loud blast from the harbor. At once I saw her turn in her chair and look down to the point below where a river boat was just leaving her slip, sweeping silently out of the darkness into the moonlit water. My curiosity deepened. Where *had* she been, and what was she doing, what queer kind of a girl was this? I took a seat beside her.

"Don't you remember me?" I asked. She turned her head with a quiet smile.

"Of course I do," she answered. Her low voice had a frankly intimate tone. "I did the moment I saw you. Besides, Sue told me about you."

"She's been telling me quite a lot about *you*."

"Has she? What?"

"That you know all about the harbor these days."

"Sue's wonderful," Eleanore murmured. "She's so sure her friends know everything."

"Let's stick to the harbor."

"All right, let's. I know enough about it to like it. Sue says you know enough to hate it. I wonder which of us knows more."

"I do."

"How do you know you do?"

"Because I've been here longer," I said. "I've hated it for twenty odd years."

She looked at me with interest. Her eyes were not at all like Sue's. Sue's eyes were always wrapped up in herself; Eleanore's in somebody else. They were as intimate as her voice.

"Don't you remember the evening when you took me down to the docks?" she asked.

"I do—very well," I said.

"And do you mean to tell me you didn't like the harbor then?"

"I do—I hated the harbor then. I was scared to death that Sam and his gang would appear around the end of a car."

"Who was Sam?" she asked me. "He sounds like a very dreadful small boy."

Soon she had me telling her of Sam and his gang and the harbor of thrills, from the time of old Belle and the Condor.

"I was a toy piano," I said. "And the harbor was a giant who played on me till I rattled inside. We had a big spree together."

"Not a very healthy spree, was it?" she said quietly, turning her gray-blue eyes on mine. For some reason we suddenly smiled at each other. "You're a good deal like your father—aren't you?" she said. "The same nice twinkle in your eyes. Please go on. What did the harbor do to you next?"

I thought all at once of the August day when she had lain, a girl of twelve, in the fragrant meadow beside me. And as then, so now, the drunken woman's image rose for an instant in my mind.

"It wiped the thrills all out," I said abruptly. I told how the place grew harsh and bare, how I could always feel it there stripping everything naked like itself, and how finally when later in Paris I felt I had shaken it off for life, it had now suddenly jerked me back, let me see what my father had really been, and had then repeated its same old trick, closing in on his great idea and making it look like an old man's hobby, crowding him out and handing us grimly two dull little jobs—one to live on and one to die on.

"It's getting monotonous," I ended.

While I talked she had been watching it, now a bustling ferry crossing, now a tug with a string of barges working up against the tide.

"How do you know it's so bad for you to be brought back from Paris?" she asked me, without looking around.

"Have you ever been in Paris?"

"Yes—and I want to go again. But I don't believe it will ever feel as real to me as this place does. And I shouldn't think it would to you. Because you were born here, weren't you—and you've been so close to it most of the time that you're all mixed into it, aren't you? I mean you've got your roots here. Why don't you write about *them* for a while?"

"What?"

"Your roots."

She turned and again her eyes met mine, and again for some reason or other we smiled.

"All right," I assented gravely, "I'll buy a hoe and start right in."

"That's it, hoe yourself all up. Get as far down as you can remember. Dig up Belle and Sam, and Sue and your mother and father. Then take a hoe to Paris and find out why you loved it so, and why you hate the harbor. Be sure you get all the hate there is, it makes such interesting reading. Besides, it may be just what you need—it may take the hate all out of your system."

"Who'll print it?" I demanded.

"Oh, some magazine," she said.

"Do you think this kind of thing would interest their readers?"

"It would interest *me*——"

"Thank you. I'll tell the editors that."

"You'll do no such thing," she said severely. "You'll tell the magazine editors, please, that I'm only one of thousands of girls who are getting sick and tired of the happy, cheery little tales they print for our special benefit. It's just about time they got over the habit of thinking of us as sweet, young things and gave us some roots we can grow on."

Another modern girl, I thought.

"Do you, too, want to vote?" I asked her, with a fine, indulgent irony.

"Some day I do," she answered. And then she added with placid scorn, "When I've learned all the political wisdom that *you* have to teach me." And as if that were a good place to stop, she rose from her seat.

"The others seem to have left us," she said. "I think I'd better be going home."

"Wait a minute, please," I cried. "When am I going to hear about you—and your side of this dismal body of water?"

She looked back at me serenely.

"Wait till you've got yours all written down," she replied. "You see mine might only mix you up. Mine is so much pleasanter. Good night," she added softly.

CHAPTER VI

Until late that night, and again the next day at my desk down in the warehouse, my thoughts kept drifting back to our talk. With a glow of surprise I found I remembered not only every word she had said, but the tones of her voice as she said it, the changing expressions on her face and in her smiling gray-blue eyes. Her picture rose so vividly at times it was uncanny.

"What do you think of her?" asked Sue.

"Mighty little," I replied. I did not care to discuss her with Sue, for I had not liked Sue's tone at all.

But how little I'd learned about Eleanor's life. Where did she live? I didn't know. When I had hinted at coming to see her she had smilingly put me off. What was this pleasant harbor of hers? "Wait till you've got yours all written down," she had said, and had told me nothing whatever. Yes, I thought disgustedly, I was quite a smart young man. Here I had spent two years in Paris learning how to draw people out. What had she let me draw out of her? What hadn't I let her draw out of me? I wondered how much I had told that girl.

For some reason, in the next few days, my thoughts drifted about with astonishing ease and made prodigious journeys. I roved far back to my childhood, and there the most tempting incidents rose, and solemn little thoughts and terrors, hopes and plans, some I was proud of, some mighty ashamed of. Roots, roots, up they came, as though they'd just been waiting, down there deep inside of me, for that girl and her hoeing.

Presently, just to get rid of them all, I began writing some of them down. And again I was surprised to find that I was in fine writing trim. The words seemed to come of themselves from my pen and line themselves up triumphantly into scenes of amazing vividness. At least so they looked to me. How good it felt to be at it again. Often up in my room at night I kept on working till nearly dawn. I was getting on famously now.

And so now, as was his habit, Joe Kramer came crashing into my life and as usual put a stop to my work.

Having just landed from Russia, he had "breezed over" to our house, had had a talk with Sue downstairs and had then come up to my room to surprise me—just as I had a good firm grip on one of my most entrancing roots.

"Hello, Bill," he cried. "What are you up to?"

"Hello, J. K. How are you?"

I knew that I ought to be genial, and for a few moments I did my best. I went through all the motions. I grabbed his hand, I smiled, I talked, I told him. I was tickled to death, I even tried pounding him on the back. But it was quite useless.

"Kid," he said with that grin of his, "you're up to something idealistic and don't want to be disturbed. But I'm here and it can't be helped. So out with it—what have you gone and done?"

And he jerked my story out of me.

"All right," he declared, "this has got to stop!"

"I knew it," I said. I had known it the minute he came in the room.

"You've got to throw up your ten-dollar job, quit working all night on stuff that won't sell, and come on a paper and make some real money."

"I can't do it," I snapped.

"You can," said J. K.

"But I tell you I tried! I went to a paper——"

"You'll go to a dozen before I get through!"

"J. K.—I won't do it!"

"Kid—you will!"

And he kept at me night after night. He was working for a New York paper now as a special correspondent. He had a talk with his editor and got me a chance to go on as a "cub" and write about weddings, describing the costume of the bride. At least it was a starter, he said, and would lead to divorces later on, and from there I might be promoted to graft. He talked to Sue and my father about it, persuading them both to take his side. Day by day the pressure increased. I set my young jaw doggedly and kept on writing about my roots.

"Look here," said Joe one evening. "Your sister tells me you're sore on the harbor. Then have a look at this." And he showed me a newspaper clipping headed, "Padrone System Under the Dumps."

"Well, what about it?" I asked him.

"What about it? My God! Here's a chance to show up the harbor on one of its ugliest, rottenest ideas! A dump is a pier that sticks out in the river. We'll go there at night, get down underneath it and look at the kids—Dago child-slaves working like hell. You say that weddings are not in your line—all right, here's just the opposite—stuff that'll make your women readers sit right up and sob out aloud! I don't care for tear-jerkers myself," he added. "But even tear-jerkers are better than Art."

"All right," I muttered savagely, "let's go and get a tear-jerker to write!"

If I must write of this modern harbor, at least it was some satisfaction to write about one of its ugliest sides.

We went the next night.

Joe had chosen a dump which jutted out from the Manhattan side of the river just about opposite our house. A huge, long, shadowy pile of city refuse of all kinds, we caught the sour breath of it as we drew near in the darkness. There was not a sound nor a light. We climbed down onto a greenish beam that ran along by the side underneath, about a foot from the water, and cautiously working our way outward for a hundred yards or more, we stopped abruptly and drew back.

For just before us under the dump was a cave with walls of papers and rags. A lantern hung from overhead, swung gently in the raw salt breeze, and by its light we could see a half dozen swarthy small boys. Five were intent on a game of dice, whispering fiercely while they played. Their boss lay asleep in a corner. The sixth, the smallest of them all, sat smoking in the mouth of the cave, his knees drawn up and his big dilated black eyes roving hungrily out over the water. All at once around the end of the pier, a dark, tall shadow like a spook swept silently out before him. He sprang back and fervently crossed himself, then grinned and drew on his cigarette hard. For the shadow was only a scow with a derrick. The imp continued his watching.

"Now," said J. K. a few minutes later back on shore, "you want to get their hours and wages. You want to look up the fire law about lighted cigarettes and a lantern——"

"Oh, damn your fire law," I growled. "I want to know where that kid with the cigarette was born, and what he thinks of the harbor!" Joe gave me one of his cheerful grins.

"You might get his views on the tariff," he said.

"Look here, J. K.," I implored him; "go home. Go on home and leave me alone. It's all right, I'm glad you brought me here—darned good of you, and I'll get a story. Only for God's sake leave me alone!"

"Sure," said Joe. "Only don't try to talk to those little Guineys. Their boss wouldn't let 'em say a word and you'd lose your chance of watching 'em. Make it a kind of a mystery story."

And a mystery story I made it.

Where had he been a year ago, this imp who had fervently crossed himself? In Naples, Rome or Venice, or poking his toes into the dust of a street in some dull little town in the hills? What great condor of to-day had picked him up and dropped him here? How did it look to him? What did he feel?

I came back to the dump night after night, and writing blindly in the dark I tried to jot down what he saw—gigantic shapes and shadows, some motionless, some rushing by with their dim spectral little lights, and over all the great arch of the Bridge rearing over half the sky. The lantern in the cave behind threw a patch of light on the water below, and across that patch from under the pier where the water was slapping, slapping, there came an endless bobbing procession—a whisky bottle, a broken toy horse, a bit of a letter, a pink satin slipper, a dirty white glove—things tossed out of people's lives. On and on they came. And I knew there were miles of black water like this all covered with tiny processions like this moving slowly out with the ebb tide, out from the turbulent city toward the silent ocean. One night the watchman on the dump showed me a heavy paper bag with what would have been a baby inside. Where had it come from? He didn't know. Tossed out of some woman's life, in a day it would be far out on the ocean, bobbing, bobbing with the rest. Water from here to Naples, water from here to heathen lands. Just here a patch of light from a lantern. That imp from Italy looking down—into something immense and dark and unknown.

He was having a spree with the harbor, as I had had when as small as he. I saw him watch the older boys and listen thrilled to their wonderful talk—as once I, too, had been thrilled by Sam. I watched him over a game of dice, quarreling, scowling, grabbing at pennies, slapped by some one, whimpering, then eagerly getting back to the game. It was "craps," I had played it with Sam and the gang. One night he dropped a cigarette still lighted into the rags and was given a blow by his boss that knocked him into a corner. But presently he crawled cautiously forth, and again with both hands hugging his knees he sat and watched the harbor. What a big spree for a little boy.

I put my own childhood into this imp, into him my first feelings toward this place. And so I came again to my roots. How the memories rose up now—the fascinations and terrors that I, too, had felt before something immense and dark and unknown.

Thank heaven J. K. had given me up and gone to Colorado—so I was left to work in peace. I called my sketch "A Patch of Light," and sent it to a magazine. It came back with a note explaining that, while this was a fine little thing in its way, its way wasn't theirs, it was neither an article full of facts nor a story full of romance. In short, I told myself savagely, it was neither hay nor tears! Again it went forth and again back it came. Then Sue gave it to one of her writer friends who said he knew just the place for it.

"No, you don't," I thought drearily. "Nobody knows—in this whole damnable desolate land."

But Sue's friend sold my story—for twenty-two dollars and fifty cents! And he said that the editor wanted some more!

It was curious, from my window that night, what a different harbor I saw below. Ugly still? Of course it was. But what a *rich mine* of ugliness for the pen of a rising young author like me!

CHAPTER VII

Now for something bigger. I would have a whack at the place by day. No mystery now, just ugliness. I would show it up in broad daylight, bringing out every detail in the glare. I would do this by comparing it to the harbor of long ago, and the snowy white sails of my father's youth.

His youth was gone. A thick-set and gray-headed old figure, he bent over his desk by my side, putting up a fierce, silent fight for his strength, and now slowly getting enough of it back to keep him at his job as a clerk in what had been his warehouse. Only once, coming suddenly into the room, I found him settled deep down in his chair, heavy, inert, his cigar gone out, staring vacantly out of the window.

The sails were gone. Down there at his dock, where even in days that I could remember the tall clippers had lain for weeks, I saw now a German whaleback. She had slipped in but three days before and was already snorting to get away. She was black and she wallowed deep, and she had an enormous bulging belly into which I descended one day and explored its metallic compartments that echoed to the deafening din of some riveters at work on her sides. Though short and stout, she was nine thousand tons. Hideous, she was practical, as practical as a factory. In her the romance of the sea was buried and choked in smoke and steam, in grime, dirt, noise and a regular haste. One morning as her din increased and the black, sooty breath of her came drifting in through our window, my father rose abruptly and slammed the window down.

"The damn sea hog!" he muttered.

Gone, too, were the American sailors. All races of men on the earth but ours seemed gathered around this hog of the sea. From barges filled with her cargo, the stuff was being heaved up on the dock by a lot of Irish bargemen. Italian dockers rolled it across to this German ship, and on deck a Jap under-officer was bossing a Coolie crew. These Coolies were dwarfs with big white teeth and stooping, round little shoulders. They had strange, nervous faces, long and narrow with high cheek bones and no foreheads at all to speak of. Their black eyes gleamed. Back and forth they scurried to the sound of that guttural Japanese voice.

"The cheapest sea labor there is," growled Dad. "Good-by to Yankee sailors."

The Old East with its riches was no longer here. For what were these Coolies doing? Handling silks and spices? Oh, no. They were hoisting and letting down into the hold an automobile from Dayton, Ohio, bound for New South Wales. Gone were the figs and almonds, the indigo, ivory, tortoise shells. Into the brand-new ledgers over which my father worked, he was entering such items as barbed wire, boilers, car wheels and gas engines, baby carriages, kegs of paint. I reveled in the commonplace stuff, contrasting it vividly in my mind with the starlit ocean roads it would travel, the picturesque places it would help spoil.

I filled in the scene with all its details, the more accurate, glaring and real the better—the brand-new towering skyline risen of late on Manhattan, the new steel bridge, an ugly one this, and all the modern steam craft, tugs, river boats, Sound steamers, each one of them panting and spewing up smoke. I sat there like a stenographer and took down the harbor's dictation, noting the rasping tones of its voice, recording eagerly all its smells. And all this and more that I gathered, I focussed on the sea hog.

And then toward the end of a winter's day we looked out of our window and saw her "sail." She sailed in a nervous, worrying haste to the grunts and shrieks of a lot of steam winches. Up rattled her anchor, out she waddled, tugs puffing their smoke and steam in her face. She didn't depart. Who ever heard of a hog departing? She just went. There were no songs, no last good-byes—except from a man in his shirt sleeves who called from the deck to a man on the pier, "So long, Mac, see you next Spring," and then went into the factory.

When the work of the day was over, I went down into the dock shed. My father's old place was at peace for a time, the desecration done with. She was empty, dark and silent. In her long, inward-sloping walls the eight wide sliding doors were closed. Only through the dusty skylights here and there fell great masses of soft light. Big bunches of canvas hung from above, ropes dangled out of the shadows. And there were huge rhythmic creakings that made you feel the ocean still here, an old ocean under an old, old dock. The place grew creepy with its past.

"Faint, spicy odors," I jotted down, as I stood there in the dimness, "ghosts of long ago—low echoes of old chanties sung by Yankee sailors—romance—mystery——"

I broke off writing and drew back behind a crate. My father had entered the dock shed and was coming slowly up the dock. Presently I saw him stop and look into the shadows around him. I saw a frown come on his face, I saw his features tighten. So he stood for some moments. Then he turned and walked quickly out. A lump had risen in my throat, for I thought I knew what he had seen.

"The Phantom Ship" became my title. A fine contrast to the sea hog, I thought. I asked Dad endless questions at night about the old days not only here, but all up along the coast of New England, and hungrily I listened while he glorified the rich life and color of those seaport towns now gray, those wharves now rotting and covered with moss. He glorified the spacious homes of the men who had ordered their captains to search the Far East for the rugs and the curtains, the chairs and the tables, the dishes, the vases, the silks and the laces, the silver and gold and precious stones with which those audacious old houses were stored. He glorified the ships themselves. From the quarter decks of our clippers, those marvels of cleanliness and speed, he told how those miraculous captains had issued their orders to Yankee sailors, brawny, deep-chested, keen-eyed and strong-limbed. He told what perils they had faced far out on the Atlantic—"the Roaring Forties" those waters were called!

"Yes, boy, in those days ships had men!"

In my room I eagerly wrote it all down and added what I myself could remember. Here from my bedroom window I tried to see what I had seen as a boy, the immaculate white of the tall sails, the fresh blue and green of the dancing waves. Oh, I was romancing finely those nights! And there came no Blessed Damozel to say to me gruffly, "Couches-toi. Il est tard."

When the sketch was completed at last I gave it to my father to read and then went out for a long walk. It was nearly midnight when I returned, but he was still reading. He cleared his throat.

"Son," he said very huskily, "this is a strong piece of work!" His eyes were moist as they moved rapidly down the page. He looked up with a jerk. "Who'll print it?" he asked.

"I wish I knew, Dad——"

I mailed it that night to a magazine. In the next two weeks my father's suspense was even deeper than my own, though he tried hard to joke about it, calling me "Pendennis." One day in his office chair he wheeled with a nervous sharpness, and I could feel his eyes fixed on the envelope which the postman had just thrown on my desk. God help me, it was heavy and long, it had my manuscript inside. Dismally I searched for a letter. Still I could feel those anxious eyes.

"Hold on!" I cried. "They've taken it! All they want me to do is to cut it down!"

"Then do it!" My radiant father snarled. "It ought to be cut to half its length! That's the way with beginners, a mass of details! Some day maybe you'll learn to write!"

I smiled happily back. He came suddenly over and gripped my hand.

"My boy, I'm glad, I'm very glad! I'm"—he cleared his throat and went back to his desk and tried to scowl over what he was doing.

"Dad."

"Huh?"

"They say they'll give me a hundred dollars. Pretty good for one month's work."

"Huh."

"And they want me to do some more on the harbor. They say it's a new field. Never been touched."

"Then touch it," he said gruffly. "Leave me alone. I'm busy."

But coming in late after luncheon that day, I found him reading the editor's letter.

"Boy," he said that evening, "you ought to read Thackeray for style, and Washington Irving, and see what a whippersnapper you are. Work—work! If your mother were only alive she could help you!"

And just before bedtime, taking a bottle of beer with my pipe, I caught his disapproving eye.

"Worst thing you can put in your stomach," he growled. He said this regularly each night, and added, "Why can't you keep up your health for your work?"

His own health had improved astonishingly.

"It's the winter air that has done it," he said.

CHAPTER VIII

My work, as my father saw it now, was to write "strong, practical articles" presenting the respective merits of free ships, ship subsidies and discriminating tariffs to build up our mercantile marine.

But I was growing tired these days of my father's idea, his miracle and his endless talk of the past. On walks along the waterfront he would treat it all like a graveyard. But while he pointed out the tombs I felt the swift approach of Spring. It was March, and in a crude way of its own the harbor was expressing the season—in warm, salty breezes, the odor of fish and the smell of tar on the bottoms of boats being overhauled for the Summer. Our Italian dockers sang at their work, and one day the dock was a bright-hued mass of strawberries and early Spring flowers landed by a boat from the South. Everywhere things seemed starting—starting like myself.

I had given up my warehouse job, and free at last from that tedious desk to which I once thought I was tied for years, with two sketches sold and ideas for others, so many others, rising daily in my mind, I went about watching the life of the port. Poor Dad. He was old. Could I help being young?

Without exactly meaning to, I drew away from my father to Sue. We felt ourselves vividly young in that house. We quarreled intensely over her friends and were pleased with ourselves in the process. We had long talks about ourselves. Sue let me talk to her by the hour about my work and my ideas, while she sat and thought about her own.

"If you're planning to write up the harbor," she said sleepily late one night, "you ought to cruise around a bit in Eleanore Dillon's motor boat."

I looked at her in astonishment.

"Does that girl run a motor boat?"

"Her father's." Sue yawned and gave me a curious smile. "I'll see if I can't arrange it," she said. And about a week later she told me, "Eleanore's coming to take us out to-night."

Some of Sue's friends came to supper that evening and later we all went down to the dock. There was no moon but the stars were out and the night was still, the slip was dark and empty. Suddenly with a rush and a swirl a motor boat rounded the end of the pier, turned sharply in and came shooting toward us. A boiling of water, she seemed to rear back, then drifted unconcernedly in to the bottom of the ladder.

In the small circle of light down there I saw Eleanore Dillon smiling up. She sat at her wheel, a trim figure in white—a white Jersey, something red at her throat and a soft white hat crushed a bit to one side. Beneath it the breeze played tricks with her hair.

We scrambled down into the cock-pit. It was a deep, cozy little place, with the wide open doors of a cabin in front, in which I caught a glimpse of two bunks, a table, a tiny electric cooking stove and a shaded reading light over the one small easy chair. There were impudent curtains of blue at the port holes. There was a shelf of books and another of blue and white cups and saucers and dishes. And what was that? A monkey crouching under the table, paws clutching the two enormous brass buttons on the gay blue jacket he wore, eyes watching us angrily as he chattered.

"Buttons," commanded his mistress, "come out here this minute and stop your noise. There's nothing for you to be peevish about, the water's like glass. When it's rough," she explained, "he gets fearfully seasick. Come here now, pass the cigarettes." And this her Buttons proceeded to do—very grumpily.

Then as a small, quiet hand pulled a lever, I felt a leap of power beneath me, the boat careened as she turned, then righted, there was a second pull on the lever, another surging leap of speed, and as we rushed out on the river now up rose her bow higher and higher, a huge white wave on either side. The spray dashed in our faces. Everyone began talking excitedly. Only the Buttons kept his monkey eyes fixed anxiously on his captain's face while he clasped the pit of his stomach.

"Oh, Buttons, don't be such a coward," she said. "I tell you it's smooth and you won't be sick! Go out there and stop being silly!"

Slowly and with elaborate caution the monkey crept forward over the cabin. For a moment up at the bow he paused, a ridiculous little dark-jacketed figure between the two white crests of our waves. Then with a spring he was up to his place on the top of the light, and there with gay gesticulations he greeted every vessel we passed.

I had taken a seat by Eleanore's side. She was driving her boat with eyes straight ahead. Now and then she would close them, draw in a deep breath of the rough salt air, and smile contentedly to herself. After a time I heard her voice, low and intimate as before:

"Finished up that hideous harbor of yours?"

"No," I answered hungrily, "I think I've just begun." I caught a gleam in her eyes.

"You'll be out of your rut in a moment," she said.

"What do you mean, my rut?" I demanded.

"The East River, Stupid—wait and see."

From the little East River corner I'd lived in, we sped far out on the Upper Bay, a rushing black speck on a dim expanse, with dark, empty fields of water around us, long, luminous paths stretching off to the shores, where the lights twinkled low for miles and miles and there were sudden bursts of flame from distant blast furnace fires.

"Tell me what you've been writing about this hideous place," she said.

"Who said it was hideous at night? Of course if you wrap it all up in the dark, so that you can see none of its sea hogs——"

"What's a sea hog?"

"A sea hog is a wallowing boat with a long, black, heavy snout." And mustering all that was left of my hatred I plunged into my picture. "The whole place is like that," I ended. "Full of smoke and dirt and disorder, everything rushing and jamming together. That's how it looks to me in the daytime!"

"Are you sure it does—still?"

"I am," I answered firmly. "And I'm going to write it just as it looks."

"Then look back of you," she suggested.

Behind us, at the tip of Manhattan, the tall buildings had all melted together into one tremendous mass, with only a pin point of light here and there, a place of shadowy turrets and walls, like some mediæval fortress. Out of it, in contrast to its dimness, rose a garish tower of lights that seemed to be keeping a vigilant watch over all the dark waters, the ships and the docks. The harbor of big companies.

"My father works up in that tower," she said. "He can see the whole harbor spread out below. But he keeps coming down to see it all close, and I've steered him up close to everything in it. You've no idea how much there is." She threw me a glance of pitying scorn. "There are over seven hundred miles of waterfront in this small port, and I'm not going to have you trudging around and getting lost and tired and cross and working off your grudge in your writing. You come with me some afternoon and I'll do what I can to open your eyes."

"Please do it," I said quickly.

She took me down to the sea gate at the end of a warm, still, foggy day. There in the deepening twilight we drifted without a sign of a world around us—till in from the ocean there came a deep billow, then another and another, and as our small craft darted off to one side a gigantic gray shadow loomed through the fog with four black towers of smoke overhead, lights gleaming from a thousand eyes.

"Another sea hog," murmured a voice.

"I said in the daytime," I replied.

We went out on another afternoon to watch the fisherman fleets at their work or scudding before a strong wind home with a great, round, radiant sun behind. She showed me fishers in the air, lonely fish hawks one by one flying in the late afternoon back to their nests on the Atlantic Highlands. And far out on the Lower Bay she knew where to stir up whole armies of gulls, till there seemed to be thousands wheeling in air with the bright sunshine on all the wings. The sunshine, too, with the help of the breeze, stole glinting deep into her hair. She watched me out of half-closed eyes.

"Is this daylight enough?" she demanded.

"This is simply absurd," I answered. "You know very well that this harbor is ugly in places——"

"Only in places. That's better," she said.

"In a great *many* places," I rejoined. "Please take me to Bayonne some day—at two p. m.," I added.

It seemed a good, safe, unmysterious hour, and as we neared the place next day my hopes mounted high, for there was a leaden sky overhead and loathsome blotches and streaks of oil on the gray water around us—while ahead on the Jersey shore, from two chimneys that rose halfway to the clouds, poured two foul, sluggish columns of smoke.

"Still New York harbor, I believe?" I inquired maliciously. But Eleanore was smiling. "What's the joke?" I demanded.

"The southwest wind," she softly replied. I could feel it coming as she spoke. As I watched I saw it take that sky and tear jagged rifts in it for the sun, and then as those two columns of smoke began twisting and writhing like monster snakes they took on purple and greenish hues and threw ghostly reflections of themselves down on the oily water around us, filled with blue and gold shimmerings now.

"What a strange, wonderful purple," murmured a quiet voice by my side.

Stubbornly I resisted conversion. I wanted more afternoons in that boat.

"Now it's blowing that oily odor our way," I declared in sudden annoyance. "I no sooner get to enjoying myself when along comes one of the smells of this place. And where's the beauty in *them?* Can you show me? Here's a place that should be a great storehouse of pure fresh air for the city to breathe, and—"

"Oh, hush up!" said Eleanore.

But I doggedly found other blemishes here—swamps, railroad yards and sooty tracks that filled the waterfront for miles where there should have been parks and boulevards. At the same time I assumed the tone of one who tries to be fair and patient. Whenever she showed me some new beauty in water or sky I took great pains to look at it well. When an angry little squall of wind came ruffling over the sunny waves in sweeping bands of deep, soft blues, I gazed and gazed at its wonder as though I could never have enough. And so gazing I spied floating there a sodden old mattress, a fleet of tin cans. And I said that it seemed an unhealthy thing to dump all our refuse so close to the city.

"They don't!" she retorted indignantly. "They take it out miles beyond the Hook!"

In short, I considered myself mighty clever. Day by day I prolonged my conversion, holding obstinately back—while Eleanore revealed to me the miracles worked by the sunset here, and by the clouds, the winds, the tides, the very smoke and the ships themselves, all playing weird tricks on each other. Slowly the crude glory of it stole upon me unawares—until to my own intense surprise the harbor now became for me a breathing, heaving, gleaming thing filled deep with the rush and the vigor of life. A thing no longer sinister, crushing down on a man's old age—but strangely deeply stirring.

"Look out, my friend," I warned myself. "This is no harbor you're falling in love with."

CHAPTER IX

Although at such lucid moments I would sometimes go a-soaring up into the most dazzling dreams, more often I would plunge in gloom. For Eleanore's dreams and all her thoughts seemed centered on her father. From each corner of that watery world, no matter how far we wandered, the high tower from which he looked down on it all would suddenly loom above the horizon. Over the dreariest marshes it peeped and into all our talk he came. A marsh was a place that he was to transform, oily odors were things he would sweep away. For every abuse that I could discover her father was working out some cure. With a whole corps of engineers drafting his dreams into practicable plans, there was no end to the things he could do.

"Here is a girl," I told myself, "so selfishly wrapped up in her father she hasn't a thought for anyone else. She's using me to boom his work, as she has doubtless used writers before me and will use dozens more when I'm gone. No doubt she would like to have *dozens of me* sitting right here beside her now! It's not at all a romantic thought, but think how she could use me then!" And I would glower at her.

But it is a lonely desolate job to sit and glower at a girl who appears so placidly unaware of the fact that you are glowering. And slowly emerging from my gloom I would wonder about this love that was in her. At times when she talked she made me feel small. My own love for my mother, how utterly selfish it had been. Here was a passion so deep and real it made her almost forget I was there, asking questions, hungrily watching her, trying to learn about her life.

"While I was in school," she said, in that low deliberate voice of hers, "my father and I went abroad every summer. We tramped in the Alps for weeks at a time, keeping way off the beaten paths to watch the work of the Swiss engineers. One of them was a woman. We saw the bridge she'd built over a gorge, and I became deeply excited. Until then I had never had any idea that I could go into my father's work. But now I wondered if I could. That winter in school I really worked. I was dreadfully dull at mathematics, but I wouldn't see it. I made up my mind to go to Cornell for the course on engineering. I worked like a slave for two years to get ready and just succeeded in getting in.

"Then toward the middle of Freshman year I realized that I was becoming a quite absurdly solemn young grind. There were over a hundred girls in college but I had made barely any friends. And so I firmly resolved to be gay. I made a regular business of it and worked my way into clubs and dances, hunting for the girls I liked and scheming to make them like me too. By May I was way behind in my work. I tried to make up, I began cramming every night until one or two in the morning. And I passed my examinations—but that summer I broke down. My father had to drop his work and take me abroad for an operation, and by the time we got back he had lost nearly six months of his time. I decided that as an engineer I was a dismal failure. I'd much better give my father a chance.

"So when he took up this work in New York I spent all my time on our new apartment. I loved fussing with it, I shopped like a bee, and this kept me busy all Autumn. Besides I was going about with Sue. She had managed me long ago at school and I was glad to let her now, for I was hunting for new ideas. But Sue put me on so many committees that by Spring my nerves were in shreds, and again for weeks I was flat on my back.

"One evening then—when my father came home and sat down by my bedside—it came over me all of a sudden—the wonderful quiet strength in his hand, in the look of his eyes.

" 'Where have you been?' I asked him.

" 'Down on the harbor,' he told me. Since eight in the morning he'd been in a launch exploring it all. I shut my eyes—my wretched eyelids quivering—and I made him describe the whole day's trip while I tried to see it all in my mind. Soon I was feeling deliciously quiet. 'I'm going down there too,' I thought.

"By the next evening I had the idea for this boat. When I told him he was delighted, and we both grew excited over the plans—which he drew by my bed, I made him draw dozens. At last it was built and lay at its dock, and I packed all I needed into a trunk and we came down in a taxi. It was a lovely May afternoon and we had a beautiful ride up the Hudson. And from then on through the Summer I hardly went ashore at all, I knew if I did it would spoil it all.

"Every night we slept on board in those two cozy little bunks. I learned to cook here. Soon I was able to run the boat and even to help my father a little. I knew just enough about his work to go places for him and save his time. I'd forgotten I ever had any nerves, for I felt I belonged to something now that got way down to the roots of things. Do you see what I mean? This harbor isn't like a hotel, or an evening gown or Weber and Fields. I love pretty gowns, and my father and I wouldn't miss Weber and Fields for worlds. But they're all on top, this is down at the bottom, it's one of those deep places that seem to make the world go 'round. It's right where the ocean bumps into the land. You can get your roots here, you can feel you are real.

"You see what my father is doing is to take this whole harbor and study it hard—not just the water, the shipping and docks, for when he says 'the port of New York' he means all the railroads too—and he's studying how they all come in and why it is that everything has become so frightfully snarled. A lot of big shipping men are behind him, and he's to draw up a plan for it all which they're going to give to the city to use, to make this port what it's got to be, the very first in the ocean world. It's one of those slow tremendous pieces of work, it will take years to carry it out and hundreds of millions of dollars. My father thinks there's hardly a chance that he'll ever live to see it all done. I know he will, I'm sure he will, he's the kind of a man who keeps himself young. But whether he really sees it or not, or gets any credit, he doesn't care.

"That's the kind of a person my father is," Eleanore added softly.

"My father wants to meet you," she told me toward the end of June, at one of those times when she let the boat drift while we had long absorbing talks. "He has read that thing you wrote about the German sea hog, and he thinks it's awfully well done."

"That's good of him," I said gruffly.

Somehow or other it always makes me uncomfortable when people talk about my work. When they criticize I am annoyed and when they praise I am uneasy. What do they know about it? They spent an hour reading what it took me weeks to write. They don't know what I *tried* to do, nor do they care, they haven't time. I never feel so cut off from people, so utterly alone in the world, as when some benevolent person says, "I liked that little story of yours." Instantly I shut up like a clam.

"I liked it too," said Eleanore.

"Did you?" I asked delightedly. Far from retiring into my shell, I wanted at once to open up and make her feel how much I had missed in that crude effort. Soon she had me talking about it. And while I talked on eagerly, I tried to guess from her questions whether she'd read it more than once. Finally I guessed she had. And, glancing at her now and then, I wondered how much she could ever know about me or I about her—really know. And the intimacy I saw ahead loomed radiant and boundless. I strained every nerve to show her myself, to show her the very best of myself.

But then I heard her ask me,

"Wouldn't you like to talk to my father?"

Here was a fine end to it all.

"I don't know," I answered gloomily. I could see already those engineer eyes moving amusedly down my pages. I could see her watching his face and getting to feel as he did about me. "What good would it do?" I added.

"What good would it do?" Her sharply offended tone brought me back with a jerk to try to explain.

"Don't you see what I mean?" I asked eagerly. "Why should a man as busy as he is waste his time on a kid like me? After all that you've told me about him, I feel sometimes as though all the writers on earth don't count any more, because all the really big things are being done by men like your father."

"That's much better," said Eleanore. "Only of course it isn't true. If you poor little writers want to get big and really count," she went on serenely, "all you have to do is to write about my father."

"I'll begin the minute you say so," I told her.

"Then it's arranged," said my companion, with an exceedingly comfortable sigh. "We've taken a cottage up on the Sound for the summer," she continued. "And we're moving up to-morrow. Suppose you come up over Sunday."

"Thanks. I'd love to," I replied.

"So she's to be away for months," I added dismally to myself. "No more of these long afternoons."

CHAPTER X

On the following Saturday, when I met her boat at an East River dock, at once I felt a difference. We were waiting for her father. The moments dragged and I grew glum, try as I would to be pleasant.

"Here he is," she said at last.

Tall, rather lank and loosely clothed, Dillon was coming down the pier in easy leisurely fashion, talking to a man by his side. His face lighted up when he saw us.

"Just a minute," he said.

His voice was low but it had a peculiar carrying quality. His rugged face was deeply lined, and I noticed a little gray in his hair. He was smiling straight down into the eyes of his companion, a much younger man, thin and poorly dressed, whose face looked drawn and tired.

"When I was your age," I heard Dillon remark, "I got into just the same kind of a snarl." And he began telling about it. A frightfully technical story it was, full of engineer slang that was Greek to me, but I saw the younger man listen absorbed, his thin lips parting in a smile. I saw him come out from under his worries, I saw his chief watching him, pulling him out.

"All right, Jim," he ended. "See what you can do."

"Say, Chief, just you forget this, will you?" the other said intensely. "Don't give it a thought. It's go'n' to be done!"

"It's forgotten."

Another easy smile at his man, and then Eleanore's father turned to us. I could feel him casually take me in.

"The thing I liked most in that sketch of yours," he was saying a few minutes later, when our boat was on her course, "was the way you listed that Dutchman's cargo. 'One baby carriage—to

Lahore.' A very large picture in five little words. I can see that Hindu baby now—being wheeled in its carriage to Crocodile Park and wondering where the devil this queer new wagon came from. I've been nosing around these docks for years, but I missed that part of 'em right along—that human part—till you came along with your neat writer's trick. 'One baby carriage—to Lahore.' You ought to be proud, young man, at your age to have written one sentence so long that it goes half way around the world."

As he talked in that half bantering tone I tried to feel cross, but it wouldn't do. That low voice and those gray eyes were not making fun of me, they were making friends with me, they were so kindly, curious, so open and sincere. Soon he had lighted a cigar and was telling Eleanore gravely just how she ought to run her boat.

"Why be so busy about it?" he asked.

"Oh, you be quiet!" she replied, as she sharply spun her wheel. Like an automobile in a crowded street our craft was lurching its way in short dashes in and out of the rush hour traffic. The narrow East River was black with boats. Ferries, tugs and steamers seemed to be coming at us from every side. Now with a leap we would be off, then abruptly churning the water behind us we would hold back drifting, watching out chance for another rush. Eleanore's face was glowing now, her hat was off, her neck was tense—and her blue-gray eyes, wide open, fixed on the chaos ahead, were shining with excitement. Now and then a long curling wisp of her hair would get in her eyes and savagely she would blow it back. And her lank quiet father puffed his cigar, with his gray eyes restfully on her. "The serenity of her," he murmured to me.

"Oh, now, my dear," he said gently, as we careened to starboard, "*that* was a slip. I can't say I would have done it like that."

"Have you ever run a boat in your life?" came back the fierce rejoinder.

"No," said Dillon calmly, "I can't exactly say I have. Still"—he relapsed and enjoyed his cigar.

Just a short time after this, we had the only ugly moment that I had been through in all our rides. A huge Sound steamer was ahead. Dashing close along under her port, we came suddenly out before her and met a tug whose fool of a captain had made a rush to cross her bow. It was one of those sickening instants when you see nothing at all to do. But Eleanore saw. A quick jerk on her lever, a swift spinning of her wheel, and with a leap we were right under the steamer's bow. It missed our stern by a foot as it passed and then we were safe on the other side. She made a low sound, in a moment her face went deathly white, her eyes shut and she nearly let go the wheel. But then, her slight form tightening, slowly opening her eyes she turned toward her father.

"Now?" he asked very softly. And there passed a look between them.

"All right," she breathed, and turned back to her wheel. And for some time very little was said.

But I understood her love for him now. These two were such companions as I had never seen before. And though I myself felt quite out of it all, this did not bother me in the least. For watching her father and feeling the abounding reserve of force deep under his quiet, I told myself that here was a big man, the first really big one I'd ever come close to. And I was so eager to know him and see just what he was like inside, that I had no room for myself or his daughter—because I wanted to write him up. What a weird, curious feeling it is, this passion for writing up people you meet.

On the remainder of the ride, and at supper that night on the porch of their cottage, a little house perched on a rocky point directly overlooking the water, I did my best to draw him out, and Eleanore seemed quite ready to help me. And later, when he went inside to do some work, I went on with the same eagerness, obliterating my own small self, exploring this feeling of hers for him and his dream of a future harbor.

Soon she was doing all the talking, her voice growing lower and more intense as she tried to make me feel all he meant when he said, "It's going to be the first port in the world." She told how up in his tower he made you see the commerce of this whole mighty world of peace converging slowly on this port. She told of the night two years before when he had come home "all shaken and queer" and had said to her huskily, "Eleanore, child, at last it's sure. There's to be a Panama Canal." Of other nights when he didn't come home and at last she went down to his office to fetch him and found him at midnight there with his men, "all working like mad and gay as larks!"

"When it comes to millions of dollars for his work," she said, "he's so very keen that he makes you feel like a little child. But when it's merely a question of dollars for himself to live on, he's a perfect baby. He won't look at a bill, he always turns them over to me. He won't enter a shop, he won't go to a tailor. One ready-made clothing store has his measure and twice a year I order his clothes and then have a fight to get him to wear them. He never knows what he eats except steak. One night when we had been having steak six evenings in succession I tried chicken for a change. At first he didn't know what was wrong. Every now and then he would seem to notice something. 'What's the matter with me?' I could see he was asking. Then all at once he had it. 'My dear,' he said, very coaxingly, 'could we have a nice juicy porterhouse steak for supper to-morrow evening?'"

From these and many other details slowly I got the feel of my man. Closer, more intimate he grew. All the work I had done in Paris, questioning, drawing out my friends until I could feel their inner selves coming out of them into me, was counting now. I had never done so well before, I was sliding my questions in just right, very cautiously turning her memory this way and that on her father's life, watching her grow more and more unaware of my presence beside her, although now I had her bending toward me, eagerly, close.

"And she thinks she's doing it all by herself," I thought exultingly.

But as there came a pause in our talk, she turned slightly in her seat and glanced in through the window into the lighted room behind. And instantly her expression changed. A swift look of surprise, a puzzled frown and a moment of hard thinking—and then with a murmured excuse she rose and went away quickly into the house. In the meantime I had followed her look. Sitting close by the lamp, in the room inside, Dillon was staring straight at this spot where I was invisible in the dark. And he looked old—and rigid, as though he'd been staring like that for some time. I caught just a glimpse. Then he heard her step and turned hastily back to his work. I looked at my watch. It was after twelve.

"And he never knew it was all about him," I said to myself disgustedly. "I hope this doesn't spoil it all."

But that is precisely what it did. The next morning she was coolly polite and Dillon determinedly genial. I could feel a silent struggle between them as to what should be done with me. She wanted to get rid of me, he wanted to keep us together. Gone was all his quiet strength, in its place was an anxious friendliness. He made me tell him what I was writing. He said he was glad that his press agent daughter had taken me 'round and opened my eyes. And as soon as she got through with me he himself would do all he could.

"I'm through with him," said Eleanore cheerfully. "I've shown him all I possibly can. What you need now," she added, turning to me in her old easy manner, "is to watch the harbor all by yourself and get your own feelings about it. You might begin at the North River docks."

I spent a wretched afternoon. All my plans for my work and my life assumed the most gray and desolate hues. Eleanore was taking a nap. At last she came down and gave me some tea.

"May I come out and see you now and then?" I asked her very humbly. "It would help me so much to talk over my work."

"No," she answered kindly, "I think you'd better not."

"Why not?" I blurted. "What have I done?"

She hesitated, then looked at me squarely.

"You've made my absurd young father," she said, "think that he is no longer young."

I lost just a moment in admiration. There wasn't one girl in a hundred who would have come out with it like that. Then I seized my chance.

"Why, it's perfectly idiotic," I cried. "Here's a man so big he's a giant beside me, so full of some queer magnetic force that on the way up here in the boat he made me forget that I was there. I forgot that *you* were there," I threw in, and I caught just the sign of a gleam in her eyes. "No longer young?" I continued. "That man will be young when you and I are blinking in our dull old age! He's the biggest man I ever met! And I want to know him, I want to know how he thinks and feels, I want that more than anything else! And now you come between us!"

"Are you real?" asked Eleanore. I looked back unflinchingly.

"Just you try me," I retorted.

"No," she replied with a quiet smile.

She said good-by to me that night.

The next morning at seven o'clock I met her father down at the boat. We had a quick swim together and then climbed on board. And the next minute, with a sober old seaman called "Captain Arty" at the wheel, the boat was speeding for New York while we dressed and cooked and breakfasted.

"This was Eleanore's idea," Dillon said. "It gets me to town by nine o'clock and takes me back each day at five. So I hardly miss a night at home....Did she ever tell you," he went on, "about the first week she spent in this boat?"

"She said it was a wonderful time."

"It was a nightmare," Dillon said. I looked at him quickly:

"What do you mean?"

"Her fight for her strength. She looked like a ghost—with a stiff upper lip. She fainted twice. But she wouldn't give up. She said she knew she could do it if I'd only let her stick it out. She has quite a will, that daughter of mine," he added quietly.

"You know," he went on, "that idea of hers that you tackle the North River piers isn't bad. Why don't you put in the whole Summer there, watching the big liners? I won't ask you to come to my office now, for our work is still in that early stage where we don't want any publicity." I could feel his casual glance, and I wondered whether he noticed my sharp disappointment. "When we are ready," he resumed, "we're sure to be flooded with writers. I hope there'll be one man in the lot who'll stick to the work for a year or more, a man with a kind of a passion in him for the thing we're trying to do. There's nothing we wouldn't do for that man. I hope he's going to be you."

At once a vision opened of work with Eleanore's father, of long talks with Eleanore.

"I'll try to get ready for it," I said.

"You've made a fine start," he continued, "and I think you're going to make good. But first let's see what you'll do by yourself. Get your own view of this place as it is to-day before we talk about plans for to-morrow. And don't hurry. Take your time."

As he said this quietly, I suddenly awoke to the fact that we were tearing down the river at a perfectly gorgeous speed. The river was crowding with traffic ahead, all was a rushing chaos of life and we were rushing worst of all. And yet we did not seem to hurry. Old Captain Arty sat at the wheel with the most resigned patient look in his eyes. And drawing lazily on his cigar Dillon was watching a new line of wharves.

"You know I've found," he was saying, "the only way to live in this age and get any pleasure out of life is to always take more time than you need for every job you tackle. I'm taking at least seven years to this job. I might possibly do it as well in five, but I'd miss half the fun of it all, I'd be glaring at separate parts of it, each one as it came along, and I'd never have time to see it full size and let it carry me 'round the world—to that baby carriage, for instance, over in Lahore."

We were rounding the Battery now. And in that sparkling morning light, with billowy waves of sea green all around us, sudden snowy clouds of spray, we watched for a moment the skyscraper group, the homes of the Big Companies. The sunshine was reflected from thousands of dazzling window eyes, little streamers of steam were flung out gaily overhead, streets suddenly opened to our view, narrow cuts revealing the depths below. And there came to our ears a deep humming.

"That's the brains of it all," said Dillon. "In all you'll see while exploring the wharves you'll find some string that leads back here. And you don't want to let that worry you. Let the muckrakers worry and plan all they please for a sea-gate and a nation that's to run with its brains removed. You want to remember it can't be done. You want to look harder and harder—until you find out for yourself that there are men up there on Wall Street without whose brains no big thing can be done in this country. I'm working under their orders and some day I hope you'll be doing the same. For they don't need *less* publicity but *more*."

He left me at the Battery, and as I stood looking after him I found myself feeling somewhat dazed. A question flashed into my mind. What would Joe Kramer say to this? I remembered what he had said to me once: "Tell Wall Street to get off the roof." Well, that was *his* view. Here was another. And this man was certainly just as sincere and decidedly more wise and sane, altogether a larger size.

Besides, I was in love with his daughter.

CHAPTER XI

On the Manhattan side of the North River, from Twenty-third Street down for a mile there stretches a deafening region of cobblestones and asphalt over which trucks by thousands go clattering each day. There are long lines of freight cars here and snorting locomotives. Along the shore side are many saloons, a few cheap decent little hotels and some that are far from decent. And along the water side is a solid line of docksheds. Their front is one unbroken wall of sheet iron and concrete.

I came up against this wall. Over the top I could see here and there the great round funnels of the ships, but at every passenger doorway and at every wide freight entrance I found a sign, "No Visitors Admitted," and under the sign a watchman who would ungraciously take a cigar and then go right on being a watchman. There seemed no way to get inside. The old-fashioned mystery of the sea was replaced by the inscrutability of what some muckrakers called "The Pool."

"Don't hurry," Eleanore's father had said. All very well, but I needed money. While I had been making with Eleanore those long and delightful explorations of the harbor and ourselves, at home my father's bank account had been steadily dwindling, and all that I had been able to make had gone into expenses.

"I don't know what to do," said Sue, alone with me that evening. "The butcher says he won't wait any longer. He has simply got to be paid this week."

"I'll see what I can do," I said.

I came back to my new hunting ground and all night long I prowled about. I sipped large schooners of beer at bars, listening to the burly dockers crowded close around me. I watched the waterfront, empty and still, with acres of spectral wagons and trucks and here and there a lantern. I had a long talk with a broken old bum who lay on his back in an empty truck looking up at the stars and spun me yarns of his life as a cook on ships all up and down the world. Now and again in the small wee hours I met hurrying groups of men, women and children poorly clad, and following them to one of the piers I heard the sleepy watchman growl, "Steerage passengers over there." I saw the dawn break slowly and everything around me grow bluish and unreal. I watched the teamsters come tramping along leading horses, and harness them to the trucks. I heard the first clatter of the day. I saw the figures of dockers appear, more and more, I saw some of them drift to the docks. Soon there were crowds of thousands, and as stevedores there began bawling out names, gang after gang of men stepped forward, until at last the chosen throngs went marching in past the timekeepers. Hungrily I peered after them up the long cavernous docksheds. "No Visitors Admitted."

Then I went into a lunchroom for ham and eggs and a huge cup of coffee. I ate an enormous breakfast. On the floor beside me a cross and weary looking old woman was scrubbing the dirty oil cloth there. But I myself felt no weariness. While all was still vivid and fresh in my mind, sitting there I wrote down what I had seen. A magazine editor said it would do. And so we paid the butcher.

The same editor gave me a sweeping letter of introduction to all ocean liners. This I showed to a dock watchman, who directed me upstairs. In the office above I showed it to a clerk, who directed me to the dock superintendent, who read it and told me to go downtown. I recalled what Dillon had said about strings. Here was string number one, I reflected, and I followed it down Manhattan into the tall buildings, only to be asked down there just what it was I wanted to know.

"I don't want to know anything," I replied. "I just want permission to watch the work."

"We can't allow that," was the answer of this harbor of big companies.

At every pier that I approached I received about the same reply. At home Sue spoke of other bills. And now that I was in trouble, hard pressed for money and groping my way about alone, I found myself missing Eleanore to a most desperate degree. Her face, her smiling blue-gray eyes, kept rising in my mind, sometimes with memories and hopes that permeated my whole view both of the harbor and my work with a warm glad expectant glow, but more often with no feeling at all but one of sickening emptiness. She was not here. The only way to get back to her was to make good with her father. And so I would not ask his aid or even go to him for advice. Testing me, was he? All right, I would show him.

And I returned to my editor, whom my intensity rather amused.

"The joke of it is," he said, "that they think down there you're a muckraker."

"I'll be one soon if this keeps on."

"But it won't," he replied. "As soon as you've once broken in, and they see it's a glory story you want, you can't imagine how nice they'll be."

"I haven't broken in," I said.

"You will to-morrow," he told me, "because Abner Bell will be with you. He's our star photographer. Wait till you see little Ab go to work. The place he can't get into hasn't been invented. Besides," the editor added, "Abner is just the sort of chap to take hold of an author from Paris and turn him into a writer."

And this Abner Bell proceeded to do. He was a cheerful, rotund little man with round simple eyes and a smile that went all over his face.

"You see," he said, when I met him the next day down at the docks, "you can't ask a harbor to hold up her chin and look into your camera while you count. She's such a big fat noisy slob she wouldn't even hear you. You've got to run right at her and bark."

"Look here, old man," he was asking a watchman a few moments later. "What's the name of the superintendent on the next pier down the line?"

"Captain Townes."

"Townes, Townes? Is that Bill Townes?"

"No, it's Ed."

"I wonder what's become of Bill. All right, brother, much obliged. See you again." And he went on.

"Say," he asked the next watchman. "Is Eddy—I mean Captain—Townes upstairs?"

"Sure he is. Go right up."

"Thank you." Up we went to the office. "Captain Townes? Good-morning."

"Well, sir, what can I do for you?" The captain was an Englishman with a voice as heavy and deep as his eyes.

"Why, Captain, I'm sent here by the firm that's putting Peevey's Paris Perfume on the market out in the Middle West. They're going in heavy on ads this Fall and I've got an order to hang around here until I can get a photo of one of your biggest liners. The idea is to run it as an ad, with a caption under it something like this: '*The Kaiser Wilhelm* reaching New York with twenty thousand bottles of Peevey's Best, direct from Paris.'"

"*The Kaiser Wilhelm*," said the captain ponderously, "is a German boat. She docks in Hoboken, my friend."

"Of course she does," said Abner. "And I can lug this heavy camera way over there if you say so, and hand ten thousand dollars worth of free ads to a German line, stick up pictures of their boat in little drugstore windows all up and down the Middle West. Do you know how to tell me to go away?"

Captain Townes smiled heavily.

"No," he said, "I guess I don't. Here's a pass that'll give you the run of the dock."

"Make it two," said Abner, "and fix it so my friend and I can stick around for quite a while."

"You're a pretty good liar," I told him as we went downstairs.

"Oh, hell," he answered modestly. "Let's go out on the porch and get cool."

We went out on the open end of the pier and sat down on a wooden beam which Abner called a bulkhead.

"If we don't begin calling things names," he remarked, "we'll never get to feeling we're here. Let's just sit and feel for a while."

"I've begun," I replied.

We sat in the shade of two wooden piles with the glare of a mid-summer sun all around us. The East River had been like a crowded creek compared to this wide expanse of water slapping and gleaming out there in the sun with smoke shadows chasing over it all. There was the rough odor of smoke in the air from craft of all kinds as they skurried about. The high black bow of a Cunarder loomed at the end of the dock next ours. Far across the river the stout German liners lay at their berths—and they did not look like sea hogs. What a change had come over the harbor since I had met that motorboat. How all the hogs had waddled away, and the very smoke and the oil on the waves had taken on deep, vivid hues—as I had seen through Eleanore's eyes. "What a strange wonderful purple," her low voice seemed to murmur at my side.

"She's going away from here," said Ab. I started:

"Who is?"

"That Cunarder. Look at the smoke pour out of her stacks. Got a cigarette about you?"

"No," I answered gruffly.

"Damn."

In the slip on our other side a large freight boat was loading, and a herd of scows and barges were pressing close around her. These clumsy craft had cabins, and in some whole families lived. "Harbor Gypsies." A good title. I had paid the butcher, but the grocer was still waiting. So I dismissed my motorboat and grimly turned to scows instead. Children by the dozen were making friends from barge to barge. Dogs were all about us and they too were busy visiting. High up on the roof of a coal lighter's cabin an impudent little skye-terrier kept barking at the sooty men who were shoveling down below. One of these from time to time would lift his black face and good-humoredly call, "Oh, you go to hell"—which would drive the small dog into frenzies. Most of the barges had derrick masts, and all these masts were moving. They rose between me and the sky, bobbing, tossing and criss-crossing, filling the place with the feeling of life, the unending, restless life of the sea.

An ear-shattering roar broke in on it all. Our Cunarder was starting. Smoke belching black from her funnels, the monster was beginning to move.

But what was this woman doing close by us? Out of the cabin of a barge she had dragged a little rocking chair, and now she had brought out a baby, all dressed up in its Sunday best, and was rocking expectantly, watching the ship. Thundering to the harbor, the Cunarder now moved slowly out. As she swept into the river the end of the pier was revealed to our eyes all black with people waving. They waved until she was out in midstream. Then, as they began to turn away, one plump motherly-looking woman happened to glance toward us.

"Why, the cute little baby," we heard her exclaim. And the next minute hundreds of people were looking. The barge mother rocked serenely.

Abner grabbed his camera and jumped nimbly down on the barge, where he took the baby's picture, with the amused crowd for a background.

"The kid's name," he remarked on his return, "is Violetta Rosy. She was born at two a. m. at Pier Forty-nine." He was silent for a moment and then went on sententiously, "Think what it'll mean to her, through all the storm and stress of life, to be able to look fondly back upon the dear old homestead. There's a punch to Violetta. Better run her in."

"I will," I said.

"And that little thing of mine," he queried modestly, "about the dear old homestead."

"I've got it," I replied.

"I hand quite a few little things to writers," Ab continued cheerfully. "If you'll just give me some idea of what it is you're looking for——"

"I'm looking for the punch," I answered promptly.

"Then we'll get on fine," he said. "The editor got me worried some. He said you'd trained in Paris."

"Oh, that was only a starter," I told him.

Presently he went into the dockshed on his unending quest of "the punch." And left to myself I got thinking. What did Paris know about us? De Maupassant's methods wouldn't do here. I noticed two painters in overalls at work on that large freighter. With long brooms that they held in both hands they were slapping a band of crude yellow paint along her scarred and rusted side. That was what I needed, the broom! All at once the harbor took hold of me hard. And exulting in its bigness, the bold raw splattering bigness of my native Yankee land, "Now for some glory stories," I said.

I went into the dockshed, and there I stayed right through until night, till my mind was limp and battered from the rush of new impressions. For in this long sea station, under the blue arc-lights, in boxes, barrels, crates and bags, tumbling, banging, crashing, came the products of this modern land. You could feel the pulse of a continent here. From the factories, the mines and mills, the prairies and the forests, the plantations and the vineyards, there flowed a mighty tide of things—endlessly, both day and night—you could shut your eyes and see the long brown lines of cars crawl eastward from all over the land, you could see the stuff converging here to be gathered into coarse rope nets and swept up to the liners. The pulse beat fast and furious. In gangs at every hatchway you saw men heaving, sweating, you heard them swearing, panting. That day they worked straight through the night. For the pulse kept beating, beating, and the ship must sail on time!

And now I too worked day and night. In the weeks that followed, Abner Bell came and went many times, but for me it was my entire life. Though small of build I was tough and hard, I had not been sick for a day in years, and now I easily stood the strain. Day by day my story grew, my glory story of world trade. Watching, questioning, listening here, making notes, writing hasty sketches to help keep us going at home—slowly I could feel this place yielding up its inner self, its punch and bigness, endless rush, its feeling of a nation young and piling up prodigious wealth. From the customhouse came fabulous tales of millionaires ransacking the world. Rare old furniture, rugs and tapestries, paintings, jewels, gorgeous gowns poured in a dazzling torrent all that summer through the docks. One day on a Mediterranean ship, in their immaculate "stalls de luxe," came two black Arab horses, glistening, quivering creatures, valued by the customhouse at twenty thousand dollars each. And into the same ship that week, as though in payment for these two, in dust and heavy smell of sweat I saw a thousand cattle driven, bellowing and lowing.

I exulted in these symptoms of our crude and lusty youth. I watched my countrymen going abroad. Not only through the Summer but straight on into the Fall they came by tens of thousands out of the West, people who had made some money and were going to blow it in, to buy things and to see things, to learn things and to eat things. One day at noon, on the end of a dock, when the ship was already far out in midstream and all the crashing music and cheers had died away, a meek old lady wiped her eyes and murmured very tearfully, "I suppose they'll be eating their luncheon soon." And then the loud voice of her daughter replied:

"Eat? Why, ma, God bless their hearts, they'll sit on that boat and eat all day!"

And I echoed her wish with a keen delight. God bless their hearts and stomachs. Oh, hungry vigorous Yankee land, so mightily young—eat on, eat on!

And the land ate on.

My work here rose to a climax a week or two before Christmas, when the newest liner of then all pulled off a new world's record for speed. With the company's publicity man, who had become a friend of mine, I went on the health officer's tug down the Bay to meet her, on the coldest, darkest night I've ever known on water. Shortly after nine o'clock the big boat's light gleamed off the Hook and she bore down upon us. She came close, slowed down and towered by our side, weird as a ghost with snow and ice in glimmering sheets on her steel sides. She did not stop. We caught a rope ladder and scrambled up, and at once we felt her speeding on.

And she was indeed a story that night. Bellowing hoarsely now in warning to all small craft to get out of her way, she was rushing into the harbor. Suddenly she slowed again, and three dark mail tugs ranged alongside, and through canvas chutes four thousand sacks of Christmas mail began to pour down while the ship moved on. Up her other side came climbing gangs of men who began to make ready her winches and open up her hatches. Now we were moving in close to the pier, with a whole fleet of tugs around us. Faint shouts rose in the zero night, toots and sharp whistles. One of the gang-planks was down at last and two hundred dockers came up on the run. Off went the passengers and the luggage, reporters skurrying through the crowds. But the ship did not rest. For she was to sail again the next night. This was to be a world's record for speed!

All night long the work went on, and I watched it from a deck above, going in now and then for food and hot drinks. On her dock side, forward, Christmas boxes, bales and packages were being whipped up out of her hold to the rattle of her winches. One sharp whistle and up they shot into the air till they swung some seventy feet above. Another whistle and down they whirled into the dockshed far below from which a blaze of light poured up. At the same time she was coaling. Along the black wall of her other side, as I peered over the rail above, I saw far below a row of barges crowded with Italians. Powerful lights swung over their heads in the freezing wind, swung above black coal heaps and the lapping water. It was an inferno of shifting lights and long leaping shadows.

I watched till daylight blotted out the yellow glare of the lanterns. Then I went home to get some sleep. And late that night when I came back I found her almost ready to sail.

Out of taxis and automobiles chugging down in front of the pier, the passengers were pouring in. Many were in evening clothes, some just come from dinners and others from box parties. The theaters had just let out. The rich warm hues of the women's cloaks, the gay head dresses here and there and the sparkling earrings, immaculate gloves and dainty wanton slippered feet, kept giving flashes of color to this dark freezing ocean place. Most of these people went hurrying up into the warm, gorgeous café of the ship, which was run from a hotel in Paris. What had all this to do with the sea?

"Come on," said the genial press agent. "You're the company's guest to-night."

And while we ate and drank and smoked, and the tables around us filled with people whose ripples and bursts of laughter rose over the orchestra's festive throb, and corks kept popping everywhere, he told me where they were going, these gay revellers, for their Christmas Day—to London, Brussels, Berlin and Vienna, Paris, Nice, Monte Carlo, Algiers.

"Now come with me," he said at last, and he took me along warm passageways to the row of cabins de luxe.

First we looked into the Bridal Suite, to which one of the Pittsburgh makers of steel, having just divorced a homely old wife, was presently to bring his new bride, a ravishing young creature of musical comedy fame. They had been married that afternoon. A French maid was unpacking dainty shimmering little gowns, soft furry things and other things of silk and lace, and hanging them up in closets. It was a large room, and there were other rooms adjoining and two big luxurious baths. The cost of it all was four thousand dollars for the five days. There were tall mirrors and dressing tables, there were capacious easy chairs. Low subdued lights were here and there, and a thick rug was on the floor. Over in one corner was a huge double bed of cream colored wood with rich soft quilts upon it. Beside the bed in a pink satin cradle there lay a tiny Pekinese dog.

"Next," he whispered. We peeped into the next stateroom, and there divided from her neighbors by only one thin partition, a sober, wrinkled little old lady in black velvet sat quietly reading her Bible. Soon she would be saying her prayers.

"Next," he whispered. And in the cabin on her other side we caught a glimpse of two jovial men playing cards in gay pajamas with a bottle of Scotch between them.

"Next." And as we went on down the row he gave me the names of an English earl, a Jewish clothing merchant, a Minnesota ranchman, a banker's widow from Boston, a Tammany politician, a Catholic bishop from Baltimore, a millionaire cheese maker from Troy and a mining king from Montana.

"How about that," he asked at the end, "for an American row de luxe?"

"My God, it's great," I whispered.

"There's only one big question here," he added. "Your long respectable pedigrees and your nice little Puritanical codes can all go to blazes—this big boat will throw 'em all overboard for you—if you can answer, 'I've got the price.'"

CHAPTER XII

Meanwhile, in the late Autumn, Eleanore had come back to town. I had a note from her one day.

"Come and tell me what you are writing," she said.

I went to see her that afternoon, and I was deeply excited. I had often felt her by my side when I was watching the harbor life and as often behind me while I wrote. We had had long talks together, absorbing talks about ourselves. And though now in her easy welcome and through all her cheerful questions there was not a suggestion that we two had been or ever would be anything but genial friends, this did not discourage me in the least. No fellow, I thought, could be happy as I and have nothing better than friendship ahead. The Fates could never be so hard, for certainly now they were smiling.

Here was her apartment, just the place I had felt it would be, only infinitely more attractive. High up above the Manhattan jungle, it was quiet and sunny and charming here. From the low, wide living-room windows you could see miles out over the harbor where my work was going so splendidly, and all around the room itself I saw what I was working for. Eleanore's touch was everywhere. An intimate, lovable feminine home with man-sized views from its windows—just like Eleanore herself, from whom I found it difficult to keep my hungry eyes away. To that soft bewildering hair of hers she had done something different—I couldn't tell what, but I loved it. I loved the changing tones of her voice—I hate monotonous voices. I watched the smiling lights in her eyes. She was at her small tea table now. Her motorboat, thank Heaven, was laid up for the winter, and I had her right here in a room, with nothing to do with her eyes but pay a decent amount of attention to me. Then by some chance remark I learned that she had been reading what I wrote, almost all of it, in fact. And at the slight exclamation I made I saw her color slightly and bite her lip as though she were angry with herself for having let that secret out.

"What do you want to write," she asked, "when you get through with the harbor?"

"Fiction," I said. "I want it so hard sometimes that it seems like a long way ahead. It seems sometimes," I added, "like a girl I'd fallen in love with—but I couldn't even ask her—because I'm so infernally poor."

Over the tea cup at her lips Eleanore looked thoughtfully straight into and through and behind my eyes.

"Fiction is such a broad field," she remarked. "What kind do you think you're going to try?"

"I don't know," I answered. "It still seems so far ahead. You see, I have no name at all, and this harbor at least is a good safe start. I'm afraid I'm rather a cautious sort. When I find what I want—and want so hard that it's the deepest part of me—I like to go slow. I'm afraid to risk losing it all—deciding my life one way or the other—by taking a chance." I made a restless movement. "I wasn't speaking of my work just then," I added gruffly.

I suddenly caught a glimpse of myself in the mirror back of Eleanore's chair. And I glared at myself for the fool that I was to have said all that. I hadn't meant to—not in the least! What a paltry looking cuss I was—small, tough and wiry, hair sandy, eyes of no color at all, snub nose and a jaw shut tight as in pain.

"You're a queer person," said a voice.

"I am," I agreed forlornly. "I'm the queerest fellow I ever met." I caught a grim twinkle in my eyes. Thank God for a sense of humor.

"Sometimes," she went on, reflectively, "you seem to me as old as the hills—and again so young and obvious. I'm so sorry to hear you say that you weren't talking of your work. I like to hear men talk of their work."

"I know you do," I said hungrily. "And that's one of the reasons why you're going to mean so much some day—to somebody's work—and to his whole life."

Why couldn't I stop? Had I gone insane? I rose and moved about the room. A low rippling laugh brought me back to my senses.

"But how about *me* and *my* life?" she asked. "That ought to be thought of a little, you know."

I came close beside her:

"Let me say this. Won't you? I'll promise never to say it again. Your life is going to be all right. It's going to be quite wonderful— you'll be tremendously happy. I'm sure of that. It's not only the way you always—look—it's the way you always think and feel. It's everything about you."

She had looked down at her hands for a moment. Now she looked up suddenly.

"Thank you," she said smiling, in a way that told me to smile too. I obeyed.

"I did that rather badly, didn't I," I said.

"No, you did that rather well. Especially the first part—I think I liked that best of all—the part where you promised so solemnly that you'd never do it again."

I went indignantly back to my chair.

"Do you know," I said, "I feel sometimes when I'm with you as though I were being managed! Absolutely managed!"

"I should think you wouldn't like that," she replied. Her hands were peacefully folded now and she looked at me serenely: "I should think you'd rather manage yourself."

I took the hint. From that day on, each time I came to see her, I managed myself severely. And this apparently pleased her so much that she seemed no longer the least afraid to let me know her as well as I liked. Her father, too, when I met him now and then in the evenings, was most kindly in his welcome. And as winter wore on, my hopes rose high.

But one evening, after Dillon had read my story about the Christmas Boat, he gave me a bitter disappointment.

"I like it," he said, as he handed it back. "It's a fine dramatic piece of work. But it's only a starter here. To get any idea of our problem you'll have to go all over the harbor. When you've done that for a few months more, and I get back from my trip abroad, I'll be glad to help you."

"You're going abroad?" I asked abruptly.

"Next month," he said, "with Eleanore. She seems to think I need a rest."

Back came the old feeling of emptiness. And gloomily at home that night I wondered if it was because she knew she was leaving so soon that she had been so intimate lately. How outrageous women are.

CHAPTER XIII

They sailed the middle of March.

It is easy to look back now and smile at my small desolate self as I was in the months that followed. But at the time it was no smiling matter. I was intensely wretched and I had a right to be, for I could see nothing whatever ahead but the most dire uncertainties. Did Eleanore really care for me? I didn't know. When could I ask her? I didn't know. For when would I be earning enough to ask any girl to marry me? At present nearly all I earned was swallowed up by expenses at home, and I knew that in all likelihood this drain would soon grow heavier.

For we could not count much longer on my father's salary. Already I had done my best to make him give up his position. He stubbornly resisted.

"I'm strong as I ever was," he declared, and he took great pains to prove it. He would sit down to dinner, his face heavy and gray with fatigue, but by a hard visible effort slowly he would throw it off, keenly questioning me about my work, more often quizzing me about it, or Sue about her "revolooters." He had a stock of these dry remarks and he used them over and over. When the same jokes came night after night we knew he was very tired. After dinner on such evenings, when I went with him into his study to smoke, he would invariably settle back in his chair with the same loud "Ah!" of comfort, and he would follow this up as he lit his cigar with the most obvious grunts expressive of health to prove to me how strong he was. He was always grimly delighted when I spent these evenings with him, but always before his cigar was out his head would sink slowly over his book and soon he would be sound asleep. Then as I sat at my writing I would glance over from time to time. I could tell when he was waking, and at once I would grow absorbed in my work. Soon I would hear a slight snort of surprise, I would hear him stealthily feel for his book, and then presently out of the silence——

"This is a devilish good piece of writing, boy," he would announce abruptly. "When *you* learn to hold your reader like this I'll begin to think you're a writer."

Yes, my father was aging fast, I would soon be the only bread-winner here. Sue fought hard against this idea, she was still set on finding work for herself, but each time she proposed it Dad would rise so indignantly, with such evident pain in his glaring old eyes, that she would be forced to give up her plan. In such talks I supported him, and in return when we two were alone Sue would revenge herself on me by the most cutting comments on "this inane habit of looking at girls as fit for nothing better than marriage."

These comments, I was well aware, were aimed at my feeling for Eleanore, for whom Sue had no longer any good word but only a smiling derision. Her remarks were straight out of Bernard Shaw's most ribald works, and they left me miserably wondering whether any man had ever loved in any way that wasn't the curse or the joke of his life. Sue dwelt on this glorious age of deep radi-cal changes going on, she spoke of Joe Kramer, with whom she still corresponded, and enlarged on the wonderful freedom he had to go anywhere at any time. Thank a merciful heaven *he* wasn't tied down! And if Joe would only keep his head and not marry, not get a huge family on his hands——

Sue made me perfectly wretched.

In this frame of mind I again tackled the harbor. Dillon had told me to cover it all, and this I now set out to do. On warm muggy April days I tramped what appeared to me hundreds of miles. But the regions that from Eleanore's boat had somehow had a feeling of being one great living thing, now on these dreary trudging days fell apart into remote bays and slips and rivers, hours of weary travel apart and each without any connection with any other that I could see. Railroad tracks wound in and out with no apparent purpose, dirty freight boats crawled helter-skelter this way and that. All seemed a meaningless chaos and jam.

And still worse, as I wrestled with this confusion I found it was growing stale to me. In those Spring days I was fagged and dull, my imagination would not work. And this gave me a scare. I must *not* grow stale, I must keep right on making money to meet the bills that were still piling up at home. And so for a Sunday paper I undertook a series on "The Harbor from a Police Boat." This sounded rather exciting and I hoped that it might restore the lost thrill. The harbor that it showed me made fine Sunday reading. Out of its grim waters dead bodies bobbed, dead faces leered, the sodden ends of mysteries. I wrote them and got paid for them. And I felt no thrill but only disgust. I made some more money out of rats—rats in countless ravenous hordes that had a harbor world of their own. This world extended for hundreds of miles in the dark chill places under the wharves. And the rats kept gnawing, gnawing, and slowly with the help of the waves they wore away to splinters and pulp the millions of beams and planks and piles. I found that entire mountains were denuded each year of their forests to supply food for the rats and the ocean here. I was almost a muckraker now.

Meanwhile I had gone in June to the South Brooklyn waterfront and had taken a room in a tenement near the end of a dock peninsula which jutted out into the bay. For I wanted to live in the very heart of the big port's confusion, to grapple alone with the chaos out of which Dillon's engineers were striving to bring order. Here I lived for weeks by myself, taking my meals in a barroom below.

There were no stately liners here. The North River piers with their rich life had been like a show room. I had come down into the factory now. I could see them still, those liners, but only in the distance steaming through the Narrows. Eleanore had gone that way. Here close around me were grimy yards with heaps of coal, enormous sheds, and inland one of the two narrow mouths of the crowded Erie Basin, out of which slid ugly freighters through the dirty water.

Like the Ancient Mariner I sat there dully on the pier watching the life of the ocean go past, and I would try to jot it down. But soon I would stop. "All right—who cares?" The punch was gone. It grew hot and the water smelt. And I was as blue a reporter of life as ever chewed his pencil.

But life has a way of punching up even a stale young writer. In the rooms above mine lived a man and wife who quarreled half way through the night. Night after night they railed at each other, until one horrible night of screams, in the middle of which I heard the man come running downstairs. He banged at my door.

"Come in," I cried morosely. A big figure entered the dark room.

"Look here," said a rough frightened voice. "Get up and get dressed and run for a doctor. Will you, son? I'm in a hell of a hole!"

"What's the matter?"

"My woman is havin' a baby, that's what," he answered fiercely. "We wasn't expectin' it so soon! An' there ain't a single doctor in miles! But there's a night watchman with a 'phone down there in the dockshed!"

"All right, old man, I'll do my best."

"Say!" he shouted after me, as I hurried down the stairs. "If you know a damn thing about this business come back here the minute you've 'phoned! I'm in a hole, brother, a hell of a hole!"

I came back soon, and within a few minutes after I came I saw a baby born.

I did not sleep that night. My mind was curiously clear. I had had the jolt that I needed from life—its agony and bloody sweat, its mystery. It was not dull, it was not stale. The only trouble lay in me. I must find a new angle from which to write.

Why not try becoming one of the workers? The man upstairs was a tug captain, and grateful to me for what help I had given; he now agreed to take me on his tug, where there was plenty of simple work which I did for a dollar a day and my board. And at once I felt a difference. The light work steadied my overwrought nerves and unlocked my mind which had set tight. And now at last I began to see my way out of the jungle.

For the tug belonged to a row of piers about a mile to the southward. Brand new gigantic piers they were, with solid rows of factory buildings on the shore behind them, all owned by one great company, which rented floors or parts of floors to hundreds of manufacturers here. The raw materials they required were landed from barges or ships at the piers and delivered to their doors at once, and their finished products were conveyed in the same way to all parts of the world. Here was a key to the future port of ordered combination that Eleanore's father was working toward.

Here was the place I must write up before he came back from abroad, to show him that I had found it.

And the very certainty of this increased my exasperation. For even still I could not write. Doggedly I worked at night up there in my room in the tenement, but I wrote the most tedious dismal stuff which I would tear up savagely. Inanely I would pound my head as though to put punch into it.

But another miracle happened to me.

On one of those enormous piers, roofed over, dim and cool inside, I stood one day looking out on the deck of an East Indian freighter, where two half-naked Malays were polishing the brass-work. One of them was a boy of ten. His small face was uncouth and primitive almost as some little ape's, but I saw him look up again and again with a sudden gleaming expectancy. I grew curious and waited. Now the looks came oftener, his every move was rest-less. And after a time another boy, a little New York "newsie," with a pack of evening papers, came loitering along the pier. Unconcern-edly up the gang-plank he went, while the Malay crouched in his corner, rigid and tense, his black eyes fixed. The white boy took no notice. Climbing up a ladder he sold a couple of papers to some offi-cers on a deck above, and then he went down again to the dock. Presently one of the officers yawned and threw his paper over the rail, and as it fell to the lower deck in an instant the Malay boy was upon it, devouring its headlines and its pictures with his animal eyes, with one of his small bare brown feet upon the jeweled bosom of the latest Fifth Avenue divorcee.

"Where does that kid sleep?" I asked an officer. I was shown his bunk below, and there I found I had guessed right. For the side and the top and both ends of his bunk were lined with red headlines and newspaper pictures all carefully cut and pasted on. Five of the New York "Giants" were there.

And as though the fresh fierce hungriness had passed from that small heathen's soul into my own, that day I again became a reporter of things to be seen in the port of New York.

Back into the dockshed I went, and all up and down and in and out among piles of strange and odorous stuffs. And once more I felt the wonder of this modern ocean world. I followed this raw produce of Mother Earth's four corners back into those factory buildings ashore. I saw it made into chewing-gum, toys, sofas, glue, curled hair and wall-paper. I saw it made into ladies' hats, corks, carpets, dynamos, stuffed dates. I saw it made into dirt-proof collars and shirt bosoms, salad dressing, blackboards, corsets and the like. Again I fairly reveled in lists of things and the places they came from and the places to which they were going. I saw chewing-gum start for Rio and Quaker Oats for Shanghai, patent medicine for Nabat, curled hair for Yokohama, "movy" theater seats for Sydney, tomato soup for Cape Town and corsets for Rangoon.

"From Everywhere to Anywhere" was the title of my article. It took only a week to write, and was ready when the Dillons came home.

CHAPTER XIV

They landed toward the end of July and I went to the dock to meet them.

Elated over my finished story, which I had in my pocket, and made absurdly happy by the sight of Eleanore smiling down at me over the rail, I was surprised at the greeting she gave me.

"Why, you poor boy. How terribly hard you've been working," she said. And she looked at me as though I were sick and worn to the bone. The end of it was that I accepted delightedly an invitation to spend a week up at their cottage on the Sound.

Those were seven vivid glowing days. I could not relax, I was too intensely happy, I had too much to tell her, not only about my work but about a host of other things that without rhyme or reason popped into my mind and had to be said. The range of our talk was tremendous, and the wider we ranged the closer we drew. For she too was telling things, and her things were as unexpected as mine and infinitely more absorbing. Her manner toward me had quite changed. It was that of a nurse with an invalid, she frankly ordered me about.

"Why can't you lie back on those cushions?" she asked one morning when we were out in her boat. "You ought to be dozing half the day—and instead you're as wide awake as an owl."

"I am," I admitted happily. "I'm trying to see everything." The chic little hat and the blouse she wore were adorably fresh from Paris, and as I watched her run her boat I could feel flowing into my body and soul a perfectly boundless store of new life.

"I've been thinking you over," she said.

"Have you?" I asked delightedly. I had often wondered if she had. "What do you think?" I inquired.

Eleanore frowned perplexedly.

"You're such a queer combination," she said. "You have such ridiculous ups and downs. To-day you're way up, aren't you."

"I am," I said very earnestly. She looked off placidly over the Sound.

"You're so very sensitive," she went on. "You let things take hold of you so hard. And yet on the other hand you seem to be so very—" she hesitated for a word.

"Tough," I suggested cheerfully.

"No—hungry," Eleanore said. "You're always reaching out for things—you jump right into them so hard. And even when they hurt you—and you're hurt quite easily—you hang on and won't let go. Look at the way you've gone at the harbor right from the start. And you're doing it still—you've done it all summer until it has made you look like a ghost. And I guess you'll keep on all your life. There are harbors everywhere, you know—in a way the whole world is a harbor—and unless you change a lot you're going to be hurt a good deal."

"My mother agreed with you," I said. "She wanted me to be a professor in a quiet college town."

"Please stop twinkling your eyes," Eleanore commanded. "Your mother knew you very well. You might have done that—and settled down—with some nice quiet college girl—if you had done it years ago. As it is, of course you're hopeless."

"I am not hopeless," I declared indignantly. "If I can only get what I want I'll be the happiest fellow alive!"

"I know," she answered thoughtfully. "You told me that before. You want fiction, don't you."

"Yes, fiction," I said wrathfully. "I want that more than anything else. But I don't want any quiet kind, and I don't want any quiet town," I went on, leaning forward intensely. "I want the harbor and the city—I want it thick and heavy, and just as fast as it will come. I want all the life there is in the world—all the beauty—all the happiness! And I can't wait—I want it soon!"

From under the brim of her soft white hat her bluegray eyes were fixed intently on the shore, which was miles away. But watching her I saw she knew that all the time I was saying desperately, "I want you."

I knew she did not want me to say anything like that out loud, and I felt myself that I had no right—not until I had done so much more in my writing. But I kept circling around it. Half the time on purpose and as often quite unconsciously, in all we talked about those days I kept eagerly filling in the picture of the life we two might lead. When in one of her cool hostile moods—moods which came over her suddenly—she told me almost jealously how happy she'd been with her father abroad and how together they had planned to go to India, China, Japan in the years to come, I brought her back to my subject by saying: "I mean to travel a lot myself."

"That's one advantage I have as a writer," I continued earnestly. "I'll never be tied down to one place. All my life—whenever I choose—I can pick up my work and go anywhere."

She looked straight back into my eyes.

"I wish my father could," she said.

"Look here," I said indignantly. "Your father has been four months abroad while I have been in Brooklyn! Isn't it only fair and square to let *me* travel this afternoon?" She looked at me reluctantly.

"Yes," she agreed. "I suppose it is."

"Come along," I urged, and off we went. While our boat drifted idly that long, lazy afternoon, we went careering all over the world and I kept doggedly by her side. Every now and then I would make her stop while we had a good look at each other, exploring deep into the old questions, "What are you and what do you want?"

"You can't run a motorboat all your life," I reminded her. "What are you going to tackle next?"

"Our living-room," she answered. "I'm going to have it done over next month."

That took us into house furnishings, and I gave her ideas by the score. I had never thought about this before, but now I thought hard and eagerly—until she brought me up with a jerk, by pityingly murmuring:

"What perfectly frightful taste you have. It's funny—because you're an artist—you really write quite beautiful things."

"I don't care," I answered grimly. "I can see that living-room—"

"So can I," she said cheerfully. "But so long as you like it, that's all there is to be said. You're the one who has to live in it, you know. Now my father likes a room—"

And while I looked gloomily over the water she told me what her father liked.

He came out from the city each evening by train. He refused to use the boat these days, he said he was so infernally busy that he could not spare the time. He brought out stacks of papers and plans which had piled up while he was abroad, and with these he busied himself at night. And though Eleanore from the veranda glanced in at him frequently, she never again caught him looking old. And when she went in to make him stop working he smilingly told her to leave him alone. He smoked many cigars with apparent enjoyment, his lean face wrinkling over the smoke as he turned over plan after plan for the harbor. His manner to me was if anything even kindlier than before. He began calling me "Billy" now.

On the last night of my stay he said:

"I think you're the man I've been looking for. I've just read your story and you've done exactly what I hoped. You've pictured one spot of efficiency in a whole dreary desert of waste. Come up to my office to-morrow at ten."

CHAPTER XV

So at last I went up to the tower.

His office took up an entire floor near the tapering top of the building, and as we walked slowly around the narrow steel balcony outside, a tremendous panorama unrolled down there before our eyes. We could see every part of the port below stretching away to the horizon, and through Dillon's powerful field glass I saw pictures of all I had seen before in my weary weeks of trudging down there in the haze and dust. Down there I had felt like a little worm, up here I felt among the gods. There all had been matter and chaos, here all was mind and a will to find a way out of confusion. The glass gave me the pictures in swift succession, in a moment I made a leap of ten miles, and as I listened on and on to the quiet voice at my elbow, the pictures all came sweeping together as parts of one colossal whole. The first social vision of my life I had through Dillon's field glass.

"To see any harbor or city or state as a whole," he said, "is what most Americans cannot do. And it's what they've got to learn to do."

And while I looked where he told me to, like a surgeon about to operate he talked of his mighty patient, a giant struggling to breathe, with swollen veins and arteries. He made me see the Hudson, the East River and the railroad lines all pouring in their traffic, to be shifted and reloaded onto the ocean vessels in a perfect fever of confusion and delay. Far below us you could see long lines of tiny trucks and wagons waiting hours for a chance to get into the docksheds. New York, he said, in true Yankee style had developed its waterfront pell mell, each railroad and each ship line grabbing sites for its own use, until the port was now so clogged, so tangled and congested that it was able to grow no more.

"And it's got to grow," he said. The old helter-skelter method had served well enough in years gone by, for this port had been like this whole bountiful land, its natural advantages had been so prodigious it could stand all our blind and hoggish mistakes. But now we were rapidly nearing the time when every mistake we made would cost us tens of millions of dollars. For within a few years the Big Ditch would open across Panama, and the commerce of South America, together with that of the Orient, would pour into the harbor here to meet the westbound commerce of Europe. Ships of all nations would steam through the Narrows, and we must be ready to welcome them all, with an ample generous harbor worthy of the world's first port.

"To get ready," he said, "what we've got to do is to organize this port as a whole, like the big industrial plant it is."

He began to show me some of the plans in blue-print maps and sketches. I saw tens of thousands of freight cars gathered in great central yards at a few main strategic points connected by long tunnels with all the minor centers. I saw the port no longer as a mere body of water, but with a whole region deep beneath of these long winding tunnels through which flowed the traffic unseen and unheard. I saw along the waterfronts continuous lines of docksheds where by huge cranes and other devices the loading and unloading could be done with enormous saving of time. Along the heavy roofs of steel of these continuous lines of buildings stretched wide ocean boulevards with trees and shrubs and flowers to shut out the clamorous life below. Warehouses and factory buildings rose in solid rows behind. The city was to build them all, and the city as the landlord was to invite the ships and railroads, and the manufacturers too, to come in and get together, to stop their fighting and grabbing and work with each other in one great plan.

"That's what we mean nowadays by a port," he told me at the end of our talk. "A complicated industrial organ, the heart of a country's circulation, pumping in and out its millions of tons of traffic as quickly and cheaply as possible. That's efficiency, scientific management or just plain engineering, whatever you want to call it. But it's got to be done for us all in a plan instead of each for himself in a blind struggling chaos."

I came down from the tower with a dazed, excited feeling which lasted all the rest of the day. That harbor of confusion had been for months my entire world, it had baffled and beaten me till I was weak. And now this man had swept together all its parts and showed me one immense design.

He had promised me the first use of his plans. With this to go on I drafted a scheme for a series of magazine articles on "The First Port of the World," and I soon placed it in advance at four hundred dollars an article. At last I was coming up in life, my first big story had begun!

I went with Dillon each week-end up to the cottage on the Sound. Here he talked in detail of his dreams, and Eleanore with her old passion and pride delighted to draw him out for me. And not only her father—for to help me in my work she invited out here in the evenings many of his engineer friends.

"It has always been awfully hard for me," she confided, "to understand big questions by reading about them out of books. But I love to hear about them from men who are living and working right in them. I love to feel a little how it must be to be living their lives."

She was a wonderful listener, for she had quietly studied each man until now she had a kind of an instinct for drawing the very best of him out. While he talked she would sit with her sewing, now and then putting in a question to help. Often I would glance at her there and see in her slightly frowning face how intently she was listening, thinking and planning to help me. Sometimes she would meet my look. I would grow tremendously happy.

"In a little while," I thought. But then I would pull myself up with a jerk: "Stop looking at her, you young fool, keep your mind on this engineer. You've got the chance of your life right now to make good in your work and be happy. Don't fall down! Get busy!"

And I did. I threw myself into the lives of these men who were the living embodiments of all that bigness, boldness, punch that had so gripped and thrilled me. The harbor had drawn them around it out of the hum and rush of the country, and here they were in its service, watching it, studying, planning for its even more stupendous growth. One night I heard them discuss the idea of moving the East River, making it flow across Long Island, filling in its old water bed and making New York and Brooklyn one. They talked of this scheme in a hard-headed Yankee way that made me forget for the moment its boldness, until some cool remark opened my eyes to the fact that this change would shift vast populations, plant millions of people this way and that.

But against these men of the tower, with their wide, deliberate views ahead, embracing and binding together not only this port but the whole western world depending upon it, I found in the city jungle innumerable petty men, who could see only their own narrow interests of to-day, and who fought blindly any change for a to-morrow—fellows in such mortal fear of some possible benefit to their rivals that they could see none for themselves. They were hopelessly used to fighting each other. And I came to feel that all these men, though many were still young in years, belonged to a generation gone by, to the age of individual strife that my father had lived and worked in—and that like him they were all soon to be swept to one side by the inexorable harbor of to-day, which had no further use for them.

It needed bigger men. It needed men like Dillon and behind him those mysterious powers downtown, the men he had called the brains of the nation, who read the signs of the new times, who saw that the West was now fast filling up, that the eyes of the nation were once more turning outward, and that untold resources of wealth were soon to be available for mighty sea adventures, a vast fleet of Yankee ships that should drive the surplus output of our teeming industries into all markets of the world. And the men who saw these things coming were the only ones who were big enough to prepare the country to meet them. My father's dream was at last coming true—too late for him to play a part. He had been but a prophet, a lonely pioneer.

My view of the harbor was different now. I had seen it before as a vast machine molding the lives of all people around it. But now behind the machine itself I felt the minds of its molders. I saw its ponderous masses of freight, its multitudes of people, all pushed and shifted this way and that by these invisible powers. And by degrees I made for myself a new god, and its name was Efficiency.

Here at last was a god that I felt could stand! I had made so many in years gone by, I had been making them all my life—from those first fearful idols, the condors and the cannibals, to the kind old god of goodness in my mother's church and the radiant goddess of beauty and art over there in Paris. One by one I had raised them up, and one by one the harbor had flowed in and dragged them down. But now in my full manhood (for remember I was twenty-five!) I had found and taken to myself a god that I felt sure of. No harbor could make it totter and fall. For it was armed with Science, its feet stood firm on mechanical laws and in its head were all the brains of all the strong men at the top.

And all the multitudes below seemed mere pigmies to me now. I remember one late twilight, coming back from a talk with an engineer, I boarded a ferry at the rush hour and watched the people herd on like sheep. How small they seemed, how petty their thoughts compared to mine, how blind their views of the harbor.

Here was a little Italian bride, just landed, by the looks of her. She kept her face close to her lover's, smiling dazedly into his eyes. And she saw no harbor. Here near by was a fat old gentleman with a highly painted young lady who laughed and swore softly at him as I passed. I sat down beside them a moment and listened. The old gentleman seemed quite mad with desire. He was pleading eagerly, whining. And he saw no harbor. Close by sat two tall serious men. One was deep in a socialist book, the other in news of the Giants. Both seemed equally absorbed. And they saw no harbor. I moved on to another spot, and sitting down by a thin seedy-looking Irish girl I heard her talk to her husband about having their baby's life insured according to a wonderful plan an agent had described to her. As she spoke she was frowning anxiously—and she saw no harbor. Not far away a plump flashy young creature was smiling down on the bootblack who was busily shining her small patent leather shoes. Her bright blue petticoat lifted high displayed the most enticing charms, and as now she turned to look off toward the lights of the city ahead, she smiled gaily to herself. And she saw no harbor. And alone up at the windy bow I found a squat husky laborer with his dirty coat and shirt thrown open wide, the wind on his bare hairy chest, hungrily watching the dock ahead as though for his supper—

seeing no harbor, no world's first port, no plans for vast fleets or a great canal, none of the big things shaping his life.

But I saw. Orders had gone out from the tower east and west and south and north to show me every courtesy. And with a miraculous youthful ease I understood all that I saw and heard. The details all fitted right into the whole, or if they didn't I made them fit. Here was a splendid end to chaos and blind wrestling with life. And feeling stronger and more sure than ever in my life before, I set out to build my series of glory stories about it all, laying on the color thick to reach a million pigmy readers, grip them, pull them out of their holes, make them sit up and rub their eyes.

For I was now a success in life! The exuberant joy of youth and success filled the whole immense region for me. In those Fall days there was nothing too hard to try, no queer hours too exhausting, no deep corner too remote, in the search for my material. I saw the place from an old fisherman's boat and from a revenue launch at night, with its searchlight combing the waters far and wide for smugglers. I saw it from big pilot boats that put far out to sea to meet the incoming liners. I ate many good suppers and slept long nights on a stout jolly tug called *The Happy*, where from my snug bunk at the stern through the open door I could watch the stars. I went down into tunnels deep beneath the waters. I went often to the Navy Yard. I dined many nights on battleships, where the talk of the naval officers recalled my father's picture of a fighting ocean world. They too talked of the Big Canal, but in terms of war instead of peace. I went out to the coast defenses, and with an army major I made a tour of the lights and buoys.

And perhaps more often than anywhere else, I went to a rude log cabin on the side of a wooded hill high up on Staten Island, where lived a Norwegian engineer. He had a cozy den up there, with book-shelves set into the logs, two deep bunks, a few bright rugs on the rough floor, some soft, ponderous leather chairs and a crackling little stove on which we cooked delicious suppers. Later out on the narrow porch we would puff lazy smoke wreaths and watch the vast valley of lights below, from the distant twinkling arch of the Bridge to the sparkling towers of old Coney. Down there like swarms of fire-flies were countless darting skurrying lights, red and blue and green and white. Far off to the south flashed the light of the Hook, and still other signals gleamed low from the ocean.

Here I came often with Eleanore, for she had now come back to town. In her boat we went to many new spots and back to all the old ones. We found new beauties in them all. At home in the evenings we had long talks. And all the time I could feel that we two both knew what was coming, that steadily we were drawing together, that all my work and my view of the harbor took its joy and its glory from this.

"In a little while," I thought.

CHAPTER XVI

I had been little at home those days, for the house in Brooklyn disturbed me now. Poor old Dad. Since I had secured my contract he had tried so hard to help me, to be eager, interested, alive, to talk it all over with me at night. And this I did not like to do. A vague feeling of guilt and disloyalty would creep into my now boundless zest for the harbor that had crowded him out. And I think that he suspected this. One night, when with this feeling I stupidly tried to talk as though I still hated all its ugliness, its clamor, smoke and grime, I caught a twinkle of pain in his eyes.

"Boy," he broke in roughly, "I hope you'll always talk and write what you believe and nothing else! I wouldn't give a picayune for any chap who didn't!"

I could feel him watching anxiously my affair with Eleanore. In the days when she had come to the house he had grown very fond of her, and now by frequent questions, slipped in with a studied indifference, he showed an interest which in time became a deep suspense.

"Out again this evening, son?" he called in one night from the bathroom where he was washing his hands and face before going down to supper. In my room adjoining I was dressing to go out.

"Yes, Dad."

"What for?"

"Some work."

"Be out for dinner too?"

"Yes."

"Who with?"

"Oh, a pilot," I answered abstractedly. I was wondering if she would wear her blue gown. She had asked quite a number of people that night. Then I saw Dad in the doorway. Briskly rubbing his gray head with a towel, he was eyeing my evening clothes.

"Devilish polished chaps these days—pilots," he commented. I heard a low snort of glee from his room.

My sister, on the other hand, had no more patience than before with this fast deepening love of mine, which had drawn me away from her radical friends up to the men of the tower who worked for the big companies. By the most vigorous ironies, the most industrious witty remarks, she made me feel how thoroughly she disapproved of anything so deadening as marriage, home and settling down, in this glorious age of new ideas.

One morning at breakfast, when I remarked as I commonly did that I would be out for dinner that night,

"Where are you going?" she asked abruptly.

"To Eleanore Dillon's," I replied. Our eyes met squarely for a moment.

"Do you know what it means to go there so often, almost every night?" she asked.

"I do," I answered bluntly. I would finish this meddling once and for all. But Sue did not look finished.

"You'd better stay home to-night, Billy," she said.

"Why?"

"Joe Kramer is coming."

"What?"

"He telephoned me late last night. He's just come from Colorado and he sails to-morrow for England. He's awfully anxious to see you."

Of course he was, and I knew what about! I saw at once by the look on her face that Sue had told him all about me and had begged him to see what he could do. Why couldn't they leave a fellow alone, I said wrathfully to myself.

But my ire softened when I met Joe. In the year and a half since I had seen him the lines in his face had deepened, the stoop of his big shoulders had grown even more pronounced, and again I felt that wistful, frowning, searching quality in him. Beneath his gruffness and his jeers he was so honestly pushing on for what he could find most real in life. A wave of the old affection came over me suddenly without warning. Vaguely I wondered about it. Why did he always grip me so?

My father too appeared at first delighted to see him. He had shown a keen relish for J. K. from that first time in college when I had brought him home for Christmas. Since then, whenever Joe had come, he and Dad had always managed to retreat to the study together and smoke and have long dogged arguments. But to-night it was not the same. For in his growth as a radical, Joe had gone beyond all arguing now. Lines of deep displeasure slowly tightened on Dad's face. All through dinner he kept attempting to turn the talk from Joe's work to mine. But this I would have none of, I wanted to be let alone. So I nervously kept the conversation on what Joe was up to. And Sue seemed more than eager to learn.

J. K. was up to a good deal.

"This muckraking game is played out," he said. "We all know how rotten things are. All we want to know now is what's to be done." And he himself had become absorbed in what the working class was doing. As a reporter in the West he had been to strike after strike, ending with a long ugly struggle in the Colorado mines. He talked about it intensely, the greed of the mine owners, the brutality of the militia, the "bull pens" into which strikers were thrown. Vaguely I felt he was giving us a most distorted picture, and glancing now and then at my father I saw that he thought it a pack of lies. Joe made all the strikers the most heroic figures, and he spoke of their struggle as only a part of a great labor war that was soon to sweep the entire land.

Sue excitedly drew him out, and I felt it was all for my benefit. Joe said that he was going abroad in order that he might write the truth about the labor world over there. The American papers and magazines would let you write the truth, he said, about labor over in Europe, because it was at a safe distance. But they wouldn't allow it here. And then Sue looked across at me as though to say, "It's only stuff like *yours* they allow."

"Why don't you two go out for a walk?" she suggested sweetly after dinner. And I consented gladly, for there are times when nothing on earth can be worse than your own sister.

We went down to the old East River docks and walked for some time with little said. Then Joe turned on me abruptly.

"Well, Bill," he said, "I've read your stuff. It's damn well written."

"Thanks," I replied.

"If I've got any knocking to do," he went on with a visible effort, "I know you'll give me credit for not knocking out of jealousy. I'm not jealous, I'm honestly tickled to death. I was wrong about you in Paris. You and me were different kinds. What you got over there was just what you needed, it has put you already way out of my class, and it's going to give you a lot of power as a spreader of ideas. That's why I hate so like the devil to see you starting out like this, with what I'm so sure are the wrong ideas."

"How are they wrong?"

"Think a minute. Why is your magazine pushing you so? The first story of your series is only just out and they've already boomed you all over the country. Why, Bill, I saw your picture in a trolley car in Denver—and you're only twenty-five years old! It's damn fine writing, I'll say it again, but that's not reason enough for this. You've got to go down deeper and look into your magazine's policy—which is to strike a balance for all kinds of middle-class readers and for their advertisers too. They've run some radical stuff this year, and they're booming you now to balance off, to show how 'safe and sane' they can be in the way they look at life, at big business and at industry—as you do here in the harbor. You're making gods out of the men at the top, you've seen 'em as they see themselves, and you've only seen what they see here. You've missed all the millions of people here who depend on the place for their jobs and their lives. They don't count for you—"

"That's not true at all!" I interrupted hotly. "It's just for them and their children that fellows like Dillon are on the job—to make a better harbor!"

"*For* them, *for* the people!" said Joe. "That's what I'm kicking at in you, Bill—you treat us all like a mass of dubs that need gods above to do everything *for* us because we can't do it all by ourselves!"

"I don't believe the people can," I retorted. "From what I've seen I honestly don't believe they count. The fellows that count in a job like this are the fellows with punch and grit enough to fight their way up out of the ranks—"

"I know, and be lieutenants and captains in a regular army of peace, with your friend Dillon in command and Wall Street in command of him! Isn't that your view?"

"All right, it is! I don't see any harm in that. It's the only safe way that I can see out of this mess of a harbor we've got. These men are the efficient ones—they're the fellows that have the brains and that know how to work—to use science, money, everything—to get a decent world ahead. What's the matter with efficiency?"

"Your latest god," sneered J. K.

"Suppose it is! What's wrong with it? What's the matter with Dillon? Is he a crook?"

"No," said Joe, "that's just the worst of him. He's so damned honest, he's such a hard worker. I've met men like him all over the country, and they're the most dangerous men we've got. Because they're the real strength of Wall Street—just as thousands of clean hard working priests are the strength of a rotten Catholic church! They keep their church going and Dillon keeps his—he's a regular priest of big business! And he takes hold of kids like you and molds your views like his for life. Look at what he has done with you here. Does he say a word to you about Graft? Does he talk of the North Atlantic Pool or any one of the other pools and schemes by which they keep up rates? Does he make you think about low wages and long hours and all the fellows hurt or killed on the docks and in the stoke holes? Does he give you any feeling at all of this harbor as a city of four million people, most of 'em getting a raw deal and getting mad about it? That's more important to you and me than all the efficiency gods on earth. You've got to decide which side you're on. And that's what's got me talking now. I see so plain which way you're letting yourself be pulled. I've seen so many pulled the same way. It's so pleasant up there at the top, there's so much money and brains up there and refinement—such women to get married to, such homes to settle down in. Sometimes I wish every promising radical kid in the country could get himself into some scandal that would cut him off for life from any chance of being received by this damned respectable upper class!"

He stopped for a moment, and then with a gruff intensity:

"We need you, Bill," he ended. "We need you bad. We don't want you to marry a girl at the top. We don't want you anchored up there for life."

We were standing still now, and I was looking out on the river. Through the grip of his hand on my arm I could feel his body taut and quivering, his whole spirit hot with revolt. The same old Joe, but tenser now, strained almost to the breaking point. But I myself was different. In college he had appealed to me because there I was groping and had found nothing. But now I had found something sure. And so, though to my own surprise a deep emotional part of me rose up in sudden response to Joe and made me feel guilty to hold back, it was only for a moment, and then my mind told me he was wrong. Poor old J. K. What a black distorted view he had—grown out of a distorted life of traveling continually from one center of trouble to another. How could he be any judge of life?

"Look here, Joe," I said. "I'm a kid, as you say, and some day I may see your side of this. But I don't now, I can't—for since I left Paris I've been through enough to make me feel what a job living is, I mean really living and growing. And I know what a difference Dillon has made. He has been to my life what he is to this harbor. And I'm not old enough nor strong enough to throw over a man as big as that and as honest and clean in his thinking, and throw myself in with your millions of people, who seem to me either mighty poor thinkers or fellows who don't think at all. They're not in my line. I believe in men who can think clean, who have trained their minds by years of hard work, who don't try to tear down and bring things to a smash, but are always building, building! You talk about this upper class. But they're my people, aren't they, that's where I was born. And I'm going on with them. I believe they're right and I know they're strong—I mean strong enough to handle all this—make it better."

"They'll make it worse," Joe answered. And then as he turned to me once more he added very bitterly, "You'll see strength enough in the people some day."

A few moments later he left me.

I looked at my watch and found it was not yet nine o'clock. I went to Eleanore Dillon. And within an hour Joe and his world of crowds and confusion were swept utterly out of my mind.

CHAPTER XVII

I had often told Eleanore of Joe. She had asked me about him many times. "It's queer," she had said, "what a hold he must have had on you. I feel sure he's just the kind of a person I wouldn't like and who wouldn't like me. I don't think he's really your kind either, and yet he has a hold on you still. Yes, he has, I can feel he has."

And to-night when I told her that I had been with him,

"What did he want of you?" she asked.

"He wants me to drop everything," I answered. And I tried to give her some idea of what he had said.

But as I talked, the thought came suddenly into my mind that here at last was the very time to settle my life one way or the other, to ask her if she would be my wife. I grew excited and confused, my voice sounding unnatural to my ears. And as I talked on about Joe, my heart pounding, I could barely keep the thoughts in line.

"And I don't want what he wants," I ended desperately. "That nor anything like it. I want just what I've been getting—just this kind of work and life. And I want *you*—for life, I mean—if you can ever feel like that."

Eleanore said nothing. In an instant the world and everything in it had narrowed to the two of us. The intensity was unbearable. I rose abruptly and turned away. I felt suddenly far out of my depth. Confusedly and furiously I felt that I had bungled things, that here was something in life so strange I could do nothing with it. What a young fool I was to have thought she could ever care for a fellow like me! I felt she must be smiling. Despairingly I turned to see.

And Eleanore was smiling—in a way that steadied me in a flash. For her smile was so plainly a quick, strong effort to steady herself.

"I'm glad you want me like that," she said, in a voice that did not sound like hers. "I don't believe in hiding things....I'm—very happy." She looked down at her hands in her lap and they slowly locked together. "But of course it means our whole lives, you see—and we mustn't hurry or make a mistake. Now that we know—this much—we can talk about it quite openly—about each other and what we want—what kinds of lives—what we believe in—whether we'd be best for each other. It's what we ought to talk about—a good many times—it may be weeks."

"All right," I agreed. I was utterly changed. At her first words I had felt a deep rush of relief, and seeing her tremendous pluck and the effort she was making, I pitied, worshiped and loved her all in the same moment. And as we talked on for a few minutes more in that grave and unnaturally sensible way about the pros and cons of it all, these feelings within me mounted so swiftly that all at once I again broke off.

"I don't believe there's any use in this," I declared. "It's perfectly idiotic!"

"Of course it is," she promptly agreed.

And then after a rigid instant when each of us looked at the other as though asking, "Quick! What are we going to do?"—she burst out laughing excitedly. So did I, and that carried her into my arms and—I remember nothing—until after a while she asked me to go, because she wanted to be by herself. And I noticed how bright and wet were her eyes.

I saw them still in the darkness down along the river front, where I walked for half the rest of the night, stopping to draw a deep breath of the sea and laugh excitedly and go on.

Life changed rapidly after that night. I grew so absorbed in Eleanore and in all that was waiting just ahead, that it was hard not to shut out everything else, most of all impersonal things. It was hard to write, and for days I wrote nothing. I remember only intimate talks. Everyone I talked to seemed to be deeply personal.

I told my father about it the next evening before supper. I found him in his old chair in the study buried deep in his paper.

"Say, Dad—would you mind coming up to your room?" He smote his paper to one side.

"What the devil," he asked, "do I want to come up to my room for?"

"I've—the fact is I've something you ought to know." I could hear Sue in the other room.

"All right, my boy," he said nervously. As he followed me he kept clearing his throat. Sue must have guessed and prepared him. In his room he fussed about, grunted hard over getting off his shoes and, finding his slippers, then lay back on his sofa with his hands behind his head and uttered an explosive sigh.

"All right, son, now fire ahead," he said jocosely. I loved him at that moment.

"You know Eleanore Dillon," I began.

"She turned you down!"

"No! She took me!"

"The devil you say!" He sat bolt upright, staring. "Well, my boy, I'm very glad," he said thickly. His eyes were moist. "I'm glad— glad! She's a fine girl—strong character—strong! I wish your poor mother were alive—she'd be happy—this girl will make a good wife—you must bring her right here to live with us!"

And so he talked on, his voice trembling. Then out of his confusion rose the money question, and at once his mind grew clear. And to my surprise he urged me to lose no time in looking around for "some good, steady position" in a magazine office. My writing I could do at night.

"It's so uncertain at best," he said. "It's nothing you can count on. And you've got to think of a wife and children. *Her* father has no money saved."

I found he'd been looking Dillon up, and this jarred on me horribly. But still worse was his lack of faith in my writing. I was making four hundred dollars a month, and it was a most unpleasant jolt to have it taken so lightly.

I went down to Sue. As I came into the living room she met me suddenly at the door. In a moment her arms were about my neck and she was saying softly:

"I know what it is, dear, and I'm glad—I'm awfully glad. If I've been horrid about it ever, please forgive me. I'm sure now it's just the life you want!"

And that evening, while Dad slept in his chair, Sue and I had a long affectionate talk. We drew closer than we had been for months. She was eager to hear everything, she wanted to know all our plans. When I tried at last to turn our talk to herself and our affairs at home, at first she would not hear to it.

"My dear boy," she said affectionately, "you've had these worries long enough. You're to run along now and be happy and leave this house to Dad and me."

I slipped my arm around her:

"Look here, Sis, let's see this right. You can't run here on what Dad earns, and if you try to work yourself you'll only hurt him terribly. My idea is to help as before, without letting him know that I'm doing it. Make him think you've cut expenses."

It took a long time to get her consent.

The next night I went to Eleanore's father. He received me quietly, and with a deep intensity under that steady smile of his, which reminded me so much of hers, he spoke of all she had meant to him and of her brave search for a big, happy life. He told how he had watched her with me slowly making up her mind.

"It took a long time, but it's made up now," he said. "And now that it is, she's the kind that will go through anything for you that can ever come up in your life." He looked at me squarely, still smiling a little, frankly letting his new affection come into his eyes. "I wish I knew all that's going to happen," he added, almost sadly. "I hope you'll get used to telling me things—talking things over—anything—no matter what—where I can be of the slightest help."

Then he, too, spoke of money. He meant to keep up her allowance, he said, and he had insured his life for her. Again, as with my father, I felt that disturbing lack of faith in my work. I spoke of it to Eleanore and she looked at me indignantly.

"You must never think of it like that," she said. "I won't have you writing for money. Dad has never worked that way and you're not to do it on any account—least of all on account of me. Whatever you make we'll live on, and that's all there is to be said—except that we'll live splendidly," she added very gaily, "and we won't spend the finest part of our lives saving up for rainy days. We'll take care of the rain when it rains, and we'll have some wonderful times while we can."

We decided at once on a trip abroad as soon as I had finished my work. And I remember writing hard, and reading it aloud to her and rewriting over and over again, for Eleanore could be severe. But I remember, too, more trips in her boat to gather the last odds and ends. I remember how the big harbor took on a new glory to our eyes, mingled with all the deep personal joys and small troubles and crises we went through, the puzzles and the questionings and the glad discoveries that made up the swift growth of our love.

And though I never once thought of Joe Kramer, he had prophesied aright. I belonged wholly now to Dillon's world, a world of clean vigorous order that seemed to welcome me the more as I wrote in praise of its power. And happy over my success, and in love and starting life anew with all the signs so bright—how could I have any doubts of my harbor?

We were married very quietly late one April afternoon. It rained, I remember, all that day, but the next was bright and clear for our sailing. In our small stateroom on the ship we found a note from the company, a large, engraved impressive affair, presenting their best wishes and asking us to accept for the voyage one of their most luxurious cabins.

"This is what comes," said Eleanore gaily, "of being the wife of a writer."

"Or the daughter," I said softly, "of a very wonderful engineer."

"You darling boy!"

We moved up to a large sunny cabin. I remember her swiftly reading the telegrams and letters there as though to get them all out of the way. I remember her unpacking and taking possession of our first home.

"We're married, aren't we," said a voice.

There was only one more good-by to be said. On the deck, as we went out of the harbor, Eleanore stood by the rail. I felt her hand close tight on mine and I saw her eyes glisten a little with tears.

"What a splendid place it has been," she said.

CHAPTER XVIII

We found every place splendid in those weeks as we let the wanderlust carry us on. And as though emerging from some vivid dream, various places and faces of people stand out in my memory now, as then they loomed in upon our absorption.

I remember the little old harbor of Cherbourg, gleaming in the moonlight, where when we landed Eleanore said, "Let's stay here awhile." So of course we did, and then went on to Paris. We took an apartment, very French and absurdly small, from a former Beaux Arts friend of mine. I remember the kindly face of the maid who took such beaming care of us, the café in front of which late at night we sat and watched the huge shadowy carts go by on their way to the market halls, the sunrise flower market, where we filled our cab with moss roses and plants, Polin's songs in the "Ambassadeurs," delicious petites allées in the Bois, our favorite rides on the tops of the 'buses, that old religious place of mine down under the bridge by Notre Dame.

All these and more we saw in fragments, now and then, looking out with vivid interest on all the life around us, only to return to each other, *into* each other I should say, for the exploring was quite different now, there had been such hours between us that nothing intimate could be held back. Nothing? Well, nothing that I thought of then. For somehow or other, in those glad, eager afternoons and evenings, in those nights, nothing disturbingly ugly in me so much as thought of showing its head. Three years before in this stirring town I had felt guilty at being a monk. But now I felt no guilt at all. For down the Champs Élysées our cab rolled serenely now, and even our driver's white hat wore an air as though it had a place in life.

From Paris we started for Munich, but we did not stop there, we happened to feel like going on. So we went through to Constantinople, whence we took a boat to Batoum and went up into the Caucasus, which Eleanore had heard about once from an engineer friend of her father's. I remember Koutais, a little town by a mountain torrent with gray vine-covered walls around it. Shops opened into the walls like stalls. There we would buy things for our supper and then in a crazy vehicle we would drive miles out on the broad mountainside to an orchard pink with blossoms, where we would build a fire and cook, and an old man in a long yellow robe and with a turban on his head would come out of his cabin and bring us wine. And the stars would appear and the frogs tune up in the marshes far down in the valley below, and the filmy mists would rise and the mountains would tower overhead. And the effect of this place upon us was to make us feel it was only one of innumerable such vacation places that lay ahead, festival spots in long, radiant lives. We felt this vaguely, silently. So often we talked silently.

Then there would come the most serious times, when with the deepest thoughtfulness we would survey the years ahead and very solemnly place ourselves, our views and beliefs. Miraculous how agreed we were! We believed, we found, in good workmanship, in honest building, in getting things done. We believed in Eleanore's father and all those around and above him that could help his kind of work. We were impatient of soft-headedness in rich people who had nothing to do, and of heavy muddle-headedness in the millions who had too much to do, and of muckraking of every kind which only got in the way of the builders. For the building of a new, clean vigorous world was our religion. And it did not seem cold to us, because our lives were in it and because we were in love.

There was no end to the plans for ourselves, for my writing, our home, the friends we wanted, the trips, the books and the music. And through it all and from under it all there kept bursting up that feeling which we knew was the most important of all, the exultant realization that we two were just starting out.

When at last we came back home this feeling took a deeper turn. I noticed a change in Eleanore. She had far less thought and time for me now, she seemed to be strangely absorbed in herself.

Nearly all her time and strength were given to our small apartment, in the same building as that of her father. By countless feminine touches she was making it look like the home she had planned. She was getting all in order. And then one night she told me why. Her arms were close around me and her voice was so low I could barely hear:

"There's going to be another soon—another one *of us*—do you hear?—a very tiny blessed one."

I held her slowly tighter.

"Oh, my darling girl," I whispered.

Suddenly I relaxed my hold, for I was afraid of hurting her now. In a moment all was so utterly changed. And as in that brave, quiet way of hers she looked smiling steadily into my eyes, my throat contracted sharply. For into my mind leaped the memory of what the harbor had shown to me on that sultry hideous summer night in the tenement over in Brooklyn. And *that* must happen to *my wife!*

"Oh, my dear," she whispered, "if you only knew how much strength I stored up way over there in the mountains."

So she had been thinking of this even then, and yet had told me nothing!

Here was the beginning of a long anxious period. Month after month I watched her quietly preparing. Slowly we drew into ourselves, while her father and mine and Sue and our friends came and went, but mattered little. I wondered if Dillon ever felt this. As he came down to us in the evenings from the apartment upstairs, where he and Eleanore had meant so much to each other only a year before, he gave no sign that he saw any change. But one night after he had gone, Eleanore happened to pick up the evening paper which had dropped from his bulging overcoat pocket.

"Billy, come here," she said presently.

"What is it?"

"Look at this."

The President of the United States had gone with Eleanore's father that day in a revenue cutter over the harbor and had spoken of Dillon's great dream in vigorous terms of approval.

"And father was here this evening," said Eleanore very slowly, "and yet he never told me a word. He saw that I'd heard nothing and he thought I didn't care. Oh, Billy, I feel so ashamed."

But she soon forgot the incident.

My suspense grew sharp as the time drew near. I had a good doctor, I was sure of that, and he told me he had an excellent nurse. But what good were all these puny precautions? The tenement room in Brooklyn kept rising in my mind.

She sat by the window that last night, and looking down on the far-away lights of the river we planned another trip abroad.

A few hours later I stood over her, holding her hand, and with her white lips pressed close together and her eyes shut, she went through one of those terrible spasms. Then she looked up in the moment's relief. And suddenly here was that smile of hers. And she said low, between clenched teeth,

"Well, dearie, another starting out—"

CHAPTER XIX

The next morning, after the rush of relief at the news of Eleanore's safety and the strange sight of our tiny son, I felt keyed gloriously high, ready for anything under the sun. But there seemed to be nothing whatever to do, I felt in the way each time that I moved, so I took to my old refuge, work. And then into my small workroom came Eleanore's father for a long talk. He too had been up all night, his lean face was heavily marked from the strain, but their usual deep serenity had come back into his quiet eyes.

"Let's take a day off," he said, smiling. "We're both so tired we don't know it."

"Tired?" I demanded.

"Yes," he said, "you're tired—more than you've ever been in your life. You'll feel like a rag by to-morrow, and then I hope you'll take a good rest. But to-day, while you are still way up, I want to talk about your work. Do you mind?"

"Mind? No," I replied, a bit anxiously. "It's just what I'm trying to figure out."

"I know you are. You've figured for months and you've worked yourself thin. I don't mind that, I like it, because I know the reason. But I don't think the result has been good. It seems to me you've been so anxious to get on, because of this large family of yours, that you've shut yourself up and written too fast, you've gotten rather away from life. Shall I go right on?"

"Yes," I said, watching intently.

"Well," he continued, "you've been using what name you've already made and writing short stories of harbor life."

"That's what the editors want," I said. "When a man makes a hit in one vein of writing they want that and nothing else."

"At this rate you'll soon work out the vein," he said. "I'd like to see you stop writing now, take time to find new ground—and dig."

"There's not an awful lot of time," I remarked.

"My plan won't stop your making money," he replied. "I want you to write less, but get more pay."

"That sounds attractive. How shall I do it?"

"By writing about big men," he said. "I suggest that you try a series of portraits of some of the big Americans and the America they know."

I jumped up so suddenly he started.

"What's the matter?" he asked with a glance at the door. "Did you hear anything?"

"Yes," I said excitedly. "I heard a stunning title! The America They Know!"

We discussed it all that morning and it appealed to me more and more. Later on, with Eleanore's help (for she grew stronger fast those days), I prevailed upon her father to let me practice upon himself as my first subject. I worked fast, my material right at hand, and within a few weeks I had written the story of those significant incidents out of thirty years of work and wanderings east and west that showed the America he had known, his widening view. I did his portrait, so to speak, with his back to the reader, letting the reader see what he saw. This story I sold promptly, and under the tonic of that success I went into the work with zest and vim.

It filled the next four years of my life. It took the view I had had of the harbor and widened it to embrace the whole land, which I now saw altogether through the eyes of the men at the top.

The most central figure of them all, and by far the most difficult to attack, was a powerful New York banker, one of those invisible gods whose hand I had felt on the harbor.

"The value of him to you," Dillon said, "is that if you can only make him talk you'll find him a born storyteller. The secret scandal of his life is that once in a short vacation he tried to write a play."

It was weeks before he would see me, and I had my first interview at last only by getting on a night train which he had taken for Cleveland. There in his stateroom, cornered, he received me with a grim reluctance. And with a humorous glint in his eyes,

"How much do you know about banking?" he asked.

"Nothing," I said frankly. And then I took a sudden chance. "What do you know about writing?" I asked.

"Nothing," he said placidly.

"Is that true? I thought you once wrote a play." He sat up very quickly. "If you did," I went on, "you've probably read some of Shakespeare's stuff. It was strong stuff about strong men. If he were alive he'd write about you, but I'm sure that he wouldn't know about banking. That's only your job."

"What do you want of me, young man?" he inquired. "Is it my soul?"

"Not at all," I answered. "It's the America you know, expressed in such simple human terms that even a young ignoramus like me will be able to understand it. Out of this big country a good many thousands of men, I suppose, have come to you for money. Which are the most significant ones?"

And I went on to explain my idea. Soon it began to take hold of him. We talked until after midnight, and later we had other talks. It was hard at first in the questioning to dodge the technical side of it all, the widely intricate workings of that machine of credit of which he was chief engineer. But as he saw how eager I was to feel his view and become enthused, by degrees he humanized it all. And not only that, he trusted me, he gave me the most intimate glimpses into this life of big money, although when I dared to include such bits in the story that I showed him he calmly scratched them out and said:

"You're mistaken, young man. I didn't say that."

As he talked I saw again that vision I had had on the North River docks. For into this man's office had come the men of the mines, the factories and the mills, the promoters of vast irrigations on prairies, builders of railroads, real estate plungers, street traction promoters, department store owners, newspaper proprietors, politicians—the builders and boomers, the strong energetic men of the land. He showed me their power and made me feel it was still but in its infancy. He made me feel a dazzling future rushing upon us, a future of plenty still more controlled by the keen minds and wide visions of the powerful men at the top.

Of all these men and the rushing world of power they lived in, I have only a jumble of memories now. For my own life was a jumble—irregular, crowded and intense. In their offices, clubs and homes, in their motors, on yachts and trains, in Chicago and Pittsburgh and other cities, I followed them, making my time suit theirs. Some had no use for me at all, but I found others delighted to talk—like the great Dakota ranchman who ordered twenty thousand copies of the issue in which his story appeared and scattered them like seeds of fame over the various counties of wheat, corn and alfalfa he owned. And in the main I had little trouble. I met often that curious respect which so many men of affairs seem to have, God knows why, for a successful writer.

I got in where men with ten times my knowledge were barred. I remember with a touch of shame the institute of scientific research where the chief of the place took a whole afternoon to show me around, and while I looked wise and tried to feel thrilled over glass tubes and jars and microscopes through which I peered at microbes, a simple old country doctor, one of the thousands of *common* visitors, by my invitation followed humbly in my wake, murmuring from time to time,

"Miraculous, by George, astounding!" And gratefully pressing my hand at the end, "This has been the chance of a lifetime," he said.

Perhaps the principal reason why I got so warm a welcome was the name I had already made as a writer of glory stories. I liked these men; I liked to enthuse over all the big things they were doing. And still true to my efficiency god, the immense importance of getting things done loomed so high in my view of life as to overshadow everything else. My sense of moral values changed.

It was a strange unmoral world.

In the institute of science these keen laboratory gods (who had seemed so cold and comfortless to me but a few short years ago) were perfecting a cure for syphilis. Strong men were removing the wages of sin!

In Chicago I met the president of a huge industrial company who had found it necessary at times to use money on politicians. For this he had been sent to jail, but later his influence got him out. Promptly he was made treasurer of another company. In one year, through his energy, now more intense than ever, the business of that company increased some thirty-five per cent., whereupon the directors of the original corporation, after a stormy meeting in which two church deacon directors fussed and fumed considerably, unanimously decided to ask him to come back. He did. He told me the story quite frankly himself. I admired him tremendously.

The head of a mining company sat in his office one afternoon and talked of the labor problem. There was no right or wrong involved, he said, it was simply a matter of force. Once when a strike threatened he had called in a "labor expert" who had used money wholesale and there had been no strike.

"Well?" he asked, smiling. "What do you think of it?"

"I think I can't print it." He still smiled.

"Naturally not. But what do you think? If you yourself were responsible to several hundred stockholders, what would you do? Risk a strike that might wipe out their dividends? Or would you resort to bribery"—his smile slowly deepened—"which is a penal offense in this State?"

I found such questions cropping up almost everywhere I went. In their dealings with the public and still more with their rivals, there was a ruthless vigor that swept old-fashioned maxims aside. And I liked this, for it got things done! I was bored to find, as I often did, these men in their homes quite old-fashioned again to suit sober old wives who still went to church. I remember one such elderly lady and the shock I unwittingly gave her. She had deplored the decline of churches; her own, she said, was barely half full. And I then tried to cheer her by an account of my last story, which was of an advertising man, a genius who in the last two years had made churches his especial line and by his up-to-date methods had packed church after church on a commission basis. Her burst of disapproval almost drove me from the house. And there were so many homes like that. Men who were perfect giants by day would become the gentlest babies at night, allowing their wives to read to them such sentimental drivel as would have been kicked from the office by day.

"But God knows they need such vacuous homes," I reflected, "to rest in."

I had never dreamed before how strenuous men's lives could be. One day in the New York office of a big plunger in real estate I pointed to a map on the wall.

"What are all those lots marked 'vacant' for?" I asked him.

"I never saw many vacant lots in that part of town." He grinned cheerfully.

"Anything under four stories is vacant to us," he answered, "because it pays to buy it, tear it down and build something higher."

That was the way they crowded their cities, and as with their cities, so with their lives. One story that interested me most was of the weird America which a renowned nerve specialist knew. To him came these men broken down, some on the verge of insanity. He gave me stories of their lives, of his glimpses into their straining minds, he described their pathetic efforts to rest, their strenuous attempts to relax. He himself had some mysterious ailment, his hands kept trembling while he talked. His wife said he hadn't had a vacation of over a week in eleven years.

From such men I would turn to exuberant lives, like that of the Tammany leader now dead, who gave a ten-thousand-dollar banquet one night, in the Ten Eyck in Albany, in honor of the newsboy who every morning for twenty-two winters had brought morning papers to him in bed in his hotel room. Or like that of the millionaire merchant who told me with the most naïve pride of the eleven hundred electric lights in his new home on Fifth Avenue, and of how the bathrooms of both his large daughters were fitted in solid silver throughout.

"Not plated, understand," he said. "I told the architect while he was at it to put in the real solid stuff—and plenty of it!"

Through this varied throng of successes, this rich abundance of types, I ranged with an ever deepening zest. As a hunter of game I watched that endless human procession on and off the front pages of papers, the men who were for the moment news. Often small people too would be there—like the telephone girl from a suburb, who for one day, as the most important witness in a sensational case of graft, was suddenly before the whole country and then as suddenly dropped out of sight. In fact, that was now my view of the land, figures emerging from dark obscure multitudes up into a bright circle of light.

And I took this front-page view of New York. I saw it as a city where big exceptional people were endlessly doing sensational things, both in the making and spending of money. I saw it not only as a cluster of tall buildings far downtown, but uptown as well a towering pile of rich hotels and apartments, a region that sparkled gaily at night, lights flashing from tens of thousands of rooms, in and out of which, I felt delightedly, millions of people had passed through the years. I loved to look up at these windows at night, at the sheer inscrutability of them. For behind these twinkling masses I knew were all things tragic, comic—people laughing, fighting, hating, scheming, dreaming, loving, living. I thought of that row of cabins de luxe that I had seen on the Christmas boat. Here was the same thing magnified, a monstrous caravansary with but one question over its doors: "Have You Got the Price?"

Once I had seen a harbor. Then it had grown into a port. And now I saw a metropolis, the hub of a successful land.

And through this gay city of triumph I moved, myself a success, and my view of the whole was colored by that. My life as an observer was sprinkled with personal moments that made me see everything in high lights. I would watch the life of a street full of people, and I myself would be on my way to an interview with some noted man or coming away from one who had given me stuff that I knew would write up big—I knew just how! Or at a corner newsstand I would catch a glimpse of my name on the cover of some magazine. Again I would be hurrying home, or into a neighboring florist's or a theater ticket office, or diving into the jolly whirl of the large Fifth Avenue toy shop in which I took an unflagging delight. In my mind would be thoughts of a pillow fight or a long evening with Eleanore, or we would be having friends to dine or going out to dinner.

For Eleanore had been swift to use my success to broaden both our lives. Young and adorably happy, eagerly alive, she did for me what she had done for her father, filling my life with other lives. She was an artist in living. It was a joy to see her make out a list of people to be asked to dine. Her father, once watching the process, remarked to me in low, solemn tones:

"She's a regular social chemist—who has never had an explosion."

He was often on the list, and through him and his many friends and the ones I made through my writing, by degrees our circle widened. We met all kinds of people, for Eleanore hated "sets" and "cliques." We met not only successful men but (God help us sometimes) we also met their wives. We met successful writers, artists and musicians, and a few people of the stage. We met visitors from the West and from half the big cities of Europe. We furbished up our French and German, our knowledge of books and pictures and plays—*successful* books and pictures and plays.

Through Eleanore's father and his work our minds were still held to the past, to the harbor which had taken me, bruised and blind and petty, and lifted me up and taught me to live, had given me my work, my home and my new god. I was grateful, I was proud, I was in love and I felt strong. And my view of the harbor in those days was of a glorious symbol of the power of mind over matter, and of the mighty speeding up of a world of civilization and peace, a successful world, strong, broad, tolerant, sweeping on and bearing us with it.

So we adventured gaily, not deeper down, but higher and higher up into life.

actors and musicians, and a few people of the place. We had our
own from the West and from half the big cities of Europe. We the
booking out French and German, now now and then a book, and
pictures and music — music, all books and pictures and plays.

Finally, I became a author and his wife, the visitors were all
head to the past to the fashion stock had to keep up, to keep up,
published myself, and then the opaque impulse to live, back over
me, the world, my home and my new son, I was unable, I was
going over its world and their origin. And my view of the harbor
in those days was of a climate symbol of the power of mind over
matter, and of the country speedily, up to a world of mind, a
and peace, a safe, safer world, a royal, bread, to grain, savory and
on and learning to win it.

So we maneuvered and waited therein and winning, higher and higher
up into life.

BOOK III

BOOK III

CHAPTER I

We had been married four years.

At the end of a crisp November day I was just about starting home. I remember how keenly alive I felt, how tingling with bodily health, and above all how successful.

I had had such a successful day. I had written hard all morning and my work had been going splendidly. I had lunched downtown with the man whose life I was writing that month, a man of astounding fertility, who had started fifteen years ago with a small hotel in a western town, had made money, had built a larger hotel, had made money, had moved to a larger town and bought a still larger hotel, had made money, had moved to Chicago, New York, had made money. And the America he knew was made up of people who themselves had made their money so suddenly they had to come to hotels to spend it. The stories that he told me, both scandalous and otherwise, of these men and women who shot up rich and diamondy out of this booming country of ours, had a range and a richness of color that had held me delighted through many long talks. During luncheon he had told some of his best, and had given me permission to print, with a discreet twist or so to disguise them, certain intimate episodes in the first fat years of men whose names were by-words now all over the land. I could already see that story selling on the newsstands.

From this man I had come uptown to a branch of the Y. M. C. A., where after an hour of hand-ball and a plunge in the swimming tank I had gone to a room downstairs, to which ambitious youngsters came for free advice from an expert who told them how to get on in life. His room was a confessional. He would cross-examine each suppliant hard, make a diagnosis of each one and then give him advice as to what to do—whether or not to throw over his job, what kind of work he was suited for best. The America he knew was made up of these small human units, some pitiably or absurdly small, but all anxiously straining upward. And they too appealed to me.

For I was so successful now that I was growing mellow. From certain big men I had written about I had taken a spacious breadth of view that included a deep indulgence for all these skurrying pigmies. Poor little devils, give 'em a chance, especially those among them who had "bim" enough to want a chance, to wonder why they were not getting on and want to do something about it. And so I had formed the habit of dropping in often at this room, hearing its confessions and now and then helping get someone a job. As the swimming tank made my body tingle, so this place affected my soul. It warmed me to do all I could for some fellow, some decent kid who was down on his luck. Besides, some confessions were gems of their kind, glimpses into human lives, hard struggles, wild ambitions. I meant to write them up some day. In fact, I meant to write everything up, I felt everything waiting for my pen.

And as I went down to the coat-room, the thought I had had so often lately came again into my mind. I too would soon throw over my job, leave articles and write fiction—my old Paris dream. But what a wide and varied experience of life I had gathered since those ingenuous Paris days. Yes, I would do it real and big, out of the big life I had known. And my heroes would no longer be watching at my elbow to point to the choicest bits and say, "You're mistaken, young man, I never said that." No, all those lifelike human touches would stay in. Stories kept coming up in my mind, one especially of late. As I stood in line for my hat and coat I thought of it now and grew so absorbed I forgot that I was standing in a line of insignificant clerks—until the one ahead of me, who had just come in from the street, asked the chap in front of him:

"Say, Gus, did you see the suffragettes? Their parade's just going by."

This brought me down from the clouds with a jerk. For I had meant to see that parade. Sue was in it, in it hard. Suffrage was her latest fad.

"Naw," growled Gus. "If I was the mayor and they came to me for a permit to march I'd tell 'em to go and buy corsets. That's their complaint. They can't get kissed so they want to vote." The other one chuckled:

"I saw one who can have my vote—and all I'll ask is a better look. Believe me, some silk stockings!"

As they went away I glared after them. "Damn little muts," I thought. I was rather in favor of suffrage, at least I felt indulgent about it. Why shouldn't I be? The great thing was to keep your mind open and kindly; to feel contempt for nothing whatever. And because I felt contempt for no thing or person in all the world, I now glared with the most utter contempt on these narrow-minded little clerks.

Then I hurried out and over to Fifth Avenue, where the throb of the drums was still to be heard. And there I found to my surprise that in a very real sense this parade was different from anything that I had ever seen before. I was more than indulgent, I was excited. And by what? Not by the marching lines of figures, fluttering banners, booming bands, nor just by the fact that these marchers were women, and women quite frankly dressed for effect, so that the whole rhythmic mass had a feminine color and dash that made it all gay and delightful. No, there was something deeper. And that something, I finally made out, was this. These women and girls were all deeply thrilled by the feeling that for the first time in their lives they were doing something all together—for an idea that each one of them had thought rather big and stirring before, but now, as each felt herself a part of this moving, swinging multitude, she felt the idea suddenly loom so infinitely larger and more compelling than before that she herself was astounded. Here for the first time in my life I felt the power of mass action.

And as presently I started home and the intensity of it was gone, there was an added pleasure to me in remembering how I had felt it. Another proof of my breadth of mind. I hurried home to dinner.

As I entered our apartment I gave a long, low mysterious whistle. And after a moment another whistle, which tried hard to be mysterious, answered mine from another room. Then there were stealthy footsteps which ended in a sudden charge, and my wee son, "the Indian," hurled me onto a sofa, where, to use his expression, we "rush-housed" each other. We did this almost every night.

When the big time was about over Eleanore appeared:

"Come, Indian, it's time for bed." She led him off protesting and blew me back a kiss from the door.

She had developed wonderfully, this bewitching wife of mine, this quiet able one in her work, this smiling humorous one in her life, this watchful, joyous, intimate one in the hours that shut everything out. Sue said I idolized my wife, that I saw her all perfection, "without one redeeming vice." Not at all. I knew her vices well enough. I knew she could get distinctly cross when a new gown came home all wrong. I knew that she could lie to me, I had caught her at it several times when she said she was feeling finely and then confessed to me the next day, "I had a splitting headache last night." In fact, she had any number of vices—queer, mysterious feminine moods when she quite shamelessly shut me out. She didn't half take care of herself, she went places when she should have stayed at home. And finally, she was slow at dressing. Placidly seated in front of her mirror she could spend an entire hour in doing her soft luxuriant hair.

I went over all these vices now as I lay back on the sofa. Idolize her? Not at all. I knew her. We were married, thank God.

Then she came back into the room. She was smiling in rather a curious way, an expectant way, and I noticed that her color was unusually high. Eleanore always dressed so well, but to-night she had outdone herself. From her trim blue satin slippers to the demure little band of blue at her throat she was more enchantingly fresh than ever. Suffragettes and that sort of thing were all very well on the Avenue. Give me Eleanore at home.

"Did you see the parade?" she inquired.

"Yes."

"Did you see me?"

I fairly jumped!

"You?" I demanded. "Were you in that march?"

"I most certainly was," she said quietly. Having shot her bolt she was regarding me gravely now, with the merest glint of amused delight somewhere in her gray-blue eyes. "Why not?" she asked. "I believe in it, I want the vote. Why shouldn't I march?

I paraded," she added serenely, "in the college section right up near the head of the line. That's why I'm home so early. I'm afraid I was quite conspicuous, for you see I'm rather small and I had to take long swinging strides to keep in step. But I soon got used to it, and I thoroughly enjoyed the cheers. We waved back at them with our flags."

"But," I cried, "my darling wife! Why didn't you tell me about it ahead?"

"Because"—she came close up to me and said quite confidentially, "we do these things all by ourselves. You don't mean to say that you mind it, dear?"

I lost about five seconds and then I did exactly right. I took her in my arms and laughed and called my wife by many names and said she couldn't worry me, that I didn't mind it in the least, was proud of her and so on. In short, to use a slang expression, I distinctly got away with it. Moreover, I soon felt what I said. I was honestly rather proud of my wife for having had the nerve to march. It must have been quite a struggle, for she was no born marcher.

And I was glad that I was proud. Another proof of my tolerance—which was the more grateful to me just now because a magazine man I admired had genially hinted the other day that I was rather narrow.

"Did you see Sue?" I inquired.

"Only for a moment," she said. "Sue was one of the marshals and she was all up and down the lines. She's coming to supper with many paraders."

"A crowd of women here? I'm off!"

"No you're not. She's bringing some men paraders too."

Men paraders! Now I could smile. I had earned the right, I had been broad. But after all, there are limits. I could see those chaps parading with women. I knew them, I had seen them before, for Sue had often brought them here. I enjoyed myself immensely—till Eleanore shot another bolt.

"Smile on, funny one," she said. "You'll be in line yourself in a year."

"I will not be in line!"

"I wonder." She looked at me in a curious way. The mirth went slowly out of her eyes. "There are so many queer new ideas crowding in all around us," she said. "And I know you, Billy, oh, so well—so much better than you know yourself. I know that when you once feel a thing you're just the kind to go into it hard. I'm not speaking of suffrage now—that's only one nice little part. I mean this whole big radical movement—all the kind of thing your friend Joe Kramer stood for." She put her arms about my neck. "Don't get too radical, husband mine—you're so nice and funny now, my love."

I regarded her anxiously:

"Has this parade gone to your head—or has Sue been talking to you again?"

"I lunched with Sue——"

"I knew it! And now she's coming here to supper—bringing men paraders!"

"And they'll all be rabidly hungry," said Eleanore with a sudden change. She went quickly in to see the cook and left me to grim meditation.

I a radical? I smiled. And my slight uneasiness passed away, as I thought about my sister.

CHAPTER II

Poor old Sue. What queer friends she had, what a muddled life compared to ours. What a vague confused development, jumping from one idea to another, never seeing any job through, forever starting all over again with the same feverish absorption in the next new radical fad. High-brow dramatics, the settlement movement, the post-impressionists, socialism, votes for women, one thing after the other pell mell. She would work herself all up, live hard, talk, organize, think and feel till her nerves went all to pieces, and then she would come to us for a rest and laugh at us for our restfulness and at herself for the state she was in. That was one thing at least she had learned—to laugh at herself—she could be deliciously humorous. And Eleanore, meeting her on that ground, would quiet her and steady her down.

We had grown very fond of Sue. We knew her life was not easy at home. Alone over there with poor old Dad and feeling herself anchored down, she would still at intervals rebel—against his sticking to his dull job, against her own dependence, against the small monthly allowance which without my father's knowledge they still had from me.

"Let me earn my own living!" she would exclaim. "Why shouldn't I? I'm twenty-six—and I'm working hard enough as it is—the Lord knows! I'm organizing every day and making speeches half my nights. Other girls take pay for that. Now Father, please be sensible. I'm going to take a good salaried job."

But then Dad, whose mind was so old and rigid, so much less tolerant than mine, would grow excited or, still worse, ashamed that he couldn't make money enough to give her all she wanted. And that desperate hungry love with which he clung to her these latter days would in the end make her give in. For under all her radical talk Sue had the kindest heart in the world.

Eleanore did her best to help. She was always having Dad over to dinner, and we had a room which she called his, where he would come and stay the week-end. At six o'clock each Saturday night he would arrive with his satchel.

"Daughter-in-law," he would announce, "my other daughter's *agin* the law, she's gone off revolooting. Can you take a decent old gentleman in out of the last century? Don't change any plans on my account. If you're going out to dinner just tell the cook to give me a snack and a cup of tea, and then I'll light a good cigar and read the works of my great son. Go right ahead as if I wasn't here."

If we had he would have been furious. Eleanore always made it his night—and no quiet evening, either. When we didn't take him out to a play she invited people to dinner—young people, for he liked them best. And late on Sunday morning the "Indian" would wake him up, would watch him shave and dress and breakfast, and then they would be off to the Park. We had named our small son after Dad and they were the most splendid chums. They had any number of secrets.

Eleanore too had made Sue use our apartment. Sue called it her Manhattan club and brought her friends here now and then—"to stir you people up," she said. But this did not disturb me, I felt too secure in life. And with a safe, amused and slightly curious attitude I found Sue quite a tonic. I liked to hear her knock my big men in her cocksure superior way. It was mighty good fun. And every now and then by mistake she would hit on something that was true.

I found something too in her ideas. This suffrage business, for example. She had stuck to this hobby quite a while, and through it she had reached the conviction that women would never get the vote until the great mass of working girls were drawn into the movement. So she had gone in for working girls' clubs, and from clubs into trade unions and from trade unions into strikes. There had been a strike of laundry girls which for a week was the talk of the town. Sue and some of her suffrage friends had organized meetings every night, and in a borrowed automobile she had rushed from meeting to meeting with two laundry women, meager forlorn-looking creatures who stood up much embarrassed and awkwardly told about their lives. One of them, a young widow, had gone home from work one night at eleven and found that her small baby had died of convulsions during her absence. It was grim, terrible stuff of its kind, and Sue was so intensely wrought up you'd have thought there was nothing else in the world. But the strike stopped as suddenly as it began, and the two women whose names she had brought into headlines were refused jobs wherever they went. Sue tried to help them for a while, until this suffrage parade came along, when she went into this equally hard and quite forgot their existence.

And then Eleanore took them up. Quietly and as a matter of course, she took their troubles on her hands, sent one to a hospital and got the other work, looked into their wretched home affairs and had them come often to see her. And this kind of thing was happening often, Sue taking up and dropping what Eleanore then took up and put through. I compared them with a glow of pride.

Eleanore's way was so sane and sure. She looked upon society much as she did upon our son, who had frequent little ailments but through them all what a glorious growth, to watch it was a perpetual joy. I remember once, when in his young stomach there were some fearful goings on, Eleanore's remarking:

"Now if Sue had a child with a stomach in trouble, I suppose her way would be to quickly remove the entire stomach and put some new radical thing in its place."

And then she went to the medicine chest, and a vastly comforted Indian was soon cheerfully sitting up in bed.

Eleanore could help others, I felt, because she had first helped herself, had tackled the mote in her own eye, from the time when she had gone down to the harbor to get her roots, as she called it. She was a wonderful manager, our budget was carefully worked out. And she had herself so well in hand she could put herself behind herself and smile clearly out on life.

"When Eleanore takes up a charity case," said her father, "she turns it into a person at once, and later into an intimate friend."

He himself took a quiet interest in all her charity cases. They would often talk them over at night, and in his easy careless way he would turn over all his spare money to help in the work.

Eleanore would protest at times, and tell him how utterly foolish he was in not putting money aside for himself. But soon, deep in another case of poignant human misery, she would throw all caution to the winds and use her father's money—every dollar he could spare. That was another vice she had.

How she hated all the red tape in that huge network of institutions by which New York City provides "relief." She never dropped a case of hers into that cumbrous relief machine and then let it slip out of her sight. She did the hard thing, she followed it up. She had learned, as I had in my work, to "get on the inside" of this secretive city, to go to the gods behind it all and so have her cases shoved. One day when one of them, a woman, was in a hospital so desperately ill that her very life depended on being moved to a private room—"It can't be done," said the superintendent. Eleanore took the subway downtown to the Wall Street office of the man who was the hospital's principal backer. She found his outer office crowded with men who were waiting to see him on business. "He can't see you," she was told. Then she scribbled this on her card:

"I want none of your money, a little of your influence and one minute of your time on behalf of a woman who is dying."

About twenty minutes later that woman was in a private room.

It is hard to stop talking about my wife. But to return to my sister:

Into my reverie that night Sue burst with a dozen radical friends. Others kept arriving, and our small rooms were soon a riot of color and chatter. Banners were stacked against the wall, bright yellow ribbons were everywhere, faces were flushed and happily tired. Eleanore sat at her coffee urn, cups and saucers and plates went around, and people still too excited to rest stood about eating hungrily. The talking was fast and furious now. I listened, watched their faces.

These "radicals," it seemed to me, had talked straight on both day and night ever since the evenings years ago when one of their earliest coteries had gathered in our Brooklyn home. And talking they had multiplied and ramified all over the town. There was nothing under heaven their fingers did not itch to change. Here close by my side were three of them, two would-be Ibsen actresses

and one budding playwright who had had two Broadway failures and one Berkeley Lyceum success. But were they talking of
plays? Not at all. They talked of the Russian Revolution. It had
died down in the last few years, and they wanted to help stir it up
again by throwing some more American money into the smolder-
ing embers. To do this they planned to whip into new life "The
Friends of Russian Freedom."

That was it, I told myself, these people were all friends of revolutions. Vaguely as I watched them now I felt I was seeing the
parlor side, the light and fluffy outer fringe, of something rather
dangerous. I thought again of that parade and my impression of
mass force. No danger in that, it was dressy and safe. But some of
these youngsters did not stop there, they went in for stirring up
people in rags, mass force of a very different kind. Here was a
sculptor socialist who openly bragged that he'd had a hand in filling Union Square one day with a seething mass of unemployed,
and then when some poor crazed fanatic threw a bomb, our
socialist friend, as he himself smilingly put it, never once stopped
running until he reached his studio.

It was this kind of thing that got on my nerves. For I pitied the
unwieldy poor, the numberless muddle-headed crowds down
there in the tenements, and it seemed to me perfectly criminal
that a lot of these young highbrows should be allowed to stir
them up. Their own thinking was so muddled, their views of life
so out of gear.

I a radical? No chance!

While they chattered on excitedly, I thought of my trip uptown
on the "El" that afternoon, a trip that I had made hundreds of
times. Coming as I usually was from some big man or other,
whose busy office and whose mind was a clean, brilliant illustration of what efficiency can be, I would sit in the car and idly
watch the upper story windows we passed, with yellow gas jets
flaring in the cave-like rooms behind them. There I had glimpses
of men and girls at long crowded tables making coats, pants,
vests, paper flowers, chewing-gum, five-cent cigars. I saw countless tenement kitchens, dirty cooking, unmade beds. These
glimpses followed one on the other in such a dizzying torrent
they merged into one moving picture for me. And that picture
was of crowds, crowds, crowds—of people living frowzily.

This was poverty. And it was like some prodigious swamp. What could you do about it? You could pull out individuals here and there, as Eleanore did. I considered that a mighty fine job— for a woman or a clergyman. But to go at it and drain the swamp was a very different matter. You couldn't do it by easy preaching of patent cure-alls, nor by stirring up class hatred through rabid attacks upon big men. No, this was a job for the big men themselves, men who would go at this human swamp as Eleanore's father had gone at the harbor—quietly and slowly, with an engineer's precision. He had been at it six solid years, but he still remarked humbly, "We've only begun."

Then from thinking of big men I thought of the one I had seen that day, and of my story about him. It was just in the stage I liked, where I could feel it all coming together. Incidents, bits of character and neat little turns of speech rose temptingly before my mind.

Presently, through the clamor around me, I heard "the Indian" crying. All this chatter had waked him up. I saw Eleanore go in to him and soon I heard the crying stop, and I knew she was telling him a story, a nice sleepy one to quiet him down.

What an infernal racket these people were making about the world. I went on thinking about my work.

CHAPTER III

"You two," said Sue, when at last her friends had gone away, "have built up a wall of contentment around you a person couldn't break through with an axe."

"Have a little," I suggested.

"Stay all night," said Eleanore.

"No, thanks," said Sue. "I promised Dad that I'd be home."

And then instead of going home she sprawled lazily on the sofa with her head upon one elbow, and settled in for some more talk. But her talk was different tonight. She usually talked about herself, but to-night she talked of us instead, of our contemptible content. And presently through her talk I felt that she had some surprise to spring. In a few moments Eleanore felt it too, I could tell that by the vigilant way she kept glancing up from her knitting.

"I think," I was remarking, "we're a pretty liberal-minded pair."

"That's it," said Sue. "You're liberals!" What utter disdain she threw into the word. "And what's more you're citizens. In all these movements," she went on, "you always find two classes—citizens and criminals. You two are both born citizens."

"What's the difference?" I inquired.

"Citizens," said Sue impressively, "are ready to *vote* for what they believe in. Criminals are ready to get arrested and go to jail."

Eleanore looked up at her.

"Who gave you that?" she asked. Sue looked a little taken back, but only for a moment.

"One of the criminals," she said. Her voice was carefully casual now but her eyes were a little excited. "He's a man who made up his mind that he wanted to get way down to the bottom, and see how it feels to be down there. So he took the very worst job he could find. For two years he was a stoker—on ships of all kinds all over the world. And now that he knows just how it feels, he has an office down on the docks where he's getting the stokers and dockers together—getting them ready for a strike—on your beloved harbor."

"Joe Kramer," said Eleanore quietly. Sue gave a sudden, nervous start.

"Eleanore," she severly rejoined, "sometimes you're simply uncanny—the way you quietly jump at a thing!"

Eleanore had gone on with her knitting. I rose and lit a cigarette. I could feel Sue's eyes upon me. So *this* was her infernal surprise! J. K. banging into my life again!

"How long has Joe been here?" I asked.

"About five months," Sue answered.

"He might have looked me up," I said.

"He doesn't want to look anyone up, I've only seen him once myself. He has simply buried himself down there. Why don't you go and see him, Billy?" she added, with a quick glance at Eleanore. "He won't amuse you the way we do. He's one of the real criminals now."

Still Eleanore did not look up.

"What's his address?" I asked gruffly. Sue gave it to me and good-humoredly yawned and said she must be getting home.

"Good-night, dear," said Eleanore. She had risen and come to the door. "What a love of a hat you're wearing. It's a new one, isn't it? I caught sight of it in the parade."

But the smile which my tall sister threw back at us from the doorway had nothing whatever to do with hats. It said as plainly as in words:

"Now, you cozy liberals, go over and touch *that* spot if you dare."

When she had gone I took up a book and tried to read. But I soon gloomily relapsed. Would J. K. never leave me alone? What was he doing with my harbor? Why should I look him up, confound him—he hadn't bothered his head about me. But I knew that I *would* look him up and would find him more disturbing than ever. How he did keep moving on. No, not on, but down, down—until now he had bumped the bottom!

"Are you going to see him?"

Glancing sharply up, I saw Eleanore carefully watching my face.

"Oh, I suppose so," I replied. She bent again to her knitting.

"He must be a strange kind of a person," she said.

CHAPTER IV

I slept little that night, and my work the next morning went badly. So, after wasting an hour or two, I decided to stop. I would go and see Joe and be done with it.

What was he doing with my harbor? The address Sue had given me was down on the North River, my old hunting ground. The weather had turned cold over-night, and when I came to the waterfront I felt the big raw breath of the sea. I had hardly been near the harbor in years. It had become for me a deep invisible cornerstone upon which my vigorous world was built. I had climbed up into the airy heights, I had been writing of millionaires. And coming so abruptly now from my story of life in rich hotels, the place I had once glorified looked bleak and naked, elemental. Down to the roots of things again.

I came to a bare wooden building, climbed some stairs and entered a large, low-ceilinged room which was evidently a meeting hall. Chairs were stacked along the walls and there was a low platform at one end. As I lingered there a moment, by habit my eyes took in the details. The local color was lurid enough. On the walls were foreign pictures, one of the anarchist Ferrer being executed in Spain, and another of an Italian mob shaking their fists and yelling like demons at a bloated hideous priest. There were posters in which flaming torches, blood-red flags and barricades and cannon belching clouds of smoke stood out in heavy blacks and reds. And all this foreign violence was made grimly real in its purpose here by the way these pictures centered around the largest poster, which was of an ocean liner with all its different kinds of workers gathered together in one mass and staring fixedly up at the ship.

Through a door in a board partition I went into a narrow room from which two dirty windows looked out upon the docks below. This room was cramped and crowded. Newspapers and pamphlets lay heaped on the floor, and in the corners were four desks, at one of which three men, whom I learned later to be an Italian, an Englishman and a Spaniard, were talking together intensely. They took no notice of my entrance, for many other visitors, burly, sooty creatures, were constantly straggling in and out.

I saw Joe at a desk in one corner. Looking doubly tall and lean and stooped, and with a tired frown on his face, he sat there with his sleeves rolled up slowly pounding out a letter on the typewriter before him. On top of his desk were huge ledgers, and over them upon hooks on the wall hung bunches of letters from other ports. It all gave me a heavy impression of dull daily drudgery. And in this Joe was so absorbed that he took no notice of my presence, although I now stood close behind him. When at last he did look up and I got a full view of his face, with its large, familiar features, tight-set jaw and deep-set eyes, I was startled at its gauntness.

"Hello, Joe——"

"Hello." A dullish red came into his face and then a slight frown. He half rose from his seat. "Hello, Bill," he repeated. "What's brought you here?"

He appeared a little dazed at first, then anything but glad to see me. The thought of our old college days flashed for a moment into my mind. How far away they seemed just now. Through our first few awkward remarks he lapsed back into such a tired, worn indifference that I was soon on the point of leaving. But that bony gauntness in his face, and all it showed me he had been through, gave him some right to his rudeness, I thought. So I changed my mind and stuck to my purpose of having it all out with Joe and learning what he was about. Persisting in my friendliness my questions slowly drew him out.

Since I had seen him five years ago he had continued his writing, but as he had grown steadily more set on writing only what he called "the truth about things," the newspapers had closed their doors. While I had gone up he had gone down, until finally throwing up in disgust "this whole fool game of putting words on paper," he had made up his mind to throw in his life with the lives of the men at the bottom. So for two years he had shoveled coal in the stokeholes of ships by day and by night, he had mixed with stokers of every race, from English, French and Germans to Russians and Italians, Spaniards, Hindus, Coolies, Greeks. He had worked and eaten and slept in their holes, he had ranged the slums of all the seas. And of all this he spoke in short, commonplace phrases, still in that indifferent tone, as though personal stories were a bore.

"But look here, Joe," I asked at the end, "what's the good of living like this? What the devil can you do?"

I still remember the look he gave me, the weary remoteness of it. But all he said was,

"Organize strikes."

"Here?"

"Everywhere."

"Of stokers?"

"No, of all industries."

"For higher pay, eh, and shorter hours."

Another brief look.

"No, for revolution," he said.

Briefly, in reply to my questions, he explained how he and his friends had already induced some twelve thousand stokers and dockers to leave their old trade unions and enroll themselves as members of this new international body, which was to embrace not only one trade but all the labor connected with ships—ships of all nations. He was here doing the advance work. As soon as the ground was made ready, he said, some of the bigger leaders would come. Then there would be mass meetings here and presently a general strike. And as the years went on there would be similar strikes in all trades and in all countries, until at some time not many years off there would be such labor rebellions as would paralyze the industrial world. And out of this catastrophe the workers would emerge into power to build up a strange new world of their own.

This was what Joe saw ahead. He seemed to be seeing it while he spoke, with a hard, clear intensity that struck me rather cold. Here was no mere parlor talk, here was a man who lived what he said.

"You comfortable people," he said, "are so damn comfortable you're blind. You see nothing ahead but peace on earth and a nice smooth evolution—with a lot of steady little reforms. You've got so you honestly can't believe there's any violence left in the world. You're as blind as most folks were five years before the Civil War. But what's the use talking?" he ended. "You can't understand all this." Again my irritation rose.

"No, I can't say I do," I replied. "To stir up millions of men of that kind and then let 'em loose upon the world strikes me as absolutely mad!"

"I knew it would."

"Look here, Joe, how are *you* so sure about all this? Hasn't it ever struck you that you're getting damnably narrow?" He smiled.

"I don't care much if I'm narrow," he said.

"You think it's good for you, being like this?"

"I don't care if it's good for me."

"Don't you want to see anything else?"

"Not in your successful world."

"Well, J. K., I'm sorry," I retorted hotly. "Because I'd like to see your world, I honestly would! I'm not like you, I'm always ready to be shown!"

"All right, come and see it. Why don't you write up Jim Marsh?" He smiled as he named the notorious leader of the whole organization. "He'll be here soon, and in his line he has been a mighty successful man. All up and down the U. S. A. Jim's name has been in headlines and Jim himself has been in jail. A successful revolutionist. So why not add him to your list? Write up the America *he* knows." There was a challenge in Joe's voice.

"All right, perhaps I will," I said. At least I had him talking now. "Come out to lunch and tell me some more."

"I don't want any lunch."

Something in the way he said that made me look at him quickly. He appeared to me now not only thin but tense and rather feverish. His nerves were plainly all on edge. He had smoked one cigarette after another.

"I've got a lot of work to-day," he added restlessly. "Not only these damn letters to write—I've got to make up our paper besides—it goes to the printer to-morrow. Here, take a copy with you."

And he handed me the last week's issue. It was a crude and flimsy affair, with its name in scarehead letters, "WAR SURE."

I glanced it over in silence a moment. What a drop for Joe, from what he had been, to this wretched violent little sheet, this muckraker of the ocean world.

"Not like the harbor *you* painted," he said.

"No," I answered shortly.

"Do you want another look at your harbor?"

I eyed him for a moment:

"All right—I'll look—"

"Fine business." He had risen now, and a gleam of the old likable Joe came for a moment into his eyes.

"Meet me to-morrow at seven a. m. And let's look at some of its failures," he said.

CHAPTER V

"Did you see him?" Eleanore asked that night.

"Yes—I saw him——"

I could feel her waiting, but I could not bring myself to talk. Eleanore wouldn't like J. K. She wouldn't like what I had told him I'd do. I was sorry now that I had, it was simply looking for trouble. I damned that challenge in Joe's voice. Why did he always get hold of me so?

"How did he look? Is he much changed?" Eleanore asked me quietly.

"Yes. He looks half sick—and old. He's been through a good deal," I answered.

"Did he talk about that?"

"Yes"—I hesitated—"and of what he wants to show me," I said. Eleanore looked quickly up.

"Are you going to see him soon again?"

"Yes—to-morrow morning—to have a look at his stoker friends. I want to have just one good look at the life that has made him what he is. That's all—that's all it amounts to——"

There was another silence. Then she came over behind my chair and I felt the cool quiet of her hand as she slowly stroked my forehead.

"You look tired, dear," she said.

Just before daylight the next morning I rose and dressed, swallowed some coffee and set out. I took a surface car downtown.

I had not been out at this hour in years. And as in my present mood, troubled and expectant, I watched the streets in the raw half-light, they looked as utterly changed to me as though they were streets of a different world. The department store windows looked unreal. Their soft rich lights had been put out, and in this cold hard light of dawn all their blandishing ladies of wax appeared like so many buxom ghosts. Men were washing the windows. Women and girls were hurrying by, and as some of them stopped for a moment to peer in at these phantoms of fashion, their own faces looked equally waxen to me. A long, luxurious motor passed with a man and a woman in evening clothes half asleep in each other's arms. An old man with a huge pack of rags turned slowly and stared after them. The day's work was beginning. Peddlers trundled push-carts along, newspaper vendors opened their stands, milk wagons and trucks from the markets came by, some on the gallop. Our car had filled with people now. Men and boys clung to the steps behind and women and girls were packed inside, most of them hanging to the straps. How badly and foolishly dressed were these girls. There must be thousands of them out. Two kept tittering inanely. All the rest were silent.

By the time that I reached the docksheds the day was breaking over their roofs. It was freezing cold, and the chill was worse in the dock that I entered. I buttoned my ulster tighter. The big place was dark and empty. The dockers, I learned from the watchman, had quit work at three o'clock, for a few tons of fruit was all the freight that remained to be loaded. The ship was to sail at nine o'clock.

The stokers had not yet gone aboard. I found about a hundred of them huddled along the steel wall of the shed. Some of them had old leather grips or canvas bags, but many had no luggage at all. A few wore seedy overcoats, but the greater part had none, they stood with their hands in their ragged pockets, shivering and stamping. Most of them were undersized, some tough, some rather sickly. A dull-eyed, wretched, sodden lot. I got the liquor on their breaths. A fat old Irish stoker came drifting half-drunk up the pier with a serene and waggish smile.

"Hello," said Joe at my elbow.

He looked more fagged than the day before. I noticed that his lips were blue and that his teeth were chattering.

"Joe," I said abruptly, "you're not fit to be here. Let's get out of this, you belong in bed." He glanced at me impatiently.

"I'm fit enough," he muttered. "We'll stay right here and see this show—unless you feel you want to quit—"

"Did I say I did? I'm ready enough——"

"All right, then wait a minute. They're about ready to go on board."

But as we stood and watched them, I still felt the chattering teeth by my side, and a wave of pity and anger and of disgust swept over me. Joe wouldn't last long at this kind of thing!

"What do you think of my friends?" he asked.

"I think you're throwing your life away!"

"Do you? How do you make it out?"

"Because they're an utterly hopeless crowd! Look at 'em—poor devils—they look like a lot of Bowery bums!"

"Yes—they look like a lot of bums. And they feed all the fires at sea."

"Are they all like these?" I demanded.

"No better dressed," he answered. "A million lousy brothers of Christ."

"And you think you can build a new world *with them?*"

"No—I think they can do it themselves."

"Do you know what I think they'll do themselves? If they ever do win in any strike and get a raise in wages—they'll simply blow it in on drink!"

Joe looked at me a moment.

"They'll do so much more than drink," he said. "Come on," he added. "They're going aboard."

They were forming in a long line now before the third-class gang-plank. As they went up with their packs on their shoulders, a man at the top gave each a shove and shouted out a number, which another official checked off in a book. The latter I learned was the chief engineer. He was a lean, powerful, ruddy-faced man with a plentiful store of profanity which he poured out in a torrent:

"Come on! For Christ's sake! Do you want to freeze solid, you —— human bunch of stiffs?"

We came up the plank at the end of the line, and I showed him a letter which I had procured admitting us to the engine rooms. He turned us over promptly to one of his junior engineers, and we were soon climbing down oily ladders through the intricate parts of the engines, all polished, glistening, carefully cleaned. And then climbing down more ladders until we were, as I was told, within ten feet of the keel of the ship, we came into the stokers' quarters.

And here nothing at all was carefully cleaned. The place was foul, its painted steel walls and floor and ceiling were heavily encrusted with dirt. The low chamber was crowded with rows of bunks, steel skeleton bunks three tiers high, the top tier just under the ceiling. In each was a thin, dirty mattress and blanket. In some of these men were already asleep, breathing hard, snoring and wheezing. Others were crowded around their bags intent on something I could not see. Many were smoking, the air was blue. Some were almost naked, and the smells of their bodies filled the place. It was already stifling.

"Had enough?" asked our young guide, with a grin.

"No," I said, with an answering superior smile. "We'll stay a while and get it all."

And after a little more talk he left us.

"How do you like our home?" asked Joe.

"I'm here now," I said grimly. "Go ahead and show me. And try to believe that I want to be shown."

"All right, here comes our breakfast."

Two stokers were bringing in a huge boiler. They set it down on the dirty floor. It was full of a greasy, watery soup with a thick, yellow scum on the top, through which chunks of pork and potato bobbed up here and there.

"This is scouse," Joe told me. Men eagerly dipped tin cups in this and gulped it down. The chunks of meat they ate with their hands. They ate sitting on bunks or standing between them. Some were wedged in close around a bunk in which lay a sleeper who looked utterly dead to the world. His face was white.

"He reminds me," said Joe, "of a fellow whose bunk was once next to mine. He was shipped at Buenos Ayres, where the crimps still handle the business. A crimp had carried this chap on board, dumped him, got his ten dollars and left. The man was supposed to wake up at sea and shovel coal. But this one didn't. The second day out some one leaned over and touched him and yelled. The crimp had sold us a dead one."

As Joe said this he stared down at the sleeper, a curious tensity in his eyes.

"Joe, how did you ever stand this life?"

My own voice almost startled me, it sounded so suddenly tense and strained. Joe turned and looked at me searchingly, with a trace of that old affection of his.

"I didn't Kid," he said gruffly. "The two years almost got me. And that's what happens to most of 'em here. Half of 'em," he added, "are down-and-outers when they start. They're what the factories and mills and all the rest of this lovely modern industrial world throw out as no more wanted. So they drift down here and take a job that nobody else will take, it's so rotten, and here they have one week of hell and another week's good drunk in port. And when the barrooms and the women and all the waterfront sharks have stripped 'em of their last red cent, then the crimps collect an advance allotment from their future wages to ship 'em off to sea again."

"That's not true in *this* port," I retorted, eagerly catching him up on the one point that I knew was wrong. "They don't allow crimps in New York any more."

"No," Joe answered grimly. "The port of New York has got reformed, it's become all for efficiency now. The big companies put up money for a kind of a seamen's Y. M. C. A. where they try to keep men sober ashore, and so get 'em back quick into holes like these, in the name of Christ.

"But there's one thing they forget," he added bitterly. "The age of steam has sent the old-style sailors ashore and shipped these fellows in their places. And that makes all the difference. These chaps didn't grow up on ships and get used to being kicked and cowed and shot for mutiny if they struck. No, they're all grown up on land, in factories where they've been in strikes, and they bring their factory views along into these floating factories. And they don't like these stinking holes! They don't like their jobs, with no day and no night, only steel walls and electric light! You hear a shout at midnight and you jump down into the stokehole and work like hell till four a. m., when you crawl up all soaked in sweat and fall asleep till the next shout. And you do this, not as the sailor did for a captain he knew and called 'the old man,' but for a corporation so big it has rules and regulations for you like what they have in the navy. You're nothing but a number. Look here."

He took me to a bulletin that had just been put up on the wall. Around it men were eagerly crowding.

"Here's where you find by your number what shift you're to work in," he said, "and what other number you have to replace if he goes down. Heart failure is damn common here, and if your man gives out it means you double up for the rest of the voyage. So you get his number and hunt for him and size him up. You hope he'll last. I'll show you why."

He crawled down a short ladder and through low passageways dripping wet and so came into the stokehole.

This was a long, narrow chamber with a row of glowing furnace doors. Wet coal and coal-dust lay on the floor. At either end a small steel door opened into bunkers that ran along the sides of the ship, deep down near the bottom, containing thousands of tons of soft coal, which the men called "trimmers" kept shoveling out to the stokers. As the voyage went on, Joe told me, these trimmers had to go farther and farther back into the long, black bunkers, full of stifling coal-dust, in which if the ship were rolling the masses of coal kept crashing down. Hundreds of men had been killed that way. In the stokehole the fires were not yet up, but by the time the ship was at sea the furnace mouths would be white hot and the men at work half naked. They not only shoveled coal into the flames, they had to spread it out as well and at intervals rake out the "clinkers" in fiery masses on the floor. On these a stream of water played, filling the chamber with clouds of steam. In older ships, like this one, a "lead stoker" stood at the head of the line and set the pace for the others to follow. He was paid more to keep up the pace. But on the fast new liners this pacer was replaced by a gong.

"And at each stroke of the gong you shovel," said Joe. "You do this till you forget your name. Every time the boat pitches, the floor heaves you forward, the fire spurts at you out of the doors and the gong keeps on like a sledge-hammer coming down on top of your mind. And all you think of is your bunk and the time when you're to tumble in."

From the stokers' quarters presently there came a burst of singing.

"Now let's go back," he ended, "and see how they're getting ready for this."

As we crawled back the noise increased, and it swelled to a roar as we entered. The place was pandemonium now. Those groups I had noticed around the bags had been getting out the liquor, and now at eight o'clock in the morning half the crew were already well soused. Some moved restlessly about. One huge bull of a creature with large, limpid, shining eyes stopped suddenly with a puzzled stare, then leaned back on a bunk and laughed uproariously. From there he lurched over the shoulder of a thin, wiry, sober man who, sitting on the edge of a bunk, was slowly spelling out the words of a newspaper aeroplane story. The big man laughed again and spit, and the thin man jumped half up and snarled.

Louder rose the singing. Half the crew was crowded close around a little red-faced cockney. He was the modern "chanty man." With sweat pouring down his cheeks and the muscles of his neck drawn taut, he was jerking out verse after verse about women. He sang to an old "chanty" tune, one that I remembered well. But he was not singing out under the stars, he was screaming at steel walls down here in the bottom of the ship. And although he kept speeding up his song the crowd were too drunk to wait for the chorus, their voices kept tumbling in over his, and soon it was only a frenzy of sound, a roar with yells rising out of it. The singers kept pounding each other's backs or waving bottles over their heads. Two bottles smashed together and brought a still higher burst of glee.

"I'm tired!" Joe shouted. "Let's get out!"

I caught a glimpse of his strained, frowning face. Again it came over me in a flash, the years he had spent in holes like this, in this hideous, rotten world of his, while I had lived joyously in mine. And as though he had read the thought in my disturbed and troubled eyes,

"Let's go up where *you* belong," he said.

I followed him up and away from his friends. As we climbed ladder after ladder, fainter and fainter on our ears rose that yelling from below. Suddenly we came out on deck and slammed an iron door behind us.

And I was where I belonged. I was in dazzling sunshine and keen frosty Autumn air. I was among gay throngs of people. Dainty women brushed me by. I felt the softness of their furs, I breathed the fragrant scent of them and of the flowers that they wore, I saw their fresh immaculate clothes, I heard the joyous tumult of their talking and their laughing to the regular crash of the band—all the life of the ship I had known so well.

And I walked through it all as though in a dream. On the dock I watched it spellbound—until with handkerchiefs waving and voices calling down good-bys, that throng of happy travelers moved slowly out into midstream.

And I knew that deep below all this, down in the bottom of the ship, the stokers were still singing.

CHAPTER VI

That same day I had an appointment to lunch with the owner of rich hotels whose story I was writing. And the interview dragged. For the America he knew was like what I'd seen on the upper decks of the ship that had sailed a few hours before. And I could not get back my old zest for it all, I kept thinking of what I had seen underneath. The faces of individual stokers, some fiery red, some sodden gray, kept bobbing up in my memory. Angrily trying to keep them down, I went on with my questions. But I caught the hotel millionaire throwing curious looks at me now and then.

I went home worried and depressed and shut myself up in my workroom. This business had to be thought out. It wasn't only stokers; it was something deep, world-wide. I had come up against the slums. What had I to do with it all?

I was in my room all afternoon. I heard "the Indian" at my door, but I sat still and silent, and presently he went away.

Late in the twilight Eleanore came. How beautiful she was to-night. She was wearing a soft gown of silk, blue with something white at her throat and a brooch that I had given her. As she bent over my shoulder I felt her clean, fresh loveliness.

"Don't you want to tell me, love, just what it was he showed you?"

"I'd rather not, my dear one, it was something so terribly ugly," I said.

"I don't like being so far away from you, dear. Please tell me. Suppose you begin at the start."

It took a long time, for she would let me keep nothing back.

"I wouldn't have thought it could hit me so hard," I said at the end.

"I'm not surprised," said Eleanore.

"I can't be simply angry at Joe," I went on. "He's so intensely and gauntly sincere. It isn't just talk with him, you see, as it is with Sue's parlor radical friends. Think of the life he's been leading, think of it compared to mine. Joe and I were mighty close once"—I broke off and got up restlessly. "I hate to think of him," I said.

"It's funny," said Eleanore quietly. "I knew this was coming sooner or later. Ever since we've been married I've known that Joe Kramer still means more to you than any man you've ever met."

"He doesn't," I said sharply. "Where on earth did you get that idea?"

"From you, my love," she answered. "You can't dream how often you've spoken about him."

"I didn't know I had!" It is most disquieting at times, the things Eleanore tells me about myself.

"I know you don't," she continued, "you do it so unconsciously. That's why I'm so sure he has a real place in the deep unconscious part of you. He worries you. He gets you to think you've no right to be happy!" There was a bitterness in her voice that I had never heard before. "I believe in helping people—of course—whenever I get a chance," she said. "But I don't believe in this—I hate it! It's simply an insane attempt to pull every good thing down! It's too awful even to think of!"

"We're not going to," I told her. "I'm sorry for Joe and I wish I could help him out of his hole. But I can't—it's too infernally deep. He won't listen to any talk from me—and as long as he won't I'll leave him alone. It's hideous enough—God knows. But if I ever tackle poverty and labor and that sort of thing it'll be along quite different lines."

The door-bell rang.

"Oh Billy," she said, "I forgot to tell you. Father's coming to dinner to-night." I looked at her a moment:

"Did you ask him here on my account?" Eleanore smiled frankly.

"Yes—I thought I might need him," she said.

I did not talk to her father of Joe—his plans for a strike were his secret, not mine. But with Eleanore pushing me on, I described the hell I had seen in the stokehole.

"You're right, it's hell," her father agreed. "But in time we'll do away with it."

"I knew it," Eleanore put in.

"How?" I asked.

"By using oil instead of coal. Or if we can't get oil cheap enough by automatic stokers—machines to do the work of men."

I thought hard and fast for a moment, and suddenly I realized that I had never given any real thought to matters of this kind before.

"Then what will become of the stokers?" I asked him.

"One thing at a time." I caught Dillon keenly watching me over his cigar. "Don't give up your faith in efficiency, Bill. If they'll only give us time enough we'll be able to do so much for men."

There was something so big and sincere in his voice and in his clear and kindly eyes.

"I'm sure you will," I answered. "If you don't, there's nobody else who can."

In a week or two, by grinding steadily on at my work and by a few more quiet talks with Eleanore and her father, I could feel myself safely back on my ground.

But one morning Sue broke in on me.

"I've just heard from a friend of Joe Kramer's," she said, "that he is dangerously ill. And there's no one to look after him. Hadn't you better go yourself?"

"Of course," I assented gruffly. "I'll go down at once."

It seemed as though the Fates and Sue were in league to keep Joe in my life.

I went to Joe's office and found the address of the room where he slept. It was over a German saloon close by. It was a large, low-ceilinged room, bare and cheaply furnished, with dirty curtains at the windows, dirty collars and shirts on the floor. It was cold. In the high old-fashioned fireplace the coal fire had gone out. Joe was lying dressed on the bed. He jumped up as I entered and came to me with his face flushed and his eyes dilated. He gripped my hand.

"Why, hello, Kid," he cried. "Glad to see you!" And then with a quick drop of his voice: "Hold on, we mustn't talk so loud, we've got to be quiet here, you know." He turned away from me restlessly. "I've been hunting for hours for that damn book. Their cataloguing system here is rotten, Kid, it's rotten!" As he spoke he was slowly feeling his way along the dirty white wall of his room. "They've cheated us, Bill, I'm on to 'em now! That's what college is really for these days, to hide the books we ought to read!"

It came over me suddenly that Joe was back in college, on one of those library evenings of ours. I felt a tightening at my throat.

"Say, Joe." I drew him toward the bed. "The chapel bell has just struck ten. Time for beer and pretzels."

"Fine business! Gee, but I've got a thirst! But where's the door? God damn it all—I can't find anything tonight!" He laughed unsteadily.

"Right over here," I answered. "Steady, old man——"

And so I got him to his bed. He fell down on it breathing hard and I brought him a drink of water. He began to shiver violently. I covered him up with dirty blankets, went down to the barroom and telephoned to Eleanore. Too deeply disturbed to think very clearly, acting on an impulse, I told her of Joe's condition and asked if I might bring him home.

"Why of course," came the answer, a little sharp. "Wait a moment. Let me think." There was a pause, and then she added quietly, "Go back to his room and keep him in bed. I'll see that an ambulance comes right down."

Within an hour after that Joe was installed in our guest room with a trained nurse to attend to him. The doctor pronounced it typhoid and he was with us for nine weeks.

The effect upon our lives was sharp. In our small crowded apartment all entertaining was suddenly stopped, and with the sole exception of Sue no one came to see us. Even our little Indian learned to be quiet as a mouse. Our whole home became intense.

Through the thin wall of my workroom I could hear Joe in his delirium. Now he was busily writing letters, now in a harsh excited voice he was talking to a crowd of men, again he was furiously shoveling coal. All this was incoherent, only mutterings most of the time. But when the voice rose suddenly it was so full of a stern pain, so quivering with revolt against life, and it poured out such a torrent of commonplace minute details that showed this was Joe's daily life and the deepest part of his being—that as I listened at my desk the ghost I thought I had buried deep, that vague guilty feeling over my own happiness, came stealing up in me again. And it was so poignant now, that struggle angrily as I would to plunge again into my work, I found it impossible to describe the life in those rich gay hotels with the zest and the dash I needed to make my story a success.

But it had to be a success, for we needed money badly, the expenses of Joe's sickness were already rolling in. So I did finish it at last and took it to my successful man, who read it with evident disappointment. It was not the glory story that I had led him to expect. My magazine editor said he would use it, but he, too, appeared surprised.

"You weren't up to your usual form," was his comment. "What's the matter?"

"A sick friend."

I started another story at once, one I had already planned, about a man who was to build a string of gorgeous opera houses in the leading American cities. This story, too, went slowly. Joe Kramer's voice kept breaking in. From time to time as I struggled on I could feel Eleanore watching me.

"Don't try to hurry it," she said. "We can always borrow from father, you know—and besides, I'm going to cut our expenses."

She was as good as her word. She dismissed the nurse, and through the last weeks of delirium and the first of returning consciousness she placed herself in Joe's borderland as the one whose presence he vaguely felt pulling him back into comfort and strength.

"No, don't talk," I heard her say to him one evening. "I don't want to hear you. All I want is to get you well. That's the only thing you and I have to talk of."

But having so thrown him off his guard, as his mind grew clearer she began cautiously drawing him out, despite his awakening hostility to this woman who had made me a success. From my room I heard snatches of their talk. She surprised J. K. by the intimate bits of knowledge about him that she had collected both from me and from his own sick ramblings. She had just enough of his point of view to rouse him from his indifference, to annoy him by her mistakes and her refusals to understand. I remember one afternoon when I went in to sit with him, his staring grimly up at my face and saying:

"Bill, that wife of yours is such a born success she scares me. Everything she touches, everything she brings me to drink, everything she does to this bed, is one thundering success. And she won't listen to anything *but* success. Your case is absolutely hopeless."

They became grim enemies, and both of them enjoyed it. She let our small son come and sit by the bed. The Indian promptly worshiped Joe as the "longest" man he had ever seen, and they became boon companions.

"It's pathetic," Eleanore told me, "the little things that appeal to him here. Poor boy, he has forgotten what a decent home is like."

As he grew stronger she read the paper to him each morning, and they quarreled with keen relish over the news events of the day. And as at the start, so now, she kept giving him little shocks of surprise by her intimate glimpses into his views. On one of these occasions, after she had come out from his room and was sitting by me reading,

"You're a wonder, Eleanore," I said. "I don't see how you've done it."

"Done what, my love?" asked Eleanore.

"Wormed all his views out of poor old Joe."

"I haven't done anything of the sort. I've learned over half of it from Sue. She comes here often nowadays and we have long talks about him. Sue seems to know him rather well."

This did not interest me much, so I switched our talk to something that did.

"What bothers me," I said with a scowl, "is this infernal work of mine. What are you smiling at?" I asked.

"Nothing," she murmured, beginning to read. "But if I were you I'd stick at my work. You're good at that."

"Not now I'm not," I retorted. "This story about the opera man isn't coming on at all! The more I work the worse it gets!"

"It will get better soon," she said.

"I'm not so sure. Do you know what I think is the matter with me? I was in to-day looking at Joe asleep, and watching the lines in that face of his it came over me all of a sudden what a wretched coward I've been." Eleanore looked up suddenly. "I know there's something in all his talk, I've known it every time we've met. His

view's so distorted it makes me mad, but there's something in it
you can't get away from. Poverty, that's what it is, and I've always
steered way clear of it as though I were afraid to look. I've taken
your father's point of view and left the slums for him and his
friends to tackle when they get the time. I was only too glad to be
left out. But that hour with J. K. and his stokers gave me a jolt. I
can feel it still. I can't seem to shake it off. And I'm beginning to
wonder now why I shouldn't get up the nerve to see for myself, to
have a good big look at it all—and write about it for a while."

"Don't!" said Eleanore. "Leave it alone!" Her voice was so
sharp it startled me.

"Why?" I rejoined. "You've tackled poverty often enough. I
guess I can stand it if you can."

"You're different," she answered. "You leave poverty alone
and force yourself to go on with your work. You've made a very
wonderful start. You'll be ready to take up fiction soon. When
you have, and when you have gone so far that you can feel sure of
your name and yourself, then you can look at whatever you like."

"I wonder what Joe would say to that."

"I know what he'll say—he'll agree with me. Why don't you
ask him and see for yourself? I'm beginning to like Joe Kramer,"
she added with a quiet smile, "because now that I understand
him I know that his life and yours are so far apart you've hardly
a point in common."

And in the talks I had with Joe this soon proved to be the case.
Eleanore brought us together now and listened with deep satisfaction as we clashed and jarred each other apart.

His old indifferent manner was gone, he was softened, grateful
for what we had done—but he held to that view of his like a rock,
and the view entirely shut me out. Joe saw society wholly as "War
Sure" between two classes, and I was hopelessly on the wrong
side. My work, my home and my whole life were bound in with
the upper class. And there could be no middle ground. My
boasted tolerance, breadth of mind, my readiness to see both
sides, my passion for showing up all men as human—this to Joe
was utter piffle. He had no use for such writing, or in fact for art
of any kind. "Propaganda" was all that he wanted, and that
could be as cheap as Nick Carter, as sentimental as *Uncle Tom's
Cabin*, if only it had the kind of "punch" that would reach to the

mass of ignorant workers and stir their minds and their passions into swift and bitter revolt. Revolution! That was the thing. The world had come to a time, he said, when talking and writing weren't going to count. We were entering into an age of force—of "direct action"—strikes and the like—by prodigious masses of men. All I could do was worthless.

These talks made me so indignant and sore, so sure that Joe and all his work were utterly wild and that only in Dillon and his kind lay any hope of solving the dreary problems of the slums—that within a few days more I was delving into my opera man with a most determined approval. He at least was a builder, he didn't want to tear everything down! In his every scheme for a huge success I took now an aggravated delight. All my recent tolerance gone, I threw into my work an intensity that I had not felt in months.

And Eleanore smiled contentedly, as though she knew what she was about. When at last the time came for Joe to leave, she was twice as friendly to him as I.

CHAPTER VII

But on coming home one evening two or three weeks later, I found Eleanore reading aloud to our son with a most preoccupied look on her face.

"Joe Kramer is coming to dinner," she said. "He called up this morning and said he'd like to see us again. Sue is coming, too, as it happens. She dropped in this afternoon."

Sue arrived a few minutes later, and at once I thought to myself I had never seen her look so well. For once she had taken time to dress. She had done her dark hair in a different way. Her color, which had been poor of late, to-night was most becomingly high, and those fascinating eyes of hers were bright with a new animation.

"She has found a fine new hobby," I thought.

Her whole attitude to us was one of eager friendliness. She made much of what we had done for Joe.

"You've no idea," she told me, "how he feels about you both." She was speaking of this when Joe came in.

He, too, appeared to me different. Into his blunt manner had crept a certain awkwardness, his gruff voice had an anxious note at times and his eyes a hungry gleam. Poor old Joe, I thought. It must be hard, despite all his talk, to see what he had missed in life, to feel what a sacrifice he had made. He had thrown everything aside, love, marriage, home, all personal ties—to tackle this bleak business of slums. The more pity he had such a twisted view. And as presently, in reply to Sue's questions, he talked about the approaching strike, my irritation at his talk grew even sharper than before.

"Your stokers and dock laborers," I interrupted hotly, "are about as fit to build up a new world as they are to build a

Brooklyn Bridge! When I compare them to Eleanore's father and his way of going to work"—I broke off in exasperation. "Can't you see you're all just floundering in a perfect swamp of ignorance?"

"No," said Joe. "I don't see that—"

"I'm mighty glad you don't," said Sue. Eleanore turned on her abruptly.

"Why are *you* glad, Sue?" she asked.

"Because," Sue answered warmly, "he's where every one of us ought to be! He's doing the work we all ought to be doing!"

"Then why don't you do it?" said Joe. His voice was low but sharp as in pain. The next instant he turned from Sue to me. "I mean all of you," he added. I looked at him in astonishment. What had worked this change in Joe? In our last talk he had shut me out so completely. He seemed to feel this at once himself, for he hastened to explain his remark. He had turned his back on Sue and was talking hard at me:

"Of course I don't mean you can do it, Bill, unless you change your whole view of life. But why shouldn't you change? You're young enough. That look at a stokehole got hold of you hard. And if you're able to feel like that why not do some thinking, too?"

"I'm thinking," I said grimly. "I told you before that I wanted to help. But you said——"

"I say it still," J. K. cut in. "If you want to help the people you've got to drop your efficiency gods. You've got to believe in the people first—that all they need is waking up to handle this whole job themselves. You've got to see that they're waking up fast—all over the world—that they're getting tired of gods above 'em slowly planning out their lives—that they don't want to wait till they're dead to be happy—that they feel poverty every day like a million tons of brick on their chests—it's got so they can't even breathe without thinking! And you've got to see that what they're thinking is, 'Do it yourself and do it quick!' The only thing that's keeping them back is that in these times of peace men get out of the habit of violence!

"But the minute you get this clear in your mind, then I say you can help 'em. Because what's needed is so big. It's not only more pay and shorter hours and homes where they needn't die off like flies—they need more than that—they need a change as much as you—in their whole way of looking at things. They've got to learn that they are a crowd—and can't get anywhere at all until all pull together. Ignorant? Of course they are! But that's where you and me come in—we can help 'em get together faster than they would if left to themselves! You can help that way a lot—by writing to the tenements! *That's* what I meant!"

Joe stopped short. And after his passionate outburst, Eleanore spoke up quietly.

"This sounds funny from you," she said. "A few weeks ago you were just as sure that Billy could do nothing. What has made you change so?"

Joe reddened and looked down at his hands.

"I suppose," he said gruffly after a moment, "it's because I'm still weak from typhoid—weak enough to want to see some one but stokers get into the job that's become my life. You see," he muttered, "I was raised among people like you. It's a kind of a craving, I suppose—like cigarettes." Again he stopped short and there was a pause.

"Rather natural," Sue murmured. Again he turned sharply from her to me.

"I say you can help by your writing," he said. "You call my friends an ignorant mob. But thousands of 'em have read your stuff!"

I looked up at Joe with a start.

"Oh they don't like it," he went on. "It only makes 'em sore and mad. But if you ever see things right, and get into their side of this fight with that queer fountainaxe of yours, you'll be surprised at the tenement friends who'll pop up all around you. The first thing you know they'll be calling you 'Bill.' That's the kind they are—they don't want to shut anyone out—all they want to know is whether he means business. If he doesn't he's no use, because they know that sooner or later they'll do it anyhow themselves. It's going to be the biggest fight that's happened since the world began! No cause has ever been so fine, so worth a man's giving his life to aid! And all you've got to decide is this—whether you're to get in now, and help make it a little easier, help make it come without violence—or wait till it all comes to a crash and then be yanked in like a sack of meal!"

Before I could speak, Sue drew a deep breath.

"I don't see how there's any choice about that," she said.

Eleanore turned to her again:

"Do you mean for Billy?"

"I mean for us all," Sue answered. "Even for a person like me!" Sue was beautiful just then—her cheeks aglow, her features tense, a radiant eagerness in her eyes. "I've felt it, oh so long," she said. "It's gone all through my suffrage work—through every speech that I have made—that the suffragists need the working girls and ought to help them win their strikes!"

"And what do *you* think, Joe?" Eleanore persisted. "Were you speaking of Billy alone just now or did you have Sue, too, in mind?"

Joe looked back at her steadily.

"I don't want to shut out the women," he said. "I've seen too many girls jump in and make a big success of it. Not only working girls, but plenty of college girls like you." He turned from Eleanore to Sue—and with a gruff intensity, "You may think you can't do it, Sue," he said. "But I know you can. I've seen it done, I tell you, all the way from here to the Coast—girls like you as speakers, as regular organizers—forgetting themselves and sinking themselves—ready for any job that comes."

"That's the way I should want to do it," said Sue, her voice a little breathless.

"But how about wives?" asked Eleanore. "For some of these girls marry, I suppose," she added thoughtfully. "At least I hope they do. I hope Sue will."

"I never said anything against that," Joe answered shortly.

"But if they marry and have children," Eleanore continued, "aren't they apt to get sick of it then, even bitter about it, this movement you speak of that takes you in and sinks you down, swallows up every dollar you have and all your thoughts and feelings?"

"It needn't do as much as that," Joe muttered as though to himself.

"Still—I'd like to see it work out," Eleanore persisted. "Do you happen to know the wives of any labor leaders?"

"I do," Joe answered quickly. "The wife of the biggest man we've got. Jim Marsh arrived in town last night. His wife is with him. She always is."

"Now are you satisfied, dear?" Sue asked. But Eleanore smiled and shook her head.

"Is Mrs. Marsh a radical, too—I mean an agitator?" she asked. Joe's face had clouded a little.

"Not exactly," he replied. Eleanore's eyes were attentive now: "Do you know her well, Joe?"

"I've met her——"

"I'd like to meet her, too," she said. "And find out how she likes her life."

"I think I know what you'd find," said Sue, in her old cocksure, superior manner. "I guess she likes it well enough——"

"Still, dear," Eleanore murmured, "instead of taking things for granted it would be interesting, I think, in all this talk to have one look at a little real life."

"Aren't you just a little afraid of real life, Eleanore?" Sue demanded, in a quick challenging tone.

"Am I?" asked Eleanore placidly.

Long after Joe had left us, Sue kept up that challenging tone. But she did not speak to Eleanore now, her talk like Joe's was aimed at me.

"Why not think it over, Billy?" she urged. "You're not happy now, I never saw you so worried and blue."

"I'm not in the least!" I said stoutly. But Sue did not seem to hear me. She went on in an eager, absorbed sort of way:

"Why not try it a little? You needn't go as far as Joe Kramer. He may even learn to go slower himself—now that he has had typhoid——"

"Do you think so?" Eleanore put in.

"Why not?" cried Sue impatiently. "If he keeps on at this pace it will kill him! Has he no right to some joy in life? Why should you two have it all? Just think of it, Billy, you have a name, success and a lot of power! Why not use it here? Suppose it *is* harder! Oh, I get so out of patience with myself and all of us! Our easy, lazy, soft little lives! Why can't we *give* ourselves a little?" And she went back over all Joe had said. "It's all so real. So tremendously real," she ended.

"I wonder what's going to happen," said Eleanore when we were alone.

"God knows," I answered gloomily. That hammering from Joe

and Sue had stirred me up all over again. I had doggedly resisted, I had told Sue almost angrily that I meant to keep right on as before. But now she was gone, I was not so sure. "I still feel certain Joe's all wrong," I said aloud. "But he and his kind are so dead in earnest—so ready for any sacrifice to push their utterly wild ideas—that they may get a lot of power. God help the country if they do."

"I wasn't speaking of the country, my love," my wife informed me cheerfully. "I was speaking of Sue and Joe Kramer."

"Joe," I replied, "will slam right ahead. You can be sure of that, I've got him down cold."

"Have you?" she asked. "And how about Sue?"

"Oh Sue," I replied indifferently, "has been enthused so many times."

"Billy."

I turned and saw my wife regarding her husband thoughtfully.

"I wonder," she said, "how long it will be before you can write a love story."

"What?"

"Sue and Joe Kramer, you idiot."

I stared at her dumfounded.

"Did you think all that talk was aimed at you?" my pitiless spouse continued. "Did you think all that change in Joe's point of view was on your account?"

I watched her vigilantly for a while.

"If there's anything in what you say," I remarked carefully at last, "I'll bet at least that Joe doesn't know it. He doesn't even suspect it."

"There are so many things," said Eleanore, "that men don't even suspect in themselves. I'm sorry," she added regretfully. "But that summer vacation we'd planned is off."

"What?"

"Oh, yes, we'll stay right here in town. I see anything but a pleasant summer."

"Suppose," I said excitedly, "you tell me exactly what you *do* see!"

"I see something," Eleanore answered, "which unless we can stop it may be a very tragic affair. Tragic for Sue because I feel sure that she'd never stand Joe's impossible life. And even worse for your father. He's not only old and excitable, and very weak and feeble, too, but he's so conservative besides that if Sue married Joe Kramer he'd consider her utterly damned."

"But I tell you you're wrong, all wrong!" I broke in. "Joe isn't that kind of an idiot!"

"Joe," said my wife decidedly, "is like every man I've ever met. I found that out when he was sick. He has the old natural longing for a wife and a home of his own. His glimpse of it here may have started it rising. I'm no more sure than you are that he admits it to himself. But it's there all the same in the back of his mind, and in that same mysterious region he's trying to reconcile marrying Sue to the work which he believes in—even with this strike coming on. It's perfectly pathetic.

"Isn't it funny," she added, "how sometimes everything comes all at once? Do you know what this may mean to us? I don't, I haven't the least idea. I only know that you yourself are horribly unsettled—and that now through this affair of Sue's we'll have to see a good deal of Joe—and not only Joe but his friends on the docks—and not even the quiet ones. No, we're to see all the wild ones. We're to be drawn right into this strike—into what Joe calls revolution."

"You may be right," I said doggedly. "But I don't believe it."

CHAPTER VIII

A few days later Joe called me up and asked me to come down to his office. His reason for wanting to see me, he said, he'd rather not give me over the 'phone.

"You're right," I told Eleanore dismally. "He's going to talk to me about Sue."

I dreaded this talk, and I went to see Joe in no easy frame of mind. But it was not about Sue. I saw that in my first glimpse of his face. He sat half around in his office chair listening intensely to a man by his side.

"I want you to meet Jim Marsh," he said.

I felt a little electric shock. So here was the great mob agitator, the notorious leader of strikes. Eleanore's words came into my mind: "We're to meet all the wild ones. We're to be drawn right into this strike—into what Joe calls revolution." Well, here was the arch-revolutionist, the prime mover of them all. Of middle size, about forty years old, angular and wiry, there was a lithe easy force in his limbs, but he barely moved as he spoke to me now. He just turned his narrow bony face and gave me a glance with his keen gray eyes.

"I've known your work for quite a while," he said in a low drawling voice. "Joe says you're thinking of writing me up."

So this was why Joe had sent for me. I had quite forgotten this idea, but I took to it eagerly now. My work was going badly. Here was something I could do, the life story of a man whose picture would soon be on the front page of every paper in New York. It would interest my magazine, it would give me a chance to get myself clear on this whole ugly business of labor, poverty and strikes. I had evaded it long enough, I would turn and face it squarely now.

"Why yes, I'd like to try," I said.

"He wants to do your picture with the America you know," said Joe. "He says he's ready to be shown."

Marsh glanced out at the harbor.

"If he'll trail around with us for a while we may show him some of it here," he drawled. And then quietly ignoring my presence he continued his talk with Joe, as though taking it for granted that I was an interested friend. I listened there all afternoon.

The thing that struck me most at first was the cool effrontery of the man in undertaking such a struggle. The old type of labor leader had at least stuck to one industry, and had known by close experience what he had to face. But here was a mere outsider, a visitor strolling into a place and saying, "I guess I'll stop all this." Vaguely I knew what he had to contend with. Sitting here in this cheap bare room, the thought of other rooms rose in my mind, spacious, handsomely furnished rooms where at one time or another I had interviewed heads of foreign ship companies, railroad presidents, bankers and lawyers, newspaper editors, men representing enormous wealth. All these rooms had been parts of my harbor—a massed array of money and brains. He would have all this against him. And to such a struggle I could see no end for him but jail.

For against all this, on his side, was a chaotic army of ignorant men, stokers, dockers, teamsters, scattered all over this immense region, practically unorganized. What possible chance to bring them together? How could he feel that he had a chance? How much did he already know?

I asked him what he had seen of the harbor. For days, I learned, he had told no one but Joe of his coming, he had wandered about the port by himself. And as a veteran tramp will in some mysterious fashion get the feel of a new town within a few short hours there, so Marsh had got the feel of this place—of a harbor different from mine, for he felt it from the point of view of its hundred thousand laborers. He felt it with its human fringe, he saw its various tenement borders like so many camps and bivouacs on the eve of a battle.

He told a little incident of how the harbor learned he was here. About nine o'clock one morning, as he was waiting his chance to get into one of the North River docks, a teamster recognized him there from a picture of him he had once seen. The news traveled swiftly along the docks, out onto piers and into ships. And at noon, way over in Hoboken, Marsh had overheard a German docker say to the man eating lunch beside him,

"I hear dot tamn fool anarchist Marsh is raising hell ofer dere in New York."

"But I wasn't raising hell," he drawled. "I was over here study-ing literature." And he drew out from his pocket a tattered copy of a report, the result of a careful investigation of work on the docks, made recently by a most conservative philanthropic orga-nization.

" 'In all the fierce rush of American industry,' " he read, with a quiet smile of derision, " 'no work is so long, so irregular or more full of danger. Seven a. m. until midnight is a common work day here, and in the rush season of winter when ships are often delayed by storms and so must make up time in port, the same men often work all day and night and even on into the following day, with only hour and half-hour stops for coffee, food or liquor. This strain makes for accidents. From police reports and other sources we find that six thousand killed and injured every year on the docks is a conservative estimate.' "

Marsh glanced dryly up at me:

"Here's the America I know."

I said nothing. I was appalled. Six thousand killed and injured! I could feel his sharp gray eyes boring down into my soul:

"You wrote up this harbor once."

"Yes," I said.

"Did you write this?"

"No. I would have said it was a lie."

"Do you say so now? These people are a careful crowd." I took the pamphlet from his hands.

"Queer," I muttered vaguely. "I never saw this report before."

"Not so queer," he answered. "I'm told that it wasn't *meant* to be seen—by you and the general public. That's the way this soci-ety works. They spend half a dead old lady's cash investigating poverty and the other half in keeping the public from learning what they've discovered. But we're going to furnish publicity to this secluded work of art.

"On Saturday afternoon," he continued, "I went along the

North River docks. I found long lines of dockers there—they were waiting for their pay. At every pay window one of 'em stood with an empty cigar box in his hands—and into that box every man as he passed dropped a part of his pay—for the man who had been hurt that week—for him or for his widow.

"And over across the way," he went on, "I saw something on the waterfront that fitted right into the scenery. It was a poster on a high fence, and it had a black border around it. On one side of it was a picture of a tall gent in a swell frock suit. He was looking squarely at the docks and pointing to the sign beside him, which said, 'Certainly I'm talking to you! Money saved is money earned. Read what I will furnish you for seventy-five dollars—cash. Black cloth or any color you like—plush or imitation oak—casket with a good white or cream lining—pillow—burial suit or brown habit—draping and embalming room—chairs—hearse—three coaches—complete care and attendance—also handsome candelabra and candles if requested.' "

As Marsh read this grisly list from his notebook, it suddenly came into my mind that in my explorations years ago I had seen this poster at many points, all along the waterfront. It had made no impression on me then, for it had not fitted into my harbor. But Marsh had caught its meaning at once and had promptly jotted it down for use. For it fitted his harbor exactly.

Vaguely, in this and a dozen ways, I could feel him taking my harbor to pieces, transforming each piece into something grim and so building a harbor all his own. Disturbedly and angrily I struggled to find the flaws in his building, eagerly I caught at distortions here and there, twisted facts and wrong conclusions. But in all the terrible stuff which he had so hastily gathered here, there was so much that I could not deny. And he gave no chance for argument. Quickly jumping from point to point he pictured a harbor of slaves overburdened; driven into fierce revolt. It was hard to keep my footing.

For his talk was not only of this harbor. It ranged out over an ocean world which was all in a state of ferment and change. Men of every race and creed, from English, Germans, Russians to Coolies, Japs and Lascars, had crowded into the stokeholes, mixing bowls for all the world. And the mixing process had begun. At Copenhagen, two years before, in a great marine convention that followed the socialist congress there, Marsh had seen the delegates from seventeen different countries representing millions of seamen. And this crude world parliament, this international brotherhood, had placed itself on record as against wars of every kind, except the one deepening bitter war of labor against capital. To further this they had proposed to paralyze by strikes the whole international transport world. The first had followed promptly, breaking out in England. The second was to take place here.

"You don't see how it can happen," said Marsh, with one of those keen sudden looks that showed he was aware of my presence. "You admit this place is a watery hell, but you don't believe we can change it. You don't see how ignorant mobs of men can rise up and take the whole game in their hands. Do I get you right?"

"You do," I said.

"Look over there."

I followed his glance to the doorway. It was filled with a group of big ragged men. Some of the faces were black with soot, some were smiling stolidly, some scowling in the effort to hear. All eyes were intent on the face of the man who had never been known to lose a strike.

"That's the beginning," Marsh told me. "You keep your eyes on their faces—from now on right into the strike—and you may see something grow there that'll give you a new religion."

As the day wore into evening the crowd from outside pressed into the room until they were packed all around us.

"Let's get out of this," said Joe at last. We went to a neighboring lunchroom and ate a hasty supper. But as here, too, the crowd pressed in to get a look at Marsh, Joe asked us to come up to his room.

"They *know* your room," Marsh answered. His tone was grim, as though he had been accustomed for years to this ceaselessly curious pressing mass, pressing, pressing around him tight. "Suppose we go up to mine," he said. "I want you fellows to meet my wife. She has never met any writers before," he added to me, "and she's interested in that kind of thing. She was a music teacher once."

I was about to decline and start for home, but suddenly I

recalled Eleanore's saying that she would like to meet Mrs. Marsh. So I accepted his invitation. And what I saw a few minutes later brought me down abruptly from these world-wide schemes for labor.

We entered a small, cheap hotel, climbed a flight of stairs and came into the narrow bedroom which was for the moment this notorious wanderer's home. A little girl about six years old lay asleep on a cot in one corner, and under the one electric light a woman sat reading a magazine. She had a strong rather clever face which would have been appealing if it were not for the bitter impatient glance she gave us as we entered.

"Talk low, boys, our little girl's asleep," Marsh said. "Say, Sally," he continued, with his faint, derisive smile, "here's a writer come to see you."

"Pleased to meet you, I'm sure," she said, then relapsed into a stiff silence. I tried to break through her awkwardness but entirely without avail. I grew more and more sure of my first impression, that this woman hated her husband's friends, his strikes, his "proletariate." She was smart, pushing, ambitious, I thought, just the kind that would have got on in any middle western town. Eleanore must meet her.

Then presently I noticed that only Marsh was talking. I glanced at Joe and was startled by the intensity in his eyes.

For Joe was watching his leader's wife. And watching, he appeared to me to be seeing her in a dreary succession of rooms like these, in cities, towns and mining camps, wherever her husband was leading a strike—and then trying to see his own home in such rooms, and Sue in his home, a wife like this. The picture struck me suddenly cold. Sue pulled into this for life! Again I remembered Eleanore's words—"Drawn into revolution."

"Say, Joe," drawled Marsh, with a sharp look at him. "Got any of that typhoid left?"

Joe laughed quickly, confusedly.

Soon after that I left them.

CHAPTER IX

The next day I went to the editor for whom I was doing most of my work. When I told him I wanted to try Jim Marsh, the editor looked at me curiously.

"Why?" he asked.

I spoke of the impending strike.

"Have you met Marsh?" he inquired.

"Yes."

"Do you like him?"

"No."

"But he struck you as big."

"Yes—he did."

"Are you getting interested in strikes?"

"I want to see a big one close."

"Why?"

"Why not?" I retorted. "They're getting to be significant, aren't they? I want to see what they're like inside." The editor smiled:

"You'll find them rather hot inside. Don't get over-heated."

"Oh you needn't think I'll lose my head."

"I hope not," he said quietly. "Go ahead with your story about Marsh. I'll be interested to see what you do."

I went out of the office in no easy frame of mind. The editor's inquisitive tone had started me thinking of how J. K. had been shut out by the papers because he wrote "the truth about things."

"Oh that's all rot," I told myself. "Joe's case and mine are not the same. The magazines aren't like the papers and I'm not like Joe. His idea of the truth and mine will never be anywhere near alike."

But what would Eleanore think of it? I went home and told her of my plan. To my surprise she made no objection.

"It's the best thing you can do," she said. "We're in this now—on account of Sue—we can't keep out. And so long as we are, you might as well write about it, too. You think so much better when you're at work—more clearly—don't you—and that's what I want." She was looking at me steadily out of those gray-blue eyes of hers. "I want you to think yourself all out—as clearly as you possibly can—and then write just what you think," she said. "I want you to feel that I'm never afraid of anything you may ever write—so long as you're really sure it's true."

I held her a moment in my arms and felt her tremble slightly. And then she said with her old quiet smile:

"Sue has asked us over to Brooklyn to-night—Joe Kramer is to be there, too."

"That affair is moving rather fast."

"Oh yes, quite fast," she said cheerfully.

"How will Dad look at it?" I asked.

"As you did," said Eleanore dryly. "He'll look at it and see nothing at all."

"I've half a mind to tell him!"

"Don't," she said. "If you did he would only get excited, become the old-fashioned father and order Sue to leave Joe alone—which would be all that is needed now to make Sue marry Joe in a week."

"Sue is about as selfish," I said hotly, "about as wrapped up in her own little self——"

"As any girl is who thinks she's in love but isn't sure," said Eleanore. "Sue isn't sure—poor thing—she's frightfully unsettled."

"But why drag Joe way over there?"

"Because she wants to look at him there. It's her home, you know, her whole past life, all that she has been used to. It's the place where she has breakfast. She wants to see how Joe fits in."

"But they'd never live *there* if they married!"

"Nevertheless," said Eleanore, "that's one of the ways a girl makes up her mind." She looked pityingly into my eyes. "Women are beyond you—aren't they, dear?" she murmured.

"J. K. isn't," I rejoined. "And I can't see him in *any* home!"

"Can't you? Then watch him a little closer the next time he comes to ours."

I went out for a walk along the docks and tried to picture the coming strike. When I came home I found Joe there, he had come to go with us to Brooklyn. He was sitting on the floor with our boy gravely intent on a toy circus. Neither one was saying a word, but as Joe carefully poised an elephant on the top of a tall red ladder, I recalled my wife's injunction. By Jove, he did fit into a home, here certainly was a different Joe. He did not see me at the door. Later I called to him from our bedroom:

"Say, Joe. Don't you want to come in and wash?"

He came in, and presently watching him I noticed his glances about our room. It was most decidedly Eleanore's room, from the flowered curtains to the warm soft rug on the floor. It was gay, it was quiet and restful, it was intimately personal. Here was her desk with a small heap of letters and photographs of our son and of me, and here close by was her dressing-table strewn with all its dainty equipment. A few invitations were stuck in the mirror. Eleanore's hat and crumpled white gloves lay on our bed. I had thrown my coat beside them. There were such things in this small room as Joe had never dreamed of.

"Oh Joe," said Eleanore from the hall. "Don't you want to come into the nursery? Somebody wants a pillow fight."

"Sure," said Joe, with a queer little start.

"By the way," I heard her add outside. "Billy told me he saw Mrs. Marsh, and I should so like to meet her, too. Couldn't you have us all down to your room some evening?"

"If you like," he answered gruffly.

"I'm honestly curious," Eleanore said, "to see what kind of a person she is. And I'm sure that Sue is, too. May we bring her with us?"

"Of course you may—whenever you like."

"Would Friday evening be too soon?"

"I'll see if I can fix it."

When Eleanore came in to me, her lips were set tight as though something had hurt her.

"That was pretty tough," I muttered.

"Yes, wasn't it," she said quickly. "I don't care, I'm not going to have him marrying Sue. I'm too fond of both of them. Besides, your father has to be thought of. It would simply kill him!"

"Yes," I thought to myself that night. "No doubt about that, it would kill him."

How much older he looked, in the strong light of the huge old-fashioned gas lamp that hung over the dining-room table. He was making a visible effort to be young and genial. He had not seen Joe in several years, and he evidently knew nothing whatever of what Joe was up to, except that he had been ill at our home. Joe spoke of what we had done for him, and Sue eagerly took up the cue, keeping the talk upon us and "the Indian," to my father's deep satisfaction. From this she turned to our childhood and the life in this old house. Dad pictured it all in such glowing colors I recognized almost nothing as real. But watching Sue's face as she listened, she seemed to me trying to feel again as she had felt here long ago when she had been his only chum. Every few moments she would break off to throw a quick, restless glance at Joe.

When the time came for us to go, my father assured us warmly that he had not felt so young in years. He said we had so stirred him up that he must take a book and read or he wouldn't sleep a wink all night. Joe did not come away with us. As we stood all together at the door, I saw Eleanore glance into Dad's study where his heavy leather chair was waiting, and then into the room across the hall where Sue had drawn up two chairs to the fire. And I thought of the next hour or two. My father already had under his arm a book on American shipping, which told about the old despotic sea world of his day, in which there had been no strikers but only mutineers.

"There's very little time to lose," said Eleanore on the way home.

"Look here," I suggested. "Why don't you talk this out with Sue, and tell her just what you think of it all?"

"Because," said Eleanore, "what I think and what you think has nothing whatever to do with the case. Sue would say it was none of our business. And she'd be quite right. It isn't."

"Aren't we making it our business?" My wife at times gets me so confused.

"I'm not *telling* them anything," she rejoined. "I'm only trying to *show* them something and let the poor idiots see for themselves. If they won't see, it's hopeless."

CHAPTER X

On Friday evening Sue sent word that she would be late and that she would meet us at Joe's room. So we went down without her.

His room had changed since I'd seen it last, I took in at once his pathetic attempts to fix it up for our coming. Gone were the dirty curtains, the dirty collars and shirts, and the bed was concealed by an old green screen borrowed from his landlady, the German saloon-keeper's wife below. The same woman had scrubbed the floor and put down a faded rag carpet in front of the old fireplace, in which now a coal fire was burning. Poor Joe had turned up all the lights to make things bright and cheerful, but it only showed things up as they were. The room was glaringly forlorn.

And now that Eleanore had come, her presence made him feel at once what a wretchedly dreary place it was. Eleanore knew what she wanted to do and she had dressed herself for the part. And as Joe took in the effect of her smart little suit, and waited for Sue and Mrs. Marsh, he became so anxious and gloomy that he could only speak with an effort. He kept glancing uneasily at the door.

"I don't like the idea," said Eleanore, "of Sue's coming down here alone at night through this part of town." Joe looked around at her quickly. "But I suppose," she added thoughtfully, "that she'd have to get used to queer parts of towns if she ever took up the life you spoke of."

"I don't think that would bother her," Joe answered gruffly.

Presently there was a step on the stairs. He jumped up and went to the door, and a moment later Sue entered the room.

Immediately its whole atmosphere changed. Sue was plainly excited. She, too, had dressed herself with care—or rather with a careful neglect. She wore the oldest suit she had and a simple blouse with a gay red tie. With one sharp glance at Eleanore, she took in the strained situation and set about to ease it.

"What a nice old fireplace," she exclaimed. "Let's turn down the lights and draw 'round the fire. You need more chairs, Joe; go down and get some."

And soon with the lights turned low and the coals stirred into a ruddy glow, we were sitting in quite a dramatic place, the scene was set for "revolution." The curtainless windows were no longer bleak, for through them from the now darkened room we looked out on the lights of the harbor. Sue thought the view thrilling, and equally thrilling she found the last issue of Joe's weekly paper, *War Sure*, which lay on the table. It was called "Our Special Sabotage Number," and in it various stokers and dockers, in response to an appeal from Joe, had crudely written their ideas upon just how the engines of a ship or the hoisting winches on a dock could be most effectively put out of order in time of strike. "So that the scabs," wrote one contributor, "can see how they like it."

"Why not have blue-penciled some of this?" I asked, with a faint premonition of trouble ahead.

"Because Joe believes in free speech, I suppose," Sue answered for him quickly.

"I'm not much of a lawyer, Joe," I said. "But this stuff looks to me a good deal like incitement to violence."

"Possibly," J. K. replied.

"You don't look horribly frightened," laughed Sue. And she wanted to hear all the latest strike news. The time was rapidly drawing near. It was now close to the end of March and the strike was expected in April.

When Marsh arrived about nine o'clock, there was an awkward moment. For behind him came his wife and their small daughter, both of whom were stiffly dressed, and with one glance at Eleanore they felt immediately out of place. Mrs. Marsh was even more hostile and curt than when I had seen her last. She was angry at having been dragged into this and took little pains to hide it.

"My husband would have me come," she said. "And I couldn't leave my little girl, so I had to bring her along." And she stopped abruptly with a look that asked us plainly, "Now that I'm here, what do you want?"

"How old is your little girl?" Eleanore inquired.

"Six last month."

"Are you going to put her in school in New York?"

And in spite of short suspicious replies she soon had Mrs. Marsh and her child talking of kindergartens and parks and other parts of the town they must see. Sue was now eagerly talking to Marsh, Joe was beside her helping her out, and both seemed wholly to have forgotten the disturbing woman behind them. But by the quick looks that Eleanore gave them now and then, I could see she was only holding back until she should have Mrs. Marsh in a mood where she could be brought into the talk and made to tell about her life.

"Don't you ever want to settle down?" she asked when there had come a pause. Marsh turned abruptly to Eleanore.

"Of course she does," he answered. "Did you ever know a woman who didn't, the minute that she got a kid? But my wife can't, if she sticks to me. She has had to make up her mind to live in any old place that comes along, from a dollar room in a cheap hotel to a shanty in a mining camp." And his look at Eleanore seemed to add, "That's the kind she is, you little doll."

Eleanore quickly made herself look as much like a doll as possible. She placidly folded her dainty gloved hands.

"I should think," she murmured in ladylike tones, "Mrs. Marsh would find that rather difficult."

"She does," said Marsh aggressively. "But my wife has nerve enough to stand up to the rough side of life—as the wives of most workingmen have to—in this rich and glorious land."

"Won't you tell us about it?" asked Eleanore sweetly. "I should be so interested to hear. It's so different, you see, from all I've been accustomed to."

"Yes," Marsh answered grimly, "I've no doubt it is. Go ahead, Sally, and tell them about it."

And Sally did. Gladly taking her husband's aggressive tone, she started out almost with a sneer. Her remarks at first were disjointed and brief, but I told her I was writing the story of her husband's life, that I wanted her side of it from the start. I promised to show her what I wrote and let her cut anything she had told me if she did not want it in print. And so in scattered incidents, with bits thrown in now and then by Marsh, the lives of these two began to come out. And we understood her bitterness.

"Mr. Marsh was born," she said, "in one of the poorest little towns in Southern Iowa. It was nothing but a hole of a place about six miles from the county seat where my father was a lawyer. But even in that little hole his family was the poorest there. I've been all over the States since then, and I've seen poor people, the Lord knows—but I want to say I've never seen people anywhere that were any worse off than my husband was when he was a boy. And yet he got out of it all by himself. He didn't need any strikes to help him."

"But of course," Sue put in smoothly, "your husband was an exceptional man." Mrs. Marsh threw her a bitter glance.

"He might have been," she answered.

"What was he like as a boy?" I asked.

"A fighter," she said. For a moment her sharp voice grew proud. "His father took diabetes and died, and they went into debt to bury him. Jim helped his mother run the farm and missed half his schooling. But his teacher loaned him text-books—and at home they had no candles, so he used to work with his back to the fire—half the night. My father used to call him a regular little Honest Abe. That's a surprise to you, isn't it," she added with a hard little laugh.

"But then the town had a sudden boom. A new branch of the railroad came through that way and houses and stores went up over night. Jim was only sixteen then, but he grabbed the chance to get into the building. In less than a year he had earned enough money so he could quit and go to school. He came over to high school in our town, walking his six miles twice a day. And that's where I met him.

"My father took a shine to him right off and promised to make him a lawyer. He loaned him law books the first year, and the second Jim worked in his office." She looked for a moment at the wall. "I expect it's not a love story you're after—so I'll leave that part of it out. Papa was mad when I broke the news—and I can't say I blame him. He was the richest man in town, the railroad lawyer of the place—and he had meant that I should go to a polishing school in St. Louis.

"Well, I did go to St. Louis, but I was eloping at the time and I became Jim's wife. We had a hard fight for a year or two, but we made up our minds we'd make it go. Jim got a job on a skyscraper which was going up at that time. I got him his breakfast at six every morning and he got home about seven at night, and right after supper he went at his Blackstone and dug into it all evening. As a rule he got to bed at one, and five hours' sleep was all he had—with a few hours extra Sundays.

"I knew a girl from home in St. Louis whose husband was making money fast. But Jim was too proud to make use of my friends or go to her home when we were invited. We missed three card parties on that account. But she helped me get some pupils and I gave piano lessons. When my baby was born I had to quit— but I thought we were out of the woods by then, for Jim was made foreman of his gang and was raised to a hundred dollars a month. We moved from our boarding house into a flat. I hired a young Swedish girl and began to feel that I knew where I was.

"But then the building workers struck. Jim had always been popular with his men, and now he wanted his boss to give them half of what they asked for. But his boss didn't see it that way at all, and he and Jim had trouble. The next week Jim decided he wouldn't manage what he called 'scabs.' So he left his employment, went in with the men and made the strike a great success. That left him leader of their union. The salary they paid him was eighty dollars instead of a hundred—so I let our Swedish girl go.

"He said his new position would give him more time to study law. But it didn't turn out quite that way. He got so wrapped up in his union affairs that he had no time for his law books. One day I put them up on a shelf and found he didn't notice it."

Eleanore suddenly tightened at this, a quick sympathy came into her eyes. Sue gave a restless little sigh.

"He'd be out at meetings most every night," Mrs. Marsh continued. "At the end of the year he was one of three leaders in a strike of all the building trades in town. All work of that kind in the city was stopped and things got very ugly. One night a man came to our flat and informed me that my husband was in jail. I went to the jail the next morning and saw him. We had quite a talk. And that afternoon I gave up our flat."

"Why?" asked Eleanore softly.

"I presumed the landlord wished it," said Mrs. Marsh without looking around. "I took a room in a cheap hotel. Mr. Marsh came out of jail with ideas that were all new to me. He had left his old trade union and gone in with a new crowd of men who stood for out-and-out revolution—which I couldn't understand. But we made the best of it. We went to the theater that night and then he took the midnight train on one of his first labor trips. At first these trips were only for a week or so, but as time went on they grew longer. As a rule I never wrote him because I never knew his address. On one trip he was away five weeks—and before he got back there was time enough for my second baby, a little boy, to be born and die of pneumonia."

Eleanore flinched as though that had hurt. I saw her turn and look at Sue, who seemed even more restless than before.

"You decided to travel with him then—didn't you?" Eleanore murmured.

"Yes," said the other gruffly. "We used to try to figure out what city he would likely be in, or at least not far away from— and then my little girl and I would find a place to board there. It has been like that for the past four years. In that time we've lived in fourteen places all the way between here and the Coast."

"Have you lived all the time at hotels?" Eleanore inquired.

"We have," said the woman curtly, "but hardly the kind you're accustomed to. As a rule, as soon as we reach a town my husband's name appears in the papers, and on that account the more refined houses wouldn't care to keep us long."

Eleanore leaned forward, her eyes troubled and intent. She seemed to have forgotten Sue.

"How do you know they wouldn't?" she asked.

"I found out by trying—twice."

I heard a sudden angry creak in the battered old chair in which Sue was sitting.

"So my little girl Lucy and I," the embittered voice went on, "go to hotels that don't ask many questions. We pass the time going to parks or museums—or now and then to a concert— where I try to give her a taste for good music."

"Do you find time to keep up your music?" I asked.

"There's time enough," came the quick reply. "You see as a rule I'm just waiting around. One night in Pittsburgh it was my birthday, and as the Grand Opera was there for a week and I had never been to one, I got Mr. Marsh to take me. We made it a regular celebration, with dinner in a first-class restaurant just for once. But my husband is generally watched, and the papers all took it up the next day. 'Marsh and wife dine and see opera after his speech to starving strikers,' or similar words to that effect."

"Do you see anything of the strikers?" I asked.

"Not much," she replied. "We used to be invited to go to parties at their homes. But most of them, even the leaders, were Irish, Germans, Italians or Jews whose wives could barely speak English. I found them not very pleasant affairs. Some of the wives drank a good deal of beer and most of them had very little to say. Strike dances were no better. The wives as a rule sat with their children around the walls—while a lot of young factory girls, Jewesses for the most part, danced turkey trots around the hall."

"There were speeches, I suppose?" Sue put in impatiently.

"Yes—Mr. Marsh and others made speeches between dances. They weren't the kind of affairs I'd been used to in our home town," said Mrs. Marsh. "I've lost track of the folks at home. I never write and they don't write me. Only once when my mother knew where I was she sent me a box at Christmas. Lucy and I got quite excited over that box, it was all the presents we'd had from outside in quite a line of Christmases. So we thought we'd celebrate."

"How did you celebrate Christmas?" Eleanore asked softly.

"We went out and bought a tree and candles, some gold balls and popcorn and all the other fixings. And we popped the corn over the gas that night. The next day we bought things for each other's stockings. Lucy was then only four years old, but I'd leave her at a counter and tell the clerk to let her have all she wanted to buy for me up to a dollar. That was how we worked it. The next night we had the tree in our room. I got Mr. Marsh to help me trim it. At last we lit the candles and let Lucy in from the hotel hall, where she'd nearly caught her death of cold. Then we opened the box from home. There was a doll for Lucy and a framed photograph of my mother for me—and for Mr. Marsh a Bible. He got laughing over that and so did I. And that ended Christmas.

"We had another Christmas last year," she said in a slow, intense sort of way as though seeing the place as she spoke, "in a mining town in Montana, where Jim had been in jail five days and the whole place was under martial law. A major of the militia came to me on Christmas Eve. He claimed that Jim had been seen by detectives traveling with another woman and that I was not his wife. They locked me up for two hours that night as an immoral woman."

Sue was sitting rigid now, her lips pressed tight. And Joe with a strained unnatural face was staring into the fire.

"But of course," Mrs. Marsh concluded, "most of the time it isn't like that. As a rule when we come to a city nothing especial happens at all. We just take a room like the one we have now and wait till the strike is over. I've got so I have a queer view of towns. I'm always there at the time of a strike, when crowds of Italians and Poles and Jews fill the streets on parade or jam into halls and talk about running the world by themselves. And I guess they're going to do it some day—but I presume not by to-morrow."

For some time while she was speaking her eyes had been fixed steadily upon Joe's only picture. It stood on the mantel, a big charcoal sketch of a crowd of immigrants just leaving Ellis Island. They were of all races. Uncouth, heavy, stolid, with that hungry hope in all their eyes for more of the good things of the earth, they seemed like some barbaric horde about to pour in over the land. With her eyes upon their faces in deep, quiet hatred this woman from the Middle West had told the story of her life.

"Well, Sally," said her husband, who had grown restive toward the end, "I guess that'll do. Let's go on home."

"I'm sure I'm ready," she quickly replied. Now that she had come out of herself she seemed angry at having told so much.

When they had left there was a silence, which Sue broke with a breath of impatience.

"What a frightful thing it must be for a man in this work," she exclaimed, "to have a wife like that! A woman so hard and narrow, so wrapped up in her own little life, with not a spark of sympathy for any of his big ideals!"

"I suppose it's the life that has done it," said Eleanore quietly, looking at Sue.

"I'd like to see some women," Sue retorted angrily, "who have been in that life for years and years, and *have* sympathy, have *everything*, don't care for anything else in the world!" She turned suddenly to Joe. "You said there were hundreds, didn't you?"

Joe looked back at her a moment. There was a startled, groping, searching expression in his eyes.

"Yes," he said. "There are hundreds."

"Are many of them married?" Eleanore inquired.

"Some of them are," he answered.

"When a woman who, as Sue has just said, throws herself into this heart and soul, marries a man who is in it, too, how much of their time can they spend together?"

"That depends on the kind of work," he said. Eleanore held his eyes with hers.

"In some cases, I suppose," she went on, "like yours, for example, where the man's work keeps him moving—if the woman's work wouldn't let her go with him they would have to be half their time apart."

"Yes."

"As Mrs. Marsh and her husband were at the time when her second baby was born."

"Yes," said Joe, still watching her.

"Aren't there a good many, too, who don't exactly marry—but marry just a little—one woman here, another there, and so on?"

"Yes," said Joe, "there are some who do that."

"I should think," said Eleanore thoughtfully, "that in a movement of this kind a man ought not to marry at all—or else marry a little a good many times—so as always to be free for the Cause."

"Unless," said Joe, quite steadily, "he finds a woman like some I've known, whose feeling for a man, one man, seems to be planted in her for life—who can easily stand not being with him because she herself is deep in her own job, and her job is about the same as his—and because the two of them have decided to see the whole job through to the end."

His eyes went up to the charcoal sketch.

"It's a job worth seeing through," he said.

Sue was leaning forward now.

"Where did you get that picture, Joe?" she asked.

"It was an illustration," he said, "for a thing I once had in a magazine." And then as though almost forgetting us all, his eyes still upon those immigrant faces, he said with a slow, rough intensity:

"I know every figure in it. I know just where they're strong and where each one of 'em is weak. I've never made gods out of 'em. But I know they do all the real work in the world. They're the ones who get all the rotten deals, the ones who get shot down in wars and worked like dogs in time of peace. They're the ones who are ready to go out on strike and risk their lives to change all this. They're the people worth spending your life with. But it's a job for your whole life—and before a man or a woman jumps in they want to be sure they're ready."

He did not look at Sue as he spoke. He seemed barely able to hold himself in. His relief was plain when we took her away.

Sue took a car to Brooklyn and we started homeward. Eleanore wanted to walk for a while. She walked quickly, her face set.

"What do you think of it?" I asked.

"I wasn't thinking of Sue," she said. "I was thinking of Mrs. Marsh. I've never tormented a woman like that and I never will again in my life—not for Sue or anyone else—she can marry anybody she likes!"

"Well, she won't marry Joe," I said. "Did you see his face—poor devil? You've certainly settled that affair."

"Have I?" she asked sharply. And then her curious feminine mind took a long leap. "And what are *you* going to be," she asked, "in a year from now?" I smiled at her.

"Not a second Marsh," I said. "But even if I were the man in the moon, you'd make a success of being my wife."

"I think I would," said Eleanore. "It must be so quiet up there in the moon."

CHAPTER XI

"Come over here at once." My father's voice over the telephone, one morning a few days later, sounded thick and unnatural.

"What about?" I asked.

"Your sister."

When I reached the house in Brooklyn he came himself to let me in and took me into the library. I was shocked by his face, it was terribly worn, quite plainly he had been up all night. As he began speaking his voice shook and he leaned forward, every inch of him tense.

Sue had told him the night before that she was going to marry Joe Kramer. In reply to his anxious questions she had given him some of the facts about what Joe was doing. And Dad had stormed at her half the night.

"She wants to marry him, Billy," he cried. "She's got her mind set on a man like that! What has he got to support her with? Not a cent, not even a decent job! He's not writing now. Do you know what he's doing? Stirring up strikes—of the ugliest kind—of the most ignorant class of men—foreigners! I know such strikes— I've fought 'em myself and I know how they're handled! That young man will land in jail! And it's where he belongs! Do you know what he's up to right here on the docks?"

"Yes, I know——"

"Why didn't you tell me? Why did you let him come to the house?"

"I was doing my best to stop it, Dad."

"You were, eh—well, you'll stop it now! Understand me, Billy, he's your friend—you brought him here—way back at the start. You've got to put a stop to this——"

"But how?" I asked, trying to steady my voice. "What do you think that I can do?"

"You can talk to her, can't you? God Almighty! Make her see this will ruin her life!"

"I can't do that."

"Can't you?" He rose and bent over me gripping my arms, and I felt his violent trembling. "If you don't, it's the end of me," he said.

"Steady, Dad—now steady—this is coming out all right, you know——" I got him back into his chair. "I'm going to do all I possibly can. I'm going to see Joe Kramer now—he's the only one who can influence her. I'm going to get him to come to Sue and help me make her feel what's ahead—the hardest, ugliest parts of his life. Now promise you'll keep out of it, promise you'll leave her alone while I'm gone."

He agreed to this at last and I left him. But as I went into the hall Sue came to me from the other room. Her face was white and strained.

"Well, Billy?" she said. My throat tightened. She looked so piti-fully worn.

"I'm sorry, Sue——"

"Is that all you have to say to me?" she cut in with a quick catch of her breath.

"No, no." I took her in my arms. "Dear old Sue—don't you know how I feel? I want to see you happy. I'm trying to see what on earth we can do."

"Why can't you all leave me alone?" she demanded, in low bro-ken tones. "That's all I want—I'm old enough! I love him! Isn't that enough? To be treated like this—like a bad little child! If you'd been here and heard him—Dad, I mean—I tell you he's half out of his mind! I'm afraid to be left alone with him!"

"Sue?" It was our father's voice. He had come out close behind us.

"Leave me alone!" Sue started back, but he caught her arm:

"You'll stay right here with me till he comes."

"Till who comes?"

"Kramer."

"Who said he was coming?"

"Your brother."

"Billy!"

"Now, Sis, I'm going to talk to Joe and try to persuade him to see you and me together, that's all—quietly—over in our apartment."

"No," said our father. "He'll see her right here!"

"Now, Dad——"

"Careful, son, don't get in my way. I'm standing about as much as I can. Kramer is to come right here. If there's any seeing Sue to be done it's to be in her home, where she belongs. I won't let her out of it—not for an hour out of my sight!"

"You'll lock me in here?" she panted. He turned on her.

"You can call the police if you want to." He let go his hold and turned to me. "I'm thinking of her mother. If she sees this man at all again I'll see him too."

"Can't you leave us?" I implored her. "Sue—please! Go up to your room!"

When she'd gone I tried to quiet him. And now that Sue was out of the way I partly succeeded. But he stuck to his purpose. Joe must come and see Sue here.

"I want to be on hand when she sees him," he insisted. "I don't want to talk—I've done all that—I won't say a word—but I want to be here. You think you know her better than I do because you're younger—but you don't. We've lived right here together—she's been my chum for twenty-five years, and I know things about her you don't know. She's wilful, she's as wild as a hawk—but she can't hold out, she hasn't it in her."

"She will if you act as you did just now——"

"But I won't," he said sharply. "That was a mistake—and I won't let it happen again. When he comes you do the talking, boy—and if we're beaten I won't try to keep her, she goes and it's ended, I promise you that. But, son, don't make any mistake about this—I have an influence over this girl that you haven't got and nobody has. I want her to feel me beside her."

He went over this again and again, and with this I had to leave him.

I found Joe in his office. He rose abruptly when I came in, and reached for his hat.

"Let's go out for a walk," he said. Down in the street he turned on me: "Sue has just 'phoned me you were there. She thought you were going to help her, Bill, she thought that you'd stand by her. She didn't get any sleep last night—she's been through hell with that father of hers——"

"Oh, I've been all through Sue's sufferings, Joe. Don't give me any more of that."

"You mean you think she's faking?"

"No. But to be good and brutally frank about it, what she suffers just now doesn't count with me. It's what her whole life may be with you."

"That's not exactly your business, is it?"

"It wouldn't be if I didn't know Sue."

"What do you know?"

"I know that in spite of all her talk and the way she acts and honestly feels whenever she's with you," I replied, "Sue wants to hang on to her home and us. She isn't the heroic kind. She can't just follow along with you and leave all this she's used to."

Joe's face clouded a little.

"She'll get over that," he muttered.

"Perhaps she will and perhaps she won't. How do you know? You want to know, don't you? You want her to be happy?"

"No, that's not what I want most. Being happy isn't the only thing——"

"Then tell her so. That's all I ask. I'll tell you what I've come for, Joe. You've always been more honest, more painfully blunt and open than any man I've ever known. Be that way now with Sue. Give her the plainest, hardest picture you can of the life you're getting her into."

"I've tried to do that already."

"You haven't! If you want to know what you've done I can tell you. You've painted up this life of yours—and all these things you believe in—with power enough and smash enough to knock holes through all I believe in myself. And I'm stronger than Sue—you've done more to her. What I ask of you now is to drop all the fire and punch of your dreams, and line out the cold facts of your life on its personal side—what it's going to be. I'll help draw it out by asking you questions."

"What's the use of that? I know it won't change her!"

"Maybe it won't. But if it won't, at least it'll make my father give up. Can't you see? If you and I together—I asking and you answering—paint your life the way it's to be, and she says, 'Good, that's what I want'—he'll feel she's so far away from him then that he'll throw up his hands and let her go. He can rest then, we can help him then—Eleanore and I can—it may save the last years of his life. And Sue will be free to come to you."

"You mean the more ugly we make it the better."

"Just that. Let's end this one way or the other."

"All right. I agree to that."

When Joe and I came into the library my father rose slowly from his chair and the two stood looking at one another. And by some curious mental process two memories flashed into my mind. One was of the towering sails that my father had told me he had seen on his first day on the harbor, when coming here a crude boy from the inland he had thrilled to the vision of owning such ships with crews to whom his word should be law, and of sending them over the ocean world. Such was the age he had lived in. The other was of the stokers down in the bottom of the ship, and Joe's tired frowning face as he said, "Yes, they look like a lot of bums—and they feed all the fires at sea." What was there in common between these two? To each age a harbor of its own.

"Well, young man, what have you to say to me?"

"Nothing."

Sue came into the room. Briefly I explained to her what our father had agreed upon, that she was to do the deciding and that he would abide by her decision. Then I began my questions to Joe. I felt awkward, painfully the intruder into two other people's lives. And I felt as though I were operating upon the silent old man close by. "The uglier the better," I kept repeating to myself.

"Let's take up first the money side, Joe. Have you any regular salary?"

"No."

"Such as it is, where does it come from?"

"Out of the stokers."

"How much do you get?"

"One week twenty dollars and another ten or five," he said. "One week I got three dollars and eighty-seven cents."

"Is that likely to grow steadier?"

"Possibly—more likely worse."

"But can two of you live on pay like that—say an average of ten dollars a week?"

"I know several millions of people that have to. And most of them have children too."

"And you'd expect to live like that?"

"No better," was his answer. My father turned to him slowly as though he had not heard just right.

"But as a matter of fact," I went on, "you wouldn't have to, would you? You'd expect Sue to earn money as well as yourself."

"I hope so—if she wants to—it's my idea of a woman's life."

"And the work you hope she'll enter will be the kind you believe in—organizing labor and taking an active part in strikes?"

"Yes. She's a good speaker——"

"I see. And if you were out of a job at times you'd be willing to let her support you?"

Sue angrily half rose from her chair, but Joe with a grim move of his hand said softly, "Sit down and try to stand this. Let's get it over and done with." Then he turned quietly back to me.

"Why yes—I'd let her support me," he said.

"You mean you don't care one way or the other. You'd both be working for what you believe in, and how you lived wouldn't especially count?"

"That's about it."

"What do you believe in, Joe? Just briefly, what's your main idea in stirring up millions of ignorant men?"

"Mainly to pull down what's on top."

"As for instance?"

"All of it. Business, industry and finance as it's being run at present."

"A clean sweep. And in place of that?"

"Everything run by the workers themselves."

"For example?" I asked. "The ships by the stokers?"

"Yes, the ships by the stokers," he said. And I felt Dad stiffen in his chair. "As they will be when the time comes," Joe added.

"How soon will that be?"

"I'll see it," he said.

"The working people in full control. No restraints whatever from above."

"There won't be anyone left above. No more gods," he answered.

"Not even one?"

"Is there one?" he asked.

"You're an atheist, aren't you," I said.

"Yes, when I happen to think of it."

"And Sue would likely be the same."

"Isn't she now?" he inquired. I dropped the point and hurried on.

"How about Sue's friends, Joe? In a life like that—always in strikes—she'd have to give them up, wouldn't she?"

"Probably. Some of 'em think they're radicals, but I doubt if they'd come far out of the parlor."

"So her new friends would be either strikers or the people who lead in strikes. Her life would be practically sunk in the mass."

"I hope so."

"You may be in jail at times."

"Quite probably."

"Sue too?"

"Possibly."

I caught the look in my father's face and knew that I had but a few moments more.

"Do you want to marry her, Joe?" I asked.

"Yes, I'll go down to City Hall—if a large fat Tammany alderman can make our love any cleaner."

"You mean you don't believe in marriage."

"Not especially," he said.

"And so if either gets sick of the other he just leaves without any fuss."

"Naturally."

There was a pause. And then Joe spoke again.

"You're a better interviewer than I thought you were," he said. "You've made the picture quite complete—as far as you can see it. Of course you've left all the real stuff out——"

"What is the real stuff, as you call it, young man?" My father's voice had a deadly ring. Joe turned and looked at him as before.

"You couldn't understand," he said.

"I think I understand enough." Dad rose abruptly and turned to Sue. "Sue," he said. "Shall I ask your anarchist friend to go?"

I could feel Sue gather herself. She was white.

"I'll have to go with him," she managed to say. A slight spasm shot over our father's face. For a moment there was silence.

"You've heard all he said of this life of his?"

"Yes."

"And what he wants and expects you to do?"

"I heard it."

"And just how he wants you to live—with nothing you've been used to—nothing? No money but what a few drunken stokers throw your way, no decent ideals, no religion, no home?"

Again a pause.

"I want to go with him," she brought out at last.

Dad turned sharply and left the room.

I heard a deep breath behind me. It came from Joe Kramer, whose face was set in a frown of pain.

"He's so damn old," Joe muttered. "You operated on him hard."

Suddenly Sue threw herself on the lounge. She huddled there shaking and motioned us off.

"Leave me alone, can't you, go away!" we heard between her sobs. "It's all right—I'm ready—I'll come to you, Joe—but not now—not just now! Go away, both of you—leave me alone!"

Joe left the house. Soon after that Eleanore arrived and I told her what had happened. She went in to Sue, I left them together and went up to my father's room. He lay on the bed breathing quickly.

"You did splendidly, son," he said. "You slashed into her hard. It hurt me to listen—but it's all right. Let her suffer—she had to. It hit her, I tell you—she'll break down! If we can only keep her here! Get Eleanore!"

He stopped with a jerk, his hand went to his heart, and he panted and scowled with pain.

"I sent for her," I told him. "She's come and she's in Sue's room now. Let's leave them alone. It's going to be all right, Dad."

I sent for a doctor who was an old friend of my father's. He came and spent a long time in the room, and I could hear them talking. At last he came out.

"It won't do," he said. "We can't have any more of this. We must keep your sister out of his sight. She can't stay alone with him in this house, and she can't go now to your anarchist friend. If she does it may be the end of your father. Suppose you persuade her to come to you."

But here Eleanore joined us.

"I have a better plan," she said. "I've been talking to Sue and she has agreed. She's to stay—and we'll move over here and try to keep Sue and her father apart."

"What about Joe?" I asked her.

"Sue has promised me not to see Joe until the strike is over. It will only be a matter of weeks—perhaps even days—it may break out to-morrow. It's not much of a time for Joe to get married—besides, it's the least she can do for her father—to wait that long. And she has agreed. So that much is settled."

She went home to pack up a few things for the night. When she came back it was evening. She spent some time with Sue in her room, while I stayed in with father. I gave him a powder the doctor had left and he was soon sleeping heavily.

At last in my old bedroom Eleanore and I were alone. It was a long time before we could sleep.

"Funny," said Eleanore presently, "how thoroughly selfish people can be. Here's Sue and your father going through a perfectly ghastly crisis. But I haven't been thinking of them—not at all. I've been thinking of us—of you, I mean—of what this strike will do to you. You're getting so terribly tense these days."

I reached over and took her hand:

"You don't want me to run away from it now?"

"No," she said quickly. "I don't want that. I've told you that I'm not afraid——"

"Then we'll have to wait and see, won't we, dear? We can't help ourselves now. I've got to keep on writing, you know—we depend on that for our living. And I can't write what I did before—I don't seem to have it in me. So I'm going into this strike as hard as I can—I'm going to watch it as hard as I can and think it out as clearly. I know I'll never be like Joe—but I do feel now I'm going to change. I've got to—after what I've been shown. The harbor is so different now. Don't you understand?"

I felt her hand slowly tighten on mine.

"Yes, dear," she said, "I understand——"

CHAPTER XII

The events of that day dropped out of my mind in the turbulent weeks that followed. For day by day I felt myself sink deeper and deeper into the crowd, into surging multitudes of men—till something that I found down there lifted me up and swept me on— into a strange new harbor.

Of the strike I can give only one man's view, what I could see with my one pair of eyes in that swiftly spreading confusion that soon embraced the whole port of New York and other ports both here and abroad. War correspondents, I suppose, must feel the same chaos around them, but in my case it rose from within me as well. I was like a war correspondent who is trying to make up his mind about war. What was good in this labor rebellion? What was bad? Where was it taking me?

From the beginning I could feel that it meant for me a breaking of ties with the safe strong world that had been my life. I felt this first before the strike, when I went to my magazine editor. He had taken my story about Jim Marsh, but when I came to him now and told him that I wanted to cover the strike,

"Go ahead if you like," he answered, a weary indulgence in his tone, "I don't want to interfere in your work. But I can't promise you now that we'll buy it. If you feel you must write up this strike you'll have to do it at your own risk."

"Why?" I asked. For years my work had been ordered ahead. I thought of that small apartment of ours, of my father sick at home—and I felt myself suddenly insecure.

"Because," he answered coolly, "I'm not quite sure that what you write will be a fair unbiassed presentation of the facts. I've seen so many good reporters utterly spoiled in strikes like this. They lose their whole sense of proportion and never seem to get it quite back."

This little talk left me deeply disturbed. But I was unwilling to give up my plan, and so, after some anxious thinking, I decided to free-lance it. After all, if this one story didn't sell I could borrow until I wrote something that did. And I set to work with an angry vim. The very thought that my old world was closing up behind me made my mind the more ready now for the new world opening ahead.

From the old house in Brooklyn I once more explored my harbor. All day and the greater part of each night I went back over my old ground. Old memories rose in sharp contrast to new views I was getting. From the top I had come to the bottom. Crowds of sweating laborers rose everywhere between me and my past. And as between me and my past, and between these masses and their rulers, I felt the struggle drawing near, the whole immense region took on for me the aspect of a battlefield, with puffs and clouds and darting lines of smoke and steam from its ships and trains and factories. Through it I moved confusedly, troubled and absorbed.

I saw the work of the harbor go now with an even mightier rush, because of the impending strike. The rumor of its coming had spread far over the country, and shippers were hurrying cargoes in. I saw boxes and barrels by thousands marked "Rush." And they were rushed! On one dock I saw the dockers begin at seven in the morning and when I came back late in the evening the same men were there. At midnight I went home to sleep. When I came back at daybreak the same men were there, and I watched them straining through the last rush until the ship sailed that day at noon. They had worked for twenty-nine hours. In that last hour I drew close—so close that I could feel them heaving, sweating, panting, feel their laboring hearts and lungs. Long ago I had watched them thus, but then I had seen from a different world. I had felt the pulse of a nation beating and I had gloried in its speed. But now I felt the pulse-beats of exhausted straining men, I saw that undertaker's sign staring fixedly from across the way. "*Certainly* I'm talking to you!" Six thousand killed and injured!

I saw accidents that week. I saw a Polish docker knocked on the head by the end of a heavy chain that broke. I saw a little Italian caught by the foot in a rope net, swung yelling with terror into the air, then dropped—his leg was broken. And toward the end of a long night's work I saw a tired man slip and fall with a huge bag on his shoulders. The bag came down on top of him, and he lay there white and still. Later I learned that his spine had been broken, that he would be paralyzed for life.

But what I saw was only a part. From the policemen's books alone I found a record for that week of six dockers killed and eighty-seven injured. I traced about a score of these cases back into their tenement homes, and there I found haggard, crippled men and silent, anxious women, the mothers of small children. Curious and deeply thrilled, these children looked at the man on the bed, between his groans of pain I heard their eager questions, they kept getting in their mother's way. One thin Italian mother, whose nerves were plainly all on edge suddenly slapped the child at her skirts, and then when it began to cry she herself burst into tears.

These tragic people gripped me hard. The stokers down in their foul hole in the bottom of the ship had only disturbed and repelled me. But these crippled dockers in their homes, with their women and their children, their shattered lives, their agony, starvation looming up ahead—they brought a tightening at my throat—nor was it all of pity. For these labor victims were not dumb, I heard the word "strike!" spoken bitterly here, and now I felt that they had a right to this bitter passion of revolt.

But still I felt their way was wrong. How could any real good, any sure intelligent remedies for all this fearful misery, come out of the minds of such people as these, who were rushing so blindly into revolt? I went into saloons full of dockers and stokers, and out of the low harsh hubbub there the word "strike!" came repeatedly to my ears, recklessly from drunken tongues. Wherever I went I heard that word. I heard it spoken in many languages, in many tones. Anxious old women said "strike!" with fear. Little street urchins shouted it joyously. Even the greenest foreigner understood its meaning. A little Greek, who had broken his arm and was one of the cases I traced home, understood none of my questions. "You speak no English?" He shook his head. "Strike!" I ventured. Up he leaped. "Yo' bet!" he cried emphatically.

What was it deep within me that leaped up then as though to meet that burning passion in his eyes?

"Keep your head," I warned myself. "To change all this means years of work—thinking of the clearest kind. And what clear thinking can these men do? The ships have got them down so low they've no minds left to get out of their holes!"

And yet—as now on every dock, that "strike feeling" in the air kept growing tenser, tenser—its tensity crept into me. What was it that lay just ahead? I felt like a man starting out on a journey— a journey from which when he comes back he will find nothing quite the same.

I had a talk about the strike one day with Eleanore's father. I can still see the affectionate smile on his face, he looked as though he were seeing me off.

"My dear boy," he said, in his kind quiet voice, "don't forget for even a minute that the men who stand behind my work are going to stamp out this strike. This modern world is too complex to allow brute force and violence to wreck all that civilization has done. I'm sorry you've gone into this—but so long as you have, as Eleanore's father, I want you now to promise you won't write a line until the strike is over and you have had plenty of time to get clear. Don't let yourself get swamped in this—remember that you have a wife and a small son to think of."

My father had put it more sharply. He was out of bed now and he seemed to take strength from the news reports that he eagerly read of the struggle so fast approaching.

"At sea," he said, "when stokers try to quit their jobs and force their way on deck, they're either put in irons or shot down as mutineers. You'll see your friend Kramer dead or in jail. No danger to your sister now. Only see that *you* keep out of it!"

I did not tell him of my work, for I knew it would only excite him again, and excitement would be dangerous.

"Now you and Eleanore must go home," said Sue that night. "You'll have enough to think of. I'll be all right with father—he knows there's nothing to do but wait, and he's so kind to me now that it hurts. Poor old Dad—how well he means. But he's the old and we're the new—and that's the whole trouble between us." A sudden light came in her eyes. "The new are bound to win!" she said.

But I was not so sure of the new. To me it was still very vague and chaotic. After we had moved back to New York, at the times when I came home to sleep, Eleanore was silent or quietly casual in her remarks, but I felt her always watching me. One night when I came in very late and thought her asleep, being too tired to sleep myself, I went to our bedroom window and stood looking off down into the distant expanse of the harbor. How quiet and cool it seemed down there. But presently out of the darkness behind, Eleanore's arm came around me.

"I wonder whether the harbor will ever let us alone," she said. "It was so good to us at first—we were getting on so splendidly. But it's taking hold of us now again—as though we had wandered too far away and were living too smoothly and needed a jolt. Never mind, we're not afraid. Only let's be very sure we know what we are doing."

"We'll be very sure," I whispered, and I held her very close.

"Let's try to be sure together," she said. "Don't leave me out— I want to be in. I want to see as much as I can—and help in any way I can. If you make any friends I want to know them. Remember that whatever comes, thy people shall be mine, my dear."

The next day the strike began.

Out of the docks at nine in the morning I saw dockers pour in crowds. They moved on to other docks, merged themselves in other crowds, scattered here and gathered there, until at last a black tide of men, here straggling wide, here densely massed, moved slowly along the waterfront.

In and out of these surging throngs I moved, so close that in the quiver of muscles, the excited movements of big limbs, the rough eagerness of voices that spoke in a babel of many tongues, such a storm of emotions beat in upon me that I felt I had suddenly dived into an ocean of human beings, each one of whom was as human as I. I caught a glimpse of Joe hurrying by. And I thought of Sue, and of Joe's appeal to her and to me to throw in our lives with such strangers as these whose coarse heavy faces were pressing so close. And I thought of Eleanore at home. "Thy people shall be mine, my dear."

Teamsters drove clattering trucks through the crowds. Some of them did not unload, but others dumped piles of freight by the docks. The dam had begun. All day long the freight piled up, and by evening the light of a pale moon shone down upon acres of barrels and boxes. Then the teamsters unharnessed their teams, left the empty trucks with poles in air, and the teamsters and their horses and all the crowds of strikers scattered by degrees up into the tenement regions. Bursts of laughter and singing came now and then out of the saloons.

Silence settled down over the docks. Walking now down the waterfront I met only a figure here and there. A taxi came tearing and screeching by, and later down the long empty space came a single wagon slowly. A smoky lantern swung under its wheels, and its old white horse with his shaggy head down came plodding wearily along. He alone had no strike feeling.

Battered and worn from the day's impressions I wanted to be alone and to think. I made my way in and out among trucks and around a dockshed out to a slip. It was filled with barges, tugs and floats jammed in between the two big vessels that loomed one at either pier. It was a dark jumble of spars and masts, derricks, funnels and cabin roofs, all shadowy and silent. A single light gleamed here and there from the long dark deck of the Morgan coaster close to my right. She was heavily loaded still, for she had come to dock too late. Smoke still drifted from her stout funnel, steam puffed now and then from her side. Behind her, reaching a mile to the North, were ships by the dozen, coasters and great ocean liners, loaded and waiting to discharge or empty and waiting to reload. And to the South were miles of railroad sheds already packed to bursting. I thought of the trains from all over the land still rushing a nation's produce here, and of the starlit ocean roads, of ships coming from all over the world, the men in their fiery caverns below feeding faster the fires to quicken their speed, all bringing cargoes to this port. More barrels, boxes, crates and bags to be piled high up on the waterfront. For the workers had gone away from their work, and the great white ships were still.

"What has all this to do with me?"

There came into my mind the picture of a little man I had seen that day, a suburban commuter by his looks, frowning from a ferryboat upon a cheering crowd of strikers. I laughed to myself as I thought of him. He had seemed so ludicrously small.

"Yes, my friend," I thought, "you and I are a couple of two-spots here, swallowed up in the scenery."

I thought of what Joe had said that day: "When you see the crowd, in a strike like this, loosen up and show all it could be if it had the chance—that sight is so big it blots you out—you sink—you melt into the crowd."

Something like that happened to me. I had seen the multitudes "loosen up," I had felt myself melt into the crowd. But I had not seen what they could be nor did I see what they could do. Far to the south, high over all the squalid tenement dwellings, rose that tower of lights I had known so well, the airy place where Eleanore's father had dreamed and planned his clean vigorous world. It was lighted to-night as usual, as though nothing whatever had happened. I thought of the men I had seen that day. How crassly ignorant they seemed. And yet in a few brief hours they had paralyzed all that the tower had planned, reduced it all to silence, nothing. Could it be that such upheavals as these meant an end to the rule of the world from above, by the keen minds of the men at the top? Was that great idol which had been mine for so many glad years, that last of my gods, Efficiency, beginning to rock a little now upon its deep foundations?

What could these men ever put in its place? I recalled the words of an old dock watchman with whom I had talked the evening before. From the days of the Knights of Labor he had been through many strikes, and all had failed, he told me. His dog sat there beside him, a solemn old red spaniel, looking wistfully into his master's face. And with somewhat the same expression, looking out on the moonlit Hudson, the old striker had said slowly:

"Before these labor leaders will do half of what they say—a pile of water will have to go by."

A sharp slight sound behind me jerked me suddenly out of my thoughts. I jumped as though at a shot. How infernally tight my nerves were getting. The sound had come from a mere piece of paper blown by the wind—a rough salt wind which now blew in from the ocean as though impatient of all this stillness. From below came a lapping and slapping of waves. Above me a derrick mast growled and whined as it rocked. And now as I looked about me all those densely crowded derricks moved to and fro against the sky. I had never felt in this watery world such deep restlessness as now.

"I wonder if you'll ever stop heaving," I thought half angrily. "I wonder what I'll be like when you finally get through with me. When will you ever let me stand pat and get things settled for good and all? When stop this endless starting out?"

CHAPTER XIII

What could such men as these raise up in place of the mighty life they had stilled?

At first only chaos.

As I went along the waterfront I felt a confused disappointment. Deep under all my questioning there had been a vague subconscious hope that I would see a miracle here. I had looked for an army. I saw only mobs of angry men. They were "picketing" the docks, here making furious rushes at men suspected of being "scabs," there clustering quickly around some talker or some man who was reading a paper, again drifting up into the streets of teeming foreign quarters, jamming into barrooms, voicing wildest rumors, talking, shouting, pounding tables with huge fists. And to me there was nothing inspiring but only something terrible here, an appalling force turned loose, sightless and unguided. What a fool I had been to hope. The harbor held no miracles.

The strike leaders seemed to have little control. Headquarters were in the wildest disorder. Into the big bare meeting hall and through the rooms adjoining drifted multitudes of men. There were no inner private rooms and Marsh saw everyone who came. He was constantly shaking hands or drawling casual orders, more like suggestions than commands. I caught sight of Joe Kramer's face at his desk, where he was signing and giving out union cards to a changing throng that kept pressing around him. Joe's face was set and haggard. He had been at that desk all night.

"It's hopeless. They can do nothing," I thought.

But when I came back the next morning I felt a sudden shock of surprise. For in some mysterious fashion a crude order had appeared. The striker throng had poured into the hall, filled all the seats and then wedged in around the walls. They were silent and attentive now. On the stage sat Marsh and his fellow leaders. Before them in the first three rows of seats was the Central Committee, a rough parliament sprung up over night. Each member, I found, had been elected the night before by his "district committee." These district bodies had somehow formed in the last two days and in them leaders had arisen. The leaders were here to plan together, the mass was here to make sure they planned right. And watching the deep rough eagerness on all those silent faces, that vague hope stirred again in my breast.

Presently I caught Joe's eye. At once he left his platform seat and came to me in the rear of the hall.

"Come on, Bill," he said. "We want you up here." And we made our way up to the platform. There Marsh reached over and gripped my hand.

"Hello, Bill, glad you're with us," he said. I tingled slightly at his tone and at a thousand friendly eyes that met mine for an instant. Then it was over. The work went on.

What they did at first seemed haphazard enough. Reports from the districts were being read with frequent interruptions, petty corrections and useless discussions that strayed from the point and made me impatient. And yet wide vistas opened here. Telegrams by the dozen were read from labor unions all over the country, from groups of socialists East and West, there were cables from England, Germany, France, from Russia, Poland, Norway, from Italy, Spain and even Japan. "Greetings to our comrades!" came pouring in from all over the earth. What measureless army of labor was this? All at once the dense mass in the rear would part to let a new body of men march through. These were new strikers to swell the ranks, and at their coming all business would stop, there would be wild cheers and stamping of feet, shrill whistles, pandemonium!

Gradually I began to feel what was happening in this hall. That first "strike feeling"—diffused, shifting and uncertain—was condensing as in a storm cloud here, swelling, thickening, whirling, attracting swiftly to itself all these floating forces. Here was the first awakening of that mass thought and passion which swelling later into full life was to give me such flashes of insight into the deep buried resources of the common herd of mankind, their resources and their power of vision when they are joined and fused in a mass. Here in a few hours the great spirit of the crowd was born.

For now the crowd began to question, think and plan. Ideas were thrown out pell mell. I found that every plan of action, everything felt and thought and spoken, though it might start from a single man, was at once transformed by the feeling of all, expressed in fragments of speech, in applause, or in loud bursts of laughter, or again by a chilling silence in which an unwelcome thought soon died. The crowd spoke its will through many voices, through men who sprang up and talked hard a few moments, then sat down and were lost to sight—some to rise later again and again and grow in force of thought and expression, others not to be seen again, they had simply been parts of the crowd, and the crowd had made them rise and speak.

On the first day of this labor parliament, up rose a stolid Pole. He was no committeeman but simply a member of the throng.

"Yo' sand a spickair to my dock," he said. "Pier feefty-two— East Reever. I t'ink he make de boys come out." He sat down breathing heavily.

"You don't need any speaker, go yourself," an Irishman called from across the hall.

"I no spick," said the Pole emphatically.

"You're spicking now, ain't you?" There was a burst of laughter, and the big man's face grew red. "You don't need to talk," the voice went on. "Just go into your dock and yell 'Strike!' You've got chest enough, you Pollock."

The big Pole made his way out of the hall. In the rear I saw him light his pipe and puff and scowl in a puzzled way. Then he disappeared. The next day, in the midst of some discussion, he rose from another part of the hall.

"I want to say I strike my dock," he shouted. Nobody seemed to hear him, it had nothing whatever to do with the subject, but he sat down with a glow of pride.

A Norwegian had arisen and was speaking earnestly, but his English was so wonderful that no one could understand.

"Shut up, you big Swede, go and learn English," somebody said.

"He don't have to shut up." The voice of Marsh cut in, and the mass backed up his curt rebuke by a murmur of approval. He had risen and come forward, and now waited till there was absolute silence. "Everyone gets a hearing here," he said. "We've got nine nationalities, but each one checks his race at the door. Every man is to have a fair show. What we need is an interpreter. Where's someone who can help this Swede?"

There was a quick stirring in the mass and then a man was shoved out of it. He went over to the speaker, who at once began talking intensely.

"The first thing he wants to say," said the interpreter at the end of the torrent, "is that he'd rather be dead than a Swede. He says he's a Norwegian. His second point is that all bad feeling between nationalities ought to be stopped if the strike's to be won. He says he's seen fights already between Irish and Eyetalians."

Up leaped an enormous negro docker who sounded as though he preached often on Sundays.

"Yes, brothers," he boomed, "let us stop our fights. Let us desist—let us refrain. We are men from all countries, black and white. The last speaker came from Norway—he came from way up there in the North. My father came from Africa——"

"He must have come last Monday," said a dry, thin voice from the back of the hall, and there was a laugh.

"Brothers," cried the black man, "I come here from the colored race. At my dock I got over sixty negroes to walk out. Is there no place for us in this strike? If my father was a slave, is my color so against me?"

"It ain't your color, it's your scabbing," a sharp voice interrupted. "They broke the last strike with coons like you. They brought you up in boats from the South. And you scabbed—you scabbed yourself! Didn't you? You did! You —— of a nigger!"

A little Italian sprang up in reply. He did not look like a docker. He was gaily dressed in a neat blue suit with a bright red tie:

"Fellow workers—I am Italian man! You call me Guinney, Dago, Wop—you call another man Coon, Nigger—you call another man a Sheeny! Stop calling names—call men fellow workers! We are on strike—let us not fight each other—let us have peace—let us have a good time! I know a man who has a big boat—and he say now we can have it for nothing—to take our wives and children and make excursions every day. On the boat we will have a good time. I am a musician—I play the violin on a

boat till I strike—so now I will get you the music. And we shall
run that boat ourselves! We have our own dockers to start it from
dock—we have our own stokers, our own engineers—we have
our own pilots—we have all! And it will be easy to steer that
boat—for we have made the harbor empty—we shall have the
whole place to ourselves! Some day maybe soon we have all
the boats in the world for ourselves—and we shall be free! All
battle boats we shall sink in the sea—we stop all wars! So now
we begin—we stop all our fighting—we take out this boat—all
our comrades on board! No coons, no niggers, no sheenies, no
wops! Fellow workers—I tell you the name of our boat! *The
Internationale!*"

The little man's speech was greeted with a sudden roar of
applause. For the crowd had seen at once this danger of race
hatred and was eager to put it down. *The Internationale* made
her first trip on the following day, and after that her daily cruise
became the gala event of the strike. Both decks of the clumsy
craft were packed with strikers, their wives and their children,
and all up and down the harbor she went. The little Italian and
his friends had had printed a red pamphlet, "Revolutionary
Songs of the Sea," the solos of which he sang on the boat while
the rest came in on the chorus. A new kind of a "chanty man"
was he, voicing the wrongs and the fierce revolt and the surging
hopes and longings of all the toilers on the sea—while this ship
that was run by the workers themselves plowed over a strange
new harbor. I watched it one day from the end of a pier. It
approached with a swelling volume of song. It drew so near I
could see the flushed faces of those who were singing, some with
their eyes on their leader's face, others singing out over the water
as though they were spreading far and wide the exultant proph-
ecy of that song. It passed, the singing died away—and still I sat
there wondering.

"We shall have all the boats in the world for ourselves—and
we shall be free! All battle boats we shall sink in the sea! We stop
all wars! So now we begin!"

Was it indeed a beginning? Was this the opening measure of
music that would be heard round the world? My mind rejected
the idea, I thought it merest madness. But still that song rang in
my ears. What deep compelling force was here—this curious

power of the crowd that had so suddenly gripped hold of this simple Italian musician, this fiddler on excursion boats, and in a few short days and nights had made him pour into music the fire of its worldwide dreams?

I saw it seize on others. One day a young girl rose up in the hall. A stenographer on one of the docks, she was neatly, rather sprucely dressed, but her face was white and scared. She had never made a speech before. She was speaking now as though impelled by something she could not control.

"Comrades—fellow workers." Her voice trembled violently. She paused and set her teeth, went on. "How about the women and babies?" she asked. "I know of one who was born last night. And that's only one of a lot. We have thousands of kids and old people—sick people too, and cripples and drunks—all that these lovely jobs of ours have left on our backs. They've got to be carried. Who's to take care of 'em, feed 'em, doctor 'em? If we're going to run the earth let's begin at home. What does anyone know about that?"

She sat down with a kind of a gasp of relief. Her seat was close to the platform, and I could see her bright excited eyes as she listened to what she had started here. For the crowd, as though it had only been waiting for this girl to speak its thought, now seized upon her question. Sharp voices were heard all over the hall. Some said they could get doctors, others knew of empty stores that could be had for nothing and used as free food stations. An assistant cook from an ocean liner told where his chief bought wholesale supplies. And the girl who had roused this discussion, her nervousness forgotten now, rose up again and again with so many quick, eager suggestions, that when the first relief station was opened that evening she was one of those placed in charge.

I saw her grow amazingly, for now I came to know her well. Her name was Nora Ganey. At home that night when Eleanore said, "Remember, dear, I want something to do that will let me see the strike for myself"—I thought at once of this work of relief. Eleanore would be good at this, she had trained herself in just such work. And it appealed to her at once. She went down with me the next morning, and she and Nora Ganey, though their lives had been so different, yet proved at once to be kindred souls. Eleanore gave half her time to the work, and these two became fast friends.

Before the strike Nora had sat all day in an office pounding a typewriter, several nights a week she had gone to dances in public halls, and that had made her entire life. In the strike she was at her food station all day, and each evening till late she visited homes, looking into appeals for aid and if need be issuing tickets for food. She heard the bitterest stories from wives of harbor victims, and she began telling these stories in speeches. Soon she was sent out over the city to speak at meetings and ask for aid. With Eleanore I went one night to hear this young stenographer speak to twenty thousand in Madison Square Garden. And the strike leader who made that speech was not the girl of two weeks before. Her life had been as utterly changed as though she had jumped to another world.

Through Marsh and Joe, in those tense days, I was fast making striker friends. With some I had long intimate talks, I ate many kitchen suppers and spent many evenings in tenement homes. But though by degrees I felt myself drawn to these men who called me "Bill," when alone with each one I felt little or none of that passion born of the crowd as a whole. With a sharp drop, a sudden reaction, I would feel this new world gone. Its strength and its wide vision would seem like mere illusions now. What could we little pigmies do with the world? Its guidance was for Dillon and all the big men I had known. Often in those days of groping, knotty problems all unsolved, with a sickening hunger I would think of those men at the top, of their keen minds so thoroughly trained, their vast experience in affairs. I would feel myself in a hopeless mob, a dense, heavy jungle of ignorant minds. And groping for a foothold here I would find only chaos.

But back we would go into the crowd, and there in a twinkling we would be changed. Once more we were members of the whole and took on its huge personality. And again the vision came to me, the dream of a weary world set free, a world where poverty and pain and all the bitterness they bring might in the end be swept away by this awakening giant here—which day by day assumed for me a personality of its own. Slowly I began to feel what It wanted, what It hated, how It planned and how It acted. And this to me was a miracle, the one great miracle of the strike.

For years I had labored to train myself to concentrate on one man at a time, to shut out all else for weeks on end, to feel this man so vividly that his self came into mine. Now with the same intensity I found myself striving day and night to feel not one but thousands of men, a blurred bewildering multitude. And slowly in my striving I felt them fuse together into one great being, look at me with two great eyes, speak to me with one deep voice, pour into me with one tremendous burning passion for the freedom of mankind.

Was this another god of mine?

CHAPTER XIV

The great voice of the crowd—incessant, demanding of me and of all within hearing to throw in our lives, to join in this march to a new free world regardless of all risk to ourselves—grew clear to me now.

I felt myself drawn in with the rest. I was helping in the public-ity work, each day I met with the leaders to draw up statements for the press. And these messages to the outside world that I wrote to the slow and labored dictation of some burly docker comrade, or again by myself at dawn to express the will of a meeting that had lasted half the night—slowly became for me my own. Almost unawares I had taken the habit of asking:

"How much can *we* do? How sane and vigilant can *we* be to keep clear of violence, bloodshed, mobs and a return to chaos? How long can we hold together fast? How far can we march toward this promised land?"

In order to see ourselves as a whole and feel our swiftly swell-ing strength, having now burst the confines of our hall, we began to hold meetings out on "the Farm." There are many "farms" on the waterfront, for a "farm" is simply the open shore space in front of a dock. But this, which was one of the widest of all, now came to be spoken of as "the Farm," and took on an atmosphere all its own. For there were scenes here which will long endure in the memories of thousands of people. For them it will be a great bright spot in the times gone by—in one of those times behind the times, as this strange world keeps rushing on.

From the top of a pile of sand, where I stood with the speakers at the end of a soft April day, I saw the whole Farm massed solid with people. This mass rose in hummocks and hills of humanity over the piles of brick and sand and of crates and barrels dumped by the trucks, and out over the water they covered the barges and the tugs, and there were even hundreds upon the roofs of dock-sheds. The yelp of a dog was heard now and then and the faint cries of children. But the mass as a whole stood motionless, with-out a sound. They had stood thus since two o'clock, and now the sun was setting. To the west the harbor was empty, no smoke from ships obscured the sun, and it shone with radiant clearness upon eleven races of men, upon Italians, Germans, French, on English, Poles and Russians, on Negroes and Norwegians, Lascars, Malays, Coolies, on figures burly, figures puny, faces white and faces swar-thy, yellow, brown and black. The sun shone upon all alike—except where that Morgan liner, still lying unloaded at her dock, threw a long dark creeping shadow out across the throng.

Thirty thousand people were here. Thirty thousand intensely alive. As I eagerly watched their faces it was not their poverty now but their boundless fresh vitality that took hold of me so hard. I had read many radical books of late, in my groping for a foothold, and I had found most of them dry affairs. But now the crowd through its leaders had laid hold upon the thoughts in these books, had made them its own and so given them life. In the pro-cess the thoughts had been twisted and bent, some parts ignored and others brought out of all their nice proportions. Exaggera-tion, sentiment, all kinds of crudity were here. But it was crudity alive, a creed was here in action. Out of all the turmoil, the take and give, the jar and clash back there in the meeting hall, had come certain thoughts and passions, hopes and plans, that the multitude had not ignored or hooted but had caught up and cheered into life. And these ideas that they had cheered were now being pounded back into their minds. Monotonous repetition, you say? Yes, monotonous repetition—slow sledgehammer blows upon something red hot—pounding, pounding, pounding—that when it cooled its shape might be changed.

Nora Ganey was speaking.

"Look at those ocean liners!" she cried. Her voice was sharp and strident. "They're paralyzed now, and because they are they're costing the big companies millions of dollars every day. That's what their time is worth to their owners. But what are those ships worth to you? Ten dollars a week and a broken arm—or a leg or a skull, you can take your choice. Six thousand of you men were crippled or crushed to death last year—and that, let me remind you, was only in the port of New York. Why was it? Why did it have to be? And why will it always have to be until you make these ships your own? Because, fellow workers, the time of the ships is worth so much to their owners that the work has got to be rushed day and night—and in that rush somebody's bound to get hurt—if he isn't killed he's lucky! And as for the rest, when at last you're through and dead tired—they point to the saloons and say, 'Now have a few drinks! We won't need you again till next Tuesday'! Do you know what all this means in your homes? It means drunks, cripples, sick and poor! It means such sights as I'll never forget. I've seen 'em all—just lately!

"I never thought of such things before. I liked my office job on the dock and all the jobs around me—and when sailing time drew near I liked the last excitement. I liked the rich furs and dresses and the cute little earrings and slippers and dogs that were attached to the women who came. I liked to see them pile out of their motors and laugh and make eyes at the men they belonged to. I liked to peep into the cabins they had—get on to all the luxuries there.

"But out of all this magnificence, friends, and this work that keeps it going—I saw one day a man come on a stretcher. He was dead. And that started me thinking. That's why I came out when the strike was called. And in the strike I've gone into your homes. I've seen what those soft expensive female dolls and all the work that makes them costs. And I've got a thrill of another kind! It's a thrill that'll last for the rest of my life! And in yours, too, fellow workers! For I believe that you'll go right on—that you'll strike and strike and strike again—till you make these tenements own these ships—and a life won't be thrown away for a dollar!"

She stopped sharply and stepped back, and there burst out a frenzy of applause, which died down to be caught up and prolonged and deepened into a steady roar, as Marsh came slowly forward. He stood there bareheaded, impassive and quiet, listening to the great voice of the mass. At last he turned to the chairman. The latter picked up a whistle, and at that piercing call to order slowly the cheering began to subside. Faces pressed eagerly closer. Marsh looked all around him.

"Fellow workers," he began, "it's hard for a man to be understood when he's talking to men from all over the world." He pointed down to a cluster of Lascars with white turbans on their heads. "*You* don't understand me. But some of your comrades will give you my speech, for we are all strike brothers here. On the ship there is no flag—on the ship there is no nation—on the ship there is only work—on the ship there are only the workers!

"For a ship may be equipped with the most powerful engines to drive her—she may have the best brains to direct her course—but the ship can't sail until you go aboard! You're the men who make the ships of use, you're the men who give value to the stock of all the big ship companies! You are the ship industry—and to you the ship industry should belong!

"I want you now to think of a tombstone. Out in the Atlantic, two miles down they tell me, a big ship is stuck with her bow in the ooze of the ocean floor and her stern six hundred feet up in the water. In the cold green light down there she looks like a tombstone—and she is packed with dead people inside. She is there because where she should have had lifeboats she had French cafés instead, and sun parlors for the ladies. Some of these ladies went down with the ship, and we heard a lot about their screams. But we haven't heard much of the cries for help of the thousands of men who go down every year in rotten old ships upon the seas! Nor have we heard of the millions more who are killed on land—on the railroads, in the mines and mills and stinking slums of cities!

"But now we've decided that cries like these are to be heard all over the world. For we've only got one life apiece—we're not quite sure of another. And because we do all the work that is done we want all the life there is to be had! All the life there is to be had—that's what we are striking for! That is our share of the life in this world! And until we get our share this labor war will have no end! Other wars may come and go—but under them all on land and sea this war of ours will go steadily on—will swallow up all other wars—will swallow up in all your minds all hatred of your brother men! For you they will be workers all! With them you will rise—and the world will be free!"

When the long stormy din of cheers had little by little died away Joe Kramer began the last speech of the day. He had eaten and slept little, he had lived on coffee and cigarettes, and there was a strained look in his deep eyes as he rose up lean and gaunt by my side.

"I'm here to-day to speak to the men who work in stokeholes naked," he said. "I'm here to talk of the lives you lead—the lives that millions before you have led—for a few brief years—and then they have died. For lives in stokeholes are not long. And before I begin I propose that we stand for a moment with uncovered heads." He looked out over the multitude as though seeing far beyond them, and his voice was as harsh as the look in his eyes. "As a tribute to all the dead stokers," he said.

And in a breathless silence the multitude did what he had asked. Joe broke this silence sharply.

"Now for life and the living," he said. "Why was it that those men all died? What has the change from sails to steam done to the lives of the men at sea?

"The old sailor at least had air to breathe. But what you breathe is red hot gas—I know because I've been there. There is a gong upon the wall, and when it clangs you heave in coal, and if when it clangs faster you don't keep quite up to its pace, a white light flashes out of the wall, and that light is the Chief Engineer's way of saying, 'God damn you, keep up those fires down there! Time is money! Who are you?'

"The old-time sailor lived on deck. He had the winds, the sun and the stars. But you live down between steel walls—with only the glare of electric lights in which you sleep and eat and sweat. You work at all kinds of irregular hours, for you there is no day or night. You don't know whether the millionaire and his last and loveliest wife are drinking champagne before going to bed, in their cabin de luxe above you, or taking their coffee the next day at noon. You don't know about anything way up there—unless you go up as I've seen you do, half out of your senses from the heat, and make a sudden jump for the rail. The cry is heard—'Man overboard!'—then shrieks and a chorus of 'Oh-my-God's!' And then somebody says, 'It's only a stoker.'"

He stopped short, and at the sudden roar of the crowd I saw him frown and quiver. He drew a deep, slow breath and went on:

"They threw off all the good in the ship with sails—but they carefully kept all that was bad. The old mutiny laws—they kept all that. Undermanning of crews—they kept all that. The water-front sharks—they kept all that. But there was one thing they couldn't keep—the old sailor's habit of standing all this! He had run away to sea as a boy, he'd been kicked all his life by the bucko mate into a state where he couldn't kick back. But with you men it is not so. Among all the thousands standing here most were on shore a few years ago, and you took your land views with you on board. You organized seamen's unions. The one in this country was meek and mild. It did not strike, it went on its knees to Congress instead, and here's part of the written petition it made. 'We raise our manacled hands in humble supplication—and we pray that the nations of the earth issue a decree for our emancipation—restore us our rights as brother men.' But Congress had no ear for you then. Sailors are men who have no votes. And so you failed in your pleading.

"But in the labor movement there seems to be no such word as fail! You have not given up your union—instead you have formed one of a kind more dangerous to your masters! You have not made smaller your requests—no, you are now demanding more! And instead of asking for merciful laws you are saying, 'We are done with your laws, will have none of your laws, will break your laws when they come in our way!'

"And what do your masters answer? Here are thousands of deserters—every man here has broken the law by leaving his ship! But have they tried to arrest you? No! They're afraid to arrest twenty thousand men, they're afraid of this strike, they're afraid of you! They're so almighty scared downtown that though we've been only a week on strike they've already sent their commands to their Congress to give us what merciful laws we like. They're scared because we've thrown over their laws—because they know that we now see our power—to stop all their ships and the trade of their land and send their stock market into a panic!

"And now do you know what I want you to do? I want you to look at their ships, at their docks, at their harbor, men—and laugh—laugh! Don't you see there's no need of violence? Laugh! In old times the people built barricades. You don't need barricades nor any guns—all you've got to do is to stand here and laugh! Look at all you have done to your bosses—and laugh! To this town, to this nation—and laugh, laugh! Look—and think— of what you *can* do—all you—and you—and you—and you—by just folding your arms! Think of all you *will* do! And laugh— laugh! Laugh! Laugh!"

He broke off with both arms raised, and there followed one moment without a sound. Then suddenly, quick and hard and clear, from a corner of this human ocean, I heard a single peal of laughter. In an instant scores joined in. Rising in outbursts here and there, deepening, rushing out over the Farm, it gathered and rolled in wave on wave, rising, always rising. And it swelled into such a laugh that I saw the police feel for their clubs. Reporters scrambled for high places, turned their kodaks on it all. Women snatched up their babies in terror and ran. Marsh stepped forward, caught Joe by the arm and jerked him back to where I was standing. I gripped Joe's hand, it was icy cold.

Marsh shouted to the chairman, and the piercing whistle for order was heard. But it took a long time for that laugh to die. Long after the meeting had broken up I saw groups gather together, and presently they would begin to laugh, and their laughter would take on again that same convulsive tensity. I heard small clusters laughing, and dense throngs in hot saloons where the low rooms would echo and double the roar.

Late at night out on the waterfront, under the bow of that Morgan ship, I found two strikers smoking their pipes, and I sat down and lighted mine. One was a Lascar, the other a Pole. In the strike these wanderers over the earth had met on the waterfront under a wagon where each had come to sleep the night. Since then they had become good friends. Each spoke a little English, each one had caught bits here and there from the speeches made that afternoon—and they had been trying to pool what they'd heard, trying to find why it was they had laughed. As now I tried to give them the gist of what Joe Kramer had said, from time to time they would glance up at the big ship they had paralyzed and chuckle softly to themselves.

Then I went on to Marsh's speech. And out there in the darkness I could feel their rough faces, one white and one brown, grow deeply, eagerly intent, as these strike brothers listened to the voice that had spoken the dream of the crowd:

"Other wars may come and go—but under them all on land and sea this war of ours will go steadily on—will swallow up all other wars—will swallow up in all your minds all hatred of your brother men. For you they will be workers all. With them you will rise—and the world will be free."

CHAPTER XV

To all this, from the buildings far downtown that loomed like tall grim shadows, the big companies said nothing.

But that same night, while I sat talking to those two men, we heard a sharp excited cry. We saw a man behind us running along the line of saloons. From these and from the tenements came pouring angry throngs of men. And out of the hubbub I caught the words,

"They're bringing in the scabs! By boat!"

Past a watchman that I knew I ran into a dock-shed and out to the open end of the dock. And there I saw a weird ominous scene. Up the empty harbor, under a dark and cloudy sky, came four barges, black with negro laborers, and ahead and around and behind them came police boats throwing their searchlights upon an angry swarm of union picket dories, from which as they drew nearer I heard furious voices shouting, "Scab!" One of the barges docked where I stood and the negroes quickly slunk inside. I drew back from them as they passed, for to me too they were "scabs" that night. Afraid to face the men outside, whose jobs they had taken, these strikebreakers were to live on the dock, under cover of police. Soon half of them lay snoring on long crowded rows of cots. Food and hot coffee were served to the rest. Then I heard the harsh rattle of winches, I saw these negroes trundling freight, the cargo went swooping up into the ship—and with a deep dismay, a sharp foreboding of trouble ahead, I felt the work of the harbor begun.

I heard a quick voice at my elbow:

"Say. What the hell are *you* doing here?" I turned to the Pinkerton man by my side:

"I'm reporting this strike."

"No you're not, you're in here to report what you see to the strikers. Now don't let's have any words, my friend, we've seen you in their meeting-hall and we've all got your number. Go on out where you belong!"

So I went out where I belonged.

I went out to the crowd—but I found it changed, split up into furious swarms of men, I found the beginning of chaos here. And the world that I had left behind, the old world of order and rule from above, which I had all but forgotten of late, now sharply made its presence felt. For the god I had once known so well was neither dead nor sleeping. Behind closed doors, the doors that had flown open once to show me every courtesy, it had been silently laying plans and sending forth orders or "requests" to all those in its service.

The next day the newspapers changed their tone. Until now they had given us half the front page. Every statement I had written had been printed word for word. The reporters had been free to dig columns of "human interest stuff" out of the rich mine of color here, and they had gone at it hungrily, many with real sympathy. You would have thought the entire press was on the side of the strikers, at times it had almost seemed to me as though the entire country had risen in revolt. But now all this was suddenly stopped, and in its place the front pages were filled with news of a very different kind. "Big Companies Move at Last," were the headlines, "Work of Breaking Strike Begun." The first ship would sail that evening, three more would be ready to start the next day, and within a week the big companies hoped to resume the regular service. They regretted the loss to shippers of all the perishable produce which to the value of millions of dollars had been rotting away at the docks. They deplored the inconvenience and ruin which had been brought on the innocent public by these bodies of rough, irresponsible men who had openly defied the law. With such men there could be no arbitration, and in fact there was no need. The port would be open inside of a week.

So the big companies spoke at last. And as I read the papers, at home that day at breakfast, I remembered what Eleanore's father had said: "Don't let yourself forget for one minute that the men behind me are going to stamp out this strike." Not without a fight, I thought. But I was anxious and depressed. Dillon had not come of late, he had felt that we wanted to be alone. As now I glanced at Eleanore, whose eyes were intent on the news of the day, I saw with a rush of pity and love how alone she suddenly felt in all this. A moment later she looked up.

"Pretty bad, isn't it, dear?" she said.

"It doesn't look very fine just now."

"Are you going down to the docks?"

"Yes, they'll want me," I replied, "to write some answer to this stuff."

"Can you wait a few moments?" Eleanore rose. "I'll get on my hat. I promised Nora Ganey I'd run her relief station for her to-day." I took her a moment in my arms:

"You're no quitter, are you?" I said.

"We're in this now," she answered, just a little breathlessly. "And so of course we'll see it through."

So we went down together.

The waterfront looked different now. In front of the docks where work had begun a large space had been roped off. Inside the rope was an unbroken cordon of police. And without, but pressing close, the multitude of people for whom in a day so much had been changed, moved restlessly, no longer sure of its power, no longer sure of anything but a fast rising hatred of the men who had taken their jobs. As at times the police lines tightened and the negroes came out for more freight, thousands of ominous eyes looked on. Standing here at one such time, I saw a negro striker pass. His head was down and he walked quickly— for race feeling had begun.

The first ship sailed that evening. Tens of thousands watched her sail. And a bitter voice beside me said,

"Laughing ain't going to be enough."

Among men on strike there are two kinds of attitudes toward those who take their places. The first is the scorn of the man who is winning. "You are a dirty scab," it says. "You're a Judas to the working class and a thief who is trying to steal my job. But you won't get it, we're bound to win, and you're barely worth kicking out of the way." The second is quite a different feeling. In this is the fear of the man who is losing—and fear, as an English writer has said, is the great mother of violence. "You *may keep* my job! And if you do I'll be left with nothing to live on!" It is this second attitude which is dreaded by strike leaders, for it leads to a loss of all control, to machine guns and defeat.

With a deepening uneasiness I saw this feeling now appear. Starting in small groups of men, I saw it spread out over the mass with the speed of a prairie fire. I felt it that afternoon on the Farm, changing with a startling speed that sure and mighty giant, the crowd, into a blind disordered throng, a mottled mass of groups of men angrily discussing the news. Threats against "scabs" were shouted out, the word "scab" arose on every side. Bitter things were said against "coons," not only "scabs" but "all of 'em, God damn 'em!" There were hints of violence and open threats of sabotage, things done to dock machinery.

But presently, by slow degrees, as though by a deep instinct groping for the giant spirit that had been its life and soul, I felt the crowd now gather itself. Slowly the cries all died away and all eyes turned to the leader. Facing them with arms upraised, Marsh stood on the speakers' pile, his own face imperturbable, his own voice absolutely sure.

"Boys," he said, when silence had come, "one lonesome ship has gone to sea—so badly loaded, they tell me, that she ain't got even a chance in a storm. She was loaded by scabs."

A savage storm of "booh's" burst forth. He waited until it subsided and then continued quietly:

"We have no use for scabs, black or white. But we have use for strikers, *both* black and white—our negro brothers are with us still, and we'll show them we know that they are our brothers. We're going to stand together, we won't let the bosses split us apart. And when we read the papers to-morrow we're going to ask if the news is all there—not the little news in big headlines about a ship or two leaving port, but the big news in a little paragraph, that you have so stopped this nation's trade that now its Congress is demanding that your masters come to terms! And as for this lonesome ship that has sailed, if you want to see just how much that means, go down and look at Wall Street. They say down there, 'We're all right now.' But their market prices say, 'We're all wrong!' "

Suddenly out of the multitude there came a high, clear voice:

"You seem to know Wall Street, Brother Marsh. Have you been selling short down there? Who's your private broker?"

Instantly there was a rush toward the questioner, but a group of police formed quickly around him and he was hurried out of the way.

"Get after that, Jim, get after it quick!" said Joe by my side. And Marsh lost not a moment.

"Let that man go!" he shouted. "He was sent here to try to stir up a riot. That lie was framed up 'way downtown! But it is a lie and you all know it—you know how I live and how my wife lives—we don't exactly roll in wealth! But even if I were a crook, or if I were dead, this strike would go on exactly the same—for think a minute and you'll see that whatever has been done in this struggle has been done each time by you. It's you who have decided each point. It's you who have been called here to-day to decide the one big question. Congress has said, 'Arbitrate.' It's for you all to decide on our answer. This is no one-man union, there is no one man they can fix, nor even a small committee. We're a committee of fifty thousand here to make our own laws for ourselves. As you lift up your hands and vote, so it will be decided. But before you do I want to say this. I care so little for Wall Street and I am so sure we'll win this strike, that with all the strength I have in me I beg you to answer, 'No arbitration, nothing half way! All or nothing!' If this is your answer, hold up your hands!"

Up went the hands by thousands, the crowd was all together now and again it spoke in one great roar. And with a sudden rush of hope I told myself, "It's still alive! This fight has only just begun!"

"That is our answer to Congress," said Marsh, when again quiet had been restored. "That is the law which we have enacted. This strike is to be fought through to the end. We are not to be scared by Wall Street or worked upon by their hired thugs and so resort to violence. I am not afraid of violence," he continued sharply, "I am here to preach it. But the only violence I preach is the violence of folded arms. You have folded your arms and their ships are dead. No other kind is so deadly as that. Only hold to this kind of violence, and though they may send out a ship here and there, this great port of New York will stay closed—bringing ruin all over the land—till the nation turns to Wall Street and says, 'We cannot wait! You will have to give in!'"

As he ended his speech, it seemed to me as though he were

reaching far out, gripping that throng and holding it in. But for how long could he hold them?

Every paper that they read had suddenly turned against them and prophesied their swift defeat. Two more ships sailed that night. And as Marsh had foretold, their sailing was played up in pictures and huge headlines, while the statement that I wrote was cut to one small paragraph and put upon the second page.

That night, with the eager aid of strikers of five nationalities, I wrote a message to the crowd, translated it into German and French, Spanish, Italian and Polish. A socialist paper loaned us their press, and by noon our message was scattered in leaflets all up and down the waterfront. This message went out daily now. For the greater part of each night I sat in strike headquarters and wrote direct to the tenements.

The next day Marsh proposed a parade, and the Farm took it up with prompt acclaim. He challenged the mayor of the city to stop it. To friends who came to him later he said:

"You tell the mayor that I'm doing my best to give these men something peaceful to do. If he wants to help me, all well and good. If he don't, let him try to stop this parade."

And the mayor granted a permit.

The next afternoon the Fifth Avenue shops all closed their doors, and over the rich displays in their windows heavy steel shutters were rolled down. The long procession of motors and cabs with their gaily dressed shoppers had disappeared, and in their place was another procession, men, women and children, old and young. All around me as I marched I heard an unending torrent of voices speaking many languages, uniting in strange cheers and songs brought from all over the ocean world. Bright-colored turbans bobbed up here and there, for there was no separation of races, all walked together in dense crowds, the whole strike family was here. And listening and watching I felt myself a member now. Behind me came a long line of trucks packed with sick or crippled men. At their head was a black banner on which was painted, "Our Wounded." Behind the wagons a small cheap band came blaring forth a funeral dirge, and behind the band, upon men's shoulders, came eleven coffins, in which were those dock victims who had died in the last few days. This section had its banner too, and it was marked, "Our Dead."

But at one point, late in the afternoon, some marcher just ahead of me suddenly started to laugh. At first I thought he was simply in fun. But he kept on. Those near him then caught the look on his face and they all began to laugh with him. Each moment louder, uglier, it swept up the Avenue. And as it swelled in volume, like the menace of some furious beast, the uncontrollable passion I heard filled me again with a sharp foreboding of violence in the crisis ahead.

"Why are you here?" I asked myself. "You can't join in a laugh like that—you're no real member of this crowd—their world is not where you belong!"

But from somewhere deep inside me a voice rose up in answer:

"If the crowd is growing blind—is this the time to leave it? Wait."

CHAPTER XVI

Five more vessels sailed that day. And in the evening Eleanore said:

"The women who came to our station to-day kept asking, 'Why can't they close up the saloons? They're just the places for trouble to start.'"

"We'll try," I said, and that same night Marsh sent word through a friend to the mayor asking him to close all barrooms on the waterfront during the strike. The mayor sent back a refusal. He said he had no power.

Late that night I went down the line and found each barroom packed with men who were talking of those ships that had sailed. And they talked of "scabs." Speakers I had not heard before were now shouting and pounding the bar with their fists. The papers the next morning ran lurid accounts of these saloons and the open threats of violence there. They censured the mayor for his weakness and called for the militia. Why wait for mobs and bloodshed?

To that challenge I heard the reply of the crowd, on the Farm that afternoon, in their applause of the fiery speech of a swarthy little Spaniard. Francesco Vasea was his name.

"They are sending hired murderers who will come here to shoot us down! But when they come," he shouted, "I want you to remember this! A jail cell is no smaller than our holes in the bottoms of their ships, the food is no worse than the scouse we shall eat if we give in and go back to our jobs! And so we shall not be driven back! When the militia come against us, armed with guns and bayonets, then let us go to meet them armed——"

He stopped short, and from one end to the other of that motionless mass of men there fell a death-like silence. Then he grimly ended his speech:

"Armed with patience, courage and a deep belief in our cause."

In the sudden storm of cheers and "booh's" I leaned over to Joe at my side:

"Why did you let that man speak?"

The frown tightened on Joe's face.

"Because he's one of us," he said.

Seven more ships had sailed by that night.

In front of the dock-sheds, outside the double line of police, the throng had grown denser day by day, and each time the "scabs" came out there had been a burst of imprecations, a fierce pressing forward. The police had repeatedly used their clubs. Now late in the afternoon a red hospital ambulance came clanging down the waterfront. It was greeted by triumphant shouts. "Some black bastard hurt at last!" There was a quick gathering of police and a lane was formed reaching into the dock. Through this lane drove the ambulance, and as presently it emerged it was greeted by tumultuous cheers.

The papers the next morning said that a raging, howling mob had tried to reach the injured man. Cries of "Sabotage!" had been heard. Two men, they said, had been injured and one killed on the docks the day before. Was this Sabotage? Had the strikers fixed the winches with the purpose of killing strike-breakers? Why not? Their leaders had openly preached it. Not only the Spaniard but Marsh himself was quoted as favoring violence, and from that special Sabotage Issue of Joe Kramer's paper long extracts were reprinted. Were not these three leaders responsible for the death of that innocent black man? And should leaders such as these be allowed to go on preaching murder? Put them in jail! Quell this insurrection while still there was time! So spoke the press.

The rumor quickly spread about that Marsh and the Spaniard and Joe Kramer were to be arrested that day. All three remained at strike headquarters, and a dozen burly strikers kept the throng from pouring in. "Go on home," I could hear them shouting. But far from going, the throng increased until it filled the whole street outside. Suddenly we heard their cries rise into a raging din.

"Well, boys," said Marsh, "I guess they're here." He gave a few more sharp directions to his aides and then went out into the hall. A dozen Central Office police in plain clothes were just coming in at the door.

"All right," said Marsh, "we're ready. But unless you men were sent here with the idea of starting trouble, suppose you leave here now without us. Each one of us will meet you at any place and time you say."

"We can't take your orders, Mr. Marsh."

"You mean you *were* sent here for trouble?"

"I mean I have warrants for the arrest of yourself, Joseph Kramer and Francesco Vasca on a charge of incitement to murder."

And in less than a minute I saw Marsh, the Spaniard and Joe Kramer each handcuffed to two men, one on either side. As they left the hall I came close behind with a score of eager reporters.

The crowd, to my excited eyes, was like a crouching tiger now, glaring out of countless eyes. Through the solid mass of men that packed the street from wall to wall, the police had forced a narrow lane from the patrol wagon to the door. On either side of this lane I saw a line of faces, eyes. Some looked anxious, frightened, and were trying to press back, but at the sight of their leaders now with a roar the multitude swept in. In a moment the lane was gone, and some fifty police had formed in a circle around the prisoners. Quickly their clubs rose and fell, and men dropped all around them. But furious hundreds kept rushing in from every side, women and children caught in the tide were swept helplessly forward, came under the clubs and went down with the rest, and still the mass poured over them. Now at last the circle of bluecoats was broken, policemen alone and in small clusters were rushed and whirled this way and that. Outnumbered twenty to one, they began to go down in the scrimmage.

Then I heard a quick shout:

"Use your guns!"

After that, two pistol shots. Then more in a sharp, steady crackle. The mass began breaking, out on the edges I could see men starting to run. But down the street came a troop of mounted police on the gallop, and straight through the multitude they rode. I saw the three prisoners seized and surrounded and thrown into the wagon. I saw it go rapidly away. The police were now making wholesale arrests. That deep strident roar of the crowd had died down and broken into panting voices, everywhere were struggling forms.

Just before me the throng opened and I saw a woman at my feet. Her face was bleeding from a club. As I stooped to lift her, I felt a big hand grip my arm and then a heavy, crushing weight press down upon my head. I felt myself sink down and down into an empty darkness.

When I came to, I was being half pushed and half thrown by police up into one of their wagons. I remember a blurred glimpse of more fighting forms around me. Then a gong clanged and our wagon was off. And in a few moments we had emerged out of all this turbulence into the quiet commonplace streets of a city of every-day business life.

In the wagon a voice began singing. I looked up and saw our Italian musician, the leader of those gay excursions on *The Internationale*. Now he was singing the song of that name. And as all came in on the chorus, I caught a glimpse of his face. One cheek was bleeding profusely and with one hand he was keeping the blood from trickling down. With the other hand he was beating time. And his black eyes were blazing.

Soon after, we came to Jefferson Market and stopped at the entrance of the jail. As we were hustled out of the wagon, and in the stronger light our cuts and swelling bruises came suddenly in view, two young girls among us began to laugh hysterically. In a moment we were inside the jail and shoved into a striker group that had come in wagons ahead of ours. A grim old sergeant at the desk was taking down names and addresses and sending the prisoners to their cells.

I found my cell a cool relief after all that fever of cries. With surprise I noticed it was clean. I had thought all cells were filthy holes. Still in a daze, I sat down on my cot and felt the big bruise on my head.

"Where am I? What has happened? What has all this to do with me? What is it going to mean in my life?"

I heard a nasal voice from somewhere say:

"I know this pen. They're putting the girls with the prostitutes."

I heard clanging gongs outside and soon the banging of steel doors as more prisoners were put into cells. And little by little, through it all, I made out a low, eager murmur.

"Say," inquired a drunken old voice. "Who are all you damn fools? What is this party, anyhow?"

"It is a revolution!" a sharp little voice replied. And at that, from all sides other voices broke out. Then from his cell our musical friend again started up the singing, his strained tenor voice rising high over all. The song rose in volume, grew more intense.

"Heigh! Quit that noise!" a policeman shouted.

"Aw, let 'em alone," said another. "They'll soon work it off."

But we seemed to be only working it up. Up and up, song followed song, and then short impassioned speeches came out of cells, and there was applause. A voice asked each one of us to name his nationality, and we found we were Americans, Irish, Scotch and Germans, Italians and Norwegians, and three of us were Lascars and one of us was a Coolie. Then there were cheers for the working class all over the world, and after that a call for more singing. And now, as one of the songs died away, we heard from the woman's part of the jail the young girls singing in reply.

And slowly as I listened to those songs that rose and swelled and beat against those walls of steel, I felt once more the presence of that great spirit of the crowd.

"That spirit will go on," I thought. "No jail can stop the thing it feels!"

And at last with a deep, warm certainty I felt myself where I belonged.

CHAPTER XVII

Early in the evening I was taken out to the visitor's room, and there I found Eleanore's father. When he saw me, Dillon smiled.

"Do you know where you are?" he asked. "You're not in the Bastille—or even Libby Prison. You're in the Jefferson Market Jail."

"It hasn't felt that way," I said.

"Probably not. But it is that way, and there's Eleanore to be thought of."

"Eleanore will understand."

I saw his features tighten. I noticed now that his face was drawn, as though he, too, had been through a good deal.

"Yes," he said, "she understands. But it's a bit tough on her, isn't it? Jail is not quite in her line."

I felt my throat contracting:

"I know all that. I'm sorry enough—on her account——"

"Then let's get out of this," he said. "I've brought you bail. No use staying in here all night."

"None at all," I agreed. "I want to get back to the waterfront. We're going to issue an answer to this. They'll need me for the writing."

Dillon watched me a moment.

"You won't be allowed to do that," he said. "They're under martial law down there."

I looked up at him quickly:

"The troops are here?"

"Yes," he replied, and there was a pause.

"These arrests, this riot," I said a little huskily.

"Weren't they all framed up ahead? They needed the riot to get in the troops."

"The troops are here."

"Rather damnable. Do you think the people on the docks will just sit back and take it all?"

"They'll have to," he said gently. "The world's work has been clogged up a little. It's to go on again now."

On the street outside he took my hand:

"My boy, when this is over we'll get together, you and I."

"All right—when it's over," I said.

The Farm that night again changed to my eyes. It was now an orderly village of tents, two regiments of militia were here, and their sentries reached for a mile to the north watching the big companies' docks.

I walked up along the line and had talks with some of the sentries. I remember one in particular, a thin, nervous little man, a shoe-clerk in a department store. Every work-day for six years he had fitted shoes on ladies' feet; he had been doing it all that morning. And now here he was down on the waterfront with only the stars above him and great shadowy spaces all around, out of which at any moment he expected rushes by strikers. These strikers to him were not human, they were "foreigners," for the moment gone mad, to be treated very much as mad dogs. And here he was all by himself, his nerves on edge, with a gun in his hands. The absurdity of that gun in his hands! And the serious danger.

I went into many tenements, into homes I had come to know in the strike. And they, too, were different now. Their principal leaders taken away and their headquarters closed by the police, the disorganization was complete. That spirit they had relied upon, that strange new spirit of the mass which they had created by coming together, was now dead—and each one felt the weakness of being alone, the weakness of his separate self. Blindly they fought against their despair. I found them packing tenement rooms, gathering instinctively in search of their great friend, the crowd.

But from such gatherings as these, the weaker, the more timid and the wiser kept away. Rash spirits led these meetings, and here was the same hot passion that I had felt back in the jail. These people did not want to think, the time for thinking had gone by. They wanted to act, to do something quick. Their minds were fiercely set on the "scabs," the police and the militia.

Their strike was not yet lost. Their friends and sympathizers were working hard that very night to get their leaders out on bail. In Washington a House committee was striving still to compel arbitration. Everywhere the more moderate spirits were drawing together, trying to work out something safe.

But these people did not know this. They were in their tenements, they were scattered far apart. They only knew how they had been clubbed, that three had been killed and many more wounded, and that now the troops were here. And the more fiery ones among them were feeling only one thing now, that when you are hit you must hit back, you must show you're not scared, you must show you're a man.

And so on the next morning, no women and no children but huge, silent throngs of men drifted out of the tenements down to the docks and moved slowly along the sentry lines.

The change to show they were not afraid came late in the afternoon. The clear, sweet call of a bugle came floating gaily on the air, then the long, hard roll of drums, and from their camp on the Farm the troops came on the double-quick up along the waterfront. Now thousands of strikers were running that way. From the foot of a city street across the wide open space to a pier the militia formed in two double lines, each line facing outward. Then down that street came mounted police and behind them a score of trucks loaded with freight.

At first I had hopes that the mass would not move. But out of the silence came angry shouts and those behind pushed forward. Those in front were pressed close up to the sharp lines of bayonets, were prodded savagely by the troops. Militia youngsters but half trained, in two thin lines opposing what appeared to them a furious sea of faces, fists and angry cries—no wonder they were nervous. Bricks came flying from all sides and even heavy paving-stones, and then a few pistol shots out of the mass. I saw a militia man drop on one knee and slowly topple over. I saw an excited young officer shout at his men and wave his sword. I saw long rows of guns make quick rhythmic movements, then level straight out, and there were two long flashes of fire.

Disordered throngs were running now. Only a few men here

and there turned to fire their pistols or to shout back frenzied, quivering oaths. Behind them a few soldiers were still shooting without orders. Near the sandpile on which I stood I saw a young militia man enough like that little shoe-clerk to have been his brother. His face was white and his eyes wild, he was panting, pumping his lever and blindly firing shot after shot.

"God damn 'em, slaughter 'em, slaughter 'em!"

An officer knocked up his gun.

That night the waterfront was still. Only the long, slow moving line of the figures of sentries was to be seen. The troops were back in their camp on the Farm. Bivouac fires were burning down there, but up here was only a dark, empty space.

Here scattered about on the pavement, after the firing had ceased, I had seen the dark inert bodies of men. Most of them had begun to move, until fully half were crawling about. They had been picked up and counted. Thirty-nine wounded, fourteen dead. These, too, had all been taken away.

From the high steel dock-sheds there came a deep, harsh murmur made up of faint whistles, the rattle of winches, the shouts of the foremen, the heavy jar and crash of crates. A tug puffed smoothly into a slip with three barges in her wake. I walked slowly out that way. The tugmen and the bargemen talked in quiet voices as they made fast their craft to the pier. Below them the water was lapping and slapping.

"The world's work has been clogged up a little. It's to go on again now."

The next day three heavy battleships steamed sluggishly through the Narrows and came to anchor in the bay. When interviewed by reporters, their commanders were vastly amused. No, they said, the United States Navy was not governed as to its movements by strikes. They simply happened to be here through orders issued weeks ago. But their coming was featured in headlines.

I saw something else in the papers that night, a force greater than all battleships. As a week before I had felt a whole country in revolt, I felt now a country of law and order, a whole nation of angry tradesmen impatiently demanding an end to all this "foreign anarchy."

"We want no more of your strikes," it said. "None of your new crowd spirit, none of your wild talk and dreams! We want no change in this country of ours!"

The authorities obeyed this will. Bail was denied to Marsh, Vasca and Joe, and for them a speedy trial was urged. The press now held them responsible not only for that first negro's death, but for all the deaths since their arrest. Let them pay the full penalty! Let them be made an example of! Let this business of anarchy be dealt with and settled once and for all!

The work of crushing the strike went on. More troops were brought to the harbor. On the docks there were not only negroes now, thousands of immigrant laborers were brought from Ellis Island and put to work at double pay, and on every incoming vessel the stokers were all kept on board. Among the strikers there was a break that swiftly spread and became a stampede. And in the following week the work of the harbor went on as before, with its regular commonplace weekly toll of a hundred killed and injured. Peace had come again at last.

On Saturday morning of that week I stood on the deck of a ferryboat packed with little commuters who waved and cheered a huge ocean liner bound for Europe. Lying deep in the water, her hold laden heavy with the products of this teeming land, her decks thronged with travelers with money in their pockets, her band playing, her flags streaming out, and over all on the captain's bridge the officers up there in command—she was a mighty symbol of order and prosperity and of that Efficiency which to me had been a religion for so many years. We all followed the great ship with our eyes as, gathering headway, she steamed out past the Statue of Liberty toward the battleships beyond.

"Well," said an amused little man close by me, "I guess that'll be about all from the strikers."

"Oh my smiling little citizen—you've only seen the beginning," I thought.

What were the strikers thinking now, and what would they be thinking soon? They had wanted easier lives, they had wanted to feel themselves powers here. Caught up in the tide of democracy now sweeping all around the earth, they had wanted to feel themselves running themselves in all this work they were doing. So they had come out on strike and become a crowd, and in the crowd they had suddenly found such strength as they never dreamed could be theirs. And they would not easily forget. The harbor was already seeing to that, for already its work had gone on with a rush, and all its heavy labor was weighing down upon them—"like a million tons of brick on their chests." I remembered what Joe Kramer had said: "It's got so they can't even breathe without thinking."

Was the defeat of this one strike the end?

The grim battleships answered, "Yes, it is the end."

But the restless harbor answered, "No."

What change was coming in my life? I did not know. Of one thing only I was sure. The last of my gods, Efficiency, whose feet had stood firm on mechanical laws and in whose head were all the brains of all the big men at the top, had now come tottering crashing down. And in its place a huge new god, whose feet stood deep in poverty and in whose head were all the dreams of all the toilers of the earth, had called to me with one deep voice, with one tremendous burning passion for the freedom of mankind.

BOOK IV

BOOK IV

CHAPTER I

Once I saw the harbor in a February storm. And in the wind and skurrying snow I saw it all together like one whirling thing alive. But the next morning the storm had died away, and a wind from the south had brought banks of fog that moved sluggishly low down on the water dividing the whole region into many separate parts. And from above, a dazzling sun shone down upon three objects near me, a ferryboat, a puffing tug, and a tramp which lay at anchor, shone so brightly on these three they seemed alone, with nothing but mist all about them.

So it was now for a time with me. The strike, which had so suddenly drawn me into its whirling crowd-life, now as suddenly dropped away. And personal troubles piled one on the other. In place of that mass of thousands, I saw only a few people I loved, and I saw them so intensely that for a time we were quite alone, with nothing but mist all around us.

Sue sent for me one morning and I went over to our house. I was startled by the change in her face. It looked not only tired, it looked so disillusioned, done, so through with all the absorbing ideas and warm enthusiasms that had given it abundant life.

"I'm not going to marry Joe Kramer," she said. "And I want you to tell him so."

I started at her blankly.

"I'm sorry," I said.

"Are you?" There was just a worn shadow of her old smile.

"I don't know why I said that," I replied. "My head's rather dull this morning. All right, Sis, I'll tell him." Still I watched her pityingly. Poor old Sue. What a crash in her life.

"I'd like you to tell him the whole truth," my sister went on

sharply, "just why I've decided as I have. Don't say it's because of
father. When I wanted Joe, Dad didn't count, he was nothing to
me but a back number. But I *don't* want him now—Joe, I mean—
I don't love him any more. If I went to him to-day in his cell and
said I'd stick by him no matter what happened because he was
the man I loved—I'd be lying—that wouldn't be me. The real me
is a much smaller person than that. I don't love Joe because I've
been scared—because he's in a common jail—waiting to be tried
for murder." Her face contracted slightly. "I suppose it's the way
I've been brought up."

"But Sue——"

"Don't stop me, Billy, let me talk!" And she talked on intensely,
so absorbed in this fierce impulsive confession that she seemed to
forget I was there. "I've been thinking what's to become of me.
I've been thinking about all the things I've been in, and none
seem real any longer—I wanted a thrill and I got it—that's all.
Then I met Joe and I got it again, I got a thrill out of all his life
and the big things it was made of. I got a *great* thrill out of the
strike. Don't you remember how I talked three weeks ago when
you were here? Dad was the Old and I was the New. I saw everything beginning. I read Walt Whitman's 'Open Road' and I felt
like Joe's 'camarado.' Well, and I kept on like that. And like a
little idiot I couldn't keep it to myself, I went and told some of my
friends. That's what's really the hardest now, what hurts the
most—I told my friends. I posed as a young Joan of Arc. I was
going to marry, give up everything, chuck myself into this fight for
the people, into revolution! Thrills, I tell you, thrills and thrills!

"But then Joe got arrested. I knew he was in a cell in the
Tombs, in Murderers' Row. And that drove all the thrills away.
That was real. Dad made it worse. He talked about the coming
trial, Sing Sing and the death house there. One morning he tried
to read to me an account of an execution. I ran away, but I came
back and read it myself, I read all the hideous details right up to
the iron chair. And just because there was a chance of Joe's being
like that, all at once I stopped loving him. Not just because I was
frightened, it wasn't so simple as a scare. It was something inside
of me shuddering, and saying 'how revolting!' I tried to shake
it out of me, I tried to keep on loving him! But I couldn't shake it
out of me! Joe had become—revolting, too! It's because of the

way I've been brought up and because of the way I've always lived! I can't stand what's real—if it's ugly! That's me!"

She broke off and looked down. I came and sat beside her, and took her cold, quivering hands in mine:

"I guess I *am* sorry, Sue old girl——"

"Don't be," she retorted. "I'm too sorry for myself as it is! That's another part of me!" Again she broke off with a hard little laugh. "Let's forget me for a minute. What has this sweet strike done to *you*?"

"I'm not sure yet," I answered. "Where is Dad?"

"Up in his room."

"Tell me about him," I said. Sue drew an anxious little breath:

"Oh Billy, he has been getting so queer. It has all been such a strain on his mind. Every day he kept reading the news of the strike—and some days he would stamp and rage about till I was afraid to be with him. He talked about that death cell until I thought that I'd go mad. Sometimes when we were talking I thought that we had both gone mad."

I went upstairs and found him in a chair by the window. With unnatural, clumsy motions he rose and came to meet me.

"I'm all right, my boy." His voice had a mumbling quality and I noticed the strangeness in his eyes. "I'm all right. I'm glad to see you." Then his face clouded and hardened a little, and he tried to speak to me sternly:

"I'm glad you're clean out of that strike and its notions—glad you've come to your senses," he said. "You're lucky in having such a wife. She's been over here often lately—and she's worth a dozen like you and Sue. Have you seen Sue?"

"Yes."

"Well, *she's* all right."

I said nothing to this, and he shot a sidelong look at me:

"I had quite a time, my boy—I had to keep right at her." Another quick look. "I suppose she's told you how I went at her."

"Never mind, Dad, it's over now."

"I had to make her feel the noose, I mean the chair," he went on in those thick, mumbling tones, "and that she'd have to choose between that and a decent Christian home—like the home her mother had. She was a wonderful woman, your mother," he wandered off abruptly. "If she'd only understood me—seen what it

was I was trying to do—for American shipping—Yankee sails!"
He sank down in his chair exhausted, and I noticed he was
breathing hard. "I'm all right, my boy, I'm quite all right——"

With a sudden rush of pity and of love and deep alarm, I bent
gently over him:

"Of course you are—why Dad, old boy—just take it easy—
quiet, you know—we're going to pull right out of this——"

The tears welled suddenly up in his eyes:

"I'm lonely, boy—I'm glad you're here!"

Presently I went down to Sue:

"When is the doctor coming next?"

"Not till this afternoon," she said.

"I'll be home to-night for supper. Phone me what he says."

"All right—where are you going now? To Joe?"

"Yes, Sis," I said.

She turned and went quickly out of the room.

In the Tombs, when Joe was brought out to me, I saw that he,
too, had been through a deep change. He had been quiet enough
all through the strike, except for that one big speech of his—but
he had been *tensely* quiet. Now the tension appeared to be gone.
He seemed wrapped up in thoughts of his own.

"Have you seen Sue?" he asked me at once.

"Yes Joe, I've just been with her."

"What did she say?"

I began to tell him.

"I knew it," he interrupted me. "I made up my mind to this the
first night I spent here in my cell. It couldn't have happened, it
wouldn't have worked. Tell her I understand all about it, tell her
that I'm sure she's right. Tell her—it's funny but it's true—tell her
this infernal pen has worked the same way on me as on her. I
mean it has made me not want her now. I feel sorry for her and
that's all—deeply and infernally sorry. I was a fool to have let her
into it. My only excuse for being so blind was that damned fever
that left me so weak. At any other time I would have seen what a
farce it was. I wasn't booked for a life like that. It doesn't fit in
with this job of mine." He smiled a little bitterly. "I used to say,"
he continued, "that if I had time I'd like to do something yellow
enough so that I'd be cut off for life from any chance of church

bells. And I guess I've done it this time—no danger of getting respectable now."

"How do you look at this, Joe?" I asked him. "What do you think they'll do to you?"

"I don't know." Again he smiled slightly and wearily. "And I can't say I *care* a damn. I feel like those fellows over in Russia, the revolutionist chaps I met, who didn't know if they'd croak in a month and didn't care one way or the other. But as a matter of fact," he added, "I think this time it's mainly bluff. They wanted to get us away from the crowd and keep us away while they broke the strike. Now that it's over you'll probably find they'll let us all off with light sentences. Of course the murder charge can't hold. . . . By the way," he added, smiling, "I hear they got you, too."

"Yes," I answered, smiling back. "The Judge fined me ten dollars and let me go. He said he hoped this would be a lesson."

Joe looked at me curiously:

"How much of a lesson, Kid, do you think this strike has been to you?"

"Quite a big one, Joe," I said.

"What are you going to do about it?"

"I haven't decided."

"How is Eleanore taking it all?"

"She's not saying much and neither am I. We're both doing some thinking before we talk."

"You're a quiet pair," J. K. remarked. "I shouldn't wonder if you'd nose along quite a distance before you get through—I mean in our direction."

"That's what we're thinking about," I replied. Again he turned to me curiously:

"You two can think together—without talking—can't you?"

"Yes—sometimes we can."

"I never got that far with Sue." All at once he came closer, his whole manner changed: "Say, Bill—tell her all I've said—will you? I'm sorry! Honest Injun! Make her feel how damnably sorry I am that I ever let her in for this!"

When I left him I went off for a walk, for I wanted to be alone awhile. I wondered just how sure Joe felt about his fast approaching trial. It seemed to me that he had a good chance of going where Sue had pictured him.

CHAPTER II

That evening I learned that my father was worse, and I spent the next day by his bedside. He had had a stroke in the morning and was not expected to live through the night.

I found him mumbling fast to himself and making slight, restless efforts to move. At last he grew quiet, and presently his half-open gnarled right hand came groping out over the covers. I took it in mine, and at once I felt it close on mine with a quick, convulsive strength. His hand was moist, his eyes saw nothing. I sat there thus for a long time. Then suddenly,

"Good boy," he muttered thickly. "Good boy—good—always good to your mother!" He kept repeating this over and over, with pauses between, then again with an effort, fiercely, as though from a distance his mind were set on getting this message over to me, over from an age that was dying into an age that was coming to life, a last good-by to hold me back.

Soon he was only mumbling figures, names of ships and distant ports, freight consignments. Now and then his finger would go to his lips, as he turned phantom pages in feverish haste. Again, in gasping whispers, he would break out into arguments for the protection of Yankee sails.

"Protection!" he would whisper. "Damn fools not to see it! Discriminating tariffs! Subsidies! A Navy! . . . Don't forget the Navy! Remember War of 1812! . . . Nothing without fighting!"

"Nothing without fighting." He had been learning this all his life—and after he had said it now, he stopped speaking and grew still. Little by little his movements grew weaker. Finally he lay like a log, and the doctor said he would be so until dead.

I went up to my old bedroom and sat down by the open window. It was a beautiful night. From the garden below, where long ago I had felt such shivers over the ocean and heathen lands, a graceful poplar rose. Behind it from the river the huge, dim funnel of a steamer rose over the roof of the warehouse. Overhead to the right swept the Great Bridge of my childhood. But behind it were other bridges now, and off across the river the buildings of Manhattan loomed in loftier masses to their apex in the tower of lights. How changed it all was since I was a boy. And yet how like. On the harbor still the hurrying lights, yellow, blue and green and red. The same deep, restless hum of labor. And from the waterfront below the same puffs and coughs of engines, the same sharp toots and treble pantings, the same raucous whine of wheels.

There came a rough salt breeze from the sea, and it made me think of billowy sails and the days of my father's boundless youth, and of the harbor of long ago that had so gripped and molded him—as I felt mine now molding me. And for what? I asked. To what were we both adventuring—out of these little harbors of ours?

Toward dawn a tramp came down the river. Dimly as she passed below I could see how old she was, how worn and battered by the waves. A desolate and lonely craft, the smoke draggled out of her funnel. I watched her steam into the Upper Bay and pass around Governor's Island. I watched till in the first raw light of day I could see only her smoke through the Narrows. Then even this became but a blur, which crept away in that strange dawn light out into the wide ocean.

A few hours later my father died.

One by one, from different parts of the port, the queerest old men came into our house on the day of my father's funeral—men who still believed in American ships, still thrilled to the dream of the Stars and Stripes wherever there is an ocean breeze; men who still believed in ships that had sails and moved along with the force of the winds; who still believed that cabin boys could rise by the sheer force of their wills to be powers in the ocean world; men who had for the common crowd only the iron discipline, the old brute tyranny of the sea. These strange old men stood with their white heads bowed, a little group, looking down into my father's grave.

"He was a magnificent fighter," I heard one of them say as we left. "He wrecked his own business for what he believed in. How many of us would go that far?"

From the grave Sue came to our apartment. Eleanore had packed her trunk.

"Sue must keep out of that dreary old house," she told me. "Luckily she has a friend out of town whom she's going to visit. When she comes back we must have the house closed, and I hope she'll live with us for a while."

We talked of this that evening, for Sue seemed to want to talk. We stayed up until late and planned and planned. Many different kinds of work for Sue were taken up and discussed by us all. She surprised me by the brave effort she made.

"I've got to want something—that's sure," she said. "I can't just yet. I've wanted so many things so hard, one after the other for nearly eight years, that now I feel as though I'd used up all the wanting that I've got. But of course I haven't. If I have I'm a back number—and I'd a great deal rather be dead. So don't you people worry. Depend upon it, in less than a year I'll be all wrapped up in something new. I'll be tremendously enthused," she ended, smiling wearily.

She agreed with me that the house be sold, and after she had left us I made every effort to sell it at once. I found it was heavily mortgaged now, but when at last I made a sale there was enough to clear off all debts and leave about two thousand dollars for Sue. She would have at least something to start on.

As we set about to dismantle the house, various things thickly covered with dust came out of closets, drawers and shelves. And these objects brought near again to me my mother's life and that hunger of hers for the things that were "fine," that hospitable door which had waited for friends from the handsome old homes all around us. These homes all along the street had now lost their quiet dignity. Some were empty and marked for sale, others that had already been sold were cheerless boarding houses. The most handsome home of all, with its ample yard where I used to play, was gone, and in its place rose an apartment building which made the old houses all seem dwarfs.

Her world and his were both slipping away. Her life and his, her creed and his, were little now but memories—memories which in Sue and in me must take their chance with the warm, new feelings, the cravings, hopes, loves, doubts and dreams of this absorbing world of our own. For the harbor was still molding lives.

How anxious Eleanore seemed to be though, I thought a little bitterly.

CHAPTER III

But Eleanore had good reason. When at last the house had been closed, back at home one evening she told me what she had known for weeks but had kept to herself until I should be free from other things. We were to have another child.

The news was a shock, it frightened me. "Where's the money to come from?" flashed into my mind. In an instant it had passed and I was holding her tight in my arms. But she must have caught that look in my face, for I could feel her trembling.

"The same funny old world, my dearest one," she whispered, "with its same old trick of starting out. But oh my dear, in spite of it all—or because of it all—how good it is to be alive! More than ever—a hundred times!"

"You darling girl," I whispered back, "you're the bravest one of all!"

Her father came to us the next night, and after Eleanore went to bed he and I talked long together. He looked worn and tired, but the same quiet affection was in his eyes.

"Let's see where we are," he said, "and what we've got to go on. To begin with, thank God, you and I are still friends. Then there's Eleanore and your small son and the smaller one that's coming. We're just starting in on a long, hot summer. She must of course be got out of town. How much have you in the bank?"

"Thirty-seven dollars," I said.

He looked thoughtfully at his cigar.

"You've never yet taken money from me," he continued, after a moment. "Still, you'd do it if you had to—because this is *our* affair. But unluckily, just at present, I'm nearly as high and dry as yourself. The men who have backed my harbor work have lost so heavily in the strike that they feel now they must recoup. I've already proposed to them a plan which they have as good as accepted. They'll provide enough money to pay the rent of a smaller office. I can borrow enough to pay half my men. The rest I'll have to let go for a time."

"And *your* salary?" I ventured.

"Is left out," he answered. "I mean it is if I stay here. I want to stay here, I want to put through this job if I can, you see it has taken six years of my life. And besides," he added wistfully, "in a very few weeks they'll finish the work at Panama—and the ships of the world will begin to crowd into a harbor that isn't ready here—we haven't even completed our plans. It's not a good time to stop our work. But of course if you and Eleanore get into a hole that is serious—as I said before and you'll agree, you'd have to let me help you—even if to do it I should have to give up my work for a while and take up something that will pay."

"No sir!"

"Yes sir," he replied. "Unless you can earn enough money yourself."

We looked at each other a moment.

"You know how to bring pressure, don't you?" I said.

"Yes, I'm bringing pressure. I want to see you go on as before."

"That won't be easy," I remarked.

"Shall we talk it over a little?"

"Yes."

"All right," he said. "Since that talk we had together the day Eleanore's first child was born, what a splendid start you made in your writing. You were not only earning big pay, you were doing fine work, work that was leading somewhere. I could see you learning to use your tools, getting a broad, sane view of life— and of yourself—training yourself and building yourself. You were right on the threshold of big results. But then your friend Kramer came along. He had not built himself, he had chucked himself over, neglected himself, his health included. So he took typhoid and came to your home. His being there was a drain on your pocket and a heavy strain on your nerves. He got you unsettled. Then came the strike. And what has it done? It has taken your time, health, money. It has left two good workmen stranded—you and me. And I don't see that it's done the crowd any good. What has the strike given you in return for all it has taken away?"

"A deeper view of life," I said. "I saw something in that strike so much bigger than Marsh or Joe or that crude organization of theirs—something deep down in the people themselves that rises up out of each one of them the minute they get together. And I believe that power has such possibilities that when it comes into full life not all the police and battleships and armies on earth can stop it."

The look in Dillon's eyes was more anxious than impatient.

"Billy," he said, "I've lived a good deal closer than you have to the big jobs of this world. And I know those jobs are to get still bigger, even more complex. They're to require even bigger men." I smiled a bit impatiently.

"Still the one man in a million," I said.

"Yes," said Dillon, "his day isn't over, it has only just begun. He may have his bad points—I'll admit he has—but compared to all the little men his vision is wide and it goes deep. And if they'll only leave him alone and give him a chance, he'll take me and the other engineers, and the chemists and doctors and lawyers, and he'll make a world—he's doing it now—where ignorance and poverty will in time be wiped completely out."

"They're not going to leave him alone," I said. "I'm sure of that now. Whether he grafts or whether he's honest won't make any difference. The crowd is going to pull him down. Because it's not democracy. The trouble with all your big men at the top is that they're trying to do for the crowd what the crowd wants to do for itself. And it may not do it half so well—but all the time it will be learning—gathering closer every year—and getting a spirit compared to which your whole clean clear efficiency world is only cold and empty!"

He must have caught the look in my eyes.

"You're thinking that I'm getting old," he said softly. "I and all the men like me who have been building up this country. You're thinking that we're all following on after your father into the past." As I looked back I felt suddenly humble. Dillon's voice grew appealing and kind. "But you belong with us, Billy," he said. "It was under us you won your start. And what I want now," he added, "is not only for Eleanore's sake, but your own. I want you to try to write again about all the work we are doing and see what it will do for you. Why not give it another chance? You're not afraid of it, are you?"

"No," I said, "I'm not afraid—and I'll give it another chance if you like—I don't want to be narrow about it, God knows. But before I tackle anything else I'll finish my story of the strike."

"All right," he agreed. "That's all I ask. Now suppose you take Eleanore up to the mountains and write your strike article up there. Let me loan you a little just at the start."

"How much money have *you* in the bank?"

"Enough to send Eleanore where she belongs."

"Eleanore belongs right here," said a voice from the other room, and presently Eleanore appeared. She surveyed us both with a scorn in her eyes that made us quake a little. "I never heard," she went on calmly, "of anything quite so idiotic. Go home, Dad, and go to bed, and please drop this insane idea that I'm afraid of July in New York, or of August or September. Do you know what you're going to do to-morrow, both of you poor foolish boys? You're going sensibly to work and worry about nothing at all. And to-morrow night we're all three of us going to forget how it feels to work or think, and get on an open trolley and go down and hear Harry Lauder. Thank Heaven he happens to be in town. To hear you talk you'd think the whole American people had forgotten how to laugh.

"Now Billy," she ended smoothly, "go to the icebox and get two bottles of nice cool beer—and make me a tall glass of lemonade. And don't use too much sugar."

CHAPTER IV

The next day and the next evening Eleanore's program was carried out. But after that night the laughing stopped. For Joe Kramer was coming to trial.

I had not seen Joe for over two weeks, and I had taken his view of his case, that there was no serious danger. But now I learned from a good source that Joe and both his colleagues were to be brought to trial at once, while the public feeling was still hot against them. As the time of the trials drew near every paper in town took up the cry. Let these men be settled once and for all, they demanded. Let them not be set free for other strikes, for wholesale murder and pillage. Let them pay the full penalty for their crimes!

In the face of this storm, I found myself on Joe's defense committee, the best part of my time each day and evening taken up with raising money, helping to find witnesses and doing the press work for parades and big mass meetings of labor.

Through this work, in odd hours, I finished my story of the strike. It all came back to me vividly now and I tried to tell what I had seen. I took it to my editor.

"Print that?" he said when he'd read it. "You're mad."

"It's the truth," I remarked.

"As you see it," he said. "And you've seen it only from one side. If this story had been written and signed by Marsh or your friend Kramer, we might have run it, with a reply from the companies. But I don't want to see *you* stand for this—in our magazine or anywhere else—it means too much to you as a writer. Look out, my boy," he added, with a return to the old brusque kindliness which he had always shown me in the years I had worked under him. "We think a lot of you in this office. For God's sake don't lose your head. Don't be one more good reporter spoiled."

I took my story of the strike to every editor I knew, and it was rejected by each in turn. They thought it all on the side of the crowd, an open plea for revolution. Then I took it to Joe in the Tombs.

"Will you sign this, Joe?" I asked, when he had read it.

"No," he replied. "It's too damn mild. You've given too much to the other side. All these bouquets to efficiency and all this about the weak points of the crowd. The average stoker reading this would think that the revolution won't come till we are all white-haired."

"I don't believe it will," I said.

"I know you don't. That's why you're no good to us," he said. "We want our stuff written by men who are sure that a big revolution is just ahead, men who are certain that a strike, to take in half the civilized world, is coming in the next ten years."

"I don't believe that."

"I know. You can't. You're still too soaked in the point of view of your efficiency father-in-law."

"So you don't feel you can sign this?"

"No."

That day I sent my story to a small magazine in New England, which from the time of the Civil War had retained its traditions of breadth of view. Within a week the editor wrote that he would be glad to publish it. "Our modest honorarium will follow shortly," he said at the end. The modest honorarium did. Meanwhile I had sent him a sketch of Nora Ganey which I had written just after the strike. I received a letter equally kind, and another honorarium. I began to see a future of modest honoraria.

In the meantime, to meet our expenses at home, I had borrowed money and given my note. And the note would soon fall due. Those were far from pleasant days. On the one side Joe in his cell waiting to be tried for his life; on the other, Eleanore at home waiting for a new life to be born. By a lucky chance for me, Joe's trial was again postponed, so I could return to my own affairs. I had to have some money quick. I went back to my magazine editor and asked for a job in his office.

"I'm ready now to be sane," I said.

"Glad to hear it," he replied. "I'll give you a steady routine job where you can grind till you get yourself right."

"Till I get back where I was, you mean?"

"Yes, if you can," he answered.

I went for a walk that afternoon to think over the proposition he'd made.

"I have seen three harbors," I said to myself. "My father's harbor which is now dead, Dillon's harbor of big companies which is very much alive, and Joe Kramer's harbor which is struggling to be born. It's an interesting age to live in. I should like to write the truth as I see it about each kind of harbor. But I need the money—my wife is going to have a child. So I'll take that steady position and try to grind part of the truth away."

"What have you been doing?" Eleanore asked when I came home. "You look like a ghost."

"Not at all," I replied. "I've been getting a job."

"Tell me about it."

I told her part. She went and got her sewing, and settled herself comfortably for a quiet evening's work. Eleanore loved baby clothes.

"Now begin again and tell me all," she ordered. And she persisted until I did.

"It won't do," she said, when I had finished.

"It will do," I replied decidedly. "It's the best thing in sight. It will see us through till the baby is born. After all, it's only for a year."

"It's a mighty important year for you, my love," said Eleanore. She thoughtfully held up and surveyed a tiny infant's nightgown. "If you do this you'll be giving up. It's not writing your best. It's giving up what you think is the truth. And that's a bad habit to get into."

"It's settled now. Please leave it alone."

"Oh very well," she said placidly. "Let's talk of what I've been doing."

"What *you've* been doing?"

"Precisely. I've taken a little apartment downtown, over by the river. The rent is twenty-eight dollars a month. It's on the top floor and has plenty of air, and there's a nice roof for hot summer evenings. You're to carry two wicker chairs up there each night after supper."

"I'll do nothing of the kind," I rejoined indignantly. "You're going to pack up at once and go to the mountains! And when you come back you're coming right here!"

"Oh no I'm not," she answered.

"Don't be an idiot, Eleanore! Think of moving out of here now! In your condition!"

"It's better than moving out of your work. Dad has kept right on with his, even when they stopped his pay. Well, now they've stopped your pay, that's all, and we've got to do the best we can. We've simply got to live for a while on modest honorariums. Now don't talk, wait till I get through. You've got to work harder than ever before but for much less money. But with less money than before we're going to be happier than we've ever been in all our lives. And you can't do a thing to stop it. If you do take that office work and bring a lot of money home, do you know what I'll do? I'll move to that little flat just the same, and all the extra money you bring will go to Mrs. Bealey."

"Who in God's name is Mrs. Bealey?"

"One of my oldest charity cases. She was here this afternoon. The trouble with you is, my dear," my wife continued smoothly, "that you've been so wrapped up in your own little changes you haven't given a thought to mine. Well, I've done some changing, too. Every time that Sue or you have taken up a new idea I've taken up a Mrs. Bealey. I did the same thing in the strike. I went with Nora Ganey into the very poorest of all the tenements down by the docks. I saw the very worst of it all—and I tried to do what I could to help. But I felt like a drop in the ocean. And that's how I've changed. Things are so wrong in the tenements that big reforms are needed. I don't know what they are and I'm not sure anyone else does. But I'm sure that if any reforms worth while are to be made, we've got to see just where we are. And that means that quite a number of people—you for instance—have got to tell the truth exactly as they see it. So I'd rather put our money in that and let old Mrs. Bealey forget our address. That's another reason for moving.

"There's nothing noble about it at all," she said as she threaded her needle. "I mean to be perfectly comfortable. I saw this coming long ago, and since the strike was over I've spent weeks picking out a nice place where we can get the most for our money.

About thirty thousand babies, I'm told, are to be born in the city this summer—and their mothers aren't going first to the mountains or even for a walk in the Park. I don't see why I shouldn't be one. As a matter of fact I won't be one, my baby won't be born until Fall, and I'll have a clean, comfortable flat with one maid instead of a dirty tenement with all the cooking and washing to do. You'll probably find magazines who'll pay enough honorariums to make a hundred dollars a month, which is just about three times as much as Mrs. Bealey lives on. So that's settled and we move this week."

We moved that week.

CHAPTER V

One night about a month later, when we had ensconced ourselves for the evening out on the roof of our new home, where the summer's night was cooled by a slight breeze from the river, our maid came up and told me there was a strange gentleman below. I went down and brought him up, I was deeply pleased and excited. For he was the English novelist whom I most admired these days. He had come to me during the strike and had been deeply interested in the great crowd spirit I had found. He was going back to England now.

"I'm curious," he told me, "to see how much your striker friends have kept of what they got in the strike—what new ideas and points of view. How much are they really changed? That, I should think, is by far the most valuable part of it all."

"It's just what I've been trying to find out for myself," I replied.

"Really? Will you tell me?"

I told him how on docks, on tugs and barges, in barrooms and in tenements, I was having talks with various types of men who had been strikers, how I was finding some dull and hopeless, others bitter, but more who simply felt that they had bungled this first attempt and were already looking forward to more and greater struggles. The socialists among them were already hard at work, urging them to carry their strike on into the political field, vote together in one solid mass and build up a government all their own. Through this ceaseless ferment I had gone in search of significant characters, incidents, new points of view. I was writing brief sketches of it all.

"How did you feel about all this," the Englishman asked, "before you were drawn into the strike?" And turning from me to Eleanore, "And you?" he added.

Gradually he got the stories of our lives. I told how all my life I had been raising up gods to worship, and how the harbor had flowed silently in beneath, undermining each one and bringing it down.

"It seems to have such a habit of changing," I ended, "that it won't let a fellow stop."

"Lucky people," he answered, smiling, "to have found that out so soon—to have had all this modern life condensed so cozily into your harbor before your eyes—and to have discovered, while you are still young, that life is growth and growth is change. I believe the age we live in is changing so much faster than any age before it, that a man if he's to be vital at all must give up the idea of any fixed creed—in his office, his church or his home—that if he does not, he will only wear himself out butting his indignant head against what is stronger and probably better than he. But if he does, if he holds himself open to change and knows that change is his very life, then he can get a serenity which is as much better than that of the monk as living is better than dying."

We talked of books being written in England and France, in Germany and Russia, all dealing with deep changes in the views and beliefs and desires of men.

"Any man," he said, "who thinks that modern Europe will go smoothly, quietly on, needs a dose of your harbor to open his eyes."

He turned to me with a sudden thought.

"Why don't you write a book," he asked, "about this harbor you have known?"

Eleanore made a quick move in her chair.

"That's just what you ought to do!" she exclaimed.

"I wonder if I could," I said. "It would be hard to see it now, as it looked at all the different times."

"You'll hardly be able to do that," the Englishman answered quietly. "Because to each one of us, I suppose, not only his present but his past is constantly changing to his view. But I wouldn't let that bother you. What would interest me as a reader would be your view of your life as you look back upon it to-day—in this present stage of your growth.

"I was raised in the Alps myself," he went on. "So *my* picture of life is the mountain path. As I climb and turn now and then to look back, the twisting little path below appears quite different each time. But still I keep on writing—my changing view of the slope behind and of the rising peaks ahead. And now and then by working my hardest I've felt the great joy of writing the truth. As you know, it isn't easy. But year by year I've felt my readers grow in number. I believe they are going to grow and grow, not mine nor yours but the readers of all the chaps like ourselves, the readers who pick up each new book with the hope that one more fellow has done his best—not to please them but to please himself—by telling of life as he has seen it—his changing life through his changing eyes."

After he left us there was a long silence. Both of us were thinking hard. And as Eleanore looked up to the stars I saw their brightness in her eyes.

"Yes," she said at last, "I'm sure. I'm sure you'd better take his advice—and write as truthfully as you can the whole story as you see it now—of this strange harbor you have known."

We talked long and eagerly that night.

CHAPTER VI

I began my story of the harbor. Every hour that I could spare from the stories and sketches of tenement life by which I made a scant living those days, I spent in gathering memories of my long struggle with this place, arranging and selecting and setting them in order for this record of the great life I had seen.

But this wide world has many such lives, many heaving forces. And ever since I had been born, while I had been building for myself one after the other these gods of civilization and peace—all unheeded by my eyes a black shadow had been silently creeping over the whole ocean world. Now from across the water there came the first low grumble of war. Within one short portentous week that grumble had become a roar, and before all the startled peoples had time to realize what was here, vast armies were being rushed over the lands, all Europe was in chaos—and the world was on the eve of the most prodigious change of all.

And like the mirror of the world that it had always been to me, the harbor at once reflected this change. Only a little time before, I had seen it almost empty, except for that crude boat of the crowd, the *Internationale*, with its songs of brotherhood and of a world where wars should cease. Now I saw it jammed with ships from whose masts flew every flag on the seas, and from the men who came ashore I heard of how they had been chased, some fired upon, by battleships—I heard of war upon the seas. I felt my father's world reborn, an ocean world where there was nothing without fighting, and where every nation fought. Ours had already entered the lists, with a loud clamor for ships of our own in which to seize this sudden chance for our share of the trade of the world. The great canal was open at last, and Europe in her turmoil had had not even a moment to look. The East and South lay open to us—rush in and get our share at last! Make our nation strong at sea!

And while in blind confusion. I groped for some new footing here, strove to see what it was going to mean to that fair world of brotherhood which I had seen struggling to be born—suddenly as though in reply there came a sharp voice out of the crowd.

Joe Kramer came to trial for his life. Before his case went to the jury, Joe rose up and addressed them. And he spoke of war and violence. He spoke of how in times of peace this present system murders men—on ships and docks and railroads, in the mills and down in the mines. And as though these lives were not enough, the powers above in this scramble for theirs for all the profits in the world, all the sweated labor they could wring out of humankind, had now flown at each others' throats. And the blood of the common people was pouring out upon the earth.

"My comrades over the water," he said, "saw this coming years ago. They worked day and night to gather the workers of Europe together against this war that will blacken the world. For that they were called anti-patriots, fiends, men without a country. And some were imprisoned and others were shot. And over here—where in times of peace the number of killed and wounded is over five hundred thousand a year—for rebelling against this murder they have called me murderer—and have placed me here on trial for my life.

"And what I want to ask you now is that you take no halfway course. Either send me out of this dock a free man or up the river to the chair. For this is no year for compromise. Am I a murderer? Yes or no. Decide with your eyes wide open. If you set me free I shall still rebel. I shall join my comrades over the sea who already are going about in the camps and saying to the rank and file—'You can stop this slaughter! You can save this world gone mad! You can end this murder—both in time of war and peace!'"

And the jury set Joe free.

Early in the following week I went down to his room by the docks for a last evening with him there. Joe was sailing that same night. Under a name not his own he had taken passage in the steerage of the big fast liner which was to sail at one o'clock. Into his room all evening poured his revolutionist friends, and the chance of revolution abroad was talked of in cool practical terms. Nothing could be done, they said, in the first few months to stop this war. Years ago the man in France, who had led the anti-war movement, had predicted that if war broke out every government rushing in would force on its people the belief that this was no war of aggression but one of defense of the fatherland from a fierce onrushing foe. And so in truth it had come about, and against that appeal to fight for their homes no voice of reason could stem the tide.

The socialists had been swept on with the rest. By tens and hundreds of thousands they had already gone to the front. But it was upon this very fact that Joe and his friends now rested their hopes. For just so soon as in the camps the first burst of enthusiasm had begun to die away, as the millions in the armies began to grow sick of the sight of blood, the groans and the shrieks of the wounded and dying, the stench of the dead—and themselves weary of fighting, worn by privation and disease, began to think of their distant homes, their wives and children starving there—then these socialists in their midst, one at every bivouac fire, would begin to ask them:

"Why is it that we are at war? What good is all this blood to us? Is it to make our toil any lighter, life any brighter in our homes—or were we sent out by our rulers to die only in order that they in their scramble might take more of the earth for themselves? And if this is true why not rise like men and end this fearful carnage?"

Already these thousands were in the camps. Into Joe's room that evening came men to give him the names and regiments of those comrades he could trust. Joe with a few hundred others was to make his dangerous way into the camps and the barracks, wherever that was possible, of French and Russians and Germans alike, to carry news from one to the other, to make ready and to plan.

Now and then, in the talk that night, I felt the thrilling presence of that rising god, that giant spirit of the crowd, not dead but only sleeping now to gain new strength for what it must do. And again in gleams and flashes I saw the vision of the end—the world for all the workers. For in this crowded tenement room, forgotten now by governments, this rough earnest group of men seemed so sure of this world of theirs, so sure that it was now soon to be born.

One by one they went away, and Joe and I were left alone. Slowly he refilled his pipe. I thought of the talks we had had in ten years.

"Well Bill," he inquired at last, "what are you going to do with yourself?"

"Write what I see in the crowd," I said, "from my new point of view—this year's point of view," I added. I went on to tell him what the English writer had said. And I told of my book on the harbor.

"Well," said Joe when I was through, "I guess it's about the best you can do. You've got a wife to think of."

"You don't know her," I rejoined, and I told him how she had changed our home in order not to stop my work.

"But don't you see what she's up to?" said Joe.

"What the devil do you mean?" I asked indignantly. Joe blew a pitying puff of smoke.

"You poor blind dub of a husband," he said with his old affectionate smile, "she's making you love her all the more. You're anchored worse than ever. *You* can't go over to Europe and take a chance at being shot. Don't you see the hole you're in? You've got to care what happens to you."

"I'm not so sure of that, Joe," I said. "Things in this world are changing so fast that it's hard for any man in it to tell where he'll be in a year from now—or even a few short months from now. It's the year that no man can see beyond."

"You mean you're coming over?" he asked.

"I'm not sure. Just now I'm going to finish this book. I'm going to see Eleanore through till the baby is born. But after that—if over in Europe the people rise against this war—I don't just see how I can keep out."

Joe looked at me queerly. And with a curious gruffness,

"I hope you will keep out," he said. "There aren't many women like your wife."

He pulled an old grip from under his bed and began throwing in a few books and clothes. From a drawer he swept a few colored shirts, some underclothes and a small revolver.

"J. K.," I said, "I've been thinking about us. And I think our youth is gone."

"What's youth?" asked Joe indifferently.

"Youth," I replied, "is the time when you can think anything, feel anything and go anywhere."

"I'm still going anywhere," he remarked.

"But you can't think anything," I rejoined. "You say I'm tied to a wife and home. All right, I'm glad I am. But you're tied, too. You're tied to a creed, Mister Syndicalist—a creed so stiff that you can't think of anything else."

"All right, I'm glad I am," he echoed. "I'm sorry youth lasted as long as it did."

He closed his grip and strapped it. Then he took up his hat and coat and threw a last look about the room where he had lived for a year or more.

"Breaking up home ties," he said with a grin. "Don't come to the boat," he added downstairs. "She don't sail for an hour or two and I'll be asleep in my bunk long before."

"All right. Good-by, J. K.—remember we may meet over there——"

Again that gruffness came into his voice:

"If you do, you'll be taking a mighty big chance," he said. "Good-by, Bill—it's just possible we may never meet again. Glad to have made your acquaintance, Kid. Here's wishing you luck."

He turned and went off down the Farm with that long swinging walk of his, his big heavy shoulders bent rather more than before. And as I stood looking after him I thought of the lonely winding road that he was to travel day and night, into slums of cities and in and out among the camps.

I walked slowly back through the tenements toward the new home among them that Eleanore had made.

In the summer's night the city streets were still alive with people. I passed brightly lighted thoroughfares where I saw them in crowds, and I knew that this tide of people flowed endlessly through the hundreds of miles of streets that made up the port of New York. Hurrying, idling, talking and laughing, quarreling, fighting, here stopping to look at displays in shop windows, there pouring into "Movies"—and walking, walking, walking on.

Going up into their tenement homes to eat and drink, love, breed and sleep, to wake up and come down to another day.

So the crowd moved on and on, while the great harbor surrounding their lives and shaping their lives, went on with its changes unheeded.

I tried to think of this harbor as being run by this common crowd—of the railroads, mines and factories, of the colleges, hospitals and all institutions of research, and the theaters and concert halls, the picture galleries, all the books—all in the power of the crowd.

"It will be a long time," I thought. "Before it comes the crowd must change. But they will change—and fast or slow, I belong with them while they're changing."

Something Joe had once said came into my mind:

"They're the ones who get shot down in wars and worked like dogs in time of peace."

And I thought of the crowds across the sea—of men being rushed over Europe on trains, or marching along starlit roads, or tramping across meadows. And I thought of long lines of fire at dawn spurting from the mouths of guns—from mountainsides, from out of woods, from trenches in fast blackening fields—and of men in endless multitudes pitching on their faces as the fire mowed them down.

And with those men, it seemed to me, went all the great gods I had known—gods of civilization and peace—the kind god in my mother's church and the smiling goddess in Paris, the clear-eyed god of efficiency and the awakening god of the crowd—all plunging into this furnace of war with the men in whose spirits all gods dwell—to shrivel and melt in seething flame and emerge at last in strange new forms. What would come out of the furnace?

I thought of Joe and his comrades going about in towns and camps, speaking low and watching, waiting, hoping to bring a new dawn, a new order, out of this chaotic night.

And I heard them say to these governments:

"Your civilization is crashing down. For a hundred years, in all our strikes and risings, you preached against our violence—you talked of your law and order, your clear deliberate thinking. In you lay the hope of the world, you said. You were Civilization. You were Mind and Science, in you was all Efficiency, in you was Art,

Religion, and you kept the Public Peace. But now you have broken all your vows. The world's treasures of Art are as safe with you as they were in the Dark Ages. Your Prince of Peace you have trampled down. And all your Science you have turned to the efficient slaughter of men. In a week of your boasted calmness you have plunged the world into a violence beside which all the bloodshed in our strikes and revolutions seems like a pool beside the sea. And so you have failed, you powers above, blindly and stupidly you have failed. For you have let loose a violence where you are weak and we are strong. We are these armies that you have called out. And before we go back to our homes we shall make sure that these homes of ours shall no more become ashes at your will. For we shall stop this war of yours and in our minds we shall put away all hatred of our brother men. For us they will be workers all. With them we shall rise and rise again—until at last the world is free!"

The voice had ceased—and again I was walking by myself along a crowded tenement street. Immigrants from Europe, brothers, sons and fathers of the men now in the camps, kept passing me along the way. As I looked into their faces I saw no hope for Europe there. Such men could take and hold no world. But then I remembered how in the strike, out of just such men as these, I had seen a giant slowly born. Would that crowd spirit rise again? Could it be that the time was near when this last and mightiest of the gods would rise and take the world in his hands?

At home I found Eleanore asleep. For a time I sat at my desk and made some notes for my writing. I read and smoked for a little, then undressed and went to bed. But still I lay there wide awake— thinking of this home of mine and of where I might be in a few months more, in this year that no man can see beyond. For all the changes in the world seemed gathering in a cyclone now.

I was nearly asleep when I was roused by a thick voice from the harbor. Low in the distance, deep but now rising blast on blast, its waves of sound beat into the city—into millions of ears of sleepers and watchers, the well, the sick and the dying, the dead, the lovers, the schemers, the dreamers, the toilers, the spenders and wasters. I shut my eyes and saw the huge liner on which Joe was sailing moving slowly out of its slip. Down at its bottom men shoveling coal to the clang of its gong. On the decks above them, hundreds of cabins and suites de luxe—most of them dark and empty now. Bellowing impatiently as it swept out into the stream, it seemed to be saying:

"Make way for me. Make way, all you little men. Make way, all you habits and all you institutions, all you little creeds and gods. For I am the start of the voyage—over the ocean to heathen lands! And I am always starting out and always bearing you along! For I am your molder, I am strong—I am a surprise, I am a shock—I am a dazzling passion of hope—I am a grim executioner! I am reality—I am life! I am the book that has no end!"

THE STORY OF PENGUIN CLASSICS

Before 1946 . . . "Classics" are mainly the domain of academics and students; readable editions for everyone else are almost unheard of. This all changes when a little-known classicist, E. V. Rieu, presents Penguin founder Allen Lane with the translation of Homer's *Odyssey* that he has been working on in his spare time.

1946 Penguin Classics debuts with *The Odyssey*, which promptly sells three million copies. Suddenly, classics are no longer for the privileged few.

1950s Rieu, now series editor, turns to professional writers for the best modern, readable translations, including Dorothy L. Sayers's *Inferno* and Robert Graves's unexpurgated *Twelve Caesars*.

1960s The Classics are given the distinctive black covers that have remained a constant throughout the life of the series. Rieu retires in 1964, hailing the Penguin Classics list as "the greatest educative force of the twentieth century."

1970s A new generation of translators swells the Penguin Classics ranks, introducing readers of English to classics of world literature from more than twenty languages. The list grows to encompass more history, philosophy, science, religion, and politics.

1980s The Penguin American Library launches with titles such as *Uncle Tom's Cabin* and joins forces with Penguin Classics to provide the most comprehensive library of world literature available from any paperback publisher.

1990s The launch of Penguin Audiobooks brings the classics to a listening audience for the first time, and in 1999 the worldwide launch of the Penguin Classics Web site extends their reach to the global online community.

The 21st Century Penguin Classics are completely redesigned for the first time in nearly twenty years. This world-famous series now consists of more than 1,300 titles, making the widest range of the best books ever written available to millions—and constantly redefining what makes a "classic."

The Odyssey continues . . .

The best books ever written

PENGUIN 🐧 CLASSICS

SINCE 1946

Find out more at www.penguinclassics.com

Visit www.vpbookclub.com

CLICK ON A CLASSIC
www.penguinclassics.com

The world's greatest literature at your fingertips

Constantly updated information on more than a thousand titles,
from Icelandic sagas to ancient Indian epics, Russian drama to
Italian romance, American greats to African masterpieces

•

The latest news on recent additions to the list, updated
editions, and specially commissioned translations

•

Original essays by leading writers

•

A wealth of background material, including biographies
of every classic author from Aristotle to Zamyatin, plot
synopses, readers' and teachers' guides, useful Web links

•

Online desk and examination copy assistance for academics

•

Trivia quizzes, competitions, giveaways, news on
forthcoming screen adaptations